REVENGE

Coming from the latrine, Holly jogged across open ground to the cover of Hut 5. Wrapped in newspaper were the frozen waste lumps he had fashioned to the width of the water pipe. He caught his breath, then ran for the hole. His fingers groped for the junction of the pipes.

In the morning the water would run along a main pipe until it met with an obstruction and the water would eat away at the mass that blocked it. Chisel it, and then carry that mass in particles to the taps, basins, sinks, and cooking saucepans of the enemy in the barracks . . .

"A gripping adventure tale."
—ALFRED HITCHCOCK'S MYSTERY MAGAZINE

Charter Books by Gerald Seymour

ARCHANGEL
THE CONTRACT

ARCHANGEL

GERALD SEYMOUR

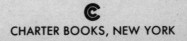

CHARTER BOOKS, NEW YORK

This Charter Book contains the complete
text of the original hardcover edition.
It has been completely reset in a typeface
designed for easy reading, and was
printed from new film.

ARCHANGEL

A Charter Book/published by arrangement with
E.P. Dutton, Inc.

PRINTING HISTORY
E.P. Dutton edition 1982
Charter edition/October 1983

ISBN: 0-441-02884-5

Charter Books are published by The Berkley Publishing Group,
200 Madison Avenue, New York, N.Y. 10016
PRINTED IN THE UNITED STATES OF AMERICA

to Gillian, Nicholas and James

His form has not yet lost
All her original brightness, nor appear'd
Less than Archangel ruin'd, and th' excess
Of glory obscured.

—JOHN MILTON
Paradise Lost

Prologue

The Aeroflot was eighty minutes late.

For "operational reasons," the girl at Information explained. Eighty minutes late out of Moscow, and she had that sweet Swiss haughty stare which seemed to say that he was lucky the damn thing was airborne at all.

Alan Millet stood close to a television monitor screen that would tell him when the Ilyushin was on final approach. He might seem calm, but it was a sham. He was nervous and excited.

The passenger would be in the back seat of the tourist section, in the center of three, with security on either side. Sometimes the passenger was handcuffed for the length of the flight, sometimes only until it had left Soviet airspace, sometimes just up the aircraft steps at Sheremetyevo.

He looked at his watch. There was time for another coffee, but he had already been three times to the coffee shop. He would wait. He would watch the passengers as they came through the silent-opening glass doors. His passenger would not be delayed by baggage collection. Just a grip bag, a holdall, or a plastic sack. There wasn't much to bring, where this one was coming from. The security men would stay on the aircraft, and there would be some insult or jibe, then their noses would be back into their magazines, the stewardesses would bring them another drink, and they would prepare themselves for four hours flying time back to Moscow.

Letters and figures raced across the width of the monitor screen. The Aeroflot was announced. He felt a dribble of sweat on the skin at his back.

It was good of the deputy undersecretary to have sent him. There could have been a consul dispatched from the Berne embassy, there could have been a local Century staffer. Better that it was Alan Millet, that it should be he who sealed the file on Michael Holly.

Alan Millet had thought many times of Michael Holly in the months since those first sparse reports had seeped into Century House from the camps at Barashevo. It had seemed so bright, so promising, the opening of the Holly file. But the brightness had been scrubbed clear and all because a man had been struck by coronary failure in his cell in a London jail.

Millet lit a cigarette, drew once on it, dropped it, and crushed it under his foot. He walked toward the "Arrivals" door. It would not be hard to identify the passenger.

Chapter 1

The distance between the steel-faced door and his bed mocked the man. A few moments before he might have quarried the strength to crawl across the floor to the door, might have gathered the will to beat his fists below the spy hole. But the chance had gone. He lay on his tousled blanket and the soft pillow, and the pain in him swelled and blustered like an autumn stormcloud.

There was always a light burning from the ceiling of a cell for men like him. Bright in the evening, dimmed in the night after lockup. A dull light now, but his eyes fastened on the wire webbing around it, as if that small bulb was a talisman. A terrifying loneliness because he could not reach the door, and his voice had fled in defeat from the surging agony that consumed his chest and left arm, and that ebbed at the pit of his throat.

His mind was alive. Thoughts and memories competed with the crushing weight on his upper ribs, the pressure of a pitiless binding that pinioned him to his bedding. Thoughts of the guard who would be sitting in his cubicle at the end of the landing with the central heating pipe against his feet and his newspaper on the table. Memories that were laced in a foreign tongue, wreathed in foreign smells, dinned by foreign sounds, wrapped in foreign tastes. The thoughts and the memories were the intruders because the pain was creeping wider and would win.

There was no one to listen for his whimpered call. He was isolated from the living, breathing world of a thousand souls who eked out their existence beyond his cramping cell. He wrapped his arms around his body, squeezing at the pressure that engulfed his heart, as if he might spirit away the growing wound.

But he was no fool, this man. He knew the meaning of the pain. A few brief hours earlier, he could have described to his companions in the exercise yard or the recreation hall the classic symptoms of the cardiac attack. Often they came to him as a counselor, tapping at what they regarded as his superior knowledge. He told one man of the treatment necessary for hernia and abscess, he told another man of the letter he should write to the lawyer who had acted in his defense, he told another how he should conduct himself at the next visit with the wife who was being screwed by the truck driver next door . . . All the cons came to his cell. They asked and he answered. He would know the signposts of the coronary. It would have been expected of him.

He lay very still on his bed because movement aggravated the pain and his legs were useless things.

A man lying in an upper-landing cell of Her Majesty's Prison, Wormwood Scrubs, and watching death scurry closer.

Just a small snapshot kept him company, a wallet-sized picture stuck to the cream-painted brickwork beside his face. A woman with fluffy blonde hair that had been combed before the wind caught at the strands. A woman in a short-sleeved blouse and a dowdy gray skirt. The photograph had been sent to him after conviction and sentence, after the stripping of his cover. The photograph dug out his buried history. The woman posed before the red-stone mausoleum containing the few earthly remains of Vladimir Ilyich Lenin. He had taken her there on the last day before he had left Moscow. A spring day with summer closing on them quickly, and they had made the pilgrimage down the steps into the hushed sepulcher, made themselves a microcosm of the slow shuffling line. Afterward, when the sunlight had again recaptured them, he had positioned her so that the edifice of the tomb peeped over her shoulders. He had used the foreign-made Instamatic which his position permitted him to purchase in the foreign currency shop at the hotel down from the square. When they had brought him to this place and slammed a door on his freedom, she had sent him her photograph. Pretense had no more value.

He gazed at the photograph, looked on it, loved with it. He would not see the woman again. He would see nothing of the past again. Not the wastelands of Sheremetyevo airport, nor the Lubyanka offices behind the curtain of guards, nor the primly ordered sleeping-quarters of the training camp at Ryazan, nor the small apartment on the outer span of the Prospekt Mir. It was only a small apartment, but adequate for a man who traveled, and for his woman who would wait a year or a month for his return, or eternity. A good woman, laced with Georgian temper . . . and the pain ripped again deep into his chest, and he gasped, and his voice rattled a call for help and his body was swept in wetness.

He heard the footsteps far away on the landing. Steps that paused and halted. The guard was checking the spy holes. Sometimes he would look into each cell, sometimes into the first three, sometimes a random selection from all those on the landing.

Shit. So unfair.

Three years in this place, three years of desiccating boredom, and they kept saying that soon he would go, and he had dreamed of nothing beyond the aircraft and the car to his apartment, and the body of the woman who had stood before the mausoleum for his camera. And now he would be cheated. No sound from the landing. The guard might have returned to his cozy room, he might have opened one of the other cells and stepped inside to take a cigarette with a lifer. On this landing all men were solitaries. Why should he bother to peep through the other spy holes, at men who slept or played with themselves or read trash books? Why bother to look in on a man whose chest was crushed by a granite weight?

He called again and could not hear the reed voice. There was no echo from the shining white tower of the corner lavatory, nor from the oakwood table made by an earlier generation of prisoner, nor from the metal chair, nor from the books, nor from the transistor radio. A silence kept company with his short bursts of breath, and he thought he could hear the perspiration running to the pits of his arms. He was dying and there was no witness.

The footsteps dragged closer to his door. Measured, confident steps. No way to stop the pain, and his body could not outlast the hurt. They would find him dead. They would stand in the cell and talk in quiet, controlled whispers of his age, fifty-one years. They would speak of his weight, fifteen pounds over. Of his smoking, two packets minimum a day. Of his exercise, the least that he could escape with. Of his eating, all that was put before him, and wiping up with bread the slicks of fat left on his plate. Textbook abuse and textbook penalty.

To die alone, that was an obscenity. To die without a hand to hold.

The footsteps reached his door.

The man tried to move on his bed, he failed. He tried again to shout, and there was only the thin wheeze of his breath.

There was the scrape of a drawn bolt, the hiss of a turned key in an oiled lock, the tinkling of a light chain cascading loose. He saw the face, shadowed by the steep black peak of the cap. Ironed shirt, pressed uniform, polished boots, bright splash of a medal ribbon. The man saw all of that and could not speak. A voice was directed toward him, there was the command for an answer. Slowly he moved his head as if that were a gesture of respect in itself. The moving of his head brought new agony, and his cheeks twisted. The uniform spun into a blur as it stepped back into the brightness of the landing. The man heard the voice, registered the urgency.

"Mr. Jones . . . It's Demyonov . . . gray as a bloody battle-ship. Reckon it's one for the medic. . . ."

Another set of pounding feet.

Another shadowed face at the door. Another strident call, and the man could not respond.

"Come on, Demyonov, let's have you. What's the matter? Lost your bloody voice for once?"

His lips fluttered. There was a kaleidoscope of thoughts in his mind, and none could slide to his tongue. He peered back at the men at the door, and his eyes bled for attention.

"Get the medical orderly, and I should say a bit of speed about it." Mr. Jones was senior duty officer. The "cons" stood up when Mr. Jones came into their cells. He liked to say that he ran a tidy landing. No messing, no back talk. But the man could not rise, could not speak, and the burden of pain over-whelmed him.

"Not feeling so good, Demyonov? Well, not to worry. Med-ic's coming over to have a look at you. You're a bit gray, I'll say that."

From far down on the bed he heard the voice. He stared at

Mr. Jones's knees, and saw the careful darn of a short rip beside the knife crease. He remembered that it was said that Mr. Jones had a kindly way with him. The cons reckoned there was a softness hidden behind the booming mouth and florid lips. The cons said that he'd learned a garrulous friendliness when he was young and had done shifts in the Pentonville death cell. They said that when things were really grim, like hideous and worse, that then Mr. Jones could make himself almost a human. The old cons reckoned he'd have had a bright word for the lad who was being tripped through the door and up the steps and onto the platform as the clock chimed. He'd heard all those things about Mr. Jones. You heard everything about everybody when you'd done three years in the Scrubs.

He raised his eyes. He saw the care of the afternoon shave, the eruption of worming veins on the cheeks, the nervousness flickering at Mr. Jones's mouth.

"Don't you worry, Demyonov, Medic's on the way. Can't have you going under, can we? Not when you're going home. Well, that's the talk, isn't it?" The medical orderly was puffing by the time that he reached the cell door. The warder stayed outside, and the orderly took Demyonov's fingers from Mr. Jones. It was a cursory check, the wiping of the damp sheen from the prisoner's forehead, an open hand laid across his chest, two fingers on the wrist for the pulse.

"I'm going to get the doctor in."

"Drag him in from home?" queried Mr. Jones.

"I'm not taking the rap for shifting this one . . ."

The orderly turned from his patient to the warder in the doorway.

". . . Get yourself down to the telephone, tell Admin that I want the doctor. Make sure he knows who he'll be seeing, that'll bring him fast enough. Better get the deputy governor up too, but the doctor first."

And then there was nothing to do but wait and watch. The orderly crouched over the bed, wincing at the man's pain, and Mr. Jones paced on tiptoe the short length of the solitary cell, and both wondered how long he would last. If he moved the man and killed him, he'd be subject to inquiry and inquest; if he let him be and allowed him to slip, the brickbats would fall as hard. This man above all others. Everyone knew him in the

Scrubs. Oleg Demyonov . . . described in chorus by the Attorney General and the Lord Chief Justice as the most dangerous individual threat to the security of the state of the last decade. A pudgy little bugger, overweight and balding, ready with a riposte to anyone. Hold out, you little creep, hold out until the doctor gets here. It was cold in the cell. Had to be, because for the last two years they'd shut the central heating down earlier. Not that Demyonov was shivering, he'd enough on his plate without feeling the chill of a January evening. The orderly was cold, only the short white coat over his shirt, and his ears strained for sounds on the iron staircases.

The doctor was young, with the aloof stamp of his trade. Into the cell, opening his bag, taking the place of the orderly. The deputy governor hovered behind him. The doctor enacted his routine. Pulse, blood pressure wrap on the arm, stethoscope to the chest. He spoke gently to the man who had been a spy, reacting to the faintest twitches of the eyebrows.

"Where's the pain, Demyonov . . . ? Just in the chest . . . ? In the left arm as well . . . ? Does the pain go further . . . ? Problem with breathing . . . ? Has this ever happened before . . . ?"

The doctor eased away from the bed, stripped off the wrap, laid the passive hand back across the man's chest.

"I want a 999 for an ambulance—he might have a chance at the Hammersmith. He's none here. His blood pressure's down in his boots."

"If he's to go out of here to hospital, Home Office has to sanction it."

"If he doesn't get to the Hammersmith, he'll be going out of here in a box."

"It has to be cleared . . ."

"The ambulance or he's dead," snapped the doctor.

It was not a quick affair, the transfer of Oleg Demyonov some eight hundred yards from the Scrubs to the Hammersmith Hospital. Authorization to be granted, the patient to be carried tortuously on a stretcher down the steep staircase from the upper landing, locked gates to be negotiated. The prison was a whispering murmur of information by the time that the high wooden gates reluctantly swung open, and the ambulance roared into a left turn past the gaunt homes of the jail's staff. As if sensing freedom, the driver played a tattoo on his siren, though the road ahead was well lit and clear of traffic.

Into the medical block, into the lift, into the Coronary Care unit. The doctor peeled away as the plastic double doors flapped shut in the wake of the wheeled stretcher. The deputy governor was at his shoulder.

"I wouldn't go in there if I were you. I mean he's not going to run away, is he? They're going to have their work cut out. He's not going to make a dash for the fire escape."

The deputy governor and Mr. Jones fidgeted in mutual discomfort. It went against the grain of their lives to let a prisoner out of sight. They heard through the doorway staccato shouts for jelly, for drip, for ECG. A small stampede of men charged past them and through the door. They heard the whining of a buzzer, the noise of fists beating on flesh.

"Cardiac Arrest team. They're walloping his chest now, trying to beat it back into action. . . . Being who he is I suggest you give the Home Office another call. That's my lot, good night."

The deputy governor followed the doctor down the stairs.

Mr. Jones was abandoned in the deserted corridor, hands folded across his stomach, skirted by passing nurses and doctors. A bloody shame for old Demyonov, he thought. Even a bloody Russian would look forward to going home, wouldn't he, even if it meant traipsing back to Moscow? Funny thing was that he wasn't a bad chap, and they'd miss him at the Scrubs whether he went out in a box or with a one-way airline ticket.

From his tunic pocket Mr. Jones took a set of clippers and started to tidy his nails. There would be a few minutes before the storm broke.

He walked from East Acton underground station through the estate of Council homes, where the walls were daubed with tribal soccer slogans and teenagers fumbled in the entries to the garages with their girlfriends' zippers.

Past the prison with its floodlit walls topped with barbed wire coils, past the twin towers of the gate house, past the surveillance cameras. His hands were deep in his overcoat pockets, and in the rush out of his home he had forgotten the scarf that was a month-old Christmas present. He had been lucky with his connections, had caught the trains quickly. God alone knew how he was going to get back to Century, but Alan Millet's wife always took the car on a Saturday night to her bridge session. He'd have to go back into Century, after a thing like this it would be expected of him. Of course, all the business could have been managed at the end of a telephone, but that wasn't the way of the Service. Not that Alan Millet could complain. Holly was his man, and once, long ago, Holly had been his pride.

The lights of the hospital blazed down on him as he turned off the pavement and threaded his way through the car park.

The medical block had a certain venerable charm, and the warmth cascaded around him. He was stopped by a porter. What was his business? Coronary Care, first floor, he was expected. Alan Millet ignored the uncertain statement that visitors were not permitted this late at night. In his wallet he carried the authority of a polaroid-printed identity card that governs entry to Century House. He hesitated for a moment at the top of the stairs, looked both ways down the corridor, and saw the upright figure of a uniformed prison officer.

He nodded a courtesy greeting and pushed his way through the doors. He saw two occupied beds and, from the pillows, pairs of concerned eyes peered at him. They were the living, they could resent the circus arrival that had been summoned to the curtained camp in the far corner. There was a trolley beside the semi-concealed bed, its top stretcher surface empty. A nurse was detaching electrodes from their cables, another was writing her notes busily. Two young doctors stood close to each other, their eyes hollowed by tiredness. A pair of West Indian porters, expressionless, wheeled the trolley away across the open-plan unit and out through the door.

"Doubtfire, Home Office." A sharp voice behind Millet. "You're a bit late, old chap."

"Millet..." he paused, "...Foreign and Commonwealth. What's happened to him?"

"Just gone on the trolley. There's a box underneath the top, they put them in there, doesn't upset people that way. About twenty minutes ago they gave up. Not a chance, everything done that could have been, he had the red carpet."

"They said he hadn't long when they called me at home. I

suppose I was sort of hoping . . . they're sometimes wrong."

"Good riddance. What'll he get, Hero of the bloody Soviet Union?"

A nursing Sister approached the two men. The message was bright in her eyes. This was an operational area.

Doubtfire had a car and driver. Night duty officer for the Home Office, a traveling fire brigade. He was returning to his cubbyhole in Whitehall and the telephone that he prayed would stay silent, and a thermos of instant coffee. Millet was thankful to accept a lift. In the back of the car they talked in desultory fashion. Two practiced civil servants, uncertain of the other's role and standing, and cautious of confidences. Millet was dropped in Great Charles Street at the entrance to the Foreign and Commonwealth Office, which left him a long walk along the river to Century House.

The wind whipped at Alan Millet's legs as he hurried along the empty pavements. The sleet pecked at the skin of his cheeks, fluttered his close-cut hair. He was obsessed with a man called Michael Holly. A tall man, alive with enthusiasm, total in self-containment. Memories more than a year old. He supposed that every desker felt a stifling involvement with his field man. Like the first whore of a man's life, never forgotten, never to be escaped from. There was a pub across the river, where he had taken Holly—he always called himself that, never bothered with his given name—where they had sipped their drinks and nibbled at the tired bread and ham, where Holly had asked the expected question. What happens if . . . ? No problem, Alan Millet had said, no problem there. The ransom money's under lock and key in the Scrubs, and a bloody good laugh he'd had as he said it. Nothing for Holly to worry himself with, and of course it wouldn't come to that anyway. A bloody good laugh. . . . The street lights picked out the man who stood against the river parapet, and who stared down at the ruffled water. Must have been the antibiotics he had been taking to stifle the influenza bug, must have been that which had loosened his tongue. A field man should never have been given a guarantee.

But Millet had offered Holly a promise.

It won't happen, of course . . . but there's a man in a cell at Wormwood Scrubs. Of course it won't happen . . . but if it did, well there'd just have to be a swap.

Bloody marvelous, wasn't it? And all the spadework done

through Belgrade, all the ribbons tied. All ready for the flight to Berlin, and the only haggle was over which crossing-point, what time, which day.

Michael Holly for Oleg Demyonov. Them happy and us happy.

But now a man lay in the mortuary of the Hammersmith Hospital and Alan Millet's promise was a worthless thing.

Chapter 2

His weapon against the rusty binding of the bolt was a fifty kopeck coin.

For more than an hour he had crouched on the floor, bracing himself as the speed changes of the train and the unevenness of the track destroyed the momentum of his painstaking work. With the milled edge of the coin he chipped at the red-brown crust that had formed between the lower lip of the cap of the bolt and the metal sheet plate of the carriage flooring. He had something to show for his effort. A tiny pile of dust debris was collected beside his knee, and some had stained the material of his gray trousers.

Those who had known Michael Holly at his home in the southeast of England, or had shared office and canteen space with him at the factory on the Kent fringes of London, might not now have recognized their man. A year in the jails had left its mark. The full flesh of his cheeks and chin had been scalped back to the bone. A bright confidence at his eyes had been replaced by something harsher. Clothes that had hung well now fell shapelessly like charity handouts. A ruddiness in his face had given way to a pallor that was unmistakably the work of the cells. His full dark hair had been cropped in the barber's chair of the holding prison to a brush without luster.

This was an old carriage, but still well capable of performing the task set for it when it had first joined the rolling-stock in the year that Holly had been born. It had carried many on this journey. It had brought them in their hundreds, in their thousands, in their tens of thousands along this track. It was a carriage of the prison train that ran twice weekly from the capital city to the interior depths of the Autonomous Soviet Socialist Republic of Mordovia. On the floor, in the filth and

the watery amber half-light, he scraped at the bolt that had felt
the boots and slippers and sandals of the prisoners who had
encompassed his lifetime. Not easy to pry at the rim of the
bolt, because this was a purpose-built carriage. No ordinary
carriage, not subject to any hasty conversion to ensure its use-
fulness, but out of the railway factory yards of Leningrad and
designed only for transporting the prisoners. A walkway for
the guards, and compartments to separate the convicts into
manageable groups, each fitted with small hatches for the dropping of their black bread rations, and unmovable benches and
shelves for a few to sleep on. The carriages had their name.
The *Stolypin* carriage carried the name of the Tsarist minister
struck down by an assassin seventy years before. The new men
of the Kremlin were not above the simplicity of taking a former
idea and adapting it to their needs. The walls, the bars, the
bolts and the locks remained; only the prisoners of the regime
had changed.

They had brought Holly by car from the Lefortovo jail to
the train while Muscovites still slept. He had barely slept after
the meeting with the consul from the Embassy and the escort
of men in the khaki uniforms of the *Komitet Gosudarstvennoi
Bezopasnosti* had taken him still drowsy from the back seat to
the train at a far platform. The one who wore on his blue
shoulder flash the insignia of major's rank had shaken his hand
and grinned a supercilious smile. Into the carriage, the door
slammed, the bolt across, the key turned.

Two other men for company. Perhaps they had been loaded
on the train many hours before Holly, because they seemed to
him to be sleeping when he had first seen them in the darkened
carriage. He had not spoken then, they had not spoken since.
A barrier existed between them. But they watched him. All
through the morning, as they sat on the makeshift bunks, they
stared without comment at the kneeling figure who ground away
at the rust around the bolt.

The work at the bolt, mindless and persistent, allowed the
thoughts of Michael Holly to flow unfettered. The week before
had stretched the distance of a lifetime. And the lifetime had
ended in a death, and death was the carriage that rolled, shaking
and relentless, toward the east.

Where to go back to, where to find the birth? Months,

weeks, days—how far to go back? The coin had found the central stem of the bolt, the rust shell was dispersed. The bolt was not strong, arthritic with age and corrosion. How far to go back?

Not the childhood, not the parentage, that was a different story, that was not the work of the last crowded hours. Forget the origins of the man.

What of Millet? Complacent, plausible Millet. But neither was Millet a part of these last days, nor was the journey to Moscow, nor the rendezvous that was aborted, nor the arrest and the trial. Millet had a place in the history of the affair, but that place was not in its present, not in its future.

Where did the present begin?

Michael Holly, now on his knees on a *Stolypin* carriage floor, and unshaven because they would not permit him a razor, and with the hunger lapping at his belly, had been a model prisoner in the Vladimir jail 200 kilometers east of the capital. A foreigner, and housed on the second floor of the hospital block in the cell that it was said had held the pilot Gary Powers and the businessman Greville Wynne. Down for espionage, given fifteen years by the courts. Everyone from the governor to the humblest creeping "trusty" knew that Michael Holly would serve only a minimal proportion of those fifteen years. There was a man in England, there would be an exchange. So they gave him milk, they gave him books to read, they allowed food parcels from the Embassy. They waited, and Michael Holly waited, for the arrangements to be made. The political officer at Vladimir said that it would not be too long, and the interrogations had been courteous, and the warders had been correct. When they had taken him from the hospital block with his possessions and spare clothes in a cloth sack he had smiled and shaken hands and believed that the flight was close, Berlin he had thought it would be. In Lefortovo holding prison he had learned the truth across a bare scrubbed table from the consul sent by the Embassy. An obsequious little man the consul had been, crushed by the message that he brought. The consul had stumbled through his speech and Holly had listened.

". . . It's not that it's anyone's fault, Mr. Holly, you mustn't think that. It's just terribly bad luck, it's the worst luck I've heard of since I've been here, that's eight years. It was all set up—well, you know that. People had worked very hard on this matter, you really have to believe that. . . . Well, we can't deliver. That's what it's all about now. A swap is a swap, one man to be exchanged for another. It was you and this fellow, and we can't deliver. . . . I'm dreadfully sorry, Mr. Holly, it's the most extraordinary thing but the chap's dead, snuffed it. He had the best medical treatment—well, you'll not be interested in that . . ."

The bolt shifted. Holly strained with his fingers to twist the coin under the lip of the bolt. The bolt had moved a millimeter, perhaps two.

". . . But I can assure you that people back in London were really most upset at this development . . . I'm afraid the Soviets are going to take rather a hard line with you now, Mr. Holly. There's no point in my not being frank. . . . The Foreign Ministry informs us now that, since your parents were both born Soviet citizens, under Soviet law you are a Soviet citizen also. I know, Mr. Holly . . . you were born in the United Kingdom, you were brought up there, you were in possession of a valid British passport when you traveled to Moscow. The Soviets are going to disregard all that. We've had a hell of a job getting this degree of consular access. I want you to know that. We said they couldn't have the corpse if we didn't get it—that's by the by—but it's understood by both sides that this is the last of such meetings. You're being transferred to the Correctional Labor Colonies, but you won't be classified as a foreigner, you won't be in the foreigner's camp. They're going to take you beyond our reach. . . . Mr. Holly, you've always proclaimed your innocence of the charges and accusations made against you. From our side, the Foreign and Commonwealth Office have been very firm too. You are innocent as far as Her Majesty's Government is concerned. We're not wavering from that position. You understand that, Mr. Holly? We deny absolutely that you were involved in any nonsensical espionage adventure. It's very important that we continue to take that line, you can see that, I'm sure. Mr. Holly, the British government knows that you have supported your parents most generously during their retirement. Your parents will not be abandoned by us, Mr. Holly, just as we will not abandon the stance that you were completely innocent of trumped-up charges. You do understand me, Mr. Holly . . . ?"

The bolt rose a centimeter.

There was a dribble of sweat at Holly's forehead. Too much space now for the coin to be useful, his finger could slide under the lip. The rough metal edge cut into his fingertip. An eddy of chill air swirled into the carriage, fastening on his knuckles. He heard, louder than before, the dripping clatter of the wheels on the rails beneath him.

". . . Look, Mr. Holly, I've painted the picture black, because that's the only honest thing to do. We'll keep trying, of course, that goes without saying, but in the present climate of relations there's little chance of your situation altering dramatically. You'll be going to the camps and you have to come to terms with that. What I'm saying is—well, you have to learn to live in those places, Mr. Holly. Try and survive, try and live with the system. Don't kick it, don't fight it. You can't beat them. I've lived here long enough to know. In a few years things may change, I can't promise that, but they may. And you have my word that you won't be forgotten, not by Whitehall, not by Foreign and Commonwealth. It's going to boil down to keeping your pecker up, looking on the best side of things. You'll do that, won't you, old chap . . . There's not really any-thing more for me to say. Only I suppose, good luck. . . ."

That was what the present had on offer to Michael Holly. A furtive junior diplomat bowing and scraping his way out of the interview section of the Lefortovo, ogling the KGB man and thanking him for a fifteen-minute access to a prisoner for whom the key was now thrown far away.

Forget the present, Holly, reckon on the future. The future is a plate of steel floor covering that creaks and whistles as it is dragged clear of the supports to which it was bolted down thirty years before.

That's the future, Holly.

A steel plate above the stone chippings and wood sleepers that mark the track from Moscow to the East through Kolomna and Ryazan and Spassk-Ryazanski. The chippings are coated in fine snow, and the cold blusters into the carriage through the draught gap. Behind him the men swore softly, breaking their silence.

The train was not running fast. He could sense the strain of the engine far to the front. There was a dawdle in its pace, and there had been times when it had halted completely, other times

when it had slowed to a crawl. The daylight was fleeing from
the wilderness that he could not see but whose emptiness beyond the shuttered windows he understood. Barely audible
above the new-found noise of the wheels, he heard the sharp
step of feet in the corridor and close to the door of their compartment. There was the flap of the food hatch swinging on its
hinge one door away from his. Holly pushed the steel plate
down, eased the bolt back into its socket with his toe.

The flap of the door flipped jauntily upward. A sneering
face gazed at the caged men. Three brown paper bags were
pushed through the hatch to tumble to the carriage floor. The
flap fell back. The two men moved at stoat's speed past Holly.
One bag into the hand of the man who was gross and white-
skinned, a second for the man with the beard. For a fleeting
moment he braced himself for confrontation, suspecting that
they would want all three bags, but they left him his. They
darted back to their bunk and behind him was the sound of
ripping paper. Animals . . . poor bastards, pitiful creatures. But
then at Vladimir, Holly had been segregated from the mass of
the *zeks,* the convicts who formed the greatest part of the prison
population. At Vladimir, Holly had been categorized as a foreigner, he had been on the second floor of the hospital block
and allowed special food and privileges. There was nothing
special for these men. These were the *zeks*—they might be
killers or thieves or rapists or parasites or hooligans. At Vladimir, Holly had been different from these men.

But not any longer. The stammered words of the consul
flooded back to him. He was to be classified as a Soviet citizen,
he was being sent to the Correctional Labor Colonies. . . . Try
and live with the system, don't kick it and don't fight it, you
can't beat them. You'll hear of me, you bastard, you'll hear
of Michael Holly.

He reached out across the floor, snatched the last paper bag.
A slice of black bread, supple as cardboard. A mouthful of
sugar held in a torn square of newspaper. A fillet of dry smoked
herring. It might have been better at Vladimir for Holly than
for the *zeks* herded into the communal cell blocks, but he had
learned to eat what food was provided. He had been taught the
hard lesson that you eat where there is food, because food is
sustenance and without it there is failure and collapse. Always

he felt sick when he ate, but he had been taught and he had learned, and his eyes squinted shut and he swallowed. The last meal for how long?

Holly grimaced.

Not much to eat in the snow beside the tracks, nor in the forests that would skirt the railway line.

They'll come with dogs, Holly, dogs and guns and helicopters. The compartment of the carriage is the small camp, everything out there is the big camp. The big camp is vast, colossal, but even beyond the hugest encampment there is still the wire and the watchtower and the searchlight. Live with the system, the consul had said. You'll hear of me, Mister bloody consul, you'll hear of Michael Holly.

He munched hard at the bread, biting deeply. He turned toward the two men, smiled at them for the first time. They looked away.

It was ridiculous that he should think of lowering himself through the floor of the carriage, that he should contemplate hanging for moments or minutes beneath the train, that he should consider allowing himself to fall on to the frozen stones between the wheels. Lunatic to reckon that it would work for him . . . but only as stupid as the acceptance of the alternative which was fourteen years in the camps.

His clothes were wrong. They had dressed him in the shoes and suit and overcoat that he had worn when arrested. Not the clothes for cross-country, and he would stand out like a beacon on the fringes of the villages and collectives that he must circle like a fox coming to the dustbins for food.

The distance was impossible. Nine hundred miles to the Turkish border, seven hundred to Finland. Lunatic. He wouldn't get a mile clear of the track. But there would never be another chance, not in fourteen years. Never again a time with such opportunity as from the train that plodded across the flat wilderness lands on the way to the East.

He twisted away from the two men. They whispered to each other.

Back to his knees. Fingers again under the bolt. His body straightened as he took the strain and pulled the bolt upward. Scratches of bright metal showed in its grime as the stem of the bolt edged clear. His fingers began to scrabble at the coarse

edge of the steel plate. Should have worn gloves because they
would have protected his hands, but they would have denied
him the freedom of movement that he now needed. Even the
numbed fingers could feel pain from the sharpness of the metal.
And the plate screamed as he wrenched it upward.

There's no plan, Holly.

The blueprint of the plan is to run. The plan is to fill the
lungs and run faster, run further. To run, and anywhere.

There is nowhere to go, no haven, no safety.

Better to run and be caught than the other, because the other
is fourteen years of failure.

Anything better than the prison cage. Holly smiled to himself, chuckled softly, because he saw in his mind the face of
the man who had brought the food to the hatch, and he thought
of the retribution that would fall on the cretin's shoulders. That
alone was worth it. . . . No, no, out of your bloody mind, Holly,
and he laughed again. Why not, Holly, why not be bloody
mad? He heaved again at the floor plate and there was room
for his feet to slide down toward the blurred stones between
the sleepers.

Are you going, Holly? Night's coming, you can see the
black shadow on the stones that rush past and between your
feet. The train's idling, not running fast. Are you going, Holly?
Your decision, Holly, yours and no one else's. He took a great
gulp of the fresh air, enough to sustain him. He looked once
more behind him.

The two men sat on the bunk shelf very still, and their
saucer eyes never left Holly's face.

Holly pushed his feet beneath the steel plate and the wind
caught at his socks and trousers and drove a channeled wind
against his legs and he cursed the awkwardness of his overcoat,
and his feet kicked in the space like the feet of a hanging man.
He searched for a resting place for them and they lashed in a
helplessness before finding a firm ledge out in the gray darkness
beyond his vision. Holly wriggled, squirmed, maneuvered his
body down into the hole. The stench of the floor was close to
him, the smell of vomit and of urine. The floor edge tore at
his buttocks, the cloth of his trousers ripped. The rim of the
steel plate scraped his upper thighs. Go on, Holly. . . . Don't
hesitate, don't look down, not at the stones, not at the wheels,

not at the rushing sleepers. The train's crawling. Never again the same chance, Holly, not for fourteen bastard years. Don't look down. . . .

When you fall, fall limp.

When you hit, clutch your body with your arms, don't bounce with your legs.

Remember the wheels. When you've fallen, stay still, don't move.

Is there a guardbox at the end of the train? Hadn't looked, had he? Is there a machine gunner at the end of the train? But he'll be high, and looking forward, the windows and the carriages will be his watch.

Just remember the wheels.

The train's running slow. It can be done at this speed. Leave it, and perhaps the gradient'll even out, the speed'll pick up.

Go now or you're lost, Holly.

Go.

The last effort. The last pushing pressure on the steel plate to create the space for his stomach and chest.

Past his eyes exploded the boots and ankles and shins of the big man sweeping toward the doorway of the compartment. And the smaller man was at Holly's back, his knee at Holly's shoulder blades and his fingers deep in the spare folds of Holly's overcoat, and he pulled and wrenched to drag Holly from the hole, and Holly knew his stale breath as he hissed and heaved to pry Holly clear. The big man beat on the door and shouted in the high nasal tone of the Caucasus, slammed his fist into the woodwork, demanded attention. The guard was running in the corridor. The big man turned and came fast toward Holly and caught his throat. Holly could not resist, and they squeezed him out from the hole and when his feet were clear the two men stamped together on the steel plate to flatten it back, and between his knees he could no longer see the whiteness of snow on the stones and the zebra flash of the sleepers. The bolt scraped in the door. The doorway gaped around the guard. The guard stood uncertain. His right hand was half hidden by the cover flap of the holster that he wore at his belt.

"Comrade . . ." wheedled the big man with the pleading of a comic. "We need water. Please, Comrade, we have had no water . . ."

The guard stiffened in anger. He had been made to run, and they wanted water. "Piss yourself for water."

"How long till we can have water, Comrade?"

The guard was young, a conscript. Command did not come easily to him. He dropped his eyes. "In two hours we are at Pot'ma Transit. There will be water there."

The door swung shut, the bolt ran home. Beneath Holly the wheels quickened over the rails. He felt weak and drew his knees up to his chest to contain his body warmth. The men had gone back to the bunk shelf and their feet swung, threatening and powerful, beside his face.

Holly looked up at them, into their mouths, into their eyes. The tiredness had stripped his fury.

"Why?"

The big man picked his nose.

"You have to tell me why."

The big man spoke slowly and without passion. "Because of what would have happened to us. Because of what they would have done to us."

"You could have said something. . . ." Holly's voice trailed away, beaten by the new apathy that overwhelmed him.

The small man speared Holly with his gaze. "For me it is myself first. Then it is myself second. After that it is myself third."

"If you had gone we would have been taken again before the courts. They would say that we were your accomplices, they would say that we helped you. You are a foreigner, we owe you nothing."

"A new charge, a new trial, a new sentence. . . . For what? For nothing." The small man battered his fist into the palm of his hand.

"Your escape is not worth to us one single day more in the camps. How then can it be worth five more years?"

"I understand," Holly said, little more than a whisper.

He rose stiffly to his feet, then bent and found the bolt where it had rolled against the compartment wall underneath the shuttered window. He placed it carefully into its entry, then stamped it down.

He walked to the wall of the compartment and dropped his weight against it and closed his eyes. He thought of the forest beyond the carriage walls, and the lights in small homes, and the unmarked snow.

The darkness of the long winter night had settled when the train came to an untidy halt at Pot'ma station. Holly joined the lines of men and women who formed files of fives beside the carriages and waited to be counted. The area was gaudily lit and the dogs on their short leashes yelped and strained the arms of their handlers. The dogs and the guards who cradled submachine guns formed a ring around their prisoners. Captors and captives stood in dumb impatience for the roll call to be finished.

That night they would be held in the Pot'ma Transit prison. Away to the north, curving smoothly, stretched a branch line that Holly could see illuminated by the arc lights. The two men with whom he had shared the compartment from Moscow stood away from him, as if by choice.

Holly started to murmur a tune, something cheerful. Close to him was a girl who rocked a sleeping baby and, when she caught his glance, she smiled sadly and held the baby tighter to save it from the snow flurries.

A tiny girl, but her eyes were bright and large and caring, full of the compassion that should have been a stranger in the Pot'ma railway yards. Even here, she seemed to tell him in her silence, there could be some small love for another sufferer, for a baby. When the order came she reached down to help an older woman to her feet and passed her the well-wrapped bundle, then she turned her back on the men and was swallowed by the mass of female prisoners.

. . . It's just terribly bad luck, the consul had said, it's the worst luck I've heard of since I've been here. . . .

In ragged columns they were marched between a corridor of armed men to the trucks.

Chapter 3

The western part of Mordovia is scattered with the Correctional Labor Colonies that are administered by the Ministry of the Interior in the distant capital. Mordovia is the cesspit into which are flushed the malcontents and malefactors of the Union of Soviet Socialist Republics. Flat, desolate countryside, unbroken by hills, the plain of Mordovia knows the stinking heat of a windless summer and the cruel gales of frozen winter. A place without vistas, without the opportunity or charity of hope.

To the south of the camps is the main road from Moscow to Kuibyshev and ultimately to Tashkent. Bedfellow of the road is the railway line that runs from European Russia to the desert lands of Kazakhstan. Pot'ma is a hesitation on that journey, none would stop there without business with the camps. The driver of the long-distance truck would tighten his hands on the wheel and urge his machine faster past the bleak terrain that marks fear and anxiety across the breadth of the Motherland. The passenger in the railway carriage would drop his head into his newspaper and avert his eyes from the window. The camps of Mordovia are known of by all citizens. To the north are the wild acres of the Mordovia state reservation. To the west is the Vad river. To the east flows the Alatyn.

Inside the box of the rivers and the railway and the reservation, the territory is barren, swamp-infested, poorly inhabited. The planners chose well. And having made their decision they set out with a will to forge a network of rough roads through this wilderness that would link the stockades of wire. The camps are historic, as much a part of history as Iosif Vissarionovich Dzhugashvili who was to take the name of Stalin. Iosif's tomb in The Kremlin Wall may be hard to find, but the camps remain as a headstone in perpetuity to his memory. Iosif may have been erased from the history books, but his camps still linger, refined and modernized, as a hallowed memorial to a life's work of elimination and retribution. They possessed a faint whiff of humor, those men who sat at the ankles of Iosif. Perhaps with the taint of a half-smile they named the camps of Mordovia after the pretty, sun-dappled forests around Moscow where they took their family picnics and holidays. *Dubrovlag*, that was the name they offered to the pestilence of fences and huts in Mordovia. The Oak Leaf camps. And after Iosif came Malenkov. And after Malenkov came Khrushchev. And after Khrushchev came Brezhnev. Each in his time has painted over the inheritance of his predecessor, but the Oak Leaf camps have remained because they have been necessary for each new czar's survival. Where the planners and architects of Iosif first planted their stakes and hung their wire, there remain posts and fences and watchtowers with searchlights and traversing machine guns. If it is hard to remember you, Iosif, we can come to the *Dubrovlag* and watch the slow march of the men who have replaced your prisoners in the Oak Leaf camps.

For thirty miles the branch line from Pot'ma winds north across the desolation of the prisonscape.

Past Camp 18 and Camp 6.

The hamlet of Lesnoy.

Camp 19 and Camp 7 and Camp 1.

The village of Sosnovka.

The station at Sal'khoz, across the road from Vindrey to Promzina.

Over the bridge that spans the turgid flowing stream at Lepley and past Camp 5, and sub-Camp 5 where the foreigners are held incommunicado from the domestic fodder of the Colonies.

Past the farm where the short-term prisoners work under the guard of rifles and dogs, past the fields where beet and potato sprout from the long-used soil.

Past the twins of Camp 4 and Camp 10, one to the left and one to the right of the single track line.

Through the township of Yavas, over the bridge of rusted steel that crosses the river, and past Camp 11 and Camp 2 where the Central Investigation Prison has been built with con-

crete to house those who face interrogation for misdemeanors
committed within the barbed wire and free-fire corridors.

Past more fields where the work is back-breaking and by
hand, past the station at Lesozavad and to the hamlet of Barashevo. Here is Camp 3, here is the Central Administration
complex. Here at Barashevo are buffers on the siding track
because few of the trains that run north from Pot'ma have need
to travel further.

The camps are rooted in the history of the state, but dedi-
cated also to the present, and will be a part too of the future.
They have their permanence, they have their place. They are
indestructible.

They are all criminals, of course, who ride in the *Stolypin*
carriages from Pot'ma on the way to Barashevo. All have been
convicted by legally constituted courts. There are some who
have stolen from banks, there are some who have read poetry
in Pushkin Square in Moscow. There are some who have raped
virgin teenage girls in the darkness of an alley way, there are
some who have taught their children the liturgy and practices
of the church of the Seventh Day Adventists. There are some
who have corruptly manipulated the production of state factories for their own personal gain, there are some who have
covertly passed on the writings of Aleksandr Solzhenitsyn. And
there are some who are traitors. They are all criminals, those
who live in the barracks huts of the camps, and those who will
join them when the train reaches the platforms of Barashevo.

It had been a luxury, the journey from Moscow to Pot'ma.
Only three to share a compartment. And a luxury, too, had
been the cell on the second floor of the hospital block at Vladimir. And luxuries are temporary.

There were fifteen of them in the compartment, crammed
and squashed for three hours since their loading from the Transit
jail. Difficult to move, hideous to breathe in the shuttered
carriage. The tight smell of men who have not washed their
bodies or known clean clothes. All together, elbows in ribs,
knees in calves, packed tight and swaying with the motion of
the train as it struggled north.

When he had woken from a faint sleep on the ice cold floor
of the cell, Holly had known that the lice had found him.

Creeping little bastards in the hair of his head and his stomach, and he had gouged with his fingernails at the flesh under his clothes. The men who sat or lay near to him on the floor had watched with a curiosity that a man who was held in the Transit jail at Pot'ma should concern himself with such a small matter as the pin-sharp biting of the louse. Only an old man with his white hair cropped short and worn as a Jew's cap had spoken to Holly with the wry grin of experience at his mouth. They were nothing, the lice at Pot'ma, the old man said. At the Transit at Alma-Ata there were bugs that saturated the walls of the holding cells, red and fast with their crawl, with a bite like scissors. And at the Transit at Novosibirsk there were rats, great gray pigs, a tail as thick as your little finger, and the men in the holding cells slept in a camp in the center of the floor and changed the watch in the dark hours so that always some men guarded the edge of their perimeter. So, what were a few lice? Holly had talked with the old man and realized only later that when he spoke all those who were within earshot had listened and tried to learn about him from his words. He was the outsider, he came from beyond the corrals of the big camp, from beyond the wire of the little camp. Though he spoke in Russian, the language that his parents had given him, he was from without the walls that bounded their experience. They examined him with their eyes and ears. They might have wished to touch him. They were without hostility and without friendship. They were interested in an object to which they had not before been exposed.

There had been eighty men in the cell trying to sleep away the cold of the night.

There had been fifteen men in the compartment of the train trying to endure the rattling movement on the rails. And the train had stopped. They heard the barking of the dogs, the shouting of orders, and they waited because that is the lot of prisoners.

For how long, Holly? For fourteen years.

In the cell at Pot'ma Transit the old man had kissed him, the door was opened, the guards were calling names. Holly and the majority were to travel, the old man waited for another transport to another destination. He had kissed Holly, wetly on each cheek, and he had not cared who had seen him, and

he had whispered in Holly's ear. In the *Dubrovlag,* he had
said, pity for others is always possible, but self-pity is never
possible. He had pulled Holly's ear then and crackled a laugh,
and Holly had slapped his shoulder in a kind of gratitude.

The wind swept aside the fetid air of the compartment as
the door was unbolted. The guards who waited below them
stamped their feet, beat down the snow beneath their boots.

Some from the carriage could jump down and then slither
into the lines they must form. Some must be helped.

Beyond the platform stood the camp. An outer gate was
open, an inner gate was closed. They stood in three rows of
five, to be counted and then marched forward. On the ice one
man fell and was scooped back to his feet by those who were
behind him. Not really a march, not even a brisk tramp, but a
shuffling movement forward toward the opened gate. Holly
saw the high wooden fence of vertical overlapping boards and
above it the rise of steep angled roofs and in the corners were
watchtowers built up on stilts with the platform reached by
open ladder. They kept the dogs close to the prisoners.

Put on a show, Holly....

He walked with his back straight and his shoulders firm.
And the other men saw him, and some would have sniggered
at the fall that would follow such arrogance, and a few would
have suffered in the knowledge that defiance brings only pain
and punishment, and for one or two or three the young man
who ambled erect in the first rank was a donor of comfort.

It was not the proper way of things that one man should
walk as if with indifference toward the opened gates of Camp
3 at Barashevo, and the guards watched him, and the dogs
eyed him. Self-pity is never possible; do not forget that, Holly.
Self-pity is unacceptable.

The gates were pushed shut behind them. A beam cracked
down into its sockets. More shouting, more orders. To Holly's
right, lights glowed from the warmth of the administration
block where the windows were misted and the scent of coal
smoke billowed from a brick chimney. The inner gates opened.
In front of him Holly could see the expanse of the snow-draped
camp. He had reached the Correctional Labor Colony in the
Dubrovlag with the designated administrative title of ZhKh
385/3/1. He had arrived at Camp 3, Zone 1 (Strict Regime). He

thought it was a Sunday, the eighth day after the death of a man in the Coronary Care unit of the Hammersmith Hospital.

The inner gate closed behind the new intake of prisoners.

From the window of the administration block overlooking the open ground of the camp close to the inner gates, the major watched as the prisoners were again lined in fives and counted, a necessary formality because this marked their passing from the charge of the MVD transport guard into the hands of the MVD Correctional Labor Detachment. He was a short man, barrel-built, and his physique was suited to the paratroop unit he had been a part of before his transfer from the active service troops of the Red Army, to the mind-twisting boredom of Ministry of the Interior camp supervision. Paratroops were the elite while those seconded to MVD work were the latrine cleaners of the armed forces. But a duty was a duty, a posting could not be evaded by a major who had been turned down for promotion to colonel. He would serve out his uniformed days as Commandant of Camp 3, Zone I.

The paratroop regiment that he had left eighteen months before was now bivouacked in a concrete and brick school house on the outskirts of Jalalabad and dominated the low ground of an Afghan valley. This was where his heart lay, where the helicopters waited to lift men into mountain combat, and the radio chattered the coordinates for Ilyushin strikes. He was an activist, with bluff red cheeks under his stunted pig eyes to prove his love of the outdoor life. Zone I was in its way as much of a prison for the Commandant as for the eight hundred men to whom he played a vague mutation of God and Commissar. Far from his paratroops, far from their mortars and machine guns and rocket-launchers, far from their special camaraderie, he worried like a dog with freshly stolen meat over the incessant and aching problems of the camp's discipline and routine.

The little parade that he witnessed through the steamed window of the administration block was a wound to him.

The conscript troops of the MVD could not entirely be blamed for the ill fit of their uniforms, for their slouched shoulders, for their callow and chilled faces. They were not the cream or they would not have found their way to this worthless place. Scum in uniform. . . . he yearned for a parade ground of his former troops, for the whip crack of their rifle drill, the unison stamping of their marching boots.

And the prisoners were worse, the worst. No feet picked up, just a slovenly shuffle in the snow . . . as if they knew that their scraping passage festered in the mind of the major. But he tried. He strove through all his waking hours to impose a smartness and snap on Camp 3, Zone I, that he knew had never been present before, and that during the night hours when he was alone he doubted he would ever achieve.

He was Major Vasily Kypov, thirty-three years of service behind him, and three more to endure before the blessed release of retirement.

A young man stood a pace behind him, young enough to have been his son, and his breath played the sweet stale smell of the cigarette smoker's mouth across the major's nostrils. The same uniform, but without the silver wings and blue tabs instead of red. A captain in KGB he might be, the power in the kingdom of Zone I, feared by the superior in rank and the inferior in fortune, but the major had demanded that inside the administration block in the mornings he should wear his uniform. Such were the victories available to the Commandant in his skirmishes with his political officer.

The captain smoked imported Marlboro cigarettes. They were sent to him in packages of ten cartons from Moscow. That was a display of influence, not that the major needed information on the long arm of KGB. And Major Vasily Kypov knew well that he commanded Captain Yuri Rudakov in name only. They shared their responsibilities for the smooth running of Zone I with the enthusiasm of those bound by a loveless marriage. Where possible they went their own ways. Where contact was unavoidable their relations were frosted and formal. If asked, Captain Rudakov would not have been able to recall an occasion when he had given ground, important or trivial, to Major Kypov.

With his pocket handkerchief the major wiped the window pane.

There was one among the dross people in their three ranks of fives who stood out. A tall man who gazed about him as if not yet intimidated by what he saw. Interest stirred in the major.

There were few enough who came to the camps with their heads erect, who stood their ground in the snow and fielded the threat of the gun barrels and dogs' mouths. The major's sensibilities were divided between admiration for a man with self-pride and hostility to a man who by defiance might provide a threat to the peaceful and submissive nature of the Zone.

"What do we have today, the same shit as always?" The major's breath blurred the glass, and he reached again for his handkerchief.

"The usual medley, Comrade Major. . . . Criminals mostly."

"Scum, parasites, hooligans . . ."

"And pliable and quiet, Comrade Major . . . if you want the busier life you can apply for Perm . . ."

"I don't want the politicals, I don't want Perm. I want a camp that is efficient and productive."

"Then you must have the scum, the parasites and the hooligans. From the criminals you have no argument . . . I have the files . . . thieves, one who took a knife to a postmaster's throat, one who buggered a Pioneer intake class, one who caught his wife screwing the rent official and took off half her head with a hammer—he should work well. There is only one. . . ."

"The one in the front rank," mused the major.

"Of course you are right. They cannot send us a box that is filled only with good apples, there has to be one that is bruised."

"Tell me."

"A peculiar case. His name is Holovich. Mikhail Holovich. That is the bruised apple." The captain walked back from the window toward the major's desk and tipped onto its ordered surface a bundle of buff card files. "In Moscow they have given Holovich the Red Stripe category."

The major swung away from the window. The red stripe on the file was attached only if there was believed to be a risk of escape. The red stripe demanded a special vigilance. The blue stripe was its brother and indicated that a prisoner had shown tendencies toward organization and confrontation. "Blue I can handle, blue you can see, blue is self-destructive and the posture of an idiot. The red stripe I detest. The prevention of escape is inexact. . . ."

"You haven't lost a man, not in your time."

"Not in my time. . . . Who is Holovich?"

"Quite a star, actually," the captain drawled. "Something far from the ordinary. His parents lived before the Great Patriotic War in the Ukraine. They were married there just prior to the Fascist invasion. The Germans took them, man and wife, back to their war factories. After the surrender they refused to be repatriated, and they settled in Great Britain. It is certain that they became participants within the traitor ranks of NTS . . . you know of that, Comrade Major? Narodno-Trudovoi Soyuz, an émigré organization, of course you know that. . . . They have one son, born Mikhail Holovich and now thirty years old. In the eyes of the British the boy had their citizenship, but we see the matter differently. To us he will always be a Soviet citizen. Mikhail Holovich became Michael Holly, but the change of a name does not discard nationality. He is Soviet. Holovich is an engineer, small-scale turbines. He worked for a firm in the area of London, and that company began to negotiate with one of our Ministries for the sale of their products to the Soviet Union. During his childhood, Holovich had been taught Russian by his mother and it was ostensibly for that reason that his company asked him to visit Moscow—a quite spurious reason because we supply most adequate and experienced interpreters for commercial negotiations with foreign concerns. Before arriving in the Soviet Union, Holovich was recruited by the British espionage service and was given instructions for a contact—I don't have to go into detail, these are matters available to me. He was caught and he was sentenced. In the interests of détente, because of our belief in the value of friendly relations where possible, our government agreed to return this criminal to the British in exchange for a Soviet citizen falsely accused in London. We were giving them gold, they were handing us tin. We made this offer on humanitarian grounds. The jailers of Holovich reneged on the agreement, the exchange will not take place. In Moscow, the Ministry of the Interior after consultation with the Ministry of Justice has determined that the full rigor of the law shall now be turned on Holovich. One year ago he was sentenced to a term of fifteen years imprisonment. Up to now he has known the soft ride of the foreigners' block at Vladimir. . . . From now on he will be treated as a Soviet offender, that is why he is not at

Camp 5. . . . He is a spy, he is a traitor, perhaps he is fortunate not to have faced the extreme penalty provided for in the criminal code."

The major strode back toward the window and his boots sounded drum rattle over the hollow spacing under the bare boards of his office. A spartan, soldierly room.

"This Holovich, he is a self-confessed spy?"

The Captain laughed quietly. "They were dilatory in Moscow. He is not self-confessed. That is to come. . . ."

Always when the snow had recently fallen there was a damp fog over the camp, a link between the low gray cloud and the whitened ground. It was hard for the major to see the little procession that moved away from the administration block toward the heart of the camp, but he fancied he could still make out one dark head among the hazing image of the retreating column.

There were faces at the glass of the windows watching their approach.

A timbered hut, a hundred feet long and balanced on stilts of brickwork, with smoke flowing from a central chimney. There were other huts visible as outlines in the mist of early afternoon, but it was to the hut with the figure "2" painted in yellow on the doorway that they were led. The snow had drifted at one end, at the beck of the wind, so that it reached almost to the eaves of the roof.

And the old man at Pot'ma had said that self-pity was not acceptable.

Holly kicked the snow from his shoes against the jamb of the door and climbed the few steps into Hut 2.

Chapter 4

There was a smell from Hut 2 that was unlike anything Holly had known before. Stronger than the smells of Lefortovo or Vladimir, more pervasive than the smells of the Lubyanka interrogation cells or the train. It was the smell of a hundred bodies that had not been bathed for a week, of a hundred sets of clothes that had been lived and slept in for a week, of excreta and vomit trapped by the windows that had not been opened for a week. It floated in the dull light of the hut, a wall that hung from the wooden rafters to the boards of the flooring. The smell would catch its victims as a spider's web ensnares a fly.

Holly and two others were delivered to Hut 2, the rest would be further dispersed. The door closed on his back.

He thought he would choke, he thought he would be sick. The bile ran in a bitter taste to his mouth.

The door split the center of one wall of the hut, a long wall. Holly turned slowly from left to right, gazed and absorbed.

A poster, white lettering on red background, blared from the gloom of the opposite wall. UNDER THE CONDITIONS OF SOCIALISM EVERY MAN WHO LEAVES THE PATH OF LABOR IS ABLE TO RETURN TO USEFUL ACTIVITY.

In the center of the hut stood a tall coke stove, blackened from use, deep in dust, and its chimney stack climbed to the ceiling and through its open hatch there was the glow of fuel working out a second day's burning. There were windows without curtains. What else, Holly? What else is there to see in Hut 2? Only the bunks, nothing else. The bunks are round the walls, the bunks fill the central aisle of the hut. Wooden framed and two tiered, half a yard between them. Hut 2 is a dumping-ground for bunk beds, it offers no space to any other furniture. There are no tables, chairs, cupboards. This is the place where they dump you, Holly, you and the bunk beds. This is where they leave you while your existence is hacked from the memory of the former life. This is home for the forgotten. Of course, you'd read of these places and screwed up your nose in disgust and said such things shouldn't be permitted, and why didn't someone else do something about it. But now, Holly, you're in Hut 2 of ZhKh 385/3/I, and nobody did do anything and the hut is reality. The hut breathes and lives and survives. The hut is your home, Holly.

"What is your name?"

A voice beside him, Holly spun to his right.

There were faces peering at him. Tired faces all of them, some old and some young. The men lay on the bunks, all but one. He was a small man with a puffed chest and a jutting chin. Holly saw the bright red band that was sewn to the upper arm of his tunic, the red diamond on his chest.

"What is your name . . . you, the one in the front?"

Holly knew the standing of the man. There had been similar men at Vladimir. The trusty of the Internal Order System. The toadie, the crawler, the compromiser, the one who worked for favors. The man came closer, maneuvering with the confidence of authority between the bunks.

"Holly, Michael Holly. . . ."

"We are Soviets here, we are not foreigners."

"My name is Holly."

"If you are in Camp 3 you are a Soviet. If you are in this camp you have a Soviet name. What is your name?"

"My name is Michael Holly . . . I was charged in that name, I was sentenced in that name."

And the faces stirred above the gray-blue pillows, and the bodies shifted beneath the dark blankets. A newcomer disputed with the trusty in his first moments inside the hut. That was entertainment. Like cats' eyes on a night road the pale faces beamed at Holly and his adversary through the grayness of the room.

"Smart ass, clever prick. . . . What is your name in Russian?" Anger flared in the man who was not accustomed to the answer back.

Holly smiled. "When I was born my parents called me

Mikhail Holovich. My name now is Holly. . . ."

Their eyes held, Holly's and the trusty's. The trusty looked away, far down to the recesses of the hut.

"At the end of the line you will find a bunk. . . . And Holovich, be careful, you clever shit. Learn what is the arm band, learn what is the diamond, remember them and be careful."

The faces watched him as he walked half the length of the hut, searchlights following him, and Holly went briskly as if by the speed of his step fourteen years might somehow trickle faster through the future's fingers. The two men who had stood behind him gave their names quickly, eagerly, anxious to avoid association. Holly went to the end of the hut. He had not given his name in Russian and the bunk that was allocated to him was against the wall at the furthest stretch from the narrow band of heat that the boiler might service. The two tiers of the end bunk were unoccupied. He chose the upper bunk. There was sagging wire beneath the frame, a drip of water plunged sporadically into the space where his feet would rest.

This is home, Holly. . . .

He had no possessions to swing onto the bunk, he wore them all. Two pairs of underpants, two pairs of socks, two vests, his gloves, his scarf. He shivered, wrapping his arms tight around his body.

"You are a foreigner?"

The voice was sharp, beside Holly's knee. He was little more than a boy. Vivid red hair cut back to his scalp, a sheen of stubble across his cheeks.

"My home was in England."

"Why are you not in Camp 5?"

"Long and complicated . . . I've fourteen years to find the answer for you."

"I am Anatoly Feldstein."

"Michael Holly. . . ."

"I think we know that now." The boy murmured his laughter. "You are political?"

"I didn't rob a bank."

"I am Article 70. Disseminating for the purpose of undermining or weakening the Soviet regime slanderous fabrications which defame the Soviet state and social system. I am a prisoner of conscience, I am named by Amnesty."

"That must help you to sleep sweetly," Holly said.

Above the Jewish boy lay a larger, heavier man with rougher hands and a jowled chin where the white ribbon of a healed scar ran twisting across the folds. Something dominating about the mouth, something cruel about the eyes. His head was motionless on the pillow as he spoke.

"You have tobacco, Holovich?"

"My name is Holly. . . ."

"I said—you have tobacco, Holovich?"

"Get the name right, and you have my answer."

The man jackknifed to a sitting position, the blanket fell from his chest.

"In this hut when I ask something, it is answered," he hissed. "Whatever I ask, it is answered. . . . Do you have tobacco, Holovich?"

"The name is Holly."

"This is my hut. . . ." A fleck of spittle rested on the blood blue lips of the man. "Learn that this is my hut. . . ."

"And learn my name."

Holly saw the streak of the blade exposed by a fold of the blanket.

What's in the bloody name Holly? How does a name matter? What matters when home is Hut 2 in Zone I in Camp 3 of the *Dubrovlag*? . . . He had told himself that his name was Michael Holly, he had set himself that challenge. Surrender was failure, failure is collapse, collapse is disaster. Where is the better ground to fight? In the hut, in the open snow, in the factory, the administration block, in the punishment cells, is any one of them a better ground to fight on? If once the cheek is turned then you will never fight again. His name was Michael Holly.

He saw the fingers tighten above the snatch of blade, he saw the legs ripple beneath the blanket as if in preparation for sudden attack.

Holly's hand moved, the lightning strike of the cobra. His fingers found the wrist. They gripped and savagely twisted. The knife sprang into the air, arced up a few inches as if powered by a small spring. It fell between the bunks and clattered dully in its landing. He held the man's wrist hard against the clean edge of the frame of the bunk.

"Don't threaten me, not ever again. My name is Michael

Holly..." he paused, then grinned quickly. "I have no tobacco... what is your name?"

Holly bent to the floor, picked up the knife, admired the
workmanship of the weapon, reversed it so that the string
whipped handle was toward the man, passed it back to him.

"Adimov... this is my hut."

"You can have all of it, but not me. No one has me."

A nervous, hesitant gust of laughter blew the length of the
hut.

"Remember that you sleep beside me... Holly...."

"I am a light sleeper, Adimov."

Before dusk Holly and those who had arrived that day were
taken to the bathhouse to stand for a few moments beneath the
trickle of lukewarm water. When they had dried perfunctorily
on the threadbare towels that were issued they were marched
across the stamped snow of a path to the Store for the clothing
issue. Black cotton trousers, a black tunic, a black quilted coat,
a balaclava that was padded. Boots of army style that fitted
loosely over his socks. There was a mattress to be carried away,
calico cloth and filled with straw. A blanket and a shallow
pillow. He dressed, he signed for the garments, he saw his old
clothes parceled into a plastic bag that was labeled and tossed
to the floor. He was in the uniform of the camp, he was a part
of its essence. The camp had drawn him with whirlpool force
into its mouth. He belonged in the camp, he belonged nowhere
else.

He shouldered the mattress and carried it back to Hut 2,
and slung it up onto his bunk, and threw the pillow and blanket
after it.

Adimov was sleeping.

Feldstein told Holly at what time they went over to the
kitchen for the evening's food and he spoke of the compulsory
attendance afterward at the Political Education Unit. Holly
sensed the loneliness of Feldstein in the hut, the dissident among
the *zeks*. That was a bitter punishment, the placing of this boy
amongst the criminals. The boy would have no defense against
these people.

"Adimov is the 'baron' of this hut. Nobody has spoken to
him in the way that you have, not for more than a year...."

"He broke a man's arm a year ago, snapped it like a dried twig behind his back. There are two men that you should fear here. Adimov in the hut, and Rudakov in the administration. Adimov you have seen, Rudakov you will find. In the punishment cells last week, Rudakov, who is the political officer, kicked over a man's slop bucket and the water ran all over the floor. There is no bedding in the punishment cells and no heating. The man slept on the floor, and the water that had been spilled froze on the floor. The man slept on ice. They are the two men who are feared here, they survive in their authority because we are afraid of them."

A private smile murmured on Holly's face. . . . He thanked the boy, then went out into the gathering darkness and across to the trodden path on the inner perimeter of the camp.

Ahead of him, spaced at compact intervals, other men walked the path. This was the place of aloneness, this was where a man went to talk only with himself. Out into the freezing, bitter wind. Holly stepped into the slow-moving line, took his pace from those who went before and after him, did not close and did not widen the gaps.

He walked against the clock.

Away from Hut 2. Past Hut 3, turn to the left, past the gate and administration which was now a darkened hulk, past where the roof of the camp's prison peeped over the fences, turn to the left, past Hut 4, past the old kitchen which was now a sleeping hut, past the bathhouse and then Hut 6, past the store, turn to the left, past the guardroom, turn to the left, past Hut 1 . . . three hundred and eighty-five paces . . . Away from Hut 2.

They were the margins for Holly, those were the limits.

And Camp 3 is one of the old ones, Holly, there have been thousands here before you, tens of thousands of booted and bandaged feet dragging round this path. Not the first to step onto that path and wonder in rage at four left turns adding to three hundred and eighty-five paces. The path was packed snow or worn earth before you were born, Holly. The path will see you out, see you dead and forgotten. Beside the path to his right there was a low wooden fence, a yard high he reckoned it to be, and in some places the snow had driven against it and reached its top. A fence of sawed-off, creosoted planks. Beyond the low innocence of the fence the snow was smooth, untrampled. Over the wooden fence is the deathstrip, Holly. He thought of a bullet, and he thought of the chill lead set in the brass cartridge cases of the rifles or machine guns that watched him. And after the low wooden fence and the clean snow was the barbed wire fence that stretched up on poles to the height of Holly's head. And after the barbed wire was another fence that was higher and again the floodlights played and caught on the cutting edges . . . and after the high barbed wire was a wooden fence that was three yards high. Two wooden fences, two wire fences, and all lit as day, all covered by the watchtowers standing in each corner of the compound, and over the highest of the wooden fences he could see only the roof of the prison.

A terrible silence without beauty. The silence of those without hope.

A man in front of him had stopped. He stared at the low wooden fence and the pure sward of snow yellowed by the lights, and at the low wire fence and at the high wire fence and at the high wooden fence. Holly saw his face as he passed behind him on the perimeter path, a face that was scraped with despair. Holly walked on and the man behind him was an abandoned nothing.

It can't be real, Holly. It can only be canvas. Put a knife to it and the canvas will rip. There must be another picture behind the paint.

Crap, Holly, it's real. And the bullets in the gun in the watchtower above, they're real . . . and the cold, and the sentence of the court which has fourteen years to run, and the worst luck that the consul had ever heard of . . . they're real.

He had completed another revolution of the prescribed path, and the man still stood and stared at the fences, and his shoulders were not hunched as if the cold no longer concerned him.

Where did it begin?

Where was the start of the story that brought Mikhail Holovich, who was to become Michael Holly, to this place of wire and snow, of dogs and guns?

The town called Bazar in the heart of the Ukraine was found on the fringes of thick forestland to the north of the Kiev to Zhitomir railway. In its way the town possessed a certain prosperity that was based on the quality of the nearby timber, the richness of the black soil, and the failure of central government's collectivization policy to reach with any great thoroughness into the self-sufficiency of the few thousands who lived there.

The Ukraine is not Russia. The Ukraine had struggled to preserve its identity of language, heritage, and literature. Moscow was a distant capital, a foreign overlord handing out its satraps and commissars. In spite of, and because of, the Stalinist purges of the thirties, the uniqueness of the Ukraine had not been dislodged. And where better to remember that individuality than in the town of Bazar. On the lips of every child of that town was the story of the day-long battle fought there on November 21st, 1921, between the men loyal to George Tiutiunnyk and the fledgling Red Army. A gunfight that stretched from dawn until night as the group who believed themselves to be Ukrainian patriots held out, without hope of rescue or reinforcement, against the encircling advance of Moscow's soldiers. It was an epic fight. Old rifles against mortars and machine guns and howitzers. It was followed, after the ammunition pouches of the defenders had been emptied, by total slaughter as the last line on the summit of an open hill was breached.

The sacrifice of Tiutiunnyk and his men, because sacrifice was how it was seen in Bazar, lingered for twenty years as a whispered obsession in the minds of the townspeople. From the time they could read and write and understand, Stepan Holovich and Ilya, who was to become his wife, had known of the battle.

And then in November 1941 the unimaginable happened.

The militia were gone from Bazar. The Party offices were closed and its workers speeding east in open trucks. Straggling, beaten columns of troops marched without equipment into the town and out along the main road to Kiev. And a day after them the Panzer convoys took the same road, and some of the girls and women of Bazar with great daring threw flowers onto the mud-spattered armor of the Panther heavy tanks, and some of the men cheered and the headmaster of the secondary school said that evening in the café on Lenin Street that this was a moment of deliverance.

The people of Bazar could not differentiate between the front line forces of the Wehrmacht and the garrison troops of the SS divisions. Nor could those people know that after the combat generals had moved further east into Russia that their authority over the civilian population would fall to the hands of Erich Koch, drafted to Kiev to head the Reichskommissariat.

On the afternoon of November 21st the townspeople flocked to the hill site of Tiutiunnyk's battle. They came in their best clothes as if it were a Sunday from the days before the church was closed. The headmaster made the first speech, flags flew, the town band played a medley of the tunes of the old Ukraine, a hymn was sung. In the evening the SS troops came to the homes of those who had organized such a happy day. In the morning the SS firing squads shot dead twenty-four of Bazar's most prominent citizens. The following week the train took all the young men and women of Bazar to the war factories of the Ruhr.

Stepan and Ilya Holovich were among those transported in the sealed wagons through Lvov and Krakow and Prague to Essen. They were the *Ostarbeiters*, intelligent and educated, and set to work as laborers, made to wear a badge.

Three and a half years later, the Panthers that had stormed through Bazar and the Ukraine came home in defeat.

Emaciated, servile, exhausted, Stepan and Ilya Holovich found themselves herded with a hundred thousand others into the Displacement Camps. The majority, the huge majority, were to be shipped back in the same closed trains to the motherland of Russia. The minority, the tiny minority, succeeded in persuading the American authorities that they should not be returned.

In 1947 Stepan and Ilya Holovich arrived with no money and no luggage at London's Tilbury docks on a freighter from Bremen. Stepan Holovich had sunk to his knees to kiss the rain-soaked paving of the dockside. From a single room in Kingston-upon-Thames which he rented and where he lived with Ilya, he repaired watches and clocks. When the local doctor, confounded by the sparrow size of his patients, informed the couple that they were to become parents, Ilya Holovich had dropped her lined and weary face to her chest and wept, and Stepan Holovich had jumped up from his chair and then scratched between his thin gray hair and laughed. A fortnight later the buff OHMS envelope had been delivered which

announced the granting of the naturalization papers. They were
British citizens by the time that Ilya Holovich entered Kingston
General Hospital for a difficult confinement. That it was difficult was of no surprise to the duty obstetrician. A woman of
that physique had no business producing 8 lb. 7 oz. babies.

They called the boy Mikhail.

In the year that the child first went to a nursery school his
father anglicized the family name. It was his hope that whereas
an essentially Ukrainian background would rule behind the
front door of their home, his son could become assimilated into
the society that had adopted his flotsam parents.

Michael Holly was an unremarkable boy growing up in the
suburbs of southwest London.

That is perhaps the start of the road to the perimeter path
of ZhKh 385/3/1.

A man stood, rakish and upright, and stared at the fences. The
night pressed down on the flood of the arc lights, the line of
lamp clusters rested on the outer fence of wood planks. The
snow gathered in a thin cloak on his tunic's shoulders and he
made no attempt to scatter the fall. Those who walked the
perimeter path went behind him, and no one spoke to the man
who gazed at the wall that held him. He communed in a sol-
itude, and much of his face was hidden by the quilted balaclava,
and his mind was blocked to those who passed him. When the
bell sounded and the ghost figures pitched from the huts to
form the lines at the kitchen, he remained, his attention held
all the time by the upper strands of wire and the topmost line
of the wooden fence.

From the corner of the compound the raised machine gun
and its minder watched and bided their time.

In the dining area of the bare brick kitchen there was a stirring
in the pool of lethargy. This was Sunday evening, the end of
the one day of the week when the factory was idle. The *zeks*
had rested, they had reinforced their strength by spending the
daylight hours on their bunks. They had written the letters that
would be read during the week by the camp censors, that would
be passed or slashed or shredded. They had read from the paltry
choice of books in the library. They had dreamed of somewhere

that was beyond the fence. They have been revived. Sunday is a hypodermic dose to the *zeks*.

There was a spatter of life and talks in the line that Holly joined and that stretched twice around the inside walls of the kitchen. For the first time in the day he heard men laugh freely.

At the far end from the door was a hatch at waist height, the level at which a man will naturally hold his steel tray. The man who ladles the food into the steel bowl on the tray cannot see the face of the man to whom he gives the food. He is blind to him and cannot therefore offer the favor of increased rations to a friend, reduced rations to an enemy. Except that Adimov and his fellow barons will speak their names, and the cook will respond, which is the way of survival. Their bowls will be brimming, they will head the line for the sprat of meat or fish that floats in the soup gruel. There is a rule, there will be a path around it. That is the way of Camp 3, it is the way of all camps in the *Dubrovlag*.

Adimov had not looked at Holly, he was far to the front of the slow-moving line with his cronies, the iron men of the huts. Feldstein stood half a wall's length ahead of Holly, beyond conversation.

The soup was a mash of wheatmeal flour and groats. There was a skim of grease that shone in the fluorescent light of the kitchen. A square of gray fish floated like a hostile iceberg, all but submerged. A tight chopped stalk of a cabbage plant. Different from Lefortovo, back in the dark ages from the second floor of the hospital block at Vladimir. Hot water to drink and rye bread to chew.

Holly found a place at the end of a table, extra room was made for him. He sat down, he smiled.

"You are the Englishman...the one who *insists* on his English name...I am Poshekhonov, from Hut 2. I sleep close to the stove."

Holly looked across the table at the stubby, round-faced little fellow who breathed a cheerfulness that was alien here. He could have been a bank manager from the High Street of Twickenham, he could have sold insurance policies or slashed-price holidays to Benidorm.

"Pleased to meet you—I'd rather it were elsewhere."

"The way you look at your food you are new to the camps.

You have to close your eyes, close your nose, close your guts, you swallow it down. You throw the bread on top of it, the bread is the cork. The bread holds it below till you're ready to shit. You don't eat like this in London?"

"Not everyday...."

Holly lifted the steel bowl to his mouth, tipped and tilted it, swallowed and felt the lukewarm drip in his throat and then the rising sickness, and he clamped his mouth shut, and swallowed again. More from the bowl.

"You have to feed, you must feed," said Poshekhonov somberly, and then his laughter broke again. "There is some goodness in the food. They even say there is protein, but that may be propaganda."

Holly thought he would choke. He bit at his lip and swallowed again.

"Is this the worst?"

"Not the worst and not the best, this is everyday." Poshekhonov leaned across the table and slapped at Holly's shoulder. "You will get used to it. How long do you have to learn to love our food? I once had two weeks to learn to love everything, two weeks until I was to be shot. The two men sentenced with me, they killed them, they spared me. Since that day I love to eat, I love all the food. Life here is very beautiful, to me any life is preferable to death. You understand me, Englishman?"

"Holly...yes, I understand you."

Only the grease lay at the bottom of the bowl. Holly took the bread and tugged it between his fingers and wolfed it to his mouth. Tasteless and dry, it suffocated the revulsion. The man next to him winked in a fast act of conspiracy, a runner bean of a man who then extended his hand to Holly and their fists gripped in a distant greeting, but there were no words. The camp was not a place of easy friendships. It was a place where men weighed and evaluated before they extended kindliness. They have learned to coexist, they have learned to live without a colleague. He wiped the scattered crumbs on his tray to a neat heap and then pinched them between his fingers and gobbled them. The meal had done little to staunch the hunger pains in his stomach. Hunger would be the battle. But they survived, all of these men in the kitchen hut had found a track of survival. And so, too, would Holly....

"Englishman, you have not asked me why I am here. . . ." The disappointment was flushed on Poshekhonov's face.

Holly stood up. Around him the benches emptied. When the food was finished, the tables cleared.

"Because it is not my business. Nor your business why I am here."

"Easy, Englishman, you cannot be an island, not in this place. The man who can live here is the one who reaches out to his fellows." Poshekhonov had gripped Holly's arm. "They have the guns and the dogs and the wire, they have their norms of output in the factory, they have their regulations and their camp regime. They seem to have everything. We have only our strength to laugh at them."

"And does your laughter wound them?"

"From laughter we can have small victories."

"Small victories win nothing."

"That is the answer of a man who hurries. There is nobody in this camp who runs. There is nowhere to run to. . . . It is your first night, Englishman, you have to learn of a new world, you have to be patient if it is to give up to you its secrets. I tell you now—the big victory is not possible."

"If you say so," Holly said over his shoulder. He joined the slow column heading out of the double doors of the kitchen.

Poshekhonov was still beside him. "You have yet to sleep here one night. The man from internal order is already your enemy. . . . Adimov, who is a killer, is your enemy. A man cannot be an island here if he is ever to turn his back on this place."

"Thank you," said Holly quietly.

Beyond the door the snow was falling more heavily and the men who crowded there braced themselves to run or shamble back to their huts. Holly stepped out into the bitter wind. You give yourself to no man, Holly. Myself first, myself second, myself third. Dancing shadows passed by him. No talk now, because the business was serious, crossing the open meters from the kitchen to the huts.

The shots ripped aside the murmur sound of sliding feet.

The shots dipped and gouged into Holly's consciousness.

And Holly knew where to look. The instant of clarity. God, Holly, you had forgotten him. You had been swilling food into your guts and making the small talk of camp survival, and you had lost him from your memory.... The columns of men that splintered from the kitchen to their huts were first frozen still, then drawn in concert to where the lights were brilliant, where the fences hung between the blackness and the snow.

One more shot.

You could have spoken to him, you could have offered something of yourself, but you left him there in the stinking bloody cold. You went to your fucking soup and your fucking swill and left him in the night.

Holly ran.

He barged aside those who were in front of him. He cannoned against gray-quilted bodies, his breath came in sobs and the chill caught at that breath and sucked out little gauze puffs of air. He ran, and came with the front rank to the perimeter path and the low wooden fence.

Only his arms had reached to the top strands. He hung from his arms and his body was quivering and his boots kicked at the snow. Not dead.

Around Holly there was a wail of anger that seethed across the illuminated strip and reached up to the watchtower from where the searchlight dazzled them. And there was the roaring of the dogs and shouting from across the compound and the guardroom. Afterward Holly could not explain to himself his action. He could offer no reason as to why he had stepped deliberately over the low wooden fence and onto the clean snow beside this one man's spaced footsteps. Instinct took control of him and the noise of the men behind him died to a whisper. With clean, sharp steps Holly walked to the wire.

He did not look up toward the guard in the watchtower. He did not see the guard revise his aim, away from the gathered crowd.

Two shots into the snow a meter to the right of his legs, tiny puffs in the snow.

Holly saw only the man on the wire. He reached up, took the weight of the body and lifted it higher and then wrenched the material of the tunic from the barbs of the wire. A tall and awkward body and yet light as a child's. Holly carried him cradled in his arms, retraced his steps, stretched over the low wooden fence and was back, swallowed again among the *zeks*.

Other arms took on the burden, and blood stained richly on the
sleeves of Holly's tunic. Two guards on skis had infiltrated
themselves between the high wire and the high wooden fence
and covered the growing mass of prisoners with their rifles.
From the interior of the camp, warders pitched through the
crowd with the aid of weighted staves and forced back the
crush around the prone body.

Amongst the warders was one man who wore no uniform,
but instead a warm quilted jacket. This man spared one short
glance at the crippled *zek,* then looked away, folded his gloved
hands across his stomach and set himself to wait patiently. This
one man set himself above the bloody incident in the snow and
the yelping sound of the siren. Holly watched him.

Life was ebbing fast. It was ten minutes before the stretcher
came, and then the prisoners parted and allowed this one from
their number to be taken to the opened gates.

When the gates were shut again the crowd broke, drifted
again toward the huts.

Poshekhonov was beside Holly.

"You should not have intervened, Englishman."

Holly felt a slow wave of exhaustion. "It was bloody murder."

"He is now outside the camp, that is why he climbed the
wire. He has found his freedom.... Who were you to stop
him? Who were you in your arrogance to try to save him from
his wish? That was his freedom, against the wire."

"I couldn't watch him, not like that."

"It is the way of the camp. Any man is free to go to the
wire. It is an intrusion to prevent it. You saw the man who
came in his padded coat; that was Rudakov. It was from Rudakov that our friend sought his freedom. Rudakov made an
ice rink of the floor of his punishment cell. A man who has
slept on ice, whose clothes have been ice, should not be pre-
vented by a stranger from making his journey to what freedom
he can find. You will learn that, Englishman."

On that Sunday night there should have been a film show
for the camp, but the projector was broken and the prisoner
who knew the trade of projectionist and might have repaired
it was serving his second consecutive fifteen day spell in a
SHIzo isolation cell. A concert had been organized in place of
the canceled film. A group of militia from Yavas, who formed

a choir that was well known throughout the *Dubrovlag*, sang for an hour and a quarter. With special enthusiasm they gave their pressed and numbed audience "The Party is our Helmsman," and "Lenin is always with You."

Holly knew the man who had climbed the wire would be dead before the concert was finished.

Chapter 5

The old *zeks*, the long-term men, they say that the first months in the camps are the hardest. And harder than the first months are the first weeks. And harder than the first weeks are the first days. And worst and most horrible is the first morning.

The regime of the darkness and the arc lights still rules when the loudspeakers erupt and relay the national anthem of the Union of Soviet Socialist Republics. A crackling and worn tape plays the music of the nation from the guardhouse, and it is six-thirty. It is never late, never earlier. The volume is high and the sounds of the military band with their brass and their drums rampage into the slumber of the men in the huts. No sleep will survive that wakening call. The old ones say that the first morning, the first experience of dawn in the camps, is the greatest test.

The old *zeks* say that if a man has a nightmare then he should not be disturbed because the awakened life of the camps is more awful than the pain of any dream.

The old *zeks* say that a man is weakest when he comes to the camps for the first time, when the desire for life is first squeezed from him.

They have all slept in their clothes under the one permitted blanket. They sleep in their socks and their trousers and their tunics, and still the cold bites them. They are fast out of their bunks and the hut shakes from the futile cursing. The warders and the trusties from internal order are at the doors of the huts, and the *zeks* are pitched out into the night darkness and spill to the perimeter path, and like an ant trail they wind around the compound for what is classified as exercise. Above them hovers the white wool vapor of their breath, beneath them the fresh overnight snow is beaten to another layer of ice. They

50

hear the stamping of the guard in his watchtower, they hear
the swish of the skis of the guards who are between the high
wire fence and the high wooden fence, they hear the snap bark
of the dogs. When they exercise, the *zeks* see nothing but their
feet dropping forward on the path. Head down, balaclava tight
on the face, scarf wrapped close, tunic collar raised. There is
no talk at morning exercise because no man is concerned with
his neighbor. The young go fast on the perimeter path, and the
old take the way more slowly, but each man is struggling for
speed, because speed is warmth. Exercise is for every morning.
If the tunics and trousers are wet then that is hard for the
prisoners and they will be damper and colder for the length of
the day that follows. The old cannot run, and they want the
latrine, but only after exercise are the men permitted to line
up for the privilege of the latrines. The latrines are better in
winter because the droppings under the board seats are frozen
and the ice quickly binds the smell of men's waste. After the
latrines, a wash of hands and face, but no shave because shaving
is done by the barber and that is once a week with the bath.
After the cold wash, it is breakfast of gruel swill and a cup of
hot water. After breakfast it is parade and the men stand in the
lines while the warders, who are backed by the fire power of
the guards, come with their lists to count and recount.

Seven-thirty. The start of the working day. Each morning
there is a faint stirring of excitement when the *zeks* march to
work. They must walk out through the camp gate and cross
the road and the railway line and then the file will enter the
compound of the factory. It is a brief walk, no more than a
hundred meters, but it is a sliver of freedom. The men march
with their warders and when they are clear of the confines of
the fences for those few steps they are hemmed in by the soldiers
and the dogs. The road serves the village of Barashevo and
sometimes the civilians have to stand behind the lines of the
guards and wait for the columns of criminals to go by before
they can proceed on their way. They are as much prisoners as
the *zeks*. Their jails are the villages of Barashevo and Yavas
and Lepley and Sosnovka and Lesnoy. They live between the
islands of wire and wooden walls, they exist within sight of
the watchtowers and beside the garrison barracks. Meager villages that are blighted by the camps and their factories. And

because they, too, are prisoners they detest the convicts, and their children ape their elders and shout "Fascists!" as the *zeks* walk in their guarded column between the zone and the factory. The villagers' employment is the Camp. They are the warders, the drivers, the technicians, the factory supervisors. A manacle secures them to the *Dubrovlag*. While the camps remain, the villagers are themselves captive. Against the shuffling columns, they have only the weapons of abuse and loathing.

There is a break of one hour for lunch. During that hour the *zeks* recross the railway line and the road and return to the zone, once more to be counted and to be searched. In the afternoon they return to the factory. In the evening they return again to the zone. The searches are painstaking, the roll calls are long. The men must stand in the wind and the stamped snow. Always they must wait.

The rhythm of the camp is constant, a ticking metronome.

Former major of paratroops, now seconded to MVD, Vasily Kypov had in his short time at ZhKh 385/3/1 received two commendations from the Ministry for the smooth running of the zone. The commendations are framed and hang on the wall of the Commandant's office.

The hunger comes quickly, the exhaustion is slower. But they are twins, these two, and their approach is inevitable. Ten hours work each day in the factory, three meals of hidden meat without fresh vegetables and fruit. Exhaustion and hunger will run together. They will sap his will. When he is spent by the work load, sagging from the diet, then he will be pliable and no longer make trouble. When he is beaten then he will be a *zek,* and that is the way of them all, all eight hundred in the compound.

Holly learned the code of behavior by watching others.

When the mob of Hut 2 fell from their bed bunks and went out into the blackness for exercise, Holly was with them. When the name of Holovich was called at the parades and counts, he shouted back "Holly . . . here" and the trifle of the gesture was ignored. When the columns went to the factory he was in their ranks. When he was given work at a lathe that rounded and spiraled chairs' legs he took no advice from the foreman, and instead watched the man next to him to study the working of the machine.

He ate the food that was provided with the avidness of those who sat around him. He lay on his bunk with his eyes open and staring at the rafter ceiling for all the hours that were common for the men of Hut 2. He blended. Not first in the line and not last. Not highest in the production line of the factory, not lowest. He joined the ghost ranks, became common and unremarkable.

There was interest in the Englishman, of course, in Hut 2. Something rare this one, they thought, something rare and original. They gazed with a covetousness at the scarf around his throat, the socks under his boots, the pants he stripped off in the bathhouse, wanted to hold and feel the texture of the garments of a stranger. They talked to him of their lives as if by that they smeared some ointment on their existence. They sought confidences from him. They were unrewarded.

Holly built a castle, a castle on an island, a castle on an island that is a prison camp.

A killer who slept at night half a meter from Holly came with his story to the Englishman's side. Adimov shuffled aside the moment of their first meeting.

The dissident who had been the first to speak to Holly talked the hesitant monologue of revolution. Feldstein came to Holly as if in hope of finding a kindred mind.

The fraud whose bunk was beside the stove and whose fall had been the hardest and cruelest of any sought out Holly on the perimeter path. Poshekhonov ladled out the lore of the Correctional Labor Colonies.

And there was Chernayev who was a thief, and Byrkin who had been a naval petty officer, and Mamarev who they said was an informer.

All reached for Holly's ear and all were turned aside.

He seemed indifferent. Not curt in his rejection of their stories, not rude. Indifferent and disinterested.

Adimov boasted of the planning of a robbery in Moscow.

The State Bank on Kutuzovsky Prospekt was to be Adimov's target. Himself and two colleagues, and even a car found for the escape run, and a homemade pistol that would be sufficient to unnerve the cashier clerks. Two hundred thousand rubles in the trunk and out into the street and into the car where the engine ticked snugly and into the traffic . . . and the stupid bitch had been on the pedestrian crossing, and her bags filled both hands, and she had frozen, not stepped back, and the car had hit her, swerved, crashed. Stupid bitch. Well, they weren't going to bloody stop because the walk sign was lit, not with the trunk full. Can't put the handbrake on and sit on your hands with the alarm bells ringing because a *babushka*'s on her way home with her son-in-law's dinner. Swerved and crashed into a lamp post. Three men in the car, all dazed, all half-concussed when the militia pulled them out, and the bank's door not fifty meters away. Twelve years to think on it, twelve years and not five gone. And Adimov seemed to look for admiration from Holly when he told his story. Each new man into the hut had clucked sympathy for Adimov's mishap, each had thought that wise. All except the new stranger, the Englishman.

In Holly's ear Feldstein whispered of the circulation of the *samizdat* writings.

Typescripts photocopied and distributed that carried the rivulet of dissent from eye to eye for the few who trusted in a future of change and the ultimate destruction of the monolith that controlled their lives. He was a part, he said, of the illegal and dangerous dissemination of information, dangerous because those who were arrested risked being parceled off to the Sebsky Institute for Forensic Psychiatry or thrown to the mercy of the *zeks* in the camps. Two years served and four to go because one in the chain had not owned the strength to withstand the interrogation of the KGB questioners in Lubyanka. And he was proud in his puny and isolated fight, and believed in a vague victory in the future, and a present of martyrdom. He spoke of the nobility of the struggle, not of the failure of achievement. He was known in the West, he said, he was supported in his agony by many thousands, he was comforted by their distant communion. Holly had listened with a chilled politeness and shrugged and turned away on his side for sleep.

At the tables in the kitchen, Poshekhonov found Holly.

The joint history of the camps and of his life bubbled clear as a hill stream. A spring of guarded hope and a source of amusement. Poshekhonov said that he had found the way to laugh, he had picked up the spear of ridicule. "Not too often, you understand, but enough to prick them. . . ." His fall had been fast and far, but it had been almost worthwhile, almost, and one day, one distant day, there was the dream of a flight beyond the borders of the Motherland. It waited for him in Zürich, Poshekhonov would say, the payoff. Had Holly ever been to Switzerland, because there was a bank there? He told of the Black Sea fishing collective where the catch was counted not in kilos of fish flesh but in the grams of the salted roe of the sturgeon. A cooperative company for the canning of caviar, and the plan had been brilliant in its sauce and complexity. A Dutch businessman had proposed the idea, a wonderful invention. . . . A tin of caviar but the label declared the produce to be herring, and as herring it was sold to Amsterdam before the transfer of the labels in Holland and entry to the shops of the European capitals. And the ripoff was well divided and a segment found its way to a bank account that was anonymous in all but its number. Couldn't have lasted. Brilliant but temporary, and Poshekhonov was lucky not to have been shot with his two principal collaborators. Poshekhonov could summon a short clear smile from Holly, a smile that was chained and brief.

Each in his way—Adimov, Feldstein, Poshekhonov—reached out toward Holly and waved a flag of interest or concern or friendship. All failed.

Holly was alone.

He waited, bandaged in his own thoughts, for the summons to the administration block.

A full week after Holly had been delivered to Camp 3, Captain Yuri Rudakov issued the instruction that the new prisoner was to be brought to his office.

It was not that he had been dilatory in his duty of interviewing all those sent to the camp who were in any way, minor or major, special. His own inclination would have led him toward this first interview three or four days earlier. But in the wake of the personal file of Mikhail Holovich had come further instructions and briefings over the teleprinter in his office. More material from Dzerszhinsky Street that he must assess. By the time that he felt ready to bring Holly before him, he had spent three clear days shut in that office with the door closed to all inquiries.

The captain was a young man, not yet past his twenty-eighth birthday.

There were those in the dim corridors of headquarters who said that his rise had been too fast. Rudakov knew the pitfalls, knew of the knives that waited for him. The KGB officer responsible for the security, both physical and spiritual, of the camp was a man on trial. It was his strength that he recognized the testing-ground. He had been on trial before. Aged only twenty-four he had held down the post of KGB officer attached to the 502nd Guards Armored Division stationed at Magdeburg in the German Democratic Republic. He had learned there how a full colonel could wince and supplicate in his presence. He had felt the power of his position when he had taken a bottle to the room of any major and propositioned for information on the talk in the mess when he, the KGB's ears, was not present. He had seen the tremble jelly of a captain's chin and known it was his uniform and the blue unit tabs that won it. He was rollercoasting toward a high-rise career and now they had sent him to this stinking backwater to test further his resolve and capability. If he won here too, if he came back from Barashevo without a stain of the shit and slime of this place on his tailored khaki uniform then the road upward and onward was clear to him. The captain was an egocentric man, one who believed in the great blueprints of life. He reckoned in a destiny that was mapped for his career. Fate had thrown the dice. Twin sixes had fallen, rocked, rolled for him to see them. Mikhail Holovich had been sent to Camp 3, Zone I.

The files told him their story—a tale of rare incompetence and of opportunity for him.

An agent of the British espionage services had been captured in Moscow. A strong creature and determined in his denials, but that should have been short-lived. Of course there had been interrogation sessions in the Lubyanka, but they had been flimsy affairs, for hanging over their progress had been the sword of a man's release. From the very start the question of exchange had reared. All the superiors, all the gold-braided ranking officers, had been short in their duty when it came to the breaking of this Englishman. Where the colonel generals, where the colonels, where the majors of headquarters had failed, idiot buggers, there was the opportunity for an ambitious captain to succeed.

Since the first file had arrived off the train from Pot'ma,

Yuri Rudakov had dreamed of little else than his triumph of interrogation over Mikhail Holovich.

He sat now at his desk, a manicured little man with a strength on his face, and a power about his sparse body, and a whiplash edge to his movements. A decisive and active young man. One who was going up. One on whom the sun played even through the bed of snow cloud over the roofs of the administration block. His desk was clear of the papers that were memorized and locked in his personal safe. He had told his wife that morning over breakfast in their bungalow on the edge of Barashevo and within faint sight of the outer wooden fence of Zone I, that he stood to gain a great prize . . . not tomorrow, not next week, but he had time, he had months of time to break this bastard.

As he waited he realized that he had not felt such keen anticipation and happiness since he had served in the front line at Magdeburg.

The knock at the door was respectful. Rudakov drummed his fingers on the table to count out five slow seconds, then called quietly for the prisoner to be brought into his presence.

Holly looked around him.

An office that might have been occupied by the personnel manager of the factory in Dartford. A tidy desk and behind it a man who might have come in on the Saturday afternoon for extra work. The collar of a checked shirt peeped from the neck of a thick blue sweater. A smaller table was beside the desk with a high-backed typewriter, the sign of a junior executive who has not been allocated a personal secretary and must write his own memoranda. A safe, a filing cabinet, a window that was curtained against the dusk of the camp and the reef of arc lights that surrounded it. A calendar with a color photograph of a snow scene was set between the framed painting of Lenin and the portrait of Andropov of the Politburo. But a desolate room, without carpet, without furniture of quality, without personal decoration. Yellow painted walls that were cheerless and ran with dribbles of condensation.

The warmth from the hot pipe that skirted a side wall billowed across Holly's face, rubbed at the cold that had settled under his tunic and shirt as he had walked from the compound with the trusty from internal order. One week and the changes had fastened on Holly, winter leaves sticking to lawn grass. Unthinking, he had placed himself not in front of the desk but at an angle to it so that he was closer to the pipes, and he wondered how long the interview would last because it was short of thirty minutes until the call to the kitchen for dinner and the hunger pain pinched at his stomach.

The man behind the desk would have been a little younger than himself. The man lounged easily in his chair and Holly stood. The man wore fitting and casual clothes and those of Holly were thin. The man was close-shaved, wore the scent of deodorant, and Holly was stubble-bearded and stank so that he himself could know the foulness. The man was relaxed and rested and Holly felt the tiredness brush through his mind and for nine and a half hours he had worked in the factory at the lathe that fashioned chairs' legs. The man possessed power and pressures and Holly knew no stare he could offer in competition.

And if they were together in Hampton Wick, if they were sitting in the front room of his home in southwest London, then Holly's company Fiesta would be in the road outside, and the clothes would be smart on his back, and the whisky and water in his hand, and the confidence in his talk. But this was not his ground. He stood in the damp boots that leaked the snow wet to his socks, and he hated the man who sat at the desk.

"Would you like to sit, Holovich?"

Holly straightened himself, shrugged at his shoulders to try to rid himself of the weariness, gazed back at the man's face.

"I believe it is quite hard, the work that you do as a strict regime prisoner. You would be better to sit, Holovich."

The air was filled with cigarette smoke. Different to Holly's nose from the dry dust filth of the tobacco used in Hut 2. Something from a former world, a part of a deep memory. His nostrils flicked, the smoke spiral played before his eyes.

"Forgive me, I didn't think, would you like a cigarette, Holovich?"

"I don't smoke . . . my name is Michael Holly."

"My name is Rudakov." The mouth of the captain sagged in amusement. "My papers tell me you are named Holovich, that is what the file calls you."

"Holly . . . Michael Holly."

"And it is important to you to keep an identity? You find that significant?"

Holly stared down at him.

"If your name is Holovich or Holly, that is important to you? That is my question."

His hands were clasped behind his back. Holly dug a thumbnail into the flesh of his hand. Trying to beat the tiredness and the sapping warmth of the room, and his eyes blinked when he wished them clear.

"If you want me to call you Holly, then I shall call you that. To me it is immaterial, to you it should be irrelevant. You shall be Holly, you can be Michael Holly. I will start again . . . would you like to sit down, Holly? Would you like a cigarette, Holly?"

"I will stand . . . I don't smoke."

He recognized the churlishness, saw Rudakov open his hands in the gesture of refused reasonableness.

"Then it is your choice that you don't sit, your choice that you don't smoke, am I right?"

"It is my choice."

"Your choice whether you smoke a cigarette, my choice on the name I give you. Whether I call you Holovich, or Holly, or Mister Holly, or Michael, that is my choice. Whether I call you by your number, that is my choice. I have every choice, and unless I wish it otherwise, you have no choice. That is the reality of your position. Know this. It is not important to me what your name should be. I don't give a shit, Mister Holly, what you are called. It is not something I would dispute with you; your insistence on a name amuses me. Understand this, though—if I were to dispute the matter with you, I would win. I spoke of the reality of your position, and I would like now to expand on that reality."

The muscles ached in his thighs and calves. The sweetness of the cigarette drugged his mind.

Remember that you hate him, Holly. . . .

"You have been here a week, Holly, I have been here one hundred times longer. I know a little of the camp life. I tell you something, I tell you this as a friend, because I have a sympathy for you. . . . Holly, you have to forget the past, that is what anyone who has spent time in the camps will say to you, you have to forget the past life. The name of Holly is behind you, it does nothing to help you. That you wish to be defiant and stand when you can sit, that is the attitude of your past life." He leaned across his desk, and his chin rested comfortably in the palms of his hands, and there was a gentleness that belied the cut in his words. "There is no exchange to look toward, that is in the past, just as your name is in the past. You must point toward your future, you must wonder if your future is to be fourteen years in the *Dubrovlag*. I think you are a young man now, what will you be in fourteen years, and will it matter then whether you are Holovich or Holly? Will it matter?"

Holly swayed on his feet. He looked past Rudakov's head to the curtain. He focused on the place where the draft blew a small bulge in the cotton.

"Those who sent you here, those who sent you on your mission against the people of the Soviet Union, they are from your past. Is that a lie? You are not at your home, you have not crossed a bridge in Berlin . . . you are in Mordovia, in a strict regime camp. Their arm is not long enough, not strong enough, they cannot lift you out from here. . . ."

The bell rang, metallic and screeching. The call for the camp to hurry to the kitchen. For the first in line the soup is warm, only for the first.

"Can I go now?"

"The pig swill they feed you, that is the future. You are learning well and quickly. The past has nothing for you, nothing, the past has abandoned you. Those that sent you here have forgotten you, buried you, stamped down the earth on your memory. I speak the truth, yes? If they had not abandoned you then you would not be here, you would not be wanting to run the width of the compound to drink the shit you wouldn't give your dog at home. Think on that. . . ."

"Can I go now?"

"Enjoy your dinner, enjoy your future." Rudakov leaned back in his chair and his face was happy with a smile, then he snapped to his feet. "I will take you back to the cage . . . and in the morning I will give the order that you are to be called by any name you want."

They went together into the night and, when the inner gate was opened, Rudakov called at Holly's back, "Good night, Michael Holly, good night. Think of those who sent you here, think of how they are spending their evening. Think of it when you are in the kitchen line, when you are eating, when you have gone to your bunk. Piss on them, Michael Holly."

Holly walked steadily along a stamped snow path, and the laughter from behind gusted to his ears.

"We are going to meet often, Michael Holly. You will learn that I can be a better friend to you than those who sent you here."

The inner gates of the zone scraped shut, and Holly strode on toward the doors of the kitchen where the end of the line spilled out from the light.

Chapter 6

The sunburn prickled at the deputy undersecretary's neck.

First day back from the winter holiday, the first morning that he had worn again his white shirt and knotted his tie and refound the quiet striped suit that was his favorite. Two weeks on the beach at Mombasa, not in a hotel of course, but in the bungalow of an old friend who had survived freedom and independence in Kenya and still made a living out of East Africa's import and export trade. It was many years since the deputy undersecretary had taken such a holiday; his previous inclination would have been toward fishing the west country salmon rivers or stalking the Scottish moors. But his wife had said that it was time for an opportunity to wear something other than thick tweeds. And the sunshine would do him good, she had said, would help with the arthritis that nagged at his left hip joint. Sunshine with a vengeance. Ninety degrees fahrenheit while the Century staffers were shivering in London. The deputy undersecretary had known heat before, but that was in the dim and dark ages when he had been young and ambitious, working the Counter Insurgency ticket in faraway Malaya and Kenya. Twenty years before he had known the draftless heat of temporary offices in Kuala Lumpur and Nairobi, but God, you lost the habit of it. At the direction of his wife he had taken fourteen full days in the sun that beat back from the Indian Ocean's azure. He had greased himself in oil and he had cooked and broiled and yearned for the magic hours of noon and six when he could down a life-saving tumbler of gin and lime. The company had been good, the talk relaxing and buoyant, but limited for all that. The deputy undersecretary could talk of his host's prospects and disappointments, he could learn of the problems of digging out foreign exchange and hard

62

currency in the Third World, the tribulations over the renewal
of residence permits, the difficulties of keeping reliable servants, but of his own world he must remain silent. The deputy
undersecretary headed the Secret Intelligence Service of the
United Kingdom, and that was not a subject matter for gossip
and conversation on a bougainvillea-fringed veranda as the
lights of the fishermen's dugouts floated inside the coral
reef.... No bloody way.

He was a man who could be honest with himself, and in
honesty he could say that he was both pleased and relieved to
be back at his desk on a gray Monday morning in London.
And at the same time ashamed of the affliction that he had
brought down on himself. Self-inflicted wound, that was how
they had referred to sunburn back in the old days of Counter
Insurgency. In CI days you thought twice about taking your
bloody shirt off. The deputy undersecretary had no one but
himself to blame for the irritation that his starched collar created
just below the line of his neatly cut hair. Silly and stupid, the
sort of thing he might have done as a child, pathetic for a man
of his age.

He snapped shut a file on his desk, reached for his briefcase
and extracted the small jar of Vaseline.

He heard the chatter of Maude Frobisher's typewriter in the
outer office, the pattern beat that indicated that she had steam
up, and with a slight secretiveness he loosened his collar and
pulled down his tie and wiped a smear of the Vaseline across
the offending skin. If word of the DUS's discomfort reached
beyond his office then there would be a titter around Century
House, from Library in the basement to Administration on the
tenth.

The deputy undersecretary was a recent arrival at Century.
It was less than a year since he had marched into this office,
having forsaken the job of director general of the Security
Service for what he regarded as a promotion, while the men
of Century recoiled at what they saw as a political insult.
Security and Intelligence were distant halfbrothers. Little fra-
ternal love existed between these two clandestine arms of government. The move from Leconfield House to Century House
crossed a chasm of prejudice and suspicion. Different animals
and different beings, from separate heritages and upbringing.

The movement of the deputy undersecretary had been ordered by the Prime Minister as a punishment to Intelligence, the senior service. A rare grimace could form at the deputy undersecretary's lips. It had been Intelligence's own self-inflicted wound that had lifted him from the status of a policeman to that of a ranking diplomat. Excessive secrecy, unwillingness to consult with senior politicians, reluctance to uncover the hands of cards on the table of missions and operations, and for all that covertness there had been no great efficiency and success.

"I'll not be treated as a damned security risk," the Prime Minister had said to the deputy undersecretary. "I'll not tolerate activities that can blow up in our faces which I haven't known about."

The deputy undersecretary's brief was clear and concise. The Service was to be cleansed. Intelligence was to be scrubbed free of the impurities of independent action. It would win him few friends in the offices of Century, few cosy evenings with his subordinates in the clubland of Mayfair. But with the Prime Minister at his shoulder and access to the seat of government a telephone call away, the new master in Century found such small irritations as insignificant as the raw blistered skin below his collar.

Tomorrow he would tell his wife to put out a shirt of softer cotton.

As the new man at Century wielding the new broom, he expected that decisions and policies would come to his desk. When his reorganization plan was completed then he could anticipate greater delegation, but not yet, not while he was imposing his will on the Service. The "in tray" memoranda soared in a hillock on his desk. Busily he scribbled in a scratchy copperplate hand that had been taught him by a schoolmistress from the hills of Brecon his thoughts and directives in the margins of the typed sheets. He worked briskly and with a stolid aptitude. Everything in front of him he read, down to the last words. That was the way to retain control of the job.

Among the papers was a brown folder stamped "SECRET." A reference number had been typed on white paper and glued to the folder. With an ink nib had been added the name of Michael Holly.

Of course the deputy undersecretary had not been beyond

the reach of Century House while in Mombasa. Twice a week a second secretary accompanied by a High Commission security officer had driven down from Nairobi with a gutted digest of the Service's affairs telexed from London. He had known of the death of Oleg Demyonov, he had been told of the Soviet retaliation, he had been informed of the visit by the consul to Lefortovo jail.

Before opening the file he added his initials to the readership list gummed to the top right corner.

There had not been many there before him, reading the file on Michael Holly.

But then he, himself, had never concerned himself greatly with the case of Michael Holly. The man had been recruited before the start of the deputy undersecretary's reign at Century, recruited and arrested and tried. The transfer arrangements for Holly and Demyonov had been basically a Foreign and Commonwealth matter, and rightly so. It had never been admitted that Michael Holly, small-time engineer, was anything other than a falsely accused business representative on lawful business in the Soviet capital. The wrinkle of annoyance creased the deputy undersecretary's mouth. Idiotic and dangerous to send an untrained man to Moscow . . . inadequate preparation on East Europe desk . . . incompetence . . . and now the turned bloody ankle of embarrassment. The sort of affair that would not be tolerated now that he held the stewardship of the Service.

And yet the matter had so nearly been blessed in a strange and unforeseen way, the Service had almost wriggled off the hook through no credit to itself . . . Incredible, bloody incredible, that the Service should have found itself within a whisker of escape, within a few heartbeats . . . Extraordinary that the Soviets had not already grilled and broken this man, unbelievable that they had permitted a trial for espionage to go ahead without the evidence of a confession. There was a reason why they had foregone the privilege of having a singing canary in the dock. They, along with their British colleagues and brothers across the Curtain, had thought only in terms of a swap. They had wanted Demyonov back. Perhaps it had been a decision taken by a general of KGB in the Lubyanka, perhaps the papers had gone to the Politburo or even to the President, but the matter had not been pushed.

There was an unspoken and unrecorded understanding between the two teams of far-divided intelligence men . . . anything was possible of those buggers he'd inherited. The minimum of diplomatic finger-pointing over Holly in return for the home-coming of the major operative that was Demyonov.

But Demyonov was dead. Demyonov had gone home last week in an elaborate casket dark inside the cargo hold of a Tupolev airliner.

Holly's easy ride was over.

They'd want a damned confession, they'd want exposure, they'd want to milk the man. The deputy undersecretary rubbed his nose, watched a flake of skin pirouette down to the opened pages of the file. Damn . . . what a fool he'd look if his face peeled. He anointed himself again with Vaseline, bruised the jelly into his nose. He reached for his telephone.

"Maude, I'd like Mr. Millet, East Europe desk, to come up. Soonest, please. . . ."

Whenever he spoke to the woman he regretted that he had not stamped his authority and demanded that Gwen should be released from Leconfield and transferred with him, but they had said in Century's personnel that he must have a secretary who knew the ropes of the Service, and he had acquiesced. A tepid little frog of a woman, that was his view of Maude Frobisher, and probably harboring a latent spinster love for his sacked predecessor. Because she disliked it so, he found a fleeting pleasure in calling her by her first name.

The deputy undersecretary thought that he liked the look of Alan Millet. A young man without the priggishness that the deputy undersecretary believed he could identify in all public school pupils, without the conceit of a Cambridge College.

"Sit down, Millet."

"Thank you, sir."

The deputy undersecretary warmed to respect, detested condescension. The former years in the Colonies with the regimen of rank had left their imprint.

"Michael Holly . . ."

"Yes, sir."

"Where is he now?"

"Mordovian ASSR, in the *Dubrovlag* complex, Camp 3 we think. . . ."

"That's Barashevo, right?"

"Correct, sir."

It pleased the deputy undersecretary to display his knowledge. If the chief hasn't mastered minutiae then his subordinates can hide behind the drape of his ignorance, that was a favorite theme of the deputy undersecretary.

"They're going to try to break him . . . you agree?"

"I agree he's a tough time ahead of him, yes."

"Bloody tough, Millet . . . and what's he going to do when the going's hard and bad, what's his break point?"

"Everyone has a break point, sir."

Millet shifted in his chair. It was the first time he had been alone and across the desk from the deputy undersecretary.

"That's a cliché, Millet. This man wasn't prepared for deep interrogation. You might just as well have sent him out naked round the privates. I want information, Millet, I want to know how he's going to cope. We've never admitted involvement, neither has he, I want to know if it's going to stay that way. I want to know whether we're going to be blushing when they put him up in the Foreign Ministry at a press conference and he spills."

"That's difficult to say, sir."

"Of course it's difficult to say. It's impossible, impossible because you don't know, Millet, the homework hasn't been done. When you've done that homework, then you'll come back and give me your answer."

"Yes, sir."

"I don't like to be in ignorance, Millet, I detest it. The Prime Minister doesn't like it either. There will be a bright little man at Camp 3, very clever and on the up, and your Michael Holly is going to be his pride and joy, and when he can wheel your man into that press conference he's going to be very smug. And I'll tell you what we'll be, we'll be on the floor, and it hurts down there. You understand me?"

"Yes, sir."

"When you netted this young man, unproven, untrained, did you tell him of the risks?"

"Not exactly, sir. Well, it wasn't really discussed."

"Should those risks have been discussed, Mr. Millet?"

"I didn't want to go into any more detail than absolutely

necessary. But perhaps, perhaps they should have been discussed. Yes, sir."

"And if they had been discussed then he might not have gone. That's surely worth brooding on, Mr. Millet."

"Yes, sir."

"On your way then, lad, and I'll offer you one thought to tide you over. Michael Holly didn't come to you, you recruited him. You put him where he is now. Camp 3 at Barashevo won't be fun, not in summer, not in winter. It'll be bloody awful there. You won't forget that, Millet?"

"Yes, sir." Millet was rising from his chair. "No . . . I mean, no, I won't forget that, sir."

The roof of the porch was shallow. It offered Alan Millet little protection from the rain that drove across the street and battered against his body.

He had rung the bell twice, listened to its chime and heard a distant door open and the call of voices.

He was pressed against the wood fence, his hips hard onto the letter box, and he cursed the slow reaction. Below his raincoat his trousers showed the damp, and his shoes were lusterless from their soaking.

The door opened, a few inches only, the limit of a security chain.

"My apologies for coming without warning . . . it's Mr. Holly, isn't it?"

"I am Holly, Stephen Holly."

An old man, the gray face of age, a dulled unhappiness in the eyes. A striped shirt without a collar, and trousers that were held at a slender stomach by braces, and carpet slippers in checked shades of brown, and a smell of pipe tobacco. He spoke English with the gravel accent of the Central European, and there was a tremor in his words.

"Who are you? What do you want?"

"My name is Alan Millet. I'm Foreign Office, I'd like to talk to you about Michael." He'd rehearsed that as he walked from the station, but it was still blurted. He felt a fraud.

"There is a Mr. Carpenter at the Foreign Office, we deal with him. . . ."

"It's a different department, a different matter."

The rain dribbled down Millet's socks.

"Mr. Carpenter had not told us anyone else was coming."

"I'm half drowned out here, Mr. Holly . . . I'd like to come inside." Millet mouthed what he hoped was a winning smile.

And he was admitted.

He shook his coat outside and it was carried before him by Stephen Holly along the corridor that led into the backroom where a windowed coke boiler blazed and the coat was draped across a fender. A woman with a brush of close-cut gray hair sat with her sewing close to the fire and a cat rested on her lap, and she looked at Millet with fear and seemed to warn her husband that this was an intruder. It was a tidy, precious little room, from the polished linoleum floor to the filled bookcase of works in English and Russian, from the glass-shined pictures of distant landscapes to the square table covered by plastic cloth and laid for a meal.

"It's Mr. Carpenter who comes from the Foreign Office to see us. No one else has ever come." The woman echoed her husband.

"It's a pretty big place, Mrs. Holly. We have a lot of sections there. . . ."

"What do you want from us?" For a man of such broken physique, Stephen Holly's voice carried a curious brusqueness.

What did he want? Well, you don't tell two old people that a year and a bit too late you're out to find what the sticking power of their son will be when it comes to the choicer interrogation techniques of KGB. If they use the noise machine, if he doesn't sleep for a week, if it's the rubber truncheons, if it's the electrodes, if it's a pardon in return for goodies . . . well, you don't tell two old people that. Slowly, he told himself, slowly and gently, because the flow won't come easily, and they're frightened and foreign, and alone without a breakwater to shelter behind. What did he want?

"We're very concerned about Michael, both of you must understand that. We worked very hard to get him out of the Soviet Union—well, you know all that, Mr. Carpenter will have told you, and he will have told you what went wrong. . . ."

"Mr. Carpenter told us why they would not release Michael." Stephen Holly spoke sharply as if now he regretted his decision to admit the stranger.

"I'm one of the team of people at the Foreign Office that will be constantly working on Michael's case. I thought that it was right that I should talk to you, try and build a better picture of Michael."

"You want to know whether he can survive his sentence?"

"I wouldn't put it as bluntly . . . we're very concerned, though, about Michael, Mr. Holly."

"Do you know anything of the *Dubrovlag?*"

"I know a little of it."

"You want to know whether he can live through fourteen years in the camps, whether for our son that is possible?"

"We feel that the more we know about Michael, then the more we can help him."

The cat yawned and stretched and its teeth and claws flashed, then it turned its back on Millet and settled again on the lap of Michael Holly's mother. The old woman stared at him and her eyes were bright and piercing and the silver thimble had fallen to the lap of her dress, and her fists were clenched now as if she searched for a memory, and her husband watched her anxiously as if he witnessed that she was at war within herself. Alan Millet stood with his back to the fire, feeling his inadequacy and waited for the woman to settle herself.

"You said your name was Millet . . . you said that you had come here to find out more about our son."

"Alan Millet, Mrs. Holly. Yes, I said. . . ."

She dismissed him to silence with a wave of a narrow, fleshless arm. The arm hovered before the bookcase and then darted at a book end and retrieved a bound diary. The fingers scooped at the pages as if there was a reference that was familiar.

"If you are Mr. Alan Millet then you come to us in deceit."

The world was caving around him, and he did not know yet from which quarter the disaster would fall, only that its arrival was certain.

"I don't know what you mean, Mrs. Holly."

"My son kept a diary . . . three weeks before he flew to Moscow he recorded that he met an Alan Millet . . . four days before he left he met again with Alan Millet . . . why now does this Alan Millet speak of our son as if he were not known to him? Why . . . ?"

Just a frail little thing, wasn't she, the wind could have

picked her up and tossed her away, yet she had demolished
him as surely as if she had wielded a pickax handle to his belly.

"I can't answer. You know that . . . you understand that. . . . I'm
sorry."

The silence gathered in the room around Millet. He saw the
shadows that reached from the furniture, that slipped from a
man and the woman of his life. When they had met at the pub,
and boasted of the ease of the dispatch of the packet that
Michael Holly would carry, he had never thought of a moment
such as this. He wanted only to be gone, to break out of the
circle of reproach and injury around him.

"My son will survive, Mr. Millet. That is what you want
to hear from me? Michael will survive. If he serves every day
of the sentence passed on him . . . even if you desert him . . . he
will survive. He would never bow to them. I know my son,
Mr. Millet."

The tears dribbled on her face and made bright lines across
the grayness of her cheeks and then her head was lost in her
hands.

"You should go now, Mr. Millet," Stephen Holly said. "You
should not come to us again."

Alan Millet plucked his coat from the fender and saw that
the drips had made a pool on the linoleum floor. He let himself
out of the front door and when he was beyond the shelter of
the porch he felt the sting of rain on his cheeks.

He walked on glistening pavements, across streets where the
rain spat back from the concrete. He shivered in shop doorways
as he waited for the traffic lights to give him green. He traversed
this suburb of southwest London with its roads of London brick
terraces and Snowcem semi-detached homes. A strange quest
for him, an eccentric Grail that he sought. This was a place
where the Soviet world was a thing of books and newspapers
and television shows and magazines—not tangible. And Alan
Millet traced a path to discover how well a man might withstand
the sophistication of modern interrogation at the hands of the
masters of that art. There should have been a better backcloth,
something that smacked more of the dramatic and less of the
bare ordinariness of these humble homes.

* * *

He met a schoolmaster, now retired.

Alan Millet sat in a front room filled with books of modern English history and photographs of small boys lined in the formations of the posed soccer team. He watched a man scratch back the memory of many years. He heard of a boy who was a loner—but not lonely, you know—satisfied to be with himself, happy with his own company.

"I don't think he needed the rest of the class, I don't think he even needed us, his teachers. A very self-contained child, if you know what I mean. Very strong in his own way, not swaggering or throwing his weight about, but a great inner strength. You'll appreciate that it's years back, that boys come and go for a schoolmaster, they're a bit phantom. But I remember this one. . . . No real brilliance, nothing outstanding in class or sports, but there was an individuality there. I suppose you want an example from me . . . ? Well, I'll tell you this, he wasn't exceptionally strong, but none of the other lads ever fought with him. That's a pretty poor example, but none of them ever dared to rag him. There was this sort of aura round him. The other boys shied away from him, and he didn't seem to notice an absence of their friendship . . . I'm afraid I haven't been of much help to you, Mr. Millet."

There was a lecturer in Mechanical Engineering at the Kingston Technical College across the river from Hampton Wick.

Millet took the bus to the prewar inelegance of the college close to the Thames towpath and blessed the warmth that he found on the upper deck.

The lecturer was at first impatient at being called from a tutorial session, before his vanity was fed the magical words of "Foreign and Commonwealth Office." He wore a bow tie, a corduroy jacket, and suede shoes and appeared to Millet to be well-distanced from any workshop floor. He sat his guest down in a cubbyhole office, mixed instant coffee with the help of a whistling electric kettle, and rambled into a monologue of his thoughts on Michael Holly.

"Academically there wasn't anything to shout from the ceilings. In fact I don't think that he found the work easy, but there was a dedication there that some of his contemporaries of the same ability could have used. If he didn't understand something, he was reluctant to stand up and ask, instead he'd worry it out himself, sometimes I reckoned he'd been at it all night. If I asked a question of him then he'd answer seriously, but if I floated a question and waited to see which of the students would pick it up I could guarantee that it would never be Holly. He had no thought of impressing me, or anyone else for that matter. I don't think he had many friends here, certainly none that would have lasted after he took his diploma. He was never on for "A's," not in written work or practical, but the "B's" were consistent enough. You know in a funny sort of way he was really rather prim. There was once some heroin floating round the college and there were two students who were the pushers—that's the phrase for them I think—and they were both beaten up. I don't mean they were just knocked about a bit . . . they were smashed, stitches and a fractured jaw for one, severe abdominal bruising for the other. You could see the scratches on Holly's knuckles for days afterward, and no one ever said anything about it. It was just not referred to . . . I read about the poor devil, that those buggers trumped up an espionage charge against him and he's years to serve in Russia. I hope I'm not being facetious, but they'll have a hell of a time with him . . . I'll put it another way to you, Mr. Millet. He was a little bit frightening. He could make the rest of us, adults and kids, seem rather frivolous. Nobody likes that, do they?"

On to the parish priest of St. Mary's and St. Peter's. Tea and a plain biscuit in a brick-built vicarage's front room.

"I'm not going to be able to help you, Mr. Millet. Yes, I was aware of him, but I never managed to lasso him. He never attended worship, he never came to the Youth Hall. I thought he might have had a place at the Youth, it seemed to me that he might have been a leader if he'd had the encouragement. I tried and failed, Mr. Millet. It was a disappointment to me. Well, you're always sorry if you let slip someone you think might be a leader. How did I know he was leadership stuff? You can tell, Mr. Millet, it's not something that can be hidden. All I can say is that I failed, and in this particular case I regret that failure."

He took a train back to London, and a taxi over to Charing Cross. Then another train toward the Kent commuter belt, and Dartford. Off the train before its route reached the suburbs. At the station he asked for directions to the industrial estate, and walked it in a quarter of an hour. Letterworth Engineering and Manufacturing Company, the sign said. Mark Letterworth was a tall man with the weight of the recession hanging heavy on his face and shoulders.

"I tell you this, Mr. Millet, two or three years ago I wouldn't have had the time to sit down and chatter about a chap I haven't seen for more than a year. That I've got the time is a bloody disaster. I've the bank breathing at me, and forty-two wage envelopes to fill on Friday morning, and the phone isn't ringing with customers. I'll tell you this so that you know I've problems too. Not problems like young Michael's, but I've enough to be going on with. I'll tell you this too, and this is for nothing, somebody dumped that boy right in the shit, somebody dropped him in the shit from a great old height. You see I never believe in smoke without fire, and when our man is nicked on a spying charge then I say to myself that somebody got at him, somebody asked a favor of him, somebody got round him. I don't know whether you've ever been to Russia, Mr. Millet, I have. I was regular there. Right? It's not the easiest of places, but business works there, and business is money, and money is wages, and wages are what keeps my workforce happy. Understand me, Mr. Millet? What I know of Moscow is that you keep your nose clean and do the work you've set out to achieve, and that way there's no hassle. I'll tell you this . . . three times before he went, Michael asked me for time to go up to London and said he was having problems with his visa. Three trips up to London. I've never had to have more than one trip to the Consulate for any visa of mine. Somebody lined him up, and that somebody is no friend of mine, Mr. Millet. I don't know what productivity you have to show in your job, in mine it's the order book. I needed that custom out of the Soviet Union, I needed it bloody badly. We've been frozen out there, and that order was worth a couple of million sterling, and that adds up to a hefty pile of wage envelopes. You asked me what he was like, Mr. Millet . . . I was going to make him a director, bloody good young man, tough and fair and straight. Nobody walked over him, not me, not the customer, not the workforce. It's a bloody tragedy he's where he is, and that's the truth. The place is the poorer without him . . . that what you want to know, Mr. Millet? The only thing that didn't work for him was his marriage, perhaps his wife will give you a different side . . . don't tell me that you didn't know he was married and separated, Mr. Millet . . . bit bloody thin on the groundwork, aren't you?"

Before he reached the small block of a dozen bed-sitting-room apartments, Alan Millet knew this would be his last call.

Still the rain, all week it had rained, and his coat was barely dried out from the previous evening and his shoes were still wet and had rejected the polish he had attempted over his breakfast. This would be the last call, and after that the heat of the office at Century that he shared with two others. One more visit and the picture of the man who had taken the package to Moscow would be fuller and acceptable as a memorandum to the deputy undersecretary. There had been no difficulty in finding her. A marriage certificate in London and the telephone book had done the work for him. He hadn't rung to make an appointment, better to turn up at the door and press the bell like any other cheapskate private detective. Well, he wasn't much more, was he? Padding the streets and prying into the window of a man's life, and the trail turned him toward the second-floor apartment of Mrs. Angela Holly (née Wells), two miles from the home of her former husband and parents-in-law. Eight o'clock in the morning, and if she went to work then he hoped still to be in time to catch her before she locked the front door and shut out the intrusion of a man from the Service.

A radio played inside the flat, the bell tinkled under his finger.

She was very pretty.

Straight blonde hair, slender-faced and with a wide mouth of expectancy as if everything that happened that was a surprise was excitement and welcomed. A green sweater that flattered and a knitted skirt that matched. A pretty girl and one that should be with a man, not a girl who should have sat beside a lawyer in a High Street divorce court. Millet had played the images game on the pavement outside, had anticipated a tousled woman who wore badges of failure. And the girl was lovely, lovely and fresh and anticipating.

"Yes . . . ?"

"I'm Alan Millet, Foreign and Commonwealth . . ."

"Yes . . ."

"Can I come in, please?"

" 'Course you can, but you'll be sitting on your own all day—I'm on my way out."

"Where do you go?"

"Town . . . off the Strand. Boring old Building Society."

"I'd like to come with you."

"Please yourself . . . bring the milk in, can you? . . . I'm hell's late and that's usual."

He picked up from beside his feet two cartons of milk and a plastic box of half a dozen eggs. At the end of the corridor leading from the front door was the kitchen, where he found the fridge. He heard her whistling to the radio beyond the half-closed door of what he presumed was her bedroom, and there was another door that could have led to the living room. A dwelling unit, nothing more, something that was right for a girl that was alone, right for a girl who lived without a man. She blustered out of the bedroom, and swept up a coat from a chair in the corridor. Millet grinned and stepped out onto the landing and behind him the door slammed cheerfully. He took his cue from her and they half ran and half walked the couple of hundred yards to the station, and she led and he followed. He had no ticket and she had a pass, and while he stood in line at the window they missed one train and she rolled her head and her eyes and seemed to think it a joke and when the train came there was one thought only in Millet's mind. How in God's name did this go wrong?

A commuter train, a stop at each station, all seats taken by the gray-suited men who hid from each other behind their newspapers and the film of cigarette and pipe smoke. So they stood and their hands clasped at the baggage rack above their heads, and Millet saw the eyes of a fellow traveler flit to the girl's features as if they were staring at those magazines on the high shelf behind the newsagent's counter. How could Michael Holly and this girl have broken?

"I want to talk to you about Michael."

A frown creased her forehead. "It's three years since I've seen him, long before all this business. Did you say Foreign

Office? . . . I've not seen him since the split."

"It's confidential really—but we were hoping to get him back. It hasn't worked out."

"I didn't know."

Lunatic. A train swaying between Kingston and Norbiton and New Malden, and a member of the permanent staff of the Service talking with a stranger about a freelance recruit who had been snaffled. They'd have his balls at Century for it.

"The Soviets have now transferred him to a Labor Camp."

"They're ghastly?"

"Pretty dreadful."

"I don't know how I can help you. I told you, it's been a long time . . ."

He felt a pig, a bore. He was ashamed of himself, and he leaned toward her, and the scent she had dabbed at her neck in the bedroom played at his nostrils.

"What broke it, Mrs. Holly?"

"Foreign Office, you said? That's the business of the Foreign Office?"

For the first time he saw a nervousness from her, the hesitation of the little girl lost. He was playing the bastard because that way the inner door opened.

"I said Foreign Office, Mrs. Holly. Why did it break?"

Her laugh showed a strain of fear, and the man whose elbow was lodged in Alan Millet's rib turned to the girl. She smiled and looked bravely into Alan Millet's face.

"I'll talk to you for all the time we're on this train. You don't come to the office, you don't come again to my home. . . ."

"Agreed," Millet said quietly. "You have my word, Mrs. Holly."

"I think I love him still, I think I'll love him all my life. I've never fallen out of love with him, not when he went home, not when we were in the courts, not now after three years. He's a man that a woman wants to love. You feel very proud when you're with him. He's perfect, you see, Mr. Millet. What's the silly bitch saying, that's what you're asking, isn't it? He's punctual, I'm late. He's tidy, I drop everything anywhere. He speaks when he has something to say, I'll talk about anything with anyone. He has a patience and a calmness, I lose my temper and shout and scream. I never had a chance to bitch

at him...do you know what that means? Can you imagine
what that's like...I can't express it properly. He was like a
kind of martyr, it was as if all my failings were stones that
were thrown at him and which he never complained of. If he'd
yelled at me then I'd have been delirious, then I could have
lived with him...He didn't need a wife, can you believe that?
He didn't need me, or anyone else. He's an entity on his
own...."

"I said it would be pretty dreadful where he is now, how
will he cope there?"

She giggled shrilly and swayed against him as the train
lurched on the points on the approach to Waterloo.

"I don't have to answer that, do I? I mean, well, it's pretty
obvious from what I've said...I told you that I loved him,
that's God's truth, I love him and I tell you they might have
made such a place just for him."

The train had stopped.

"I said you shouldn't come back to me, Mr. Millet, and
you agreed."

"I gave my word, Mrs. Holly, thank you."

Millet and the girl were pushed toward the door, disgorged
from the carriage.

The smile swept her face and she patted his hand, and then
she had spun on her heel and the swing was in her hips as she
walked away into the hurrying crowds.

Chapter 7

Holly worked on alone at the lathe that fashioned the chairs' legs.

Around him the other machines were silent, closed down. The saws and planes and chisels and hammers were abandoned. The benches were deserted. Only Holly was at his place. His back was to the window and he did not turn to spare a glance at the crush of the *zeks* who squirmed against the grime of the windows. There was no expression on his face, just the blank skin façade of hunger and tiredness.

At first the civilian foremen who came to the factory each morning from Barashevo village had shouted that the men should stay at their work, but their protests had made a battle that he could not win. The trusties of internal order had added their voices and they, too, were ignored. The two wings of authority had accepted defeat and then joined the workforce at the windows. Beyond the glass there was a sporadically placed ring of guards and dogs who seemed uncertain as to whether to stare back at the distorted press of faces at the glass panes, or whether to watch instead the spiral column of smoke and the flames that played at its heels. Only the roof of the Commandant's hut was visible over the high wooden fence that was the boundary of the factory compound, but the fire was high and the smoke higher. There was much for everyone to see. Like children the prisoners reveled in the spectacle, and their enjoyment was spurred by the noise of sirens and shouting and the crackle of old wood in the fire.

Holly heard above the drone of his lathe motor the scenario of sound that the fire carried, and heard too the happiness of the men who had left their benches.

"All the files, all the bastard case files, all there to burn, all gone."

"They'll only have the sand buckets, they won't have a water supply. I saw the hoses last week, they hadn't been drained, they're frozen solid in their coils."

"Did you see the pig Kypov? He came in running like a fat sow, his uniform's half burned off his fucking back."

"How could a fire start there?"

"The speed it spread, that's not electrical, it spread like tart's clap."

"Shit how it started, it did. Bugger how it started."

Holly knew.

Holly could have answered the babble over his shoulder.

He picked at another piece of raw wood that had been crudely cut in the workshop across the compound in preparation for the finishing work of the lathes.

The wood shavings and dust reached up in an awkward mess from the floor beside his legs. A great mound close to him, but the daily norm that was so precious to the administration of the camp would be found wanting that day. Bloody dangerous, this lathe, Holly thought. Wouldn't have wormed through any Factory Safety Act passed in Britain in the last fifty years, open and unshielded parts, and half of the men who used them wore the scars on their hands to prove the danger. There should have been gloves and protective goggles and face masks to field the resin and varnish dust. And the men worked without these essentials because work was food, and food was life.

Holly knew how the fire had started in the office of Major Vasily Kypov.

In his mind that was guarded by gray, disinterested eyes and his sallow tight-drawn forehead, Holly could picture the process of how a match lit in innocence had tumbled upon an incendiary device. He had looked for a loophole in their guard, he had found that crevice at the first time of asking. Smug, weren't they? Believing in their authority so totally that they could not envisage a mere prisoner, a mere item of scum, daring to kick back. Kick back with interest. And the interest was prime rate high, and the flames were falling now because little was left for them to feed from.

The foremen called again for the men to return to their work. They came when the fire had dipped below the level of the high fence. There was a rumble across the workshop floor as the motors of the machinery sluggishly coughed back to life.

The old thief, Chernayev, from Hut 2 was beside Holly. A grizzled gnome of a man with a face as white as office paper and a pepper speckle of beard growth across his jowls and chin.

"You weren't interested? You've been here three weeks— I tell you, when it is three years you will run to the window with the rest of us."

Holly did not look away from his work.

"How long have you been here?"

"This camp five years, before that twelve years in Perm. They call me Chernayev the thief. I have not been a thief for seventeen years, chance would be a thing. I did twelve years in Perm, and I was stupid...I had a tattoo done...imbecile...Brezhnev is a parasite, that was the tattoo on my arm. You know they could have shot me for that. Self-defacement, inciting anti-Soviet attitudes, it's all in the penal code. Four words and they could have shot me, that's in the book. I have four more to go.... See this...." He held out his arm and pushed back the sleeve of his overall and there was a rectangle of puckered ruddy skin. "They had to get rid of the offensive literature, they couldn't burn it, so they scraped it off and grafted back some skin from my ass.... You understand why I laugh when Kypov's hut goes down?"

Holly seemed to look at him as if the matter of a fire that destroyed the office of the Commandant was neither of occasion nor note.

"I understand why you laugh."

The foreman was behind them peering between their shoulders, and there was a sniff of impatience.

"It's not a wives' meeting, it's a workshop...and you're behind, Chernayev...."

It had been very simple once he had absorbed the mechanics of the attack.

A juvenile could have done it. They were so flabby. They believed so completely in the strength of their discipline and the spider net of submission that it secreted.

The screws that they used in the workshop came in plastic bags a few inches square. Holly had picked a discarded one

from the floor. The lathes were serviced with a light oil film,
draped in it as if to give them an overcoat protection that would
ensure their survival against age and wear. Holly had filled the
plastic bag with oil and twisted the neck tight and fastened it
with a snip of wire. The bag and the oil had nestled behind his
testicles, held in place by his underpants, as he had walked
from the factory to Hut 2, evaded the evening search. Feldstein
had given Holly a magazine and said he wanted it no longer.
In his iron mug, on the privacy of his bunk, Holly had man-
ufactured the pulp of papier-mâché as he had been taught to
by his mother when he was a small boy. He made a rough
shape that was neither a cube nor a sphere, but a wet and
hollow lump. In the night when the hut was quiet apart from
the coughing and the bed creaks and the whimpering of men
in despair, he had gone to the stove and heated his shape until
it was dried and firm. The bag that was filled with oil sat inside
its carton. He had smeared the shape with coal dust.

Each morning there was a rota of men designated to fill the
coal containers for the day—buckets for the administration
offices and the guardroom and the barracks, sacks for the huts—
from the central heap of fuel beside the compound gate. The
perimeter path was beside the coal mountain. On exercise that
morning he had tossed his offering the few inches from his
pocket to a waiting bucket. From the far side of the perimeter
path he had watched the detail at their work as they scraped
the overnight snow from the coal mountain, then shoveled the
buckets and sacks full. He did not know which building he
would raze . . . but one would go. One was doomed when a
bucket of coal was tipped on to a blazing fire and the flames
eroded the dust covering, ate at the brittle papier-mâché, flickered at the softness of the plastic bag. Really it had been very
simple. Simple and anonymous. The covert attack of the unseen
guerilla. And no one for them to strike back against. Simple
and anonymous and safe. And a beginning, Holly, only a beginning. The first shot of war. And war, once started, has a
long road to run.

At midday they were marshaled and marched back from the
work compound to the living compound to take their places in
the line for the kitchen. Holly saw the confusion of the guards'

officers and NCOs, the way that instructions were given in a
frantic pitch and confronted by the sullen amusement of the
zeks. The dogs were allowed to drag their handlers closer to
the ranks of men as the roll call was made. And those in charge
strutted along the lines and there was an anger at their faces
that Holly had not seen before. Anger at humiliation, at pride
lost. It was a bright day with thin sunshine burnishing up from
the snow and men blinked and rubbed their eyes as they crossed
the open space between the two compounds, tramping over the
road running down to the village and the railway line that
stretched far the other way to Pot'ma. The guards who sealed
the *zeks* into their corridor were restive, in poor temper. Another group of prisoners, themselves surrounded by guns and
dogs, waited for the slow column to clear the road so that they
themselves could pass on. Holly grimaced. A log jam at Barashevo, as if this forgotten end of the world was a metropolis
of movement and then he looked again at the huddle of prisoners
separated from him by two lines of uniformed guards.

Women. And Holly had not gazed on a woman for thirteen
months.

Women who wore black. Black tunics and black skirts and
black boots. Dissent and crime are not the prerogative of the
male. A chorus of shouting began around Holly. Fun for the
zeks, diversion from the tedium of the parade line and the parade
march and the parade search and the parade lunch. And the
women matched the men in earth and coarseness and the laughter pealed between the two groups. Perhaps because he was
not yet bowed with the burden of imprisonment, Holly was a
man to be noticed. Taller than those around him.

A girl had seen Holly.

A tiny creature who was muffled in a tunic with the collar
upturned and with a scarf across her mouth and a forage cap
whose peak was pulled down over her eyes. An elf and an
urchin, she had seen Holly. He stared back at her. Two people
on opposite platforms and when the trains come they will go
their different ways and not meet again. And the railway track
that divided them was lines of men in uniform who cradled
machine pistols, who held tight to dragging dogs.

He saw a name printed across the right side of her tunic.

He knew her only as Morozova. Why one girl in a crowd?

Why one girl who possessed only a hidden face and a printed name?

Poshekhonov was at Holly's side, chuckling from the side of his mouth.

"Hard for you young bastards . . . old buggers like me, we've forgotten what it's like. Not that thinking about it helps. Tie a knot, boy, that's the best."

He remembered her. Standing beside the rails at the junction at Pot'ma she had held the baby of an exhausted mother, and she had smiled at him. He could not see if she smiled now that her mouth was hidden by her scarf.

"Don't look at those beasts," Poshekhonov said. "That's the slime at the bottom of the can. They'd eat a man. . . . You don't believe me? I tell you, I'd rather go without than have that lot screw me. They're shit, in Zone 4 they're not women as we'd know them, just shit."

The column moved on. Holly surprised himself, he turned his head to watch the women cross the path. He thought he saw the girl again, but he could not be sure.

The gate stood in front of them. The girl was gone from his mind, swept aside by the burned-out office at the end of the administration block. They had done quite a good job, Holly could see that, in containing the fire. Only the Commandant's room was wrecked, gutted. He told himself that the office would have been an addition, built onto the end of what had before been an exterior wall of brick and therefore powerful enough to hold back the spread of the flames.

"You know, Holly, there was a man here once who told me an extraordinary thing about women . . ." Poshekhonov babbled as a stream runs over rocks. ". . . he said that a girl he knew once used to do it while in a handstand position. Can you believe that, Holly? I never quite knew whether to believe him. Standing on her hands with her back against the wall, and she wanted him to run at her. I could never believe that. . . . Shit, I've wanted to . . ."

Holly saw the blackened uniforms of the guards as they moved among the debris of the office that they had retrieved. Some still threw buckets of snow into the small flames that lived. There was the rich stench of charred wood, and the python hiss of water on embers. Dark on the snow, beneath the windows, were items of furniture and crumpled photograph frames and scattered wisps of paper.

He wondered whether he were pleased, excited, whether he was proud.

Poshekhonov tugged at Holly's arm, demanded further attention.

"I never knew whether I should believe that man . . . but, you know, he gave me great pleasure. He implanted the thought in me, the thought of this woman with her handstand. She changes for me each day—she is blonde and she is dark, young and mature, fat and thin—it doesn't matter. Extraordinary pleasure."

"Does the sight of the Commandant's hut flattened, busted, does that give you pleasure?" Holly asked.

They stood waiting their turn to go through the gate. Ranks of five and the counting again, and the calling of names, and across the compound the beckoning presence of the low-built kitchen.

"Why should that give me pleasure?"

"Because at worst they are hurt, at best they are inconvenienced."

"And if they are hurt, does that help me? Does that shorten my sentence? Does it soften my mattress . . ."

"I don't know."

Holly was withdrawn, private. He felt no call to share the small purseful of glory. To his left three guards had taken the strain on a rope that ran tight and stretched to the building. He heard the command, he heard the men's feet slither in the snow as they pulled. With a shriek the last beams of the roof collapsed and pitched down.

"Kypov's office is nothing. Now the handstand, that's different. I could kiss the man who told me that, two years of happiness he's given me. All I wish is that I could find out whether it's possible."

Holly smiled drily. "Anything is possible if you have the will."

"I have the will, I'm short of the bloody woman. . . ."

Poshekhonov turned to Holly to have the satisfaction of seeing his joke shared. Holly no longer looked at him, he stared back at the stunted ruin that had been the office of the Commandant.

* * *

That morning Captain Yuri Rudakov had taken his wife to the shops at Pot'ma.

By the standards of the *Dubrovlag* she had a nice home, a two-bedroomed bungalow on the outer edge of the village. With no children, two bedrooms was a privilege. Two bedrooms and the best furniture that could be made in the factory. But she hated this place. Hated it for its bleak isolation and petty preoccupation with the work of fences and confinement. She admitted to no friends among the small clutch of camp officers' wives at Barashevo. She had no companion in this snow wilderness with its circles of wire. She had been brought up in the sophistication of inner Moscow, and she had traveled to European Germany. She was an outsider and feared by the wives of the other officers of Camp 3 because her husband was KGB and because his reports could break and crush the career of any man, however senior. She urged on the days until the chance of their transfer away, she wrote waspy letters to her mother three times a week, and whenever possible she badgered her Yuri to take her to the shops at Pot'ma.

They were little enough, those shops. But to be in Pot'ma, to walk along Leninsky Prospekt, that was bliss. And when she went to Pot'ma she had the whole and unchipped attention of her man, and when he drove their car and walked with her in front of the shops he had no files, no papers. It was a victory for her each time that she wrested him away from his desk and his teleprinter and his uniform. The life of the camp consumed their married life, oppressed her from her hour of waking until the time she fell asleep. And each third Sunday of the month was the evening that she detested, when she must take the political studies lecture for Camp 3, Zone I. It was her duty, Yuri had said. She had trained as a teacher, and was the daughter of a colonel of KGB and a probationer member of the Party, it was her duty to participate in the re-education of prisoners. And they stank, stank like cattle carcasses outside an abattoir. And they had eyes, bright and pricking eyes that shredded her clothes and burrowed to the soft underwear she had purchased in the Centrum store on Magdeburg's Karl Marx Strasse. There were some who were clever, some who were stupid, and none who cared for the lecture that would take her forty-five minutes to read and three evenings to prepare. Yuri had said it was her duty. At times she believed she could make her hard man into a piece of putty, but not when he spoke of duty. Duty was his life. Duty was the bastard world of the *Dubrovlag*.

Elena Rudakov sat beside her husband, and on the back seat of the car, in plastic bags, was a new nightdress of flannelette and two shirts for Yuri to wear at home and two kilos of turnips from the open market and a small rug to go in front of the stove in their living room. He had even been attentive, Yuri, and that was rare. He had talked of a new prisoner—too much to hope that he would speak of anything other than the camp— a prisoner who was an Englishman. Guarded talk, because she was never fully in his confidence, but he had spoken of a prisoner who was special and different. He drove slowly because the rough road was always treacherous in winter and insufficiently sanded, but the inside of the car was warm and the sky alive in blue beyond the windows.

She was almost happy, almost at peace, until they saw, together, the high column of the black smoke.

She was left to take the car home. The spell was broken, the pool was rippled from its serenity by the way he snapped instructions to her and then ran to the administration block. She could have kicked a dog. He had not kissed her or looked back, just sprinted across the snow.

The sight was a hammer blow to Yuri Rudakov.

The end of the administration block was a grotesque mess.

Only the smoke now, because the flames had been suffocated. Smoke that rippled and soared.

He saw Kypov, a comedy clown with a soot-smeared face and the back of his uniform singed and brown from collar to knee-boot. There were no thoughts in his mind, no preconceptions, only the demand for information.

Empty words. "What happened?"

"Where the hell have you been?" Kypov shouted at him across the few meters that separated them, and the breath spouted white from the major's mouth. "Why were you not here?"

"I asked what happened," Rudakov said. He despised these army men, in particular those who had lost their units in exchange for secondment to MVD camp detachments.

"You should have been here."

"Will you tell me what happened or not . . . Major Kypov?"

They were all the same, all noise and sparrow fart, and if the man only knew the idiot scene he cut. . . .

"My fire exploded."

The fight had fled the major. His hands hung simply by his trouser pockets, ungloved, and Rudakov could see that they trembled.

"More."

"The fire had been lit before I came to the office. My orderly put more coal on for me. After he had gone I was standing in front of the fire, my back to it. There was a sort of an explosion, not very loud, the flames took my back. I was alight. My orderly had to roll me on the floor. He pulled me out, he saved my life."

"What have you lost?"

"I could have lost my life . . ." and the indignation was rich again in the major's voice.

"What have you lost in the fire?"

"The administration files that I kept, some of the convicts' files."

"They were not in the safe?"

"You have seen my safe. It could not hold half the papers that were in my cupboard."

The men who worked around the building acknowledged a secret circle that surrounded their camp Commandant and their camp KGB officer. None broke into the circle. They threaded a wide path round them.

"Then you will have to inform Moscow."

"And what are you going to do?"

"Try to find out why, to find how, to find who. That is what I am going to do, Comrade Commandant. And you, you should get to your quarters, and get out of those clothes. The Commandant should not be an object of ridicule to his prisoners."

There was a fleck of amusement at the corner of Captain Rudakov's mouth. He considered whether Major Kypov's commendations, so preciously framed, had perished. He walked to his own office. An accident or an attack, he wondered, and stamped the snow from his walking shoes on the steps of the main administration doorway.

* * *

The line edged forward toward the food hatch.

Holly heard only occasional talk about the burned office because the job of the men around him was to get the food inside their guts, get the warmth into their throats.

A line creeping forward, and a rabble of men leaving the hatch and hurrying for the first bench place they could find. And hungry men are pliable men, hunger wins submission, hunger is the tool of Major Vasily Kypov, hunger is the whip of the Commandant of Camp 3, Zone I. But Holly and eight hundred with him had a roof over their kitchen, and there would be a roof over Hut 2 when the freezing night came. Kypov had no roof, and the thought carried a first-found peace for Holly, lifted him from the line of men who straggled across the dirt-smeared floor boards. You did it well, Holly, bloody well.

Byrkin had been a petty officer in the Navy.

In the evenings in Hut 2 he had twice pulled Holly to a corner to tell him of his innocence.

Now he staggered toward Holly, making a path between the tables and benches and the backs of sitting men that flanked him on one side, and the waiting line on the other. Byrkin would have been tall when he was in the Navy, but the camp had bent his back and plucked his hair from a smoothed scalp. His hands shook and his balance was cruelly uncertain, a fly wheel that had lost its rhythm.

Byrkin had twice found out Holly to tell him of the sailing of the frigate Storozhevoy from the naval harbor at Riga. Mutiny by the men, and what could a petty officer do if the Ministry in Moscow determined that the sailors of the Storozhevoy should not be freed from their conscripted service after four years at sea, that they should serve another year, what could a petty officer do? Not Byrkin's fault that the mutiny disease had swept the cramped quarters of the lower decks. He had been locked in a cabin, a prisoner with the officers when the bombers came on a low-clouded November afternoon. Seven years before, and the memory still with him, bleeding him. A memory of imprisonment below the water line as the high explosive had silenced the engines of a fighting frigate, marooned its escape to Swedish waters. Fifty men dead before the turbines of a Krivak class frigate with a displacement of 3800 tons were halted. And more to die before the firing squad, and few who did not wear the gold rings of the officers to escape the penalty of imprisonment. One unguarded remark by Byrkin, one remark that had been carried back by a man with innocence on his face to those who would judge Byrkin. What did the Ministry expect, how did they think the men would react? What insensitivity from the Ministry! Ten years in the *Dubrovlag* for the private expression of a petty officer who was a captive in a cabin while the high explosive bombs rained on to the armor plate of the Storozhevoy.

They said in Hut 2 that he was mad. The *zeks* did not know of the bitter trial of the breakdown. Byrkin's balance was lost, and each step that he took was an agony of effort and fear.

Holly saw him, heard his shrieking wail as a shoulder lifted from the bench and caught square on the underneath of Byrkin's enamel soup bowl. The opaque yellow liquid floated high beside Byrkin's face then splashed on his tunic, onto the shoulder of the man who had nudged him, onto the boards of the floor. It was Byrkin who shouted. A howl of protest, of despair. The man who rose from the bench seemed to offer a grudging apology, but Byrkin would not have seen the gesture as he scrabbled on the floor for his slice of black bread. Holly looked into Byrkin's eyes witnessing the suffering. What price against that suffering was the pleasure that the Commandant had no roof to cover his office? Holly had felt pleasure, allowed it to cocoon him. Where did that pleasure stand on the scale against the misery of a man in the kitchen whose soup was spilled, whose bread was soggy from the floor's snow water?

Poshekhonov was beside Holly. Always Poshekhonov seemed to be close to him.

"Only happens to someone like Byrkin. He's doomed, damned. Mark me, Englishman, he'll go to the wire."

"He's sick," said Holly. The tranquillity had gone from his face. He moved forward to close the gap again with the tunic back in front of him and his lips were dented white where the teeth had bitten at them.

"Sick? Of course he's sick. Sick like everybody. What do you expect, a nice neat psychiatric ward? He's better here, better with us than at the Sebsky. . . ."

"I don't know of the Sebsky."

"For one who intends to stay a long time with us, Englishman, you know little of us. In Moscow is Kropotkin Lane. At Number 23 is the Sebsky Institute for Forensic Psychiatry. Ask Feldstein, our little revolutionary. He shits himself each day that they will send him there. Friend Byrkin would get robust treatment at the Sebsky. Even this place is better than some, Englishman."

They were at the hatch. Soup in a bowl, hot water in a mug, bread on the tray.

"Will you sit with me, Englishman?"

There was a wintry smile on Holly's face.

"Find a place for two of us, I'll come to you."

Holly took his tray and walked briskly back along the line of men who waited for their food. He saw ahead of him the bowed back of Byrkin, hunched head in hands with an empty bowl in front of him on the table. Holly's movement was very quick, sudden, and few would have seen the gesture. His soup bowl snaked from his tray, tipped, tilted, the liquid ran steaming to the bowl in front of Byrkin. And Holly was gone, moving to where a space waited for him beside Poshekhonov.

Adimov had seen. One of the few, but he had seen. He sat with a frown of puzzlement on his forehead, then turned back to join again the talk around him.

"Where's your soup?" Poshekhonov asked Holly as he sat down, squeezing himself over the bench.

"I had it on the way here—little enough of it."

"You shouldn't do that. You get more goodness if you take it slowly. There was a man here once, he could take half an hour to drink a bowl of soup, big as an ox. Didn't matter if it was stone cold, still took it sip by sip . . ."

Poshekhonov liked to talk. That was his happiness, to talk to a captured ear was for him the thrill of seeing the Commandant's office roofless and destroyed. Holly did not interrupt him, and broke his bread into small pieces and husbanded the crumbs.

The report that the office of Major Vasily Kypov, Commandant of ZhKh 385/3/1 in the Mordovian ASSR, had been burned to destruction in as yet unexplained circumstances was a matter of sufficient significance to be seen by a senior official at the Ministry of the Interior.

The official was a member of the staff of the procurator general who had responsibility for the smooth running of the Correctional Labor Colonies scattered across the Union of Soviet Socialist Republics.

Before giving up this half-filled sheet of paper to his file system, the official had noted well its contents. Anything extraordinary that happened in Camp 3, Zone I, was out of place. Such a well-administered camp, so little difficulty springing from it, a Commandant in whom great confidence was justly placed.

In the weeks that followed, the teleprinter messages from Barashevo were to become familiar reading to the official who now hobbled on the built-up shoe that supported his club foot toward his filing cabinets.

Chapter 8

A building has been destroyed and can be rebuilt. A roof has fallen and can be replaced.

The captain of KGB begins an investigation. The major in command is at first flustered, then morose.

There is labor in Zone I, and to spare. In a few days there will be a new office for Major Kypov at the end of the administration block.

For nearly half a century the camp has survived the storms. More than fire is required to break the regimen of ZhKh 385/3/I.

Later, those who were to piece together the events at the camp of the early months of that year, from the time of snow till the approach of spring, were to wonder what was the ambition of Michael Holly, prisoner of Hut 2, in Zone I of Camp 3 in the *Dubrovlag* complex.

For a few days there was a swirl of conversation in the camp about the fire and its likely cause, and then the talk slipped. The *zeks* had more to concern them. Interest in food, in warmth, in punishment, soon outstripped a matter as trivial as a fire. The fire was a dream, the fire was as nothing as the new bricks were slapped into cold cement and the air rang with the rasp of the carpenters' saws as they fashioned the ceiling framework.

Only for Holly did the fire live on. If he had chosen to confide in anyone then he could not have said clearly what was the summit of his aspiration. He would have fumbled for explanations. But the point was irrelevant because he had no confidant. He offered his friendship to no one. Feldstein the dissident, Chernayev the thief, Poshekhonov the fraud, all reached for the Englishman as if to draw out some spark of friendship. All were resisted.

When he walked the perimeter fence, when he worked at the bench with the wood that would become a chair's leg, when he ate in the kitchen, when he lay on the top tier of the bunk, he was alive and alert. Always watching.

Holly searched for the next opportunity to strike again at the administration of the camp that held him.

Darkness outside the hut, and beyond that darkness the ring of light from the arc lamps over the fence and the wire. The hut windows were misted as if a concerted bluster of hot air had steamed them. The lights were on inside the hut.

A few men read magazines, Feldstein was as always with a book. Another hour until lights out. Some tried already to sleep. At the end of the hut a boy waited, sitting hunched on an upper bunk, for darkness to come to the living quarters because then he could go to the mattress of the man who loved him. . . . A low drone of talk hummed in the hut, and Holly lay on his back on his bunk and gazed at the roof rafters and counted the time between each fall of a water drop to his feet.

Near to Holly, Adimov was stretched on his bunk stomach down. For a long time he had held the envelope in his chubby fingers and close to his face. He had seemed to sniff at the opened envelope as though it carried some scent, but the letter inside only peeped from the tear and was not taken out. A man seeming to fight some inner struggle. Lying still, with the fingers clenched on the envelope and the eyes saucer wide.

"Holly . . ." A hissed whisper from Adimov.

The knife had never been spoken of again. Holly did not interfere with the "baron's" running of the hut.

"Adimov . . ." No move of Holly's head.

"Come here, Holly." An instruction, a command.

"I'm very comfortable, Adimov."

"Come . . . now."

"Listen when I speak to you . . . I said I'm comfortable."

Holly heard him shift on his bunk and the mattress seemed to belch at the movement.

"Please come, Holly . . . please. . . ."

Holly jackknifed his legs over the side of the bunk, swung

himself down to the floor, dropped his feet beside Adimov's bunk. His head was close to Adimov, close enough to smell the force of the man's breath, to see the white anger of the scar on his face.

"What is it, Adimov?" spoken gently.

The toughness caved, the face of a child who is frightened.

"I had a letter this morning, a letter from my wife's mother. It is the first letter that I have had here in a year..."

"Yes."

"I can't read, Holly."

The voice grated in Adimov's throat. Holly's ear was beside Adimov's mouth.

"You want me to read it for you?"

"They read it for me in administration."

"You want me to read it again?"

"You don't know whether those pigs lie to you...."

"Give it to me, Adimov...no one here will know."

Only when Holly's hand was on the envelope did Adimov release his fingers' grip. He had held the paper as tightly as an old woman holds a rosary. Holly looked over the single sheet of paper that was covered in the large hand of one for whom writing was slow and difficult. He read the few lines through, then closed his eyes for a moment before reading aloud.

Terminal cancer, cancer of the bowel. Perhaps a month.

"Is that what they told you?"

"That is what they told me that the letter said."

Adimov sagged down onto his mattress and his head was half-buried in his pillow and there was a redness in his eyes.

"Will they let you go to her?"

There was a choking laugh from Adimov, derisive.

"Will they bring her to you?"

"Would you bring a woman to this place? Would you give to a dying woman as a last memory the sight of our camp? Would you, Holly...?"

"What can I do, Adimov?"

"I saw you with Byrkin's soup."

Holly started back and something of the kindness was lost from his face.

"I saw you, it means nothing that I saw you...I thought

you would help me, too. If you helped Byrkin, that you would
help me."

"What can I do?"

"I can't read, I can't write. . . ."

The man who dominated the hut, who controlled the tobacco
racket, who took an undisputed place at the front of the food
line in the kitchen.

"You want me to write a letter to your wife?"

"And none of these people shall know."

Because in the life of the camp, if the wife of the strongman
has terminal bowel cancer and will be dead within a month,
then that is weakness, and from weakness there cannot be
spawned authority, and without authority the man who breeds
fear throughout the hut will disintegrate.

"I will write the letter tomorrow. I'll get the paper and you
will tell me what to write."

"Thank you, Holly. I am generous to my friends."

Holly turned away, climbed again on to his bunk.

On his back he began again to count the interval between
the water drops. He wrapped the blanket round him, a sparse
level of protection against the cold. He thought of Alan Millet . . . didn't know why, couldn't place the trigger that led him
to Alan Millet and a pub in the Elephant and Castle south of
the Thames. It would be more than a week since he had thought
of Millet. More than a year since they had last spoken, and
more than a week since he had last examined his memory of
those meetings. It had been a very typical contract that Mark
Letterworth had contrived in outline for the sale of the turbine
engines to a Moscow factory. And Letterworth had said that
the deal was bogging down in that bloody stupid Olympic fracas
and the Afghan mess, and that he didn't give a shit for politics,
only for selling engines. Holly spoke the language, so he'd
better jump on an Aeroflot and get over there and chase it up
with the Ministry. All simple, all sweet. And the day after
Holly had been up to London to apply from the Consulate for
a visa there had been the telephone call at Letterworth Engineering. A call with a bad script. . . .

"You don't know me, Mr. Holly, but there's something I'd
like to meet you about when you're next in London. Hopefully
that'll be in the next week. . . ."

They met near Waterloo station because that was good for a train from Dartford. He knew about Holly, this man who called himself Alan Millet. He had read a file on Stepan and Ilya Holovich that would have come with a dust coat out of a Home Office basement reserved for the histories of aliens (naturalized). He knew of attendance by Stepan Holovich at NTS meetings in Paddington, and had the date that a father had taken his son to a house off the Cromwell Road to celebrate the National Day of the Ukrainian exiles with supermarket Italian wine and kitchen table cheese. And Alan Millet had spoken soft words....

"It's not really anything very important, Michael, it's rather a small thing we're asking of you. It helps us and it doesn't help them, if you know what I mean."

There must have been a point of no return, but Holly could not remember passing it. It had not occurred to him that he could stand up in the pub, leave the beer half-drunk, the sandwich half-eaten, walk out into the London early evening. When he thought back over it, as he lay on the bunk and water drips splattered every eleven seconds between his ankles, he could remember only a film of excitement that had wrapped him. At their next meeting instructions had been given for a rendezvous. That had been a long meeting. Long and fulfilling because Alan Millet offered the chance to bite at an old enemy whose presence pervaded the rooms of the terraced home in Hampton Wick.

Michael Holly had trusted Alan Millet implicitly. On his back, on his bunk, he doubted if he would ever trust another man again.

If Yuri Rudakov, undressing in the front bedroom of their bungalow, had not been so tired, he would have taken the time to admire the new nightdress that his wife wore as she sat against the pillows and turned the pages of a picture magazine. If he had not been halfway to sleep he would have noticed that far from washing the makeup from her face she had taken the trouble to apply the eye shadow and lipstick that her mother sent her from Moscow.

She read him. Elena Rudakov knew the signs.

"The fire . . . still the fire. . . ."

"Still the fire." Yuri Rudakov settled in the bed beside her, he made no effort to close the gap between them.

"You've let the cold in."

"I'm sorry. . . ."

"How did the fire start?"

"I don't know."

"It takes you two days and half of two nights to find out that you don't know?"

"You want to hear?"

"I've sat here two days waiting for you to come home, waiting to have a conversation with you. Yes, perhaps I want to hear."

He wanted only for the light to be put out, he waited only for darkness and sleep. He would get nothing before he had fulfilled the chore of explanation.

"Something that was inflammable was in the coal bucket. I don't know what it was, perhaps just paper with oil on it, I don't know. The room had drafts, you needed a greatcoat to stand in it. Kypov never complained, never did anything about it, seemed to think that the chiller his office the more masculine and vigorous he was. Would have made him think he was with the poor bloody troops in a tent in Afghanistan . . . I don't know. There were drafts through the window frame, under the door. He's a fat little bugger and he'd stood his backside in front of the fire. That's all I know. There wasn't a bomb, nothing like that. Just something that ignited enough to get a flame onto his seat. After that, panic. . . . He was shouting, the door is opened, somebody puts a rifle barrel through the window. Drafts all over. I know how it spread, you see. I don't know what started it."

"What are you going to do?"

"Put a couple in the SHIzo block for fifteen days, the ones who filled the buckets. That's all."

"Then you don't have to go early tomorrow?"

Her arms reached toward his head, pulled him toward her.

"I've a bastard day tomorrow. Really. . . . They've given me a major interrogation—I'd told you about the Englishman—that's what I should have been working on, not an idiot fire. The interrogation is a challenge to me. It's a compliment in itself that they've given me the chance. . . ."

He felt her body surge away from him. His head fell against the pillow. He saw her back clothed in the flannelette night-dress. He wanted to touch her, but he did not know how.

He reached up for the light switch. Sleep would be hard to find. Before his eyes would cavort the typed words in the file of Michael Holly.

A fire must have a spark, a flash of ignition. So, too, must an idea of action. There is a moment when an idea is born, the clash of a flint.

Holly was on the perimeter path.

He walked alone, deep-wrapped in his own thoughts, and the morning was colder than any of those of the week before.

The cold cut through him, summoned by the winds that had begun their journey on the far plains of Siberia and the Ural mountains and the great Kirgiz steppe.

He felt it at his face and his fingers and his back and his arms, felt it at his buttocks and privates and thighs. No snow in the air that morning, only the wind that gusted and trapped the men on the perimeter path. And the cold was worst at the feet, he thought. Michael Holly had been a prisoner of the camp for less than one month, and already he believed that he could walk this path with his eyes closed. Four turns to the left on each lap of the compound, and he fancied that he knew at which moment he must drop his shoulder, cut his stride and turn. If he knew the path blindfold after one month, how well would he know it after fourteen years?

In front of him was Chernayev who had not practiced his trade of thieving for seventeen years. Twice that morning Holly had passed Chernayev on the path. Now the old man walked in the center of the path and the way was blocked and Holly had to check his stride.

Chernayev turned his head as if he felt the breathy impatience of the man behind him.

"Holly . . . the Englishman . . . ?"

"Yes."

"And in a hurry? Is it different to you if you make four times round the path and not three?"

Holly faltered for an answer. "If I go faster then I am warmer. . . ."

"If you go faster then you are hungrier."

"Perhaps."

"I know . . . I used to go fast when I was first at Perm, and my gut punished me. Slow yourself, Michael Holly, walk with me."

"There are many you can walk with."

He could have bitten at his tongue. Crudeness and arrogance, enough to shame himself. Chernayev turned toward him, little of his face showing. The old *zek,* the one who took care of himself and who would walk out of Camp 3, Zone I, when his time came.

"Easy, Michael Holly . . . you should not forget who you are. You are not one of us, you are from outside us. In the hut we all talk of you, you know that? If a man drinks only an alcohol made from paint or varnish or polish or acetone then he will dream of vodka. If a man talks only with the prisoners of his own world then he will seek out a stranger. . . . You are important to us. You make a window for us."

"I will walk with you, Chernayev."

Holly fell into step with the old thief, clipped his pace. Holly's shoulder was high above Chernayev's. There was a distant whistle from behind Chernayev's teeth as if he tried to blow away the wind that settled on him.

"The dirt is the hardest, you find that, the filth is the hardest. . . ."

"I suppose you learn to live with it," Holly said distantly.

"I've never learned to. I hate the scum on my body. . . . And this week there will be no showers. . . ."

"Why not?"

"Look with your own eyes." Chernayev waved his arm toward the center of the compound. The snow was dirtied there, earth spattered, and a dark mound was set beside a hole. "We dug a new water pipe, two summers back, across the middle of the camp. The old pipes were cracked, leaked. Some bastard cheated, they say there was not enough binding put around the joins, again the pipe leaks. It's the main water supply for the whole camp, for us and for the barracks. They won't keep the barracks short, so *we* lose the water, *we* do without."

"Yes."

"Where they have dug the hole is a main junction, they say

it is the worst place for the leak, where the water is separated. Some goes to us from the junction, the rest goes to the barracks. The men who work in the hole say it is a pig to work there."

Holly's eyes flickered.

"Where the hole is, that is the junction between their water and ours?"

"Yes. . . . Imagine working in a pit with the water frozen round you, and you cannot wear gloves. If you wear gloves then the water will freeze on them, freeze them hard, and you cannot work. The supervisor says that they cannot wear gloves."

"After the place where they have dug the hole, after that all the water flows to the barracks and the administration?"

"Yes . . . they always cheat on materials for the camp. We earn our wages here. We work in the factory, good work is done here, and they deduct for our food and our keep. If they used the money that they take from us for the maintenance of the camp we would live like kings. It's exploitation, you agree with me?"

"I agree with you, Chernayev."

The old thief rambled on and together they completed another circuit of the perimeter path. Holly barely listened. He thought only of a water pipe, a narrow metal pipe that carried water away from the compound and under the wire and the high wooden fence and on toward the two-story barracks and the kitchens and dormitories of the guards. A slow smile played at Holly's mouth, and there was a bright happiness in his narrowed eyes.

"And the water is cut off while the men work?"

"What do you say . . . ? The water . . . ? The water . . . ? Of course it is cut off. But the bastards in the barracks have the water tower to supply them. Once a day they flush the water through the pipe so that the water tower is topped, that's why the hole is water-filled each morning when the men start work. We have only a water tanker this week, so no showers. They're right bastards who cheated on the materials. . . ."

"If they have the water then they should enjoy it."

Holly's head was doubled on his chest, and his words were spoken without sound, and Chernayev talked on from the side of his mouth, oblivious to the loss of his audience. An old man talking and a younger man who no longer listened.

*   *   *

No man lingered in the latrine wing of the bathhouse. Fear of
the rats hurried even those with the fluid stomach of embryonic
dysentery or gastroenteritis. Some said they had seen the quiz-
zical, gray-whiskered faces staring up at them as they crouched
on the two boards above the refuse pit, peering at the nervous
men from beside the walls of the cubicles and showing no
apprehension. The poison was insufficient to destroy the rat
colony. Beneath the boards on which the men squatted the
matter froze hard and solid.

Before he cleaned himself with old newspaper, Holly knew
the germ of his idea.

The prisoners shambled in an untidy mess toward the open
space between Hut 3 and Hut 4. Soon the Commandant would
come through the gates and into the compound and the orders
would be shouted for them to form their ranks for roll call and
check before the march to the factory for work.

Holly stood beside a poorly dug hole and he looked down
at a T-shaped junction of pipes and saw that the screw-fastened
aperture that gave access to the pipe join and its subsidiary was
swathed in cloth and knotted around in plastic sheeting.
The screw would be adequately protected against the night
frost. He believed he would be able to unfasten the screw turn.
His eyes roved to the perimeter fences where the lights still
shone as if in defiance of the coming day. The lights were far
away, and at their nearest points the bulk of Hut 3 and Hut 4
would shelter the hole in shadow.

A clean ice sheet at the pit of the hole was evidence that
the work was not close to completion. At the pace the *zeks*
worked, the hole would not be filled by that evening.

There was a barked shout. Without emotion the prisoners
took their places in the appointed line.

He had dressed that morning in his civilian clothes, reckoning
that military uniform was unsuitable for the work of the day.
He would not attend parade, he would avoid his Commandant.
A pleasant enough looking young man was Yuri Rudakov in
his slacks and open check shirt and loose gray jacket. His hair
was combed and carefully parted, he had shaved with a new

blade. On his way to the office he had asked for a thermos of coffee to be sent to him and two mugs and a bowl of sugar and some milk. When they had been brought he ordered that Michael Holly should be escorted to the administration building from the factory's furniture production shop. From beyond his rooms and from outside his seldom-washed windows he heard the persistent hammer blows of the carpenters astride the new roof of the Commandant's office.

"Sit down, Holly."

"Thank you, Captain Rudakov."

"Some coffee?"

"Thank you."

"A cigarette?"

"No, thank you."

"You are well, you are not ill?"

"I am not ill, not by the standards that exist here."

"You would like sugar with your coffee?"

"No."

"All the prisoners take sugar."

"Then I am different."

"You have settled here?"

"As well as I will ever settle here."

"The other men in your hut, how do they treat you?"

"I have no problems in the hut."

Rudakov leaned forward across his table, extracted a cigarette from a Marlboro carton, reached with his fingers for his lighter.

"But it's ridiculous, Holly, ridiculous and stupid."

"What is ridiculous and stupid, Captain Rudakov?"

"You are an idiot to be here, you know that Holly. It is unnecessary, it is a waste. You face fourteen years here...."

"I know the sentence of the court."

"A man like you should not be here, you have no necessity to waste your life away here. The camp will destroy you, it destroys every man. You will be an animal when you leave here."

"I am grateful for your concern, Captain Rudakov."

"Are we to work together, Holly, or are we to fight?"

"I don't imagine us as colleagues."

Rudakov drew deeply on his cigarette, let the smoke waft toward the chipboard ceiling.

"You like to be facetious, Holly. You are fond of playing with sarcasm. It is not a game that I like, it does not amuse me . . . I asked whether we should work together or whether we should fight . . . it will be your decision, Holly. If we work together then, perhaps, you will be here for a few months, if we fight then you are here for fourteen years."

"The coffee, Captain, it's foul."

"If we work together then doors will open, the road will be clear to the airport. The flight to London, everything into place, cooperation will take you home, Michael—you don't mind if I call you by your name, and I am Yuri—it would never be known in London that you have helped us, you would go home with honor. . . ."

"Don't they give a man in your position better coffee than this, Captain Rudakov?"

"In England you were a talented man. You have a good job, a good salary. You have no need to turn your back on that. You can return to your work, to your home, to your friends. In a few months you can be back. You do not belong here, Holly, not among these scum that you sleep with, not in those rags, not in a place like this camp. You understand me?"

"A child could understand you, Captain Rudakov."

"You owe them nothing, those that trapped you, sent you here. You owe them no loyalty . . . you owe my country no enmity. My country has not harmed you. We do not deserve your hatred. Do you want to stay here or do you want to go home?"

Holly held the mug between his two hands, and his palms were warmed, and he looked into the murk of the liquid. He yearned to gulp down the coffee that remained, he craved to ask for more. He looked back at his interrogator.

"I'm sorry, I wasn't listening . . . you'll have to say that again. . . ."

Rudakov's body surged up over the table, his arm snatched at the collar of Holly's tunic, pulled him up from his chair. The fingers were clamped solid as if sewn into the material. Holly felt the spatter of Rudakov's breath.

"Don't play with me, Holly . . ."

Two heads a few inches apart. Two pairs of eyes caught in the action of battle. Holly saw the red glow at Rudakov's cheeks.

"Don't do that to me again, Captain Rudakov," Holly said.

"A prisoner does not talk in that way to a camp officer . . . I do what I like with any *zek*. You are just another *zek*."

"Don't do it to me again."

"You are forbidden to speak to an officer in that fashion." But Rudakov was subsiding back into his chair and his hand had loosened the grip at Holly's collar and he panted as if the slight movement had winded him. "What would you do if I did that to you again?"

"When you are on the floor in the corner you will know what I have done, Captain Rudakov."

Holly saw the anger rise, saw the clench of Rudakov's fists, saw his chair back away on its castors.

"Article 77 Section I: striking or assaulting a member of camp administration, fifteen years to death. Remember that, Holly."

The smoke hung in the air between them. Rudakov poured more coffee into Holly's mug. The game of persuasion did not come easily to the interrogator. He spoke like a man who uses an alien language. But the chair was sliding back toward the table, back to the closeness of conspiracy and friendship.

"Holly, it is stupid that we fight . . . we have everything to offer each other. You should not be here, Holly, this is a place for filth, for criminals. Within days of helping me you would be transferred back to the hospital wing of Vladimir, within a few months you would be home . . . think on it. You do not have to survive the *Dubrovlag*, you do not have to survive anything. You can go home, if you cooperate. . . ."

"Thank you for the coffee," Holly said.

"Holly, listen to me, believe in me . . . you need me, you need my friendship . . . you do not have to be here. Help me, Michael Holly, help me and I can help you. Help me and you have the transfer. Help me and you have the flight home. . . ."

The voice across the table tapped at Holly's mind. There was nothing for him to say. He thought of the latrine and the T-junction of a water-main pipe, and a hole that had been carved from the snow and frozen earth, and a screw top cover that was lagged at night, and a place that was in shadow from the arc lamps of the perimeter fences. He thought of a fighting field that was again simple, again anonymous.

"When you came to Moscow you carried a packet, a coded packet, that you were to pass to someone. Who gave you the packet, Holly? What was the agency in London, what was the name of the man who gave you that packet? They were not very efficient, the people who prepared you in London. You can't say they were efficient, can you? The pickup was not met. You placed the packet, you returned an hour later and because the packet had not been taken you retrieved it. Who instructed you? What were your fall-back orders? Was there another collection point, Holly . . . ?"

Holly sweating, Holly who was not trained and who had laid the envelope given him by Alan Millet on the top of the wire rubbish basket beside the bench on the Lenin hills. Holly coming back to the bench after an hour's walk that had taken him to the ski jump where the young people gathered to watch the first of the winter's athletes propel themselves into the dizzy air flows. Holly finding that his packet had not been taken, retrieving it, hurrying away, and frightened to look over his shoulder and check whether he was under surveillance. The first fear, the first knowledge that involvement was real and personal and far distanced from a glass of beer and a sandwich in a pub across the Thames.

"You had to know that you would be caught. Did they not tell you that you might be held? Do they think we are stupid? They misled you, for a year you have known that. It is a kindness to them to say that they misled you, Holly, you were their plaything. Was it a senior man who briefed you? I don't think so, I think it was a boy. Did your desk officer tell you who would collect the package . . . ?"

Holly alone on the Underground, with an uncollected package. Surrounded by Muscovites, strap-hanging on a fast train that slid to its halts and was away again. Returning to the Rossiya and not daring to look at the men and women who stood and swayed beside him.

"It wouldn't even have been an important mission. They may have told you that it was, but it couldn't have been. Would they have asked you, without training, without experience, to carry an important package? Hardly, Holly..."

All so fast, so dreamlike and simple, the arrest of Michael Holly. Standing at reception at the Rossiya, asking if there had been any messages because the Ministry might have telephoned to give timings for his meeting. One moment standing at reception and then wafted, as if he were a feather fluttering, to the car on the curb. Through the swing doors, and he had not registered what was happening to him until he was out into the late afternoon cold and the open doorway at the back of the car was yawning for him. God, he'd been frightened. Terrified. A locked car, a short journey of screaming tires, a side entrance to the Lubyanka. Nothing they could do now would be worse than the fear as the high gate fell like a guillotine behind him.

"You owe it to yourself to help us to help you. It is not betrayal, it is you who have been betrayed. You owe them nothing. I think that you know I speak the truth. What do you say, my friend?"

Holly saw Rudakov leaning easily back in his chair, saw the smugness on his face.

"I think, Comrade Captain, I think you should shove yourself right up your ass..."

Rudakov laughed, richly and loudly.

"Right up your ass till you choke in your own stink."

Rudakov still laughing, and the shimmer of cracked ice across his face, and his gaze unwavering.

"Think on it, Holly. Think on it tonight, think on a transfer to Vladimir, think on a flight to London."

Holly laughed too, and their laughter mingled. There was something of pride in Holly's eyes, and there was an inkling of combat in Rudakov's eyes. But in an instant the laughter was gone from the political officer's mouth. "Be careful for yourself, Holly. Believe me you should be careful. In a few days I will send for you again. In the meantime you consider."

"Thank you for the coffee, Captain Rudakov."

Coming from the latrine, the figure hugged the shadow of the building before jogging across open ground to the cover of Hut 5. Wrapped in newspaper were the frozen lumps he had fashioned by stone to the width of the water pipe. From Hut 5 he had thirty yards of snow space to cross. He caught his breath, prepared himself, then ran for the hole. His shape joined the dark heap of earth and he landed without noise in the pit. A searchlight beam curved above him. A dog barked. He heard the voices, miserable and low-pitched, of patrolling warders. He realized with a vicious clarity that he had never considered the possibility of discovery. The light swung away, no sign or sound of the dogs, the voices faded. He trembled. His fingers groped for the junction of the pipes. It was the work of a few minutes.

Michael Holly was back inside Hut 2 a clear hour before the trusty slammed shut the hut's door, switched off the lights.

In the morning the water would run, run fast and sweet along a main pipe until it met with an obstruction and the water would eat away at the mass that blocked it. Chisel it, and then carry that mass in diminishing particles to the taps and basins and sinks and cooking saucepans of the barracks.

Chapter 9

The prisoners are quick to notice change.

Behind the listless, dulled façade their minds are keen to seek out anything which is eccentric in the camp life. It is impossible to trick these leeches. Better than those who administer the compound, the prisoners know the working of the camp ritual.

Within a day and a night of Holly making his night run to the earth hole, the huts were alive with rumor.

Another morning after and there was no longer scope for rumor. The talk now was certainty.

Of the four corner watchtowers overlooking the compound of Zone I, one was not manned as the men massed for parade and roll call.

The work of counting the prisoners and shouting the names was managed by seven warders and guards and not the familiar dozen.

The captain of KGB was on show in uniform and greatcoat, and held the clipboard for the ticking off of names, and that would normally have been the task of a junior officer of the MVD detachment.

And of those who were there, some looked sick with a yellow pallor of the face skin, and some leaned on the shoulder of the nearest colleague for support, and some during the day would duck away from their duties and run with a crabbed strut toward the barracks building.

A guard on the ski run between the high wire fence and the high wooden wall collapsed in the view of the prisoners and it was a full ten minutes before he was noticed from a watchtower and help sent to him. The *zeks* had heard his soft low call for help, turned their backs and closed their ears.

The prisoners were marched to work. They were hurried across the transit land between the compound and the factory. They were stampeded over the open space of the road and the railway line, and when they reached the workshops they found that all was normality with the full staff of civilian foremen there to harry them to the daily quota.

And the *zeks* wondered, wondered how it were possible for only guards and warders to be ill and sick, and for themselves to crawl about their work and existence immune from the microbe.

Late in the morning the word spread through the workshops. From tongue to ear, from the finish shop to the paint shop to the lathe shop the word flowed.

The word was dysentery.

Dysentery. How was it possible that an epidemic of dysentery could afflict only that minority living in the barracks, and avoid touching eight hundred men who ate and slept the short distance away over the high wooden wall and high wire fence?

How was it possible?

Major Vasily Kypov pondered that question as he walked a slow circle of the compound in the company of Captain Yuri Rudakov. When an ambulance passed them, khaki and green camouflage with the red marking on white background, he could remember that it was the third that morning to leave the barracks sleeping-quarters for the Central Hospital of the *Dubrovlag*.

And there would be an inquiry and findings and an official report that would reach the desk of the procurator in Saransk, the capital city of the Mordovian ASSR, and then join the paper chain that routed to the Ministry in Moscow. Public Health inspectors had come from Pot'ma and had sealed the kitchens of the barracks. A crate of phthalyl-sulphathiazole tablets had been flown by helicopter from Saransk. And at the hospital there was nausea and fever and diarrhea of mucus and blood, and it was said that a guard and a warder might die.

They had no answers, the major and the captain, as they walked the snow paths, only a growing sense of humiliation that the camp was now in the possession of strangers. On that morning there was no sparring between them, and Kypov could almost feel an ooze of sympathy from the young Rudakov. There had never been disease before at ZhKh 385/3/I, not even among the prisoners. The major led the way back toward the barracks, no longer able to stall the hearing of the initial reports from the experts who had invaded his territory. As they went past the factory they could hear the drone of the working engines. Half as bad only, if the prisoners had been laid down by the disease—but it wasn't the prisoners, not the scum, the filth of the huts. It was the guards and warders who rolled in drugged discomfort in their segregated wing of the Central Hospital. That was a salted wound.

The team from Public Health in Pot'ma had made the NCO's mess hall in the barracks their working area.

There were charts and diagrams spread out over a Ping-Pong table encircled by men and women in white coats. There were stool bottles for paperweights, little bottles with pen markings for identification. This was Vasily Kypov's empire, but none of the interlopers stiffened to attention at his entrance.

The man who came to him was hollow-cheeked. Wireframed spectacles sat low on a hawk nose. He gazed at the major as if he were a hostile creature, and when his eyes flickered to the younger officer beyond the Commandant and understood the blue collar tabs of KGB he seemed to look away with a smear of distaste. He gave Kypov and Rudakov the crystal impression that they interrupted his work.

"Major Kypov, the Commandant . . . ? I am Superintendent of Public Health at Pot'ma . . ."

Kypov nodded.

"You have here an outbreak of dysentery of epidemic proportions. I have worked at Pot'ma for nine years. Yours is the most serious outbreak of this disease that I have found in any of the camps during that time . . ."

Kypov's head seemed to droop against his chest.

"Dysentery, Major Kypov, does not arrive by accident. It is not obligatory, not even in a place such as you supervise. . . ."

Kypov straightened himself. He spoke with a bluff optimism, half believing the suggestions that he offered. "Some cook with filthy hands, something like that, could that be it?"

"That most definitely would not be the cause of this outbreak, Major. You have raw sewage coming directly into the water system of the barracks building. Untreated sewage flowed directly through the waterpipes . . ."

"Impossible."

"Not impossible, but proved. We have taken scrapings from several feet behind the taps, there is no area of doubt. You have a very serious situation on your hands. We believe there has been an act of sabotage. . . ."

"Impossible. . . ." But the denunciation of Major Kypov was hesitant, unsure.

"How could it be sabotage?" Rudakov said quietly. Filth in the kitchens was within the province of the camp's Commandant. Sabotage was KGB, sabotage was his own.

"From your own charts of the water-main route and that of the sewage pipes from both inside and outside the compound that lead to the general cesspit . . . they are not even close to each other. Raw sewage was introduced to the water-main. Major Kypov, I assume that the diet of your prisoners differs considerably from that of the camp officials."

"Correct."

"We have managed only a preliminary examination of the specimen from the pipes, but I am confident that a more thorough testing will show that the sewage is the product of the prisoners' feces."

The captain of KGB closed his eyes. In front of his face the palms of his hands rubbed slowly together. A man who winces at the implications of his knowledge.

Rudakov ignored his Commandant, he stretched out his hand to the Superintendent of Public Health and led him to the door. Before they went out into the compound he had draped a guard corporal's weatherproof jacket over the civilian's shoulders.

They walked to a place behind Hut 3 and Hut 4, and stopped beside a dug pit and a heap of earth. Rudakov shouted at the two *zeks* who worked in the hole and when they were slow to respond he dragged them each up from the ground heaving at their collars. The Superintendent of Public Health took the place of the *zeks,* looked hard at the pipes between his shoes that were half covered in mud water. He took a knife with a fine sliver of a blade from his pocket and first scraped at the rim of the screw top over the junction, then dropped his findings into a plastic sachet bag. Afterward he took another bag and unscrewed the top of the junction pipe and scraped again. When he had finished he looked up and shrugged, then blew into his hands to warm them.

"I said it was an act of sabotage—there is your evidence."

The prisoners marched with their snow-shuffling tread back into the compound. Midday and lunch. Eight hundred men. Blank-faced, yet devouring the sight of the captain of KGB and a civilian with a white coat peeping beneath a military jacket. Like the rustle of wind in an autumn tree the word echoed from those who could see to those who were at the back and denied sight. Rudakov scanned the faces, saw the dumb and sullen eyes of those who stared back. There was one among this mass who fought against him, one who had taken Yuri Rudakov as the target of his attack. Any battle against the life of the camp was a personal fight with the captain of KGB. He bit his lip. He pulled his cigarettes from his pocket. One of them among that mess of filth had tossed the glove into the path of the captain of KGB. And they seemed so barren of initiative, so deserted of spirit, and yet there was one. . . . He had thought Michael Holly important. Michael Holly was a luxury, an irrelevance compared to the sabotage of the water-main pipe.

Where to begin?

The eyes of the *zeks* bored into Yuri Rudakov's back as he walked away toward the administration block. He abandoned the Superintendent of Public Health to find his own way back to the barracks.

There had been a fire in the Commandant's office. Begin there.

There had been an attempt to poison the guard troops and warders living in the barracks, follow with that. He had the beginning, he had no end. He felt the eyes trace his footsteps. Fear winnowed his gut. The regime of the camp had never been challenged before. If the worm was not stopped then it would eat out the core of submission around which the camp existed.

In the months that he had been at ZhKh 385/3/I he had never known that fear that slid with him into his office.

He had the beginning, he had no end.

*   *   *

On her knees, beside her pail, a rough brush in her hand, Irina
Morozova scrubbed the floor of the corridor that led to the
ground floor wards of the hospital. At least once a week a
detachment of the Zone's prisoners were taken to the hospital
for the skivvy work. The water was cold, her hands blued, her
nails cracked, but it was welcome work. She was outside the
Zone. The work separated her from the other women of her
Zone. She would have liked a friend inside the living hut of
Zone 4, someone to share with, to talk with. She was alone in
her Zone. Her education and privilege dictated that she be
alone. Only those with calloused minds and coarse hands who
sought a lover bothered themselves with the small, pale-skinned
Morozova. Kneeling in the corridor, with her bucket and her
brush, she enjoyed the limit of freedom that could be hers.

It was not easy to clean the corridor floor.

The impatient progress of the medical staff on their way to
and from the wards caused her to pull aside her bucket, rock
back on her knees to make room for them. Each time the
wheeled stretcher squeaked past her, she had to pull the bucket
from the center of the corridor to the wall. Some of those on
the stretcher were in night clothes, some were dressed still in
full winter-issue uniforms.

And the word accompanied the stretcher and the sharp paces
of doctors and nurses. The word was disease. The word was
poison. The word was sabotage.

Disease might be accident, but not poison, not sabotage.
Poison was premeditated. Sabotage was attack. She had no
need to see the harassed faces of the medical staff to know of
the success of a premeditated attack on the administration of
the camp. She saw a boy wheeled by in his pajamas who cried
and rolled in pain. She saw a young guard taken to the wards
who spewed yellow mucus down to his waist across the buttons
of his greatcoat.

Who was doing this with poison and sabotage?

Why? To what end? To what hope of success?

In her whole life Irina had never stamped on a spider, laid
a hand on the wings of a butterfly, nor set the trap for a mouse.
Her mind rocked in argument. The camp was her enemy. The
servants of the camp were her enemies. A man had dared an
act of premeditated sabotage. Had that man the right to her
support? She scrubbed fiercely at the floor. She thought of the

pain of that boy, she thought of the sickness of that guard. She thought of a man who dared what had never been dared before. She knew no way to silence the rage of argument.

At the end of the morning, Morozova and the others of the hospital detail were taken back to Zone 4. The argument was not settled. One thing only blazed in her mind.

Who dared it?

Two more reports now fell on the desk of the senior official of the Ministry in Moscow.

News from Barashevo, again and so soon.

A report from the Superintendent of Public Health in Pot'ma on the first findings as to the causes of a dysentery epidemic. A report also from Major Vasily Kypov concerning the circumstances in which he had requested the reinforcement of his guard capability by two platoons from Central Garrison. The official did not immediately file away these two reports. He photostated them, and did the same with the earlier teleprinter sheet that gave details of a fire and the destruction of an office. Three reports now, and a file and a reference number of their own.

With the slim, new folder under his arm, the official went to the office of the procurator general. The procurator general ruled over all the Correctional Labor Colonies stretched across the State. When the whiff of trouble seeped to Moscow, then the official would carry a new file up the steps and along the passages to the presence of the procurator general.

On an upper floor, in a pleasantly furnished room overlooking the inner streets of the capital, the name of Vasily Kypov was raised, bandied, his career examined.

"But regardless of whether there have been failings in administration by Major Kypov, we have the more pressing matter," the senior official said softly. "We have an incidence of terrorism. . . ."

"I want a charge, I want a court, I want an execution," the procurator general stated. "I will not tolerate terrorism in the camps."

A lone figure on the perimeter path, Michael Holly in the evening walking the boundaries of the compound.

From the window of Hut 2 they watched him, Adimov and
Feldstein and Poshekhonov and Byrkin and Chernayev. They
stared out at the tall striding figure, lean-built in spite of the
padding of the quilted tunic. The snow flurried across the compound and sometimes he was lost to them. Something animal
about the aloofness of this man from the world of the hut on
which they all depended. Something wild and untamed. They
watched him a long time before dividing. Adimov returned to
the card school where he would be the winner, Feldstein to his
book, Poshekhonov to the bunk beside the central stove, Byrkin
to the memory of a Krivak class frigate sailing under full power
for Swedish waters. Chernayev watched him longer, then went
abruptly to his bunk and took his scarf and his woolen mittens
and his balaclava and his cap, and opened the hut's door and
went into the night. He went partly from sympathy, partly from
envy. Sympathy for the man who was alone with the temperature tumbling in the darkness. Envy for the man who could
make an island of himself. And Chernayev, the old *zek* who
had seen all the storms of the camps, felt the fear that held all
the men of Camp 3, Zone I, a fear that was based on beds
filled in the Central Hospital, a fear that was seeded on retribution to come, a fear that might be assuaged in the company
of a man who walked alone on the perimeter path. He was
honest, Chernayev, honest with his own thoughts, and the sense
of fear did not surprise him. To be afraid now was honesty.
All of the compound knew of the poison that had been introduced into the main water supply pipe to the barracks, all
waited for the fall of the counterstroke. When they caught him,
or them, it would be a shooting matter. A man would be pushed
to the snow cover of the yard inside the walls of the jail at
Yavas down the road. The hammer of a Makharov automatic
pistol would be drawn back. One bullet. One split skull, one
ripped brain. In all of the huts they were waiting for the counterstroke to fall, wondering who they would come for.

"Can I walk with you, Holly?"

"Of course."

"Why are you outside?"

"Because it suits."

"Everyone else is inside, finding what warmth they can."

"I am warm if I am moving."

"They say in the camps that a man who thinks he does not need friends is a dreamer."

"They cannot take the dream away from us."

"To dream here is to die."

"I've no intention of dying, I promise you that, Chernayev."

"Those that put shit in the pipe, they were dreamers. . . ."

"Your opinion."

"They dreamed of fighting back, of kicking at the bastard fences, of hitting Kypov."

"And that is just a dream?"

"It is impossible, it has to be a dream . . . they cannot be beaten."

"If everybody says that they cannot be beaten, then that will be true," Holly said softly.

"The compound is part of the camp, the camp is part of the *Dubrovlag*, the *Dubrovlag* is part of the Ministry, the Ministry is part of the administration, the administration is part of the State. A few men in hospital does not hurt the State."

"If you say so, Chernayev."

"What do you say, Holly?"

"I say that an old man should be beside the stove in his hut."

"Don't piss on me, Englishman."

"Then don't test me, Chernayev." Holly slapped his gloved hand on the thief's small shoulders, pulled him close, and they walked together in step. "You didn't have to come out, I appreciate that you did."

"It's suffocating in there . . . everyone is afraid. . . ."

"What are they afraid of?"

"They wonder who will be taken, and when—whether it will be a friend. . . ."

"Will they take the right man?" Holly asked distantly.

"They have to find somebody. Perhaps they will find the man who did it, quickly. If not . . ." Chernayev paused, shrugged under Holly's arm. "They must find somebody. All of Internal Order were with Kypov and Rudakov this evening. They will be very thorough, Holly, that is their way."

"Of course."

"There are informers in the huts—some we know and some we don't."

"Of course."

"It is said that in the morning they are bringing in more KGB, from other camps. They are going to interrogate every man in the compound."

"May it help them find the guilty," Holly said lightly.

"Be careful, Holly. . . ." There was a passion in Chernayev's voice, the quaver of an old man.

"Why do you say that to me?"

"Because . . . because you stand out . . . you are not in the mass of us. . . ."

"I will be careful."

Holly squeezed at Chernayev's shoulder.

And Chernayev chuckled, and his slender body that was bones in a bag shook with laughter.

"Shit in their waterpipe. I didn't know anyone was so clever. Did you see Kypov's face this morning . . . ? Shit in the pipe, and more shit landing on his pretty uniform. Think what they're saying about him in Saransk, what they're saying in Moscow. . . . But I don't like what happened to the guards, they're young, they're conscripts . . . you know that they say one may die . . . I don't hold with that. They're only boys. What's our quarrel with them?"

"Perhaps that was thought of."

"We coexist here. Most of them, the decent ones, they loathe it. All of us, we hate it. We have found a way of living with them."

"Why do you tell me that, Chernayev?"

"You may not understand the way that the camp lives."

They walked underneath a corner guardtower and they saw the barrel of the machine gun and the darkened shadow at the opened window above it. Their voices were whispered, they would not have carried to the chilled ears of the sentry.

"How often does anyone fight back against them?"

"It has happened."

"Tell me, Chernayev."

"There is a folklore of the camps. There are stories that are handed down. It is like the romances of the Tartars that have survived, never written on paper. We have our stories."

"Tell me."

"The stories are all about how the *zeks* laughed at them.

Fighting them with violence is new. They say there are eighteen men in the Central Hospital tonight, they might as well have been machine gunned. . . ."

"Tell me the stories."

"There were the skulls. Shit, we laughed at the skulls. The camps aren't new, they were built when I was a child. Sometimes they move the camps. The huts are shifted, a new compound goes up. Perhaps their maps aren't very good. A few years ago they laid out a factory compound for our Zone right on top of an old bone yard. In the thirties they died like flies in these places, epidemics and executions, they needed communal graves. You can't see it now because of the snow, but in the factory compound we are allowed to grow flowers—not vegetables, but flowers—and when they hoed the ground they found the bones, they hadn't put them down deep. There was one man who took three skulls and set them on posts and when the morning came the skulls faced the main gate, right in the eye of the sentries. We laughed till it hurt us."

"Why are you only allowed to grow flowers?"

"Because vegetables have vitamins. . . ."

"The skulls won you nothing."

"It won us a laugh and that was precious. It was a gesture and we laughed, there has been a gesture here now and we are afraid. Which is better for us, Holly, to laugh or to be afraid?"

"Tell me of another time that you laughed."

"There were the underpants . . . next to our compound is the women's camp and past that is the small camp for men, Camp 3, Zone 5. The underpants were there. . . . This man had a tenner, he didn't give a shit for them. He found a man in the hut who had just had a visit and his wife had brought new, clean pants, white pants. The tenner got the pants—I don't know how, not for gold would I give up clean pants—and he made a flag of them, and then he painted on the symbol of the United Nations, he smuggled some blue paint out of the workshop. He was an intellectual, shit knows how he knew the symbol. It was in December, the tenner said it was the Human Rights Day set aside by the United Nations, and he flew his flag from the roof of his hut. What was funny was that they didn't know what to do. The warders wanted to rip down the flag, but he said that was treason because the government of

the Soviet Union observed Human Rights Day, because the
government of the Soviet Union was a member of the United
Nations. The warders had to send for the officers, the officers
sent for the Commandant, and the flag flew all morning ... in
the afternoon they pulled it down. The flag, the pants, was
trimmed in black ribbon, they didn't know why. It was very
funny, really."

"And again you won nothing."

"There is no victory. Not even for the politicals, for the
intellectuals. Those with the brains don't win. They still rot in
Perm."

"Tell me."

They were underneath the watchtower again and this time
the guard leaned through his window as he peered down at the
two men beneath him whose shoulders wore a snow mantle
and whose heads were close as lovers'.

"The politicals went on hunger strike at Perm in '74 and
'76 ... this is only what I heard. They said they were prisoners
of conscience and they shouldn't be made to work. They said
that the heaviest work was given to them. The strike started at
Camp 35, it spread to 36 and 37. It lasted a month and then
they sent a man from Moscow to negotiate. The prisoners were
given everything they demanded, they started to eat again. So
what happened? The leaders were transferred to Vladimir, to
Chistopol. They took back what they had given, nibbled it
back. They didn't even have anything to laugh about, they had
nothing."

"Perhaps some pride," Holly said thoughtfully.

"Perm lives on. And after some man has put shit in the
water-main, our camp will live on."

The bell sounded. The call for all prisoners to be in their
huts. In a few minutes, after the hut lights had been doused,
the warders would enter the gate in pairs, and the dogs would
run loose and sniff under the stilted huts before being called
to heel.

"Thank you for your time, Chernayev."

A hoarseness captured Chernayev's voice. They were near
to the door of Hut 2. The light from a window brimmed onto
their faces. The snow was matted across their clothes. An old
thief who was hoarse and frightened. "Don't play with them,

Holly. Don't think they are fools. Be careful, all the time be careful. . . ."

Holly saw there were tears running on Chernayev's cheeks.

The arrival close to midnight in four jeeps of the interrogators from KGB was a bitter pill to Yuri Rudakov. They came with the arrogance of an outside élite, loud-voiced and heavy-booted in the corridors of the administration block. Of course, he himself could not have toothpicked through the stories of eight hundred men. Of course, he had known that an investigation on this scale must be boosted by fresh faces and fresh minds. But the manner of their coming had wounded him. A dozen men who could be spared from their own camps and from headquarters at Yavas, because there they had achieved the quiet life that enabled them to be sent to ZhKh 385/3/I. He had believed he had the quiet life until the office of the Commandant had burned, until the water of his garrison had been fouled. In their presence he had survived their cool politeness, yet he had read in the cold of their faces the contempt that they felt for a political officer who must call in help to suppress a spreading anarchy.

In the privacy of his office, deep in self-pity, he stared at the uncurtained window, at the lights and the wire and the darkened huts.

The Superintendent of Public Health had suggested that the feces were introduced to the pipe two nights before the obvious outbreak of the dysentery epidemic. The red band men, Internal Order, had provided him with the lists of those whom they thought they remembered seeing outside the huts on that evening. Not many names—some worked in the library, some had cleaning duty in the kitchen, some who walked on the perimeter path. No prisoner was allowed into a hut other than his own. There were few places for them to go after darkness, few names on the lists. . . .

Some who had walked on the perimeter path. . . . Holly, Michael Holly. . . . Internal Order said he had been out that night . . . and that evening before the arrival of the KGB interrogators he himself had seen Holly before the bell. . . . Holly who circled the perimeter, a tiger in a cage. He wouldn't have known of the waterpipes, wouldn't have known the routing

of the pipes, and wouldn't have known the drill for the filling
of the coal buckets for the administration. But in the morning
twelve new men would be siphoning the prisoners into groups
for interrogation, hard interrogation with the fist and rubber
truncheon. Rudakov thought of the hours that he had invested
in Michael Holly, thought of the prize he could win himself if
he was able to unlock the loyalties of Michael Holly.

The light blazed down from the ceiling, and the central
heating pipes were tepid behind him, and the arid lists of names
littered his table. The small, bitter hours for Yuri Rudakov.

He said aloud, "No way any of those bastards get their
hands on Holly, not on my Holly."

His words bounced back from the walls, and from the photograph of Comrade Andropov and from the reproduction print
of Lenin and from the filled ashtray and from the unwashed
coffee mug, bounced back and mocked the captain of KGB.

Holly lay on his back on his bunk and listened to the recitation
of the words. The words were spoken quietly, privately, by
Anatoly Feldstein, as if from them he could draw a strength.

The hut was silent, free from movement and sound. Only
the rhythm of the words that comforted the young Jew.

> I will go out on the square
> And into the city's ear
> I will hammer a cry of despair . . .
> This is me
> Calling to truth and revolt
> Willing no more to serve
> I break your black tethers
> Woven of lies . . .

"Who wrote that, Anatoly?"

"I didn't know you were awake. . . ."

"Who wrote it?"

"It was written by Yuri Galanskov. He read it to a group
in the Mayakovsky Square in Moscow. That was after Sin-
yavsky and Daniel were sentenced. They gave him seven years.
He was at Camp 17, it's ten kilometers from here."

"It's beautiful, beautiful and brave."

"They murdered him. He had an ulcer. They told his mother that he wasn't ill, just 'a hooligan who shirked his work,' that's what they called him. The ulcer burst, he developed peritonitis. They sent a doctor from Moscow, eventually, but too late. They murdered him."

"Good night, Anatoly."

Holly turned his back on Feldstein, lay on his side, pulled his blanket over his head, tried again to sleep.

Chapter 10

In the night a guard died at the Central Hospital.

Nineteen years old. A swarthy boy before the sickness found him. A conscript from a village of fishermen near the Black Sea's city of Sukhumi. A soldier of the MVD killed by a perforation of the intestine and severe hemorrhage from the gut.

One death, seventeen casualties for treatment. A doctor from Saransk said that he had read that dysentery was most likely to provide complications for the malnourished. He asked whether it was possible that a guard could suffer malnourishment. His question was not answered.

The news of the death reached Vasily Kypov as he dressed in his bungalow half a kilometer from the compound. There was a telephone beside his bed and, while he spoke, his orderly was brewing coffee in the kitchen and whistling a popular tune of the young people in Moscow. A breath of cheerfulness swam from the kitchen as Kypov listened to the message from the hospital. As a military man he knew of casualties. The paratroops had taken killed and wounded on the streets of Budapest when he was a junior lieutenant. As a captain he had known the pain of casualties in the old quarter of Prague. Casualties were inevitable; even on maneuvers in the German Democratic Republic or on exercise in eastern Poland there would be accidents. His former colleagues serving out time as garrison troops in Jalalabad would know the meaning of casualties — unused sleeping bags, packaged personalized belongings. Casualties were part of the paraphernalia of war.

But this was not war. This was the tedium of camp administration. This was the boredom of watching over a criminal scum.

The Hungarians had kicked back. The Czechs had struck out. The Afghans would fight with the teeth of ground-to-air missiles, rockets, medium machine guns. That was predictable, acceptable. But this?... Was he in a state of war with eight hundred scarecrow filth as an enemy? He had never thought of the *zeks* as his enemy, never believed they had the will to bite against his authority. One pig from out there had killed a young man for whom Vasily Kypov, formerly a major of para-troops, was responsible.

He had not been a hard man, he told himself that, he had never resorted to brute repression. He had been fair, and they had shown their gratitude. They had given him a boy who was dead.

His chin shook, his hand trembled with his anger. When the orderly brought his coffee the liquid slurped from the filled mug and dribbled from his jaw.

From the distant lit line that was the perimeter fence of the camp he could hear the amplified strains of the National Anthem. The night's snow lay on the track, sheeting the previous day's ice and grit. The orderly drove slowly, with great care, toward the administration block.

There was more coffee in the officers' mess.

Kypov and his own at one end and, away across the room, the huddle of the interrogators who had arrived during the night. He saw that Rudakov flitted between the two groups as if uncertain of his allegiance. If one fell then all would fall. And camp security was the one area of administration where the Commandant gave ground to the junior KGB officer on attachment.

He was buggered if he would be a prisoner in his own mess.

He strode across the room, introduced himself to the senior interrogator. The two men stood for several minutes on the no-man's-land of the central carpet, heads close, voices low. The mess was warm, the stove fire well ablaze, and when they had finished talking he found that his eyes wandered to the red coals, and he remembered the searing flash as the flames had leaped from his own fireplace, and he glanced at the coal bucket. He was afraid, in his own mess he was afraid. That was the cancer that had to be cut. He turned back to the senior interrogator.

"You have everything that you need?"

"Everything. Each man has a room allocated."

"Excellent."

"We are not patient, Major . . . there have been very firm instructions from Moscow."

"I hope you kick the shit out of them," Kypov said.

He buttoned his greatcoat, drew on his gloves. Out from the mess and into the darkness. The snow flakes nicked the skin of his cheeks. Around him were his officers and guards with machine pistols, and dogs and warders with wooden staves. In front of him the gates were pushed open, piling snow to the side. He saw the prisoners, vague through the snowfall.

He was at war, and victory in war demanded the harshest resolution. Out there was his enemy. An enemy bent in its rags against the wind. But a boy lay dead in the refrigerated mortuary of the Central Hospital, and among his enemy was that boy's murderer.

A few meters forward of the center of the front line of prisoners had been placed a wooden box, white from the snow-fall. He marched toward it and the murmur of talk died in the ranks.

As if it were a drill movement, and looking straight ahead, Kypov stepped onto the box . . . slipped . . . skidded. . . .

His arms flailed for support and could clutch at nothing.

He landed in the snow on his back, arms and legs spread, sinking in its softness. And the boots and the hems of greatcoats crowded around him, and gloved hands lifted him and beat the snow from his shoulders and his buttocks.

It started as a growl, the laughter of the men in front of him. It began as a tremor, became a quake, and as far as he could see there were mouths open in mirth. His fingers gripped tight inside his gloves. And in front of him the faces were animated, alive, bright with fun.

He turned.

The nearest man with a machine pistol. He snatched it, and still the laughter rattled in his ears. With his teeth he dragged a glove from his hand. All the time the laughter. He cocked the weapon and the crack of the metal movement was lost in the laughter's gale. He fired over their heads, his forefinger

locked to the trigger. All of the magazine. Thirty-six shots.
When the magazine was exhausted his finger was still tight on
the trigger.

The report of the gunfire beat back at him from the low
snow cloud.

The prisoners were silent. Heads down, shoulders cowed,
mouths shut.

He shouted and his words carried clearly across the compound.

"Within the last week a part of the administration block,
the property of the State, was sabotaged by fire. Within the
last forty-eight hours the water supply to the garrison has been
poisoned. As a result of the first action, property of the State
was destroyed to the value of many hundreds of roubles. As a
result of the second action the life of a young man has been
taken . . . he has been murdered. Neither of these actions was
accidental. I guarantee that the malefactors will be sought out
and will be subject to the most rigorous penalties laid down
by law. Some of you may labor under the misguided belief
that you have a duty to shield a killer and a saboteur. If we
discover that any of you have followed that road then I promise
that you, too, will feel the full harshness of the law. Every
man from this compound will be questioned by investigators.
You must cooperate fully with the investigation team. Until
we have arrested this murderer certain penalties will be imposed
on all prisoners. . . . No visits, short or long, will be permitted.
No parcels will be accepted. No incoming mail will be distributed, no outgoing mail will be despatched. The library will
be closed, all entertainments are canceled. If the culprit has
not been discovered by Sunday then a full day's work will be
performed on that day. There is one, or there are some, among
you who want to play rough with me. I, too, can play. I can
play rough with all of you."

They waited in the snow. They waited for the order to move
off toward the factory compound and the shelter of the workshops. The order was not given. They stood in their lines and
ranks and the snow fluttered to their caps and lay on the shoulders of their tunics and gathered over their thin felt boots.

Twelve from the front rank were taken to the administration block.

They watched the camp Commandant, alone and brooding, as he paced around them, and they were encircled by guards and the dogs crept close to the legs of their handlers.

Few bothered to brush the snow from their caps and tunics. They had not been forbidden to talk, but the voices of the *zeks* were dampened.

In the rear rank were the men from Hut 2.

Byrkin who had been a petty officer said, "They will never let go of this one. That is the way of the Services, they will go on until they have a body. At first they will try to have the right body, afterward they won't care. . . . My wife was to have come next week and the children. Nothing is worse than missing a visit. I can just remember what the children look like."

Mamarev who carried the stain of informer said, "Whoever did this, he had no right to involve us all. He's hiding behind us. We owe nothing to the bastard that killed a guard who hadn't harmed him."

Poshekhonov who had been a fraud said, "The man who did this, he has destroyed Kypov, he has ruined Rudakov. Perhaps not finally, but near to it. They have trouble in their camp, and what other camp has trouble? They have to call for more troops, for interrogators from outside. Now Moscow knows that this camp has trouble and they will ask why, why this camp alone? Did you see Kypov, like a bloody savage this morning? One man has beaten him. You could almost feel sorry for the pig."

Adimov who was a killer said, "It is not a man from Hut 2. I know when a mouse farts in Hut 2. Huts 3 and 4 are closest to the pit, he'll have come from them . . . I had a letter taken out that night, a little creep from the perimeter guard, I've not seen him again. He'll have the shits, he'll be in the hospital . . . their man's not from our hut."

Feldstein who considered himself the political prisoner said, "I cannot support such an action as this. The boy who died was as oppressed as we are. All the conscripts are ignorant and captive. If we strike at them with violence then we only justify the repression tactics of the Politburo, of the fascists of the monolith. It will only be by nonviolence that we win anything, by passive resistance. To attack them like this is to be as crude and vulgar as they are."

Chernayev who had not been a thief for seventeen years said, "They can do nothing to us. One only they can shoot ... perhaps he would have died of pneumonia, or coronary exhaustion, perhaps anyway he would have run for the wire.... They can't do anything. But the man who killed the guard, I hope that man knows why the guard had to die. Unless he knows why, then what he did was wasted."

The voices around Michael Holly.

In the second rank two men fell, simultaneously, as if by signal. They were pulled back to their feet by the *zeks* of the same line. Blue, blood-drained faces, fingers that could not move, feet that could not be felt.

An old man screamed. A young man sobbed without shame. The snow fell on the compound.

Kypov paced alone around his prisoners.

The first twelve came back and one bled from the nose and another from the lip and a third was helped by others. Another twelve were called, and the snow fell. Another twelve returned, and the snow fell. Another twelve were called...

No bell for lunch, no call for the kitchen line, no smoke from the iron stack on the kitchen roof.

The guards shivered and their dogs moaned.

Holly stood straight, tried not to twist his face away from the snow flurries that were channeled between the bodies and over the shoulders of the men in front of him.

Why, Holly?

What's the justification, Holly? Eight hundred men lined in ranks in the snow, and the temperature sliding, and the snow settling, and the kitchen idle. Why, Holly?

Because it's there....

There had once been a cartoon that he had seen in a London evening newspaper. A mountain of bodies, Asian and Caucasian and dead that were the casualties of the battle for South Vietnam's Khe Sanh, and on one side of the mountain was LBJ and on the other was Ho, and the caption read "Because It's There."

Everyone says you should fight them. Fight against a wrong,

fight against an evil, fight against an injustice. Everyone says that, until they are confronted themselves with wrong and evil and injustice. Different when you face it yourself. . . . And because Holly fought, then Byrkin and Mamarev and Poshekhonov and Adimov and Feldstein and Chernayev stood in the snow and shivered and were cold to the marrow and their bellies scraped in hunger like a shingle at the seashore.

You have an arrogance, Michael Holly.

Perhaps.

You have a conceit when you put these poor bastards to the agony of a day frozen in line in the snow.

Perhaps.

And one man will die, Holly. Perhaps you . . . perhaps some man that you know. Perhaps some gray creature from another hut whose life has never crossed yours. Will you cry for him, Holly? Will you, when he goes to the bullet in the yard of the Central Investigation Prison at Yavas?

God . . . God, I don't know.

When you made the bomb to go with the coal, when you forced the shit into the water-main pipe leading to the barracks, did you know of this?

No. . . . No. . . . Of course I didn't bloody know. How could I have known?

A man in his rank crumpled and slithered to the ground, and his companions pulled him back to his feet and tried to chafe his legs and cheeks and hands, and then Holly knew weakness, felt his knees cave, his strength slide.

He fought a war with proxy weapons. He used the handgun of the men of the compound, and he hadn't asked them, he hadn't won them to his flag.

A man is a better man if he fights.

You believe that, Holly?

I believe that . . . I think I believe that. Anything is better than just surviving. And if you fight then some will be hurt, that is the way of fighting, and some will know why and some won't. And this is an evil place, this place should be destroyed. Even if another place rises afterward, it should still be fought against.

Will you believe that, Holly, when they take a man to the yard at Yavas?

He watched Kypov striding his own perimeter, a short round figure made grotesque by the thickness and length of his greatcoat, made silly by the full wide cap.

Pray God I have the strength, to believe that.

In midafternoon the men who had not been questioned were sent back to their huts.

Internal Order knew the reason. The trusties reported that the interrogators had complained that the men who were being brought to them were too cold to talk, that their minds were as numbed as their feet and fingers.

Like rats after food the *zeks* struggled to get close to the central stove of the hut and the snow melted from their clothes and boots, puddling the floor. Beside the door Holly had scraped the snow from his tunic and trousers. Now he sat on his bunk, dangling his legs and listened to the skirmish of talk around the stove.

Feldstein came to his own bunk and shook his head with puzzlement.

"You know, Holly, there is a pride among the *zeks* tonight. You would expect it of the politicals, but not from the *zeks*. . . . Nobody screamed at Kypov for deliverance. There was no surrender out there. That was the strength of nonviolence. Just standing there, dumb, and staring them out, that was incredible. I didn't think the *zeks* could behave like that."

"And that matters?"

"Of course that matters. It shows them that we are people, not numbers. The more they believe we are people, then the more they will show respect toward us. Eight hundred numbers are simply an administrative question for them, eight hundred people is something else."

"But they must find one to shoot."

"I had forgotten. . . ." Feldstein spoke with a sharp sadness. He flopped down onto his mattress.

From the door of the hut the names were called.

Those that came back said the interrogators were losing heart, were bored with battering at the silence wall. The questioning was sluggish, ill-informed, they said.

The dozen from Hut 2 came to the administration block and

the long internal corridor. Hanging out from each door was a
KGB man, whores in a brothel and touting for a customer.
Holly saw that their tunic collars were unfastened, that all
pretense of smartness was abandoned. He wondered whether
they would hit him... how he would respond if they did. He
had never been hit in his life, least of all by a man with a
rubber truncheon. They had been called in alphabetical order
from the hut. After Adimov and Byrkin and Chernayev, together with Feldstein, before Mamarev and Poshekhonov. A
routine was being followed. If there were suspicion held against
him then the rhythm of the questioning would have been broken, he would have been summoned ahead of his turn. But if
they did not take Michael Holly, then they would take another.
All the men in the hut said that they must take one man. Holly
shuddered. He saw that Yuri Rudakov had come to his door
at the far end of the corridor. He heard the shout.

"Holly, to my office."

He walked past the interrogators, smelled their breath,
smelled the herring and bread they would have gulped between
the beatings, smelled the coffee that would have fortified them.

"In here, Holly."

Rudakov grabbed him by the tunic front, propelled him
through the door. The lock clicked shut.

Rudakov loosed his grip. He said pleasantly, "Sit down."

Holly sat on the straight back wooden chair in front of the
desk.

"Would you like some coffee? There's a sandwich if you'd
like it. ..."

Holly craved coffee, would have groveled for a sandwich.

"No."

"I've plenty of coffee, sandwiches too."

"No."

"Please yourself," Rudakov said.

"I don't come cheap, not as bloody cheap as that."

"Please yourself. ..."

Rudakov walked to the filing cabinet and the tray on the
top with the thermos flask and the plate. He made a song of
pouring the coffee, a dance of unwrapping the sandwiches from
waxed paper.

"... You can change your mind."

"No."

"My wife made the coffee, and the sandwiches. They're very good, she buys her meat in Pot'ma. Were you married, Holly?"

"You've read the file."

Rudakov came back to his desk. Coffee ran on his chin, crumbs fell from his mouth.

The impact of a truncheon on flesh and bone and muscle buffeted dully through the thin wall, emptied the sound into Rudakov's office.

"That'll be Feldstein. Superior little bastard, don't you think so, Michael? Going to set the world to rights, going to change the order. Just a creep, our Comrade Feldstein, don't you think?"

"Why am I in here?"

Rudakov opened his hands, rolled his eyes in disbelief, theatrical and exaggerated.

"Do you want to be with him? You want to be with those animals? They're not pretty boys with a set of rules, they've come to find who killed a guard. That's their order and they will achieve it, they will find somebody they can charge with killing a guard. You want to go to their care? I've shielded you, Michael . . . You should thank me . . . You want some coffee now?"

"No."

Through the wall Holly heard the soft moan of Feldstein. He stared back into Rudakov's eyes until they blinked and turned away from him.

"Did you think on what I said?"

"I don't remember what you said."

"A transfer to Vladimir."

"In exchange for what?"

"In exchange for a statement. Something about the work that you were sent to accomplish in our country. We would let you go for that. No one could blame you afterward for a statement of that sort—it would only be the truth . . ." Rudakov warmed to his own words, a smile of friendship snuggled at his mouth. ". . . The truth about who sent you, and who you were to meet."

"You have the statement that I made at Lubyanka."

"I have read the statement, Holly." Rudakov played the man who was disappointed. "Not a very full statement and then you persisted in the lie of innocence."

"I said in my statement that I was not a spy. . . ."

The room shook. In the next office a body had been thrown with force against a wall.

"And that was a lie, Holly."

"You say it was a lie, I do not."

He thought of Feldstein, a thin Jewish boy who would have a bleeding mouth and bruises above his kidneys. A boy who could recite in the darkness the poem of a man who had died from a burst ulcer.

"Don't you want to go home?"

He thought of Feldstein who would be in pain behind a plasterboard wall, and of Byrkin who would lose a visit, and of Adimov who would not see his wife before the cancer caught her, and of Poshekhonov, and of Chernayev.

"You must want to go home, and we are making it so easy for you. But you have a problem, Holly. You labor under an illusion. You believe you can make me impatient. Holly, I have all day, I have every day to sit with you. Actually, I value the time I spend with you. You're not getting out of here; I'm not about to be posted. I have all the time I need. It is your time that is wasted. Personally, I would like to see you go home. You should believe me, Holly. Consider, who else can you believe?"

He thought of a girl that he had seen behind a line of guns and a cordon of dogs. An elfin girl with brave, bright eyes. Morozova, the one word stamped on her tunic above a slight breast. A girl with no given name . . .

"You could be out of here within days, perhaps even hours. Listen to me, you have no need to be here."

He thought of eight hundred men lined up in the snow, the pariahs and dross of a nation. And they had stood their ground.

"I want to see you go home, Holly. I want to see you go free to lead the rest of your young life away from this place."

"Give me some coffee, please."

"That's being sensible. Have some coffee and a sandwich then we'll talk. You won't have to go back to the hut tonight, I'll find you somewhere here. . . ." Rudakov bounced across the room toward the filing cabinet, moving on his toes in a waltz of success. "We'll have you out of that hut. I don't know how you've survived with that scum."

Rudakov set the mug of coffee down in front of Holly.

Holly picked it up, pondered the coffee for a moment. He threw it in Rudakov's face.

Hot, steaming coffee ran down Rudakov's best uniform and scalded his skin, and the mug had bounced to the floor and smashed.

Rudakov blinked. Coffee droplets sprinkled from his eyebrows. He wiped furiously with his handkerchief at the growing stains on his uniform.

"If you are here fourteen years..." Rudakov spat across the table. "...If you serve fourteen years at Barashevo, remember each day the chance you were given. And remember this, too, *Mister* Holly. If I hit you, in the condition you're in, if I hit you then I break you. I can break any bone in your body. You remember that."

"I said I didn't come cheap. Not as cheap as a mug of coffee and a sandwich."

"Every day in fourteen years you will wish you had never done that."

Holly smiled.

"When you report to Moscow will you say that you failed?"

Back in the hut the limping Feldstein reported that Holly had been taken to the punishment cells.

"Rudakov offered him coffee, Holly threw it in his face..."

Some said the Englishman was an idiot, some that he had snapped. But the *zeks* do not linger on the misfortune of one man. Holly was instant interest, then replaced.

Chernayev gazed wistfully at the empty bunk, the folded blanket, then went to the window and looked across the snow to the high wire fence and the high wooden wall and the jutting roof of the prison block. He alone thought that, perhaps, he understood.

Chapter 11

"So, how will he cope there?"

"He'll cope but it will be hard for him."

"Why hard for him?"

"Because he won't lie down, that's not his way."

"But you think he can cope, whatever that means?"

"They won't destroy him, he won't be on his back with his legs in the air."

Alan Millet had been waiting for a week to see the deputy undersecretary, but that was the cross of carrying Grade II rank. The DUS could call you in and utter an instruction from the mountain summit, and you'd run your backside sore and ferret the facts he wanted, then you couldn't get back in to report. All the previous week Millet had badgered Miss Frobisher for fifteen minutes of DUS's time, and she'd put up a wall that the likes of Alan Millet couldn't scale. He'd reckoned she didn't approve of Grade II men having direct access to the DUS. It would not have been acceptable under the former regime at Century. A Grade II man would report to a principal officer or at most to an assistant secretary, never to the deputy undersecretary directly. And Miss Frobisher, damn her, believed that old ways were best ways. And chaos she caused, because the DUS was snapping his orders through and the young men couldn't get back to him with their answers. Millet had been forced to play the old-fashioned game. An early morning rise, an early morning train into London, and he was loitering outside the DUS's door a quarter of an hour before Maude Frobisher would be sharpening her pencils and dousing her hyacinth bulbs. A hell of a way to run a Secret Intelligence Service . . . But Millet had seen his man, arranged the time of a morning meeting and braved Miss Frobisher's anger when he had presented himself.

"I tell you this, Millet, and I tell you frankly, I wouldn't have sanctioned any of this Holly business if I'd been in the driver's seat. No way that it would have landed on this desk and been approved."

"A suggestion was made, sir . . . not at my level, at assistant secretary level . . . the suggestion was accepted. I was told to get on with it."

"I'm not blaming you, lad, I'm just stating the fact. I've read your report."

"I don't think we really knew that much about Holly when we roped him in."

"You seemed to have known nothing."

"Something like that, sir."

"And that's past history."

"Past history, as you say . . . I don't suppose, sir, that it's much help to anyone at this stage but, as you will see from my report, everyone I spoke with reckons that Holly is a fighter . . ."

The deputy undersecretary slammed his hand onto his desk.

"For God's sake, Millet, we're not talking about an under-age kid playing in a big boy's football game. We're talking about a man who is serving Strict Regime in a Correctional Labor Colony of the Soviet Union. They don't piss about there. Psychological torture, physical torture, nutritional deprivation, sleep deprivation. That's just for starters, Millet, and they can get better and nastier just as soon as they want to."

Millet fidgeted in his chair.

"I can only repeat, sir, what I wrote in my report."

"Am I supposed to be impressed?" The deputy undersecretary sighed in theatrical exasperation. "You talk with a retired suburban schoolmaster, with a lecturer from the Technical College, with a small time businessman who's going broke fast, with a secretary from a Building Society. Humdrum little people, and you reckon they can tell you how a man is going to cope at Camp 3, Barashevo . . . ? Am I supposed to be impressed?"

"I was impressed." There was a singe of anger in Millet's voice.

"And when they throw the book at him, he's going to keep his mouth shut?"

"I think so."

"When they go to work?"

"I think so."

"They're not very gentle, Millet . . . Michael Holly, whom you picked off the street, he can stand up to that?"

Millet hesitated. He tried to picture an interrogation room with a shining light and the turning spool of a tape recorder. He tried to imagine the bruised lip and clenched fist.

"I don't know, sir."

"Neither do I."

"I suppose we didn't think it would come to this."

"I'm sure you're right." The deputy undersecretary spoke with a soft compassion. The lilt of the Brecon hills made music of his words. "For what the Service has done to Michael Holly, the Service should feel a great sense of shame."

Millet bridled. "Of course everyone was very sorry when he was picked up."

"I'll tell you something, so that you'll learn the way I intend to run Century and the Service. I don't believe that sitting behind this desk gives me the right to play with people's lives unless the very security of our nation depends on it. I'm not a chess man, Millet, I don't like seeing grubby pawns knocked off the board and rolling on my carpet. The recruitment of Michael Holly was shabby, inexpert. You're wondering why we've gone longer than the fifteen minutes you asked for, I'll tell you . . . I care on two counts about Michael Holly. I care that a young engineer faces fourteen years in the Soviet Union's camps. I care also that we may face embarrassment and humiliation that we will have brought down on our own shoulders. You understand me?"

"Yes, sir."

It was the fragile cooperation that existed between the Security Service and Century House that had provided the name of Michael Holly.

When a British subject booked a flight reservation to Moscow, his name came to the attention of Security, and Security passes that name to Century. The field man in Moscow was never happy on drops and dispersals—too risky. All the diplomats were subject to surveillance, part and parcel of the job. The Second Secretary (Consular/Visa) at the Embassy would have wanted nothing to do with anything as vulgar as placing packets in rubbish bins. Century had an old faithful, a businessman who was a regular on the British Airways Trident to Sheremetyevo, good as gold, reliable as a Jap clock. On the plane every six weeks for a three-day trip. In a briefcase stacked full with costings and sales brochures the packets went to Moscow; in the same briefcase the material of the agent returned to Century. But the old faithful had fallen ill, pneumonia with a suspicion of pleurisy, and so faithful had the courier been that his sickness left them flattened on that section of the East Europe desk that handled the agent in the Soviet capital. So Alan Millet had sifted the names on the flight reservations for the coming month and played the computer tabs and found a cross-reference on Michael Holly, and traced back through Stepan Holovich and the case history of an alien's file. He'd described the recruitment to his assistant secretary superior as a "piece of cake." Seemed simple enough when you were high above the Thames looking at the world from behind the sealed plate-glass of Century House. Nothing ever went wrong, did it? Michael Holly in the park on the Lenin hills and all to keep a routine and a rhythm intact. All to keep a contact with a typist who worked within the Kremlin's walls, and who saw little that was important. What she typed she reported and, for what she reported, Michael Holly had been pressed into the service of his country. Alan Millet could remember the afternoon that the news had been relayed from Foreign and Commonwealth to Century House, the report that a British national had been arrested in the foyer of the Rossiya hotel and that he would face charges of espionage. He remembered that as a miserable afternoon, an afternoon when he had shivered in the face of Century's central heating. "One of yours . . . ?" the FCO had drily queried.

"That's all, Millet . . . you'll not forget him?" The deputy undersecretary turned away. The meeting was terminated.

"No, sir."

"If I thought you'd forget him I'd break your neck."

Millet let himself out of the room. As he closed the door quietly he heard the lifting of a telephone.

"Maude . . . I'd like an appointment this afternoon with the permanent undersecretary at Foreign and Commonwealth."

"PUS at FCO, I'll arrange it."

* * *

It had been an absurdly slow and uninteresting evening, even for so travel-scarred a diplomat as the Ambassador.

For close to four years he had performed his duties of office at the Kremlin's receptions. They never improved, they never crawled above the level of extreme tedium.

With the Diplomatic Corps he had stood in line for thirty-five minutes in the St. Andrew's Hall, waiting for what he usually referred to as the home team to make their appearance with their principal guest. They had been late, and he had felt around him the sweat of the Third World, the noise of the New World, the breath of the Old World.

The home team had finally emerged to lead, in ponderous convoy, the mincing clan of diplomats up the sweeping staircase. It was one of the Ambassador's tasks to watch the procession of the leaders. The order in which they formed up was of importance, who was relegated to the fourth row, who was brought from the back to the second row, who required the help of a stick. The President was heavy on his feet again, worse than last month, better than in the summer.

And so to the food.

Standing around tables laden with caviar and smoked sturgeon, holding a glass that was resolutely refilled with vodka or Armenian brandy, he waited for an opportunity to speak quietly into the ear of an interpreter should one of the great men of the regime hover close to him. He never chased after them at a function such as this, sometimes they came and sometimes they did not. He'd explained that to Foreign and Commonwealth.

The instructions from London had been quite specific. They wanted the matter raised as an informal question, not taken to the Ministry during working hours. Through an ocean of Third World faces the Minister caught the eye of the Ambassador, nodded an acknowledgment and made a path for himself through the guests. The interpreter hovered close by, treated with the respect an old man gives to his truss but indispensable for all that.

"Excellency. . . ."

"Good evening, Sir Edward . . . you are enjoying yourself?"

"As always the hospitality is extreme. I hope that soon we can reciprocate the entertainment at the Embassy."

They never came to the Embassy if they could avoid it. Juniors only for the Queen's birthday party.

"You have a Parliamentary delegation here in a few days, the arrangements are completed?"

"I am confident that the visit will be splendidly interesting to our members of Parliament."

The Ambassador had worn a monocle since he had been an undergraduate at Cambridge. For effect only, plain glass, but from his first day in Moscow the Soviets had been bemused by its eccentricity. Whenever it seemed likely to slip, the Ambassador grinned and the movement of his muscles held fast the monocle over his eye.

The Minister smiled back, perhaps he had lost a moment of humor through the passage of translation. "We must meet again soon . . ."

"Excellency. . . ."

"I have many guests to meet."

"One matter . . . briefly . . ."

The Minister laughed. The medal of the Order of Lenin flapped slightly on his breast. "Are we working tonight?"

"Excellency, it is my hope that the visit of our Parliamentarians will start to ease the climate of misunderstanding that has prevailed between our two governments in recent months . . ."

"I hope so too, Sir Edward."

"There is another matter where an action of clemency from the Soviet government would be received with great gratitude by my government."

"Clemency? In what case do you request our clemency?"

For both men the banter was concluded. The Minister looked sharply into the Ambassador's eye and monocle.

"A young British national named Michael Holly. He has served one year of a fifteen-year sentence."

"Refresh my memory."

"It was alleged in court that he was engaged in espionage activities. The allegation was strenuously denied by both my government and by the young man in question. An act of clemency now would have far-reaching effects on the relations between your government and mine."

The Minister's eyes narrowed behind his steel-lipped spectacles. The Ambassador grinned and the monocle wavered.

"A bit of paper would settle it, Sir Edward," the Minister replied crisply. "A bit of paper from your government for public release that acknowledges the involvement of this young man in espionage activities on behalf of the British secret services against my country. I would have thought that after the release of such a text we would regard your request for clemency most favorably. . . . As you see, Sir Edward, I have many who are waiting to see me . . . I hope that you enjoy the rest of your evening."

The Ambassador sought out the Australian and the Canadian. In times of adversity it was general for the old Commonwealth to stand shoulder to shoulder.

They had never beaten the Whitehall pigeons, the Foreign Secretary reflected. For all that Public Works spent in frightening the little beasts away, they returned in perpetuity to ladle their droppings over the walls and windows of the center of government. Heaven only knew what it cost to clean the ranks of FCO windows and it had been done last week with an army swinging from cradles and ladders. But the smears were back. He watched one dribble sinking on the pane through which he looked out over St. James's Park.

The view from his office was one of the great pleasures of government. In winter the sounds of the traffic flow were sealed outside, and the cars and trucks and taxis moved in a silent ballet. The troopers of the Household Cavalry tripped the length of the Mall behind the noiseless marching of a brilliantly decorated military band. The secretaries came with paper bags to feed the birds of the park's ponds. Only the bloody pigeons, wheeling and arcing and crapping, spoiled the serenity of the view. They'd have to be culled, come to that in the end, and bugger what the old ladies said.

"DUS is here, Foreign Secretary."

He turned reluctantly from the panorama. The permanent undersecretary always entered with the footfall of a ghost, as if he was above knocking.

"I did tell you he was coming, Foreign Secretary."

"Of course you did . . . about Michael Holly, yes?"

"About Michael Holly . . ."

The permanent undersecretary lowered himself into an armchair. The Foreign Secretary glared. Who ran the bloody place, PUS or Minister? The deputy undersecretary was still standing, there at least were some manners.

"Won't you sit down, DUS?"

"Thank you, sir."

"Don't call me that, for Christ's sake. I've told you that before."

The Foreign Secretary was at his desk. The deputy undersecretary sat forward on a settee. The permanent undersecretary lolled back in his armchair. Three men who had gathered in an upstairs office of Whitehall to talk of a man serving time in a Correctional Labor Colony.

"The Ambassador's not hopeful," the permanent undersecretary intoned. "In a way he had a bit of luck last night, managed to get the ear of the Foreign Minister, and that's higher than he could have hoped. The message came back loud and clear. If we admit espionage in the Holly case, then we can have him. But we have to claim him, we have to wear the hair shirt."

"Don't like that." The Foreign Secretary drummed his fingers on the desk top. "They'd trumpet it round the world. Afterward it wouldn't matter a damn how hard we retracted. If we're belting them for Afghanistan, for Angola, for Ethiopia, then we have to be clean. Apologizing for Michael Holly as a British agent is not being clean."

"Then Mr. Holly stays where he is."

The permanent undersecretary beat the bowl of his pipe into the palm of his hand. Most of the inner debris reached the ashtray, some fell to the cream-based carpet. He saw the annoyance of the Foreign Secretary.

"It's an unhappy option. . . . What are your feelings, deputy undersecretary?"

"I'd not like an admission, Foreign Secretary."

"Then, that's where he stays."

"Admissions smack of incompetence."

"This was a matter of incompetence." The permanent undersecretary spoke through a tower of smoke.

"Before my time," the deputy undersecretary said evenly. "Of course, it's not totally in our hands. We may dismiss the option of admission, but that's not to say that Mr. Holly won't get into that game himself. He could, conceivably, go public to get himself out."

"Wouldn't matter," the permanent undersecretary said with confidence. "Brainwashing and all that . . . We could stand that, not in the same league as us chipping in first and claiming him."

"In fact, it's not that likely that he'll bend."

"Tough chap, is he?" The Foreign Secretary barked the question as if his interest in the matter was revived.

"Quite tough, they say."

"Good, very good . . . because we won't be pulling him out. Perhaps we should try again in a few years, three or four, things might be easier then. Are those places really as bad as they're painted? They must have civilized themselves a trifle since Stalin."

The deputy undersecretary examined his fingernails. He was adept at hiding private pain, personal shame. He stayed silent.

Did it always rain in January in London? Alan Millet's shoes were again wet, stained with damp.

He couldn't fathom the deputy undersecretary. Incredible that he should be sent out on such a chase as this, and on the DUS's personal instructions. He'd enough work on his desk. Everyone accepted that East European carried the heaviest load at Century. But the DUS commanded and Alan Millet was paid to jump.

An insignificant sign told him that he had reached the door he wanted.

Amnesty International (British Section).

Not a place where a government civil servant was ever at ease. Fine when they were bashing the Soviets, the East Germans, the North Vietnamese, the Argentines. Awkward when they shouted against the regimes of Central America that were linked with the old ally. Impossible when they reported on the torture of Irishmen in Belfast. In the hallway he saw a poster with the motif of a candle coiled by barbed wire. The home of an organization, voluntarily funded, that struggled to win freedom for thousands of men and women, classified as prisoners of conscience, scattered in jails across the world.

He took the lift. He asked, in a waiting room littered with pamphlets and cigarette ends, for the girl whom he had telephoned for an appointment.

She came through a door that had been security locked. Jeans and sweatshirt and a baggy sweater, and he felt the daftness of his suit. She led him through a maze of passages to a room piled with unsorted papers, stacked books. She found him a chair that he thought might collapse. For a moment he pondered on young people who gave their time for a pittance to help innocents in faraway cells.

She spoke with a ladies' college accent. Her fingers were deep stained with nicotine, her hair ponytailed with an elastic band.

"You wanted to know about Camp 3, Barashevo? Right? There's a complex there, one of the largest of the whole *Dubrovlag*. There's the Central Hospital, there's a small camp for men, there's the large camp, and each of those has its own factory area. There's also a small camp for women. The larger camp for men is classified as ZhKh 385/3/I, and about eight hundred men are held there. I think that's the one you're interested in—ZhKh 385/3/I. There are six sleeping huts and the usual kitchens and bath houses and store sheds, all fairly typical of an old camp, goes right back to the purge days and prewar. The prisoners there are on strict regime. We don't have a great deal of information anymore because the people we are concerned with have mostly been moved away to the Perm camps. We have only one at Camp 3, Zone I. He's a Jewish dissident that we've adopted as a 'P of C'—that's Prisoner of Conscience. He's Anatoly Feldstein, convicted of passing *samizdat* documents,... we might get him out. They're not very interested in him or they wouldn't have let him stay there, they'd have moved him to Perm with what they call 'especially dangerous state criminals.' The Commandant is an elderly army officer, Kypov, bit of a martinet but not a sadist. The political officer, that's KGB, is quite a young chap. The name we have is Yuri Rudakov. In the factory they make..."

"Tell me about Rudakov."

"Rudakov.... We had something on him about a year ago. He's young for the job, first time in the camps from what we gather. He'll be on his way through, doing one posting and then coming out. It's a long time, as I say, since we've had up to date information . . ."

"More about Rudakov, please."

"We had something from Feldstein, but it's a year old. There was just a passing reference to Rudakov . . . that he was intelligent, that he didn't seem very interested in Feldstein."

"Does that mean he's looking for the easy life?"

"Christ, no . . . it means that Feldstein isn't a hero. There are passive and active prisoners. Some are overwhelmed, some struggle. Feldstein doesn't shout, so he's left to himself. As I say, we think we might get him out. He's not a name we push and we hope that gives him a better chance. We push with Orlov and Scharansky, people like that, because it helps them. We leave Feldstein alone."

"You don't have any more on Rudakov?"

"Only what I've told you."

Millet felt the inadequacy of his question. "It's a pretty hard place, Zone I?"

The girl pushed her papers away across the table to signify she had more important work to complete.

"You have a friend in there?"

"You could call him a friend."

"Hard as a nightmare, that's what I'd call it, Mr. Millet."

Chapter 12

The name of the punishment isolation cell is *Shtrafnoi Izolyator,* and the *zeks* have abreviated the words to SHIzo. There is a minimum-maximum spell in the SHIzo, and that is fifteen days. Men who are sent to the SHIzo are taken outside the main perimeter of the camp to a separate compound. The unit that houses the SHIzo cells is single-story and built of brick. Inside each long wall is a corridor that runs the length of the building and the cells form the core of the block and run back to back. Sometimes there are wooden framed bunks, sometimes the prisoners must sleep on the floor, rest their heads on their boots. Here is no heating, and the water runs on the peeling, whitewashed walls. There is a slop bucket for the long night hours and the cells stink with the waste smell of the prisoners. The rations fed to the men in the SHIzo cells are reduced, cut to 1750 calories per day, and they must work in a factory that is specifically for them. The SHIzo cells are the home of tuberculosis and the ulcer and infection and lice. Bedding is not issued, reading matter is not permitted, letters and parcels are not allowed, visits are canceled. The window of the cell is small and high, the light that burns round the clock is small and dimmed.

The prisoner is cold, wet, hungry and exhausted. He can believe here that he is forgotten. A man may shout and he will not be answered, he may scream and he will not be heard. The SHIzo cell is the ultimate punishment of the Correctional Labor Colony.

The name of Michael Holly was written in thin chalk on the outer surface of the cell door.

He had been in the cell for nine days. Nine days' solitary.

147

Half an hour's exercise in the morning, walking behind another's back in a yard with high cement walls and a wire net at
the top, and the exercise time must also be used for washing,
and cleaning the cell and emptying the bucket. The work is
done in the extended end cell of the corridor. The fine polishing
of wooden cases for clocks. Not like the big factory where men
could talk as they worked. There is silence in the SHIzo factory.
No civilian labor is permitted to enter the SHIzo block for
supervision work. Warders rule here, and the quota has been
set higher than in the big factory. If a man disputes, complains,
then the penalty is automatic and summary. That is a new
offense, that calls for an additional fifteen days and the sentence
will be consecutive.

Holly in a personal hell.

On the evening of the tenth day they brought company for
Holly.

He heard the sounds of their coming as he lay on the floor,
huddled and shivering. Two sets of boots beating a tattoo in
unison in the corridor and the scraping of feet that were dragged.
He had found that he always lay on the floor at the far wall to
the door, always distanced himself as greatly as possible from
the door, from the warders' entry. A bolt scraped. A prisoner
was supposed to stand when a warder entered his cell, and they
carried the truncheons to enforce the rule. Holly started to climb
to his feet, from his stomach to his hands and knees, and then
his fingers reaching up at the smoothness of the wall to give
him leverage.

He was halfway to his feet when the door opened, and the
corridor light was impeded by the dwarfing shape of the men.
They did not enter the cell, they pitched the old man in, and
in the same movement that they discarded him they slammed
shut the door. The bolt ran home. Holly rolled back onto the
floor.

The old man was close to him.

"Bastards . . ." he growled at the door. "Bastards . . .
whores. . . ."

Holly looked at him. A skinny bag of bones and tattered
uniform. A gray parchment of skin drawn across the face, a
white stubble of hair across a skull that was rivered in high
veins. A tiny man, and if they had been standing he would

have rested his forehead under Holly's chin.

"Scum . . . whoring scum."

Holly saw the bruises, red and flushed, on the old man's cheek.

The old man turned to him, maneuvered his shoulders slowly so that he stared at Holly. There was a brightness in the eyes. Holly recognized it and felt the disgrace that he had been clawing his way to his feet in submission while the old man had laid on the ground and cursed his captors. Holly had been caving, slipping, falling. If an old man could give back to them, then Michael Holly had no cause to slither upright in humility.

He had been shown a way back.

"Mikk Laas . . ."

"Michael Holly . . ."

"I've not seen you before."

"I've been here a little over a month, in the camp."

"I know everyone who comes to the SHIzo."

"My first time."

"For me it is home."

"Thank you, Mikk Laas."

"For what?"

"For showing me something that I had forgotten."

"For shouting?"

"I had forgotten."

"You are not Russian . . ."

"English."

"I am Estonian, from near Tallinn. You know where that is?"

"Only from the map."

"How old are you, Michael Holly?"

"Just past thirty."

"When you were a baby, perhaps even before you were born, they took me from Estonia."

"All the time here?"

"Here—and in 4 and in 17 and in 19."

"You have earned the right to shout at them, Mikk Laas."

"What can they do to me now? What can they do that they have not already done?"

They talked a long time, Mikk Laas who was from Estonia,

Michael Holly who was from England. They talked in quiet, concerned voices and built themselves a wall around their two bodies that curtained off the wet running walls and the harsh concrete floor and the spy hole of the door. Later, Holly pulled his tunic up from the waist and tugged his undershirt clear and dipped a pinch of it into his mug of water and moved close to the old man and wiped at the dirt that had gathered at his bruised cheek. With his eyes closed and the brightness gone, the fight went from the face of Mikk Laas and he was pathetic and worn, and Holly knew he was close to tears, tears of pity.

"You have been here thirty years?"

"Thirty years and it is a sentence of life. I will be here until I die."

"For what?"

"They call it treason, we said it was freedom . . . And you Michael Holly . . . ?"

"Fourteen years more. They call it espionage."

Mikk Laas opened his rheumy eyes. They glowed in an instant sadness.

"You are right, Michael Holly. You are right to guard yourself. You are beginning your time, it is right that you should first find who you can trust and who will betray you. It doesn't matter for me. I'm here, I stay here. You are right to have caution . . . but I tell you, Michael Holly, I'm not a 'stoolie' . . ."

"I'm sorry."

"You have nothing to be sorry for."

"Why are you in the punishment block?"

"This time . . . ? Last time . . . ?"

"This time."

"I was in the Central Hospital. I have stomach ulcers. They said I was malingering. Perhaps they were right, perhaps they are not too bad, my ulcers. I found the place where they dump the potato that they are feeding to the guards who are sick— not real potatoes, only the peelings. I was eating the peelings when I was caught. Under the blanket the bed was half-full of potato peelings."

A slow grin came to Holly's face. "Rudakov gave me some coffee in his office, proper coffee. I threw it back in his face. I think I spoiled his uniform."

Mikk Laas smiled too, and the laughter croaked in his throat.

"Always keep your pride, Michael Holly. Even if you must waste good coffee, keep your pride."

"Does your face hurt still?"

"Less . . . I kicked the bastard that hit me, kicked his balls. He hurts more. He'll whine to his woman tonight."

"What happened thirty years ago . . . ?"

Holly unlaced his boots, put them under his ear. He lay on his side and faced the wall. Over his shoulder the old man spoke. A quiet and assured voice, and their bodies were beside each other and their warmth spanned the two of them. He listened to Mikk Laas tell his story.

"I was a boy. In Tallinn my father had a small business, he sold gentlemen's clothes. Estonia was an independent country. For seven hundred years we had existed under the boot of conquerors, now for twenty-two years we knew freedom. If you set twenty-two years against seven hundred then the freedom is brief, but it was rich wine to Estonians at that time. In 1941 the Red Army came to Estonia. They had made a non-aggression pact with Germany, they had divided their spheres of influence. Estonia was to be Soviet. They purged anyone with brains, with initiative, with culture. My father went . . . anyone who might have organized public opinion was taken. I don't know whether he went to the camps or whether he was shot outside the city, we have never heard. We fought them. Not an organized fight, not soldier to soldier. We fought them as guerillas. We went to the swamps south of Tallinn to the forests around the Suur Munamagi mountain. A few of us, and with old weapons. We tried to snipe them, to harass them. Then the Germans came and the Red Army retreated. There was no choice to make between our enemies. The Germans were hideous, the Soviets were worse. We fought as partisans against the Germans. We lived rough outside the villages. We hit and we melted back. I don't know what we achieved, nothing perhaps, but at least we were Estonians fighting for Estonia. At least the people who had stayed in Tallinn and Poltsamaa and Tartu knew that the freedom of Estonia lived in the hearts of a few men. And the Germans went and the Red Army returned. They came back to crush the last breath from free Estonia. They bombed Tallinn, they shipped the young men out. We fought on from the forests. When the Germans were there we had the weapons from the Soviets who had fled. Now we used the weapons that the Germans abandoned. Perhaps it was all useless, I doubt that we hurt them. It ended near Mustvee, we were trapped on the shore of Lake Peipus. We had nowhere to run to. There was half a brigade in front of us and the lake behind. We surrendered. It is the only time in my life that I have raised my hands. They marched us through Mustvee to the army camp, the whole of the town had come out to look at us. We were in rags. No one shouted, no one gestured. There was no hate and no sympathy. They had been emasculated, those people. That is why I will never be allowed to return to Estonia. They would not permit a man who has fought against them to go back because he might again breathe something into the emptiness of those people's lives. I don't know whether I was lucky that they didn't shoot me. Twenty-five years they gave me. . . ."

Holly was near to sleep. His eyes were firm shut against the ceiling light.

"You said you had done thirty years . . ."

"After twenty years I wanted to escape."

"You waited twenty years?"

"I waited twenty years. They gave me another fifteen. . . ."

"I could not have waited twenty years."

"It is not easy . . . believe me."

Mikk Laas looked at Michael Holly's back. He watched the rhythm of the breathing. He believed the young man was asleep. He dragged his body closer and snuggled against Holly for more warmth and rested his head on his hands. A slight heat flickered between them, a slight small heat in the SHIzo cell.

A man in handcuffs was driven by jeep to the Central Investigation Prison at Yavas.

The KGB team of interrogators dispersed to their camp appointments and to headquarters.

Major Vasily Kypov stood before his prisoners and announced that he was good to his word, that the restrictions he had imposed were lifted. The new roof for his office was completed and peeped smugly over the high wooden fence and waited for a snowfall to embrace it.

In Hut 2, by an end wall and far from the stove, a bunk was empty and draped with a folded blanket. Nearby, rolled in the dream that showed to him a woman who was dying, Adimov was asleep, and Feldstein lay still with the picture of exile alive in his mind.

Captain Yuri Rudakov could concern himself again with the prize that would be won when a confession of guilt was extracted from a prisoner in the solitary cells.

The camp ticked away the hours, grudgingly maintained its motion. One man ran at the wire and when the sentry fired high, fled back to the safety of his hut. Another man hanged himself with a towel in the bathhouse and was buried without the recognition of a stone in the prisoners' cemetery. Another man tried to steal the tobacco hoard of a "baron" and was clubbed unconscious and nobody witnessed the attack and nobody stood to defend him.

In Moscow, in a high room at the Ministry, a senior official of the procurator general's staff read the report that ZhKh 385/3/I was again at peace, and wondered how it could ever have been otherwise.

Through cold days and frozen nights the camp at Barashevo wheezed an existence. The camp worked and slept, ate its food, searched for its lovers, plundered and thieved, changed the guard in the watchtowers, patrolled the wire and the high wooden wall.

And in the SHIzo cell past the perimeter fences two men found a friendship on a concrete floor.

With a new office to work from, Major Vasily Kypov returned to the administrative details that had been neglected. For ten days he had ignored the paper piles that were now heaped as a punishment on his desk. The movement of prisoners into and out of his jurisdiction. The allocation of visits. The permission for parcels to be distributed. The reports on the letters vetted by the censorship team. The order for the camp's food supplies. Of course, he had a team of clerks and officers whose job it was to oversee such business. But the Commandant was responsible.

Deep in the mound of paper was a laconic note from Captain Yuri Rudakov stating that the prisoner Michael Holly had been sent to the SHIzo "box" for fifteen days.

Kypov had not been consulted. The maintenance of discipline was the responsibility of the Commandant, yet he had not been told that a man had been punished. He had not entered the offense and the penalty on the man's security file. The slip of paper was inadequate. A matter such as this should have been brought directly to his attention, not left for him to find as he sifted the paper mass.

Vasily Kypov instructed his orderly to find Yuri Rudakov and bring him to the office. He could have gone himself, but he played the formal game and sat in full splendor behind his desk and waited for Rudakov to come.

Ten minutes he waited, and the poor humor induced by the paper mountain was fueled by the delay. And when Rudakov came, the annoyance of the Commandant verged with anger. Not even in uniform. And always with those sickly foreign cigarettes in his mouth, and a hand in his pocket.

"Captain Rudakov. . . ."

"You sent for me, Major."

"I sent for you ten minutes ago, more than ten minutes ago. . . ."

"I came as soon as I was free, Major."

The hostility billowed from the major's face.

A shadowed smirk sidled to the captain's mouth.

"A man has been sent to the SHIzo block—I was not informed."

"The SHIzo is full, two-thirds men, one-third women from Zone 4."

"You sent one man there, Michael Holly."

"I provided your clerk with a memorandum of my action."

"Which I find now, buried in my papers."

"Then the blame is with your clerk."

"All matters of discipline should be referred to me."

"You've seemed preoccupied. . . ."

Vasily Kypov stared back at the KGB captain, his pig eyes burned.

"What was the nature of the man's offense?"

"My report refers to insubordination."

"What type of insubordination?"

"He was offensive to me."

"How was he offensive?" Kypov tunneled with his questions, following a seam.

"He threw something at me. . . ." Rudakov shifted on his feet. His hand was no longer in his pocket, his fingers flicked irritably.

"What did he throw at you?"

"He threw coffee at me."

"Coffee . . . ?"

"Coffee."

"Is it a regular practice to serve coffee to your prisoners?"

"It is not."

"Why in this case did you feel it necessary to supplement this man's diet?"

"A mug of coffee is not supplementing a diet. I was interrogating this man."

"Did he have cake as well?"

"I am entitled to interrogate a man in any manner I wish. It is a matter of state security."

"Does 'state security' require that coffee be served to the enemies of the State?"

"There are various techniques of interrogation."

"And some require the serving of coffee?"

"I have been entrusted with a job of interrogation."

"We have had arson in this camp, we have had murder, now we have blatant insubordination to an officer. We are wavering on a collapse of discipline. I will not suffer insubordination."

"I think he lost his head. . . ." Rudakov spoke with desperation.

"It will not happen again."

"I will see that it does not happen again."

"No, captain, you don't understand me . . . I'm not asking you, I am telling you that it will not happen again."

Rudakov lurched to the door. Failure soared at him. Failure to handle a prisoner who could toss coffee in his face and commit his Number One uniform to the civilian dry cleaners in Pot'ma. Failure to stand up to the cretin who had been thrown from military service to work out his last days in this shit-heap camp. He was a man familiar only with having his way. He believed his rank and office guaranteed his authority. But he had been caught out and humiliated. He flung open the door and went out, he heard behind him the cavern chuckle of Kypov.

Two warders brought Michael Holly back to his cell from the workshop.

When he had seen their faces he had known what faced him. In the workshop the other prisoners had known. They had turned away, all except Mikk Laas and from him there could be only a mute sympathy.

Inside the cell they tripped Holly to the floor and as he fell he saw the squat shape of the Commandant who had waited for him to be fetched.

The palms of his hands smacked into the concrete, the roughness caught and scratched his flesh. The boots were around him. Wet, dirt-smeared, snow-soaked toecaps, and above the toecaps the bright black polish.

Boots and truncheons working on Holly's body. He rolled himself into a defensive coil, but that was poor protection. When he saved his sides, then his head and his back were defenseless. When he saved his head and his back, then his sides were open to the kidney kicks of the boots. They said nothing, and he did not cry out. Only the squelch of the boot and the thud of the truncheons disturbed the silence of the cell. They didn't pant, they didn't sweat. It was not hard work to beat a man who was on the concrete floor beside their boots. His eyes were closed, his mind circled in hatred of the men around him. There was nowhere to flee, Holly lay still until they were satiated.

When the door had slammed behind him the pain came, came in rivers, came in mountains. Pain settling in his muscles, flowing in his limbs, climbing to agony.

Holly fainted. He was on the floor and with his arms around his head when Mikk Laas returned to the cell.

The man who had come thirty years before from Estonia prised Holly's arms away from his head and cradled him in his lap. He saw the blood that caked his hair and the fierce technicolor of the developing bruises. Later, when the soup swill was brought to the door, Mikk Laas dipped bread into the warm liquid and opened Holly's mouth and put the wet bread on his tongue and massaged his throat so that he could swallow.

The afternoon had merged with the evening, the evening had slipped to night, and the old man held Holly's head and crooned a song that came from the far villages of the Baltic coast.

When Holly woke there was a moment before he felt the pain and in that time he was aware only of the old man's body and the calloused hands that held his cheeks. Then he moved, and pain swilled through him. He looked up into Mikk Laas's face.

"I didn't cry . . . I begged nothing of them," he whispered.

"Then you have beaten them."

Holly managed a bitter smile. Blood ribbons sailed on his cheeks.

"I won't wait twenty years, Mikk."

"Why do you tell me?"

"Because I look for help."

"What help?"

"I have to know everything that has been tried . . . everything that has failed, everything that has succeeded."

"There are many who say it is impossible."

"You're not one of those."

"For a certain man it is possible. In my time there have been a few . . . for a few escape is possible."

Because they spoke so quietly, whispered in each other's ears, they heard the sound of the woman sobbing. A damaged sound muffled by brickwork, but for all that the noise of a woman who was sobbing.

He had worked late and because the contents of the file still played irrationally in his mind, Yuri Rudakov was not ready to go home to his bungalow and his wife. He went to the officers' mess in the hope that a brandy, or two, or three, would relax him. He would need something to calm him before he faced Elena and the newest bitching criticism that she had for his return.

As he came through the door he knew that the Commandant was drunk.

Kypov stood with his back to the stove, telling a story, and his collar clasps were unfastened and a twist of hair draped over his forehead.

The story died on the Commandant's lips.

The young officers shuffled in guilt around Major Kypov. Nobody slackened his guard when the KGB officer was present, nobody allowed alcohol to talk when the KGB officer listened.

Rudakov went to the bar, asked the mess steward for a brandy, signed the docket, took his glass to a table, selected a magazine and sat down. Silence hung like a shroud on the room.

"Where have you been, Rudakov, working . . . ?" Kypov shouted across the carpet. A voice of slurred treacle. "Working or holding a coffee party . . . ?"

There was a titter from one of the younger officers. Rudakov stared at the printed page.

"Our Comrade from the organ of State Security likes to entertain his prisoners at coffee parties, but they are not always grateful . . ."

Rudakov snapped shut the magazine, reached for his glass. The men around Kypov backed away, rats on a ship's hawser.

"Have no fear, Comrade, he'll not do it again. He's learned. He'll not give any more cheek . . . not to you, not to me, not to anyone."

Rudakov stood up.

"How will he have learned?"

No movement in the mess. The eyes of the watchers ranged from Rudakov, erect and ice-cold, to Kypov whose hand was against the wall beside the stovepipe as if he needed support.

"The boot and the stick, that's how he's learned. The boot in the balls, the stick on the shoulder . . ." Kypov giggled, steadied himself.

"You put the boot into Michael Holly? You're a stupid bastard, Major Kypov. More stupid than I could have imagined."

The door slammed on Rudakov's back.

The room emptied. Those who a few minutes before had been happy to surround the Commandant now slipped from his company. Behind the bar the mess steward found work for himself in polishing glasses.

He was alone. What had happened? In a fortnight what had

happened in his camp? The camp that had been a model of management and efficiency. The bastard thing had fallen on his head in one fortnight. His office had been burned, his garrison incapacitated. There had been reinforcement platoons and the indignity of an interrogation squad in his compound. The KGB officer had sworn at him in the full hearing of his officers.

Kypov slumped to a chair.

The mess steward without bidding brought him a brandy and a glass of beer to chase it.

Michael Holly and Mikk Laas sat on the floor with their backs against the far wall from the door.

Beyond the wall the woman cried, in fear and isolation. Mikk Laas had said that it was always harder for the women. Long into the night, while the woman wept in a cell that backed onto theirs, Mikk Laas talked of escape and Michael Holly listened. Holly bled the experience of the old man.

". . . The escaper is not a man who is loved in the camp. Each time that he attempts the breakout, whether he succeeds or fails, he makes the life harder for those who have not been involved. On the morning of a breakout the camp is consumed with excitement, everyone waits to discover his fate—then the penalties come. For that reason when the escaper returns he has no friends. He is a sullen man, the escaper. Between each attempt he is haunted by the fear of failure. He prowls looking for a weakness in their defenses, in their wire. When he smiles, it is because he believes that he has found again the hole through which he will crawl. The desire to escape becomes obsessional. He thinks of nothing except the height of the wire, the pattern of the guard changes, the thoroughness of the counting and the checking, the identity of the 'stoolies.' If it is not an obsession he has no chance of success. There was one of our people who was an escaper—Georgi Pavlovich Tenno—he tried to break out of Lubyanka as soon as he was arrested, then from Lefortovo when waiting for the trial, then from the *Stolypin* as he was taken to the east, then from the truck that took him from the station to the camp . . . every attempt failed. It was said that he marveled at the thoroughness of the guards' procedure. He was intelligent, an officer, yet he failed. There is another kind

of escaper, a suicide. He knows that he will not break clear of
them, that they will catch him and kill him. In the philosophy
of the camp that is honorable. There are some—not the sui-
cides—who will try to recruit a fellow prisoner, others who
swear that the escaper must be alone. There is no right answer.
If there are two men perhaps they can feed from each other,
give each other strength. But there is a saying in the camps—
only fools help other people. Occasionally, very occasionally,
there has been a mass escape, all out and everyone out. Once,
in the Stalin time when the camps bulged, a whole compound
went; they walked in a snowstorm over the drift that covered
the wire . . . I am tired, Michael Holly, you have four more
days with me. In that time I will tell you what I know, all that
I know . . ."

Behind the wall a woman still cried.

"Thank you, Mikk Laas."

"You listen well, Michael Holly."

"I have the best of teachers."

Holly rubbed the back of his hand in affection across the
Estonian's jaw.

"And you have hope, and that woman believes she has
nothing."

"Have you ever cried, Mikk Laas?"

"Only when no one could hear me."

"What could you say to her?"

"That they should not hear you cry. If they hear you then
they are satisfied."

Holly struggled to his feet. It was the first time that he had
stood since the warders had brought him back to his cell from
the workshop and stiffness bit in his knees and hip. There was
weakness in his legs, and he pushed himself up with a hand
that rested on Mikk Laas's shoulder. When he was upright he
leaned on his hands and felt the damp of the walls.

"Don't cry," Holly shouted. His voice boomed around.
"Don't show them you are afraid. Don't please them with your
tears."

Silence.

It was as if Holly was alone in the punishment block. He
sank down to his knees, and in front of his eyes were the
scratches and messages of *zeks* who had gone before him.

"What is your name?" Holly called.

A small voice, the cry of a bird carried on the wind from past the line of a hill top.

"My name is Morozova. . . ."

Holly heard the advance of the warder along the corridor. There would be an eye at the spy hole. He rolled onto his side and remembered a small face trapped between the swathe of a scarf and the peak of a cap.

He did not hear the crying again that night, and when he called in the morning he was not answered.

Chapter 13

All the officers of the zone had gathered in the mess for break-fast. Only the young and unmarried would normally have taken their first meal in the mess; those who had bungalows and quarters in the village would have eaten away. But word of last night's cat fight between the Commandant and political officer had spread with speed from man to man. They must both appear at breakfast in the mess, not to show would be to admit humiliation. And every man who had the rank to gain access to the mess had made it his business to play the part of witness. Not every day that a major of paratroops was raging drunk and personally supervising the beating of prisoners—not every day that a captain of KGB felt secure enough in his position to abuse his senior in the full hearing of company.

The deputy commander, the adjutant, the guards' platoon commanders, the supervisory officers of the warders, the officer in charge of camp maintenance, the officer who oversaw camp provisions and factory materials, they were all there. They waited in a strung-out line around the central table on which was stacked bread and cereal and the coffeepot on its candle heater.

Major Vasily Kypov strode through the door. No fool, this man. He could recognize the craving for drama. He nodded brusquely to the four corners, and seemed to curl his lip as if in disappointment that one man was not yet present. He poured his coffee, elbowed away the steward who tried to offer him a cereal bowl. He wore his best uniform and the medal ribbons blinked in the dull room. Dressed as for a parade. There was a defiance about the old goat, the deputy commander thought, something that was not pretty but assuredly brave. Kypov held the center ground and watched the door.

Captain Yuri Rudakov came into the mess before his Commandant had drained that first cup of coffee. A great silence about him as he eased the door shut. Something blatant about the watchers now. They devoured him. Rudakov had taken to his uniform, and his boots were cleaned and his cap was worn jauntily. Rudakov ignored the food, took only coffee. He hesitated for a moment inside the circle beside the table, then seemed to stiffen and walked straight toward Vasily Kypov. Collectively the watchers bit at their breath, craned to listen.

"Good morning, Commandant . . . I think we'll be spared more snow today. . . ."

"I didn't hear the radio . . . we can do without snow."

They spoke with a brittle politeness. Two men who share the same lover and have met at a party.

"I have my uniform back from the cleaners." Rudakov smiled thinly.

"Put the charge on expenses . . ." Kypov felt he had made a joke, that the ice wall would soon crack.

"This once I will do that . . . it won't be stained again."

"Of course."

"I was working late last night."

"After . . . after you came into the mess?"

"Yes. I was drafting a report of my interrogation of Michael Holly. I was going to send the report, now I have decided not to."

"No?"

"I have decided that there should be no interim report. I will submit a report to Moscow when the interrogation is completed."

"I am sure you have made the right decision." The relief sighed in Kypov's mouth.

"I hope so," Rudakov said quietly. "In Moscow they put great store on this interrogation."

"A good decision."

"Last night I wrote a draft of what would have been an interim report, but I've consigned it to my safe. If the interrogation is as successful as I hope, then the interim report will become irrelevant."

"I wish you luck with your interrogation."

Rudakov looked around him. He was aware of the rampant

disappointment of those who had overheard him.

"Thank you for your encouragement, Commandant."

Rudakov offered his hand, Kypov accepted. The Commandant cuffed the political officer on the shoulder, the political officer smiled at the Commandant. There had been a public quarrel, there was now a public friendship.

But the Commandant knew who had won.

A draft report snuggled in the safe of the captain of KGB, a report that would tell of gross interference by the camp Commandant in the legitimate investigations of Yuri Rudakov, a report that if it went to Lubyanka and headquarters would spring the trap of removal and premature retirement. He felt the straps around him that would confine for all time his independence from his political officer.

"If you will excuse me, Commandant."

"Of course . . . I hope you are correct in your forecast . . . about the snow. . . ."

Rudakov turned his back on the vulture eyes and hurried out of the mess. Those bastards would still be rotting in the camp long after Yuri Rudakov had returned to Moscow or been posted to Washington or had taken a trusted place in Berlin. Rudakov was temporary, Rudakov was going through, Rudakov was on his way and the *Dubrovlag* was a diversion on that journey. Rudakov was singled out for something better than the *zek* scum of a Correctional Labor Colony. Yet his ride out of the reach of Barashevo's claws was not certain. Michael Holly was the means.

He needed the confession of the Englishman. He needed his back to climb over.

He walked past the lines of prisoners drawn up for the roll call. He saw the passive faces, the worn uniforms salvaged by shades of patchwork. He trod a path where the pack snow merged with the ocher dirt of the compound's sand. He went along the high wire and the high wooden wall and through the vague shadow of a watchtower. He came to the main gate where two sentries stood with machine pistols slung across their chests. He saw the dogs that waited beside their handlers ready to escort the prison column from the compound to the factory zone. And he wondered. Was there not another way? That the camps had been filled by the purges of the thirties was now explained by the Stalinist cult of personality. That the camps had been filled in the years after the Great Patriotic War was explained by the power of Lavrenti Beria, now executed. That the camps had been filled in the latter days of Khrushchev had been explained by the incompetence of that First Secretary. But why were the camps still filled? Why, under the benevolence of Brezhnev, had they not found another way? It was a brief thought, and he trembled because it had shadowed across his mind. They said a million men and women were held in the camps. He shook the aberration from his head, and the wind whipped at him, the gusts caught at him, and through his greatcoat he shivered.

He had not known that thought before.

Rudakov took Michael Holly from the work cell of the SHIzo block and escorted him back to his office. He saw the way the man limped, the way he had tucked his wrist between the buttons of his tunic for support, the spectacular bruises. As they went past the *zeks* there was a growl of reaction to the hobbling, bowed prisoner.

Holly scraped a smile to his face.

It hurt to lift his free arm, but he managed a half wave.

He saw Chernayev and Poshekhonov, thought he could recognize Feldstein in the back lines. He heard the few shouts of support that merged with the yelled orders for quiet and the calling of the names.

He had found friends.

It required a beating on the floor of the SHIzo cell to find friends, it took a mug of coffee thrown into the face of authority to discover comrades. And when he went back to his cell in the evening Mikk Laas would be waiting.

He followed Rudakov into the administration building and he closed the door of Rudakov's office behind them. He saw the stain of coffee on the wall beyond the swing chair.

"Sit down."

"I'd just as soon stand, thank you."

Holly recognized the strength that had been given him by the boot and the truncheon. He would not have believed it before. Mikk Laas had explained. What can they do now? he had said.

"Sit down, Holly . . . please. . . ."

Every action, every word, should be divided into the zones of victory and defeat. The political officer had used the word "please," that was victory. There could be no defeat in accepting the chair.

He saw the half-smile at Rudakov's mouth.

"Should I offer you coffee?"

"I don't need coffee."

"Would you like something to eat?"

"I don't need anything to eat."

"What happened yesterday, I had no involvement . . ."

"Should that matter to me?"

"It was on the initiative of the Commandant."

"It doesn't concern me."

"You have to make a choice, Holly. There is the way you are heading, there is the way that I am offering. Perhaps you don't know that the choice exists, so I will make it very clear to you. The way you are heading will keep you here for fourteen years, the way that will trundle you between the SHIzo block and Hut 2. There is also the opportunity for common sense, the opportunity of the flight home to London. The choice is clear. The choice would be clear to a child. . . ."

The pain came in swinging bursts to Holly's body. Rich, live pain and in its wake were the memories of the flailing boot and the falling truncheon. He thought of Mikk Laas from whom they had not yet stamped the heritage of Estonia, of a woman who cried in solitary and did not believe that she was heard. He thought of Feldstein who had passed on a *samizdat* paper, of Adimov whose wife was dying of a cancer ravage, of Chernayev and Poshekhonov who had befriended him.

"If I don't go back to the work cell I won't be able to complete my output norm," Holly said flatly.

"I have protected you, Michael. For what you did to me in here I could have put you before a court—under Article 77-I of the Criminal Code you could have had another fifteen years. Can't you see what I am doing for you?"

"What happened to your investigation team?"

"They found a man, they have left. . . . You have to think of your life. You have to think of your future. I cannot protect you forever. . . ."

"Which man did they find?"

"A maniac from Hut 4, half-mad anyway, used to work at the Water Authority in Moscow . . . it's irrelevant . . . I am protecting you now. I cannot go on doing that. Are you asking me to abandon you? Are you listening to me, Holly . . . ?"

"What will happen to this man?"

Rudakov shrugged.

"We have a penalty for murder, it does not concern you. . . . Think of your parents, they are old, in the twilight of their lives. They have one son only. They will die without ever seeing that son again. They will die in an agony of unhappiness. That is not my fault, Michael. That is not the fault of the Soviet people. It is in your hands to make those old people happy, Michael. You think that I am very crude, that I play to the emotions. The crudest argument is the best."

Holly hung his head.

He had condemned a man to die. He had consigned an elderly couple living in a London suburb to a dotage of misery. For what?

To indulge an ideal? The ideal of Michael Holly scattered casualties across the length of the compound, across the breadth of a terraced house.

When he looked up he saw the triumph large in Rudakov's face. He knew of nothing to say. Michael Holly had thought he was brave, and his bravery was paid for with another man's life, with his parents' misery. The strength ran from him, the resolve leaked away. Another man's life, his parents' misery. His head was deep in his hands, hidden.

"Captain Rudakov. . . ."

"You are going to be sensible, Michael?"

"Give me time."

"Get it over, Michael. Finish it now."

"Give me a few days. You will find I am not a fool. You will have something to send to Moscow."

"Each day you wait is a wasted day."

Rudakov beamed over the table, made a dramatic gesture by pulling from a drawer a sheet of blank paper, took his pen from his tunic pocket.

"I have to prepare myself."

"A few days only."

"Thank you." Holly seemed to brighten, as if a great decision had been taken. "I want to go back to the work cell. If
I do not go now I will not complete my output norm."

Rudakov shook his head, a tinge of sadness had gathered.
He saw the wreckage of a human being. At that moment the
sight gave him no pleasure. He could take no pride in the
destruction of a proud man. The collapse had been faster than
he would have believed possible. He was vindicated. The pen-
tothal drugs, the torture electrodes, the beatings, they were not
the only way. His approach had been correct, even humane. . . .

Holly forced himself up from the chair. He staggered toward
the door, and waited for the orderly to answer Rudakov's call
and come to escort him back to the SHIzo block.

They had ravished the supper, raped the soup and bread. They
were left now with a windy ache in the belly, a warmth in the
throat, the knowledge that if they were quiet they would not
be disturbed for the night hours. No crying from the cell through
the wall, no response to Holly's tapping. But the girl had been
an interlude, an interruption. The business of that evening, and
each evening that followed, devolved from the experience bank
of Mikk Laas.

Mikk Laas on the concrete floor beside Michael Holly and
whispering at his ear.

"You can't tunnel out of here, not in winter with twenty
degrees below and permafrost. You see that? And it's no better
a prospect in the summer. It's the matter of the water table—
it's high here. There's a top level of sand and under that runs
the water. Anywhere in the camp if you dig a hole more than
four feet deep you will have standing water. Then they have
another small sophistication—they are very thorough people,
never forget that, Michael Holly—beyond the wooden fence
there is in summer a plowed strip, they harrow it to show
footprints. Between the wooden fence and the plowed strip
they have dug into the ground a line of concrete blocks. The
blocks are a meter square and a few centimeters thick. They
have dug them down into the earth so that if it were possible
to cope with the water table and to have a tunnel running under
the fence then the weight of the blocks would collapse the
workings. Years ago we worked to place the blocks in position,

I know their weight, it took two of us to move each one. . . . Even
if you could disperse the earth, if you had the strength to manage
the digging, if you could find the collaborators that you could
trust, you still would not succeed by tunneling. Forget a tunnel."

Mikk Laas with his bony body pressed against Holly, searching his memory for precedent.

"There is a way that relies on conspiracy, but it is always
dangerous to involve others, because then the chance of the
'stoolies' hearing is widened. Back in Camp 19, ten years ago,
perhaps eleven, there was a snowstorm as the men were to be
marched back from the factory to the living zone. Two men
stayed in the factory and when their names were shouted for
the roll call others claimed their names. The two men had lifted
the floor of the factory and sheltered underneath and they had
smeared the boards with oiled cloths. They knew they would
be missed, but they needed those few hours for the trail to
grow cold. They knew that the dogs would be loosed to search
through the living zone and the factory, but they hoped that
the cloths would have dulled their scent to the dogs. It was a
Friday when they went under the boards, and they hoped that
by the Sunday the heat would have gone and with the work
place not in use they might find a place on the wire to climb
and run. I said the guards were thorough, Michael Holly. . . . They
were shot on the factory wire."

Mikk Laas would sometimes shake his old stubble-crested
head at Michael Holly, as if there was a futility in all he said.

"There have been those who have tried to smash their way
out through a broken fence. A truck will come in, to deliver
coal, materials, anything . . . the men will attempt to seize the
truck and drive it at the fence. Not the gate, because the gate
is reinforced . . . They will set the truck in gear and hide on the
floor of the cab and hope the machine gun spray misses them.
To me that plan is useless. Even if you break the fence and
clear the compound you have woken all hell and its jackals.
They will come after you with jeeps, you have aroused them.
It is a way that has been tried and it is hopeless."

Mikk Laas with his spindle fingers holding tight to Michael
Holly's hand.

"To have any chance the man must go as soon as darkness

falls. He must use the whole night of darkness to get clear of
the camp. If he goes in summer then he has a short night. If
he goes in winter he has a long night, but the snow track also.
That is the choice. There is another thing, Holly. Should you
leave the camp, should you get a kilometer clear, ten kilometers, a hundred kilometers, what have you achieved then?
Where has that taken you?"

The last night, the last night of fifteen for Michael Holly
in the SHIzo cell. He wondered whether he would ever again
see the old Estonian.

"You would go for the wire, Mikk Laas?"

"If a man is careless for his life . . . yes, I would go for the
wire."

"In the early evening?"

"Just before six in winter, before the guard change."

"Wire-cutters?"

"You would need an accomplice. There are some *zeks* who
would have the power to get cutters from a guard. . . . You
would need a 'baron.'"

"And outside the wire?"

"You should not ask me. In thirty years I have not been
outside the wire or the transport convoy."

"It is better with an accomplice?"

"You cannot do without a friend. You are blind outside the
fence."

"Mikk, Mikk Laas . . . you were a partisan . . . ?" Holly's
head was buried in his hands, and his fingers were white as
they pressed down on his skull.

"I was a partisan, or a terrorist, or a freedom-fighter . . ."

"You hit German barracks, Soviet convoys?"

"And we ran and we hid . . . sometimes we attacked, not
often . . . I am not proud, Michael Holly, I do not have to
pretend. Mostly we ran and we hid."

"When you attacked what followed your action?"

"Reprisals." Mikk Laas grated the word in hatred, spat it
from his tongue.

"When you attacked you knew that reprisals would follow?"

"We knew."

"They shot people in reprisal because of what you had done?"

"Some they shot, some they transported."

"You knew what would happen? Each time you planned an attack you knew what would happen?"

"We knew. Whether it was the Nazi or the Soviet column that we hit, the result would be the same."

"And when you knew that, how then could you justify your attack?"

"Why do you ask?" There was a fear in Mikk Laas's voice.

"How could you justify your attack?" Holly hissed the question.

"We agonized. . . ."

"How did you justify it?"

Mikk Laas looked around him as if for escape, but there was none, and the breath from the young Englishman played across his old cheeks, and his wrists were caught hard. He hesitated, then the answer flowed in the torrent of a cleaned drain.

"We thought we were right. We believed we were the guardians of something that was honor and courage. We told ourselves that even reprisal killings and transportation could not justify our inaction. It was an evil thing that we fought. That is not an easy word to use—'evil'—but we felt from the depths of our hearts that if a man is confronted by evil then he must fight against it. We thought this was the only way, that without this there could be no freedom, not ever. We decided that some had to die, some who had not chosen our course, in order that one day there might be a freedom."

"And now, what do you think now?"

Mikk Laas sighed, and his body seemed to shrivel.

"I think now that those men and women who were shot in reprisal for an action of mine died for nothing."

"You're wrong."

"I am not young. I have been here thirty years. . . ."

Holly shook him to silence. Holly's fists were buried in Mikk Laas's tunic. With all his strength he shook an old man's words from his lips.

"When you were a fighter you were right, now that you are old you are wrong!"

Like a wounded rat Mikk Laas scuffled his way to the corner of the cell. His voice was a high whine. "When I was young I knew certainty. I know that certainty no longer."

They slept separately that night, using the full width of the SHIzo cell. The gap of concrete flooring was not bridged and both were cold in their shallow sleep.

Early in the morning, before the start of the working day, Holly was escorted back to the living zone. He was in time to join the breakfast line, and then take his place in the ranks for roll call, and afterward go back to his bench and lathe in the factory. Chernayev, Poshekhonov and Feldstein all tried to begin a conversation with Holly, but they were rebuffed. He would speak to no man until the evening.

When it was dark Holly asked Adimov to come from the hut with him. Two huddled figures on the perimeter path.

"Your wife is dying. They will not let you go to her. I will give you the chance to see her before she dies. We will go out of here together. We go out this week."

When they returned to Hut 2, there were those who saw the gleam of tears on Adimov's cheeks.

Chapter 14

In all the years that Adimov had been at Barashevo no man had ever offered him the hand clasp of friendship.

Authority in plenty, friendship in minimum, for the killer of a woman on Moscow's Kutuzovsky Prospekt. From his first days in ZhKh 385/3/I he had fought to maintain that authority. Knife fights, beatings, humiliations all played their part in winning for him a pedestal position that left him respected yet friendless.

In the kitchen Adimov would never be the man who went short. In the factory Adimov would never be the man who operated the dangerous lathe. In Hut 2 Adimov would never be the man who must hide and guard his possessions. Like a new stag that disputes the territory of an old antlered stud he had overthrown the former "baron" of the hut. They still reminded him of the fight, those who wished to settle close at his side in the evenings and breathe the words they thought he wished to hear. They reminded him of the circling combat in the aisle between the lines of bunk beds when he had wrested supremacy from their former master. A lunging swaying fight when the men of the hut had stayed back on their mattresses with their eyes locked to the brightness of two steel blades. A wordless fight that soared to an instant climax when the silver of steel was blood-darkened. The old "baron" was now in Hut 4, a morose figure stripped of influence.

No man had ever come to Adimov with a proposition of partnership. No man had ever come to Adimov as an equal.

When he twisted his mind back over the months and years that he had been a prisoner in the camp he could not recollect any moment when he had entertained the thought of escape. He would have reckoned escape to be the final idiot fling of the suicide. He had thought only of making himself supreme over all others within the confines of the camp.

But a new man had come to their hut, a man who was indifferent to the power wielded by Adimov.

The power of the "baron" had been eroded by that very indifference. The new man had drawn weakness from Adimov's strength, sapped his very authority. He had asked the new man to write a letter for him when no other *zek* in the hut could be allowed to learn that Adimov was illiterate. A new man had placed Adimov in his debt. No other prisoner in the camp could boast that he was the creditor to Adimov.

The suspicion had succumbed to confusion. The confusion had been beaten back by the very confidence of Michael Holly. . . .

And Adimov would again be with his woman.

She was a blowsy creature, an untidy, tire-fat woman who was warm and kindly to Adimov. In all his life she was the only person that he had loved. He thought of her on her back in the bed of the tiny room that he had shared with her. He thought of the disease that ran through her stomach. Of course they would be watching the apartment, but he could come at night. If he could see her just once, hold her, whisper some happiness into the ear of his woman who was dying.

That bugger, the Englishman, he didn't ask for much.

Wire-cutters and food and two white sheets, and three days to find them.

The "baron" had influence. The "baron" was the puppeteer who could tug the strings.

There was a guard, a creeping, curved-shouldered youth, with more than one year served in the MVD detachment of the camp who could be owned, manipulated by Adimov. It was the power of the "baron" that he knew the flaws of the mighty and the lowly of the camp. There was a guard who brought sugar and chocolate to a trusty of Internal Order because the man was from the same suburb of Murmansk, a guard who in the innocence of his first weeks at the camp had compromised himself for all the time of his conscripted service. That guard would supply the wire-cutters.

There was a *zek* who worked on the duty rota in the kitchen and who was behind with his tobacco payments to the "baron," a bent willow of a man who could be persuaded to provide a package of bread and parboiled potato.

There was a boy who had come with a pale, tear-ridden face to his "baron" to ask for protection, a boy with slim hips and cropped blond hair who would pay every ruble and kopeck that he earned in the workshop for the privilege of sheltering under the strong arm of Adimov. There were two old bastards who wanted the kid, neither would dare to touch him while he was under the guardianship of Adimov. The boy worked in the laundry where camp uniforms and blankets were washed, and also the sheets from the garrison's barracks.

Adimov could supply wire-cutters, a supply of food, two white sheets.

He spoke to the guard who stood beside the gate of the compound, and the hissed threat of exposure was sufficient to silence his stuttered hesitation.

He spoke to the kitchen hand at morning exercise on the perimeter path in the half-light, and twisted his arm painfully up into the valley of his back.

He spoke to the laundry worker as they were marched to the factory, and the boy imagined his trousers being ripped down from his waist and the hands of an old man on his skin, and he nodded in dumb acquiescence.

Adimov could provide as Holly had asked, for the coming Sunday.

Morning roll call.

A frost gathering on the noses and eyebrows of the *zeks* in their ranks. The checking of names. Rudakov stood beside Kypov, at his shoulder. Michael Holly was always in the rear rank for roll call, and always Rudakov could see him. There was a stature that put him above the other men in the forward ranks.

"Holly. . . ." The bark of the sergeant who held the clipboard and the pencil.

"Present. . . ." The reply drifting over the heads from the back.

Another name, another answering call. Rudakov walked toward the sergeant.

"Get Holly here," Rudakov said.

The flow of the sergeant was broken.

"Holly to the front. To the political officer. Ignatiev...."

"Present. . . ."

Holly moved from his place in the rear line. He skirted the end of the rank and came slowly forward. Perhaps, Rudakov thought, there was an insolence about the way the prisoner approached. Not deliberately delaying, not hurrying.

"Isayev. . . ."

"Present. . . ."

Rudakov watched him come, noted that his tunic for all its padding hung looser now on the Englishman's body than when he had first come to the camp. And all the time that Holly walked, Rudakov could see that his eyes were on him. That was the difference with this man. Any other would have dipped his head, avoided the boldness of the close gaze.

"Isayev. . . ."

"Present. . . ."

Rudakov permitted Holly to come near to him and when he stopped, only a couple of meters short, then Rudakov stepped forward. He spoke quietly.

"You are ready?"

"Very soon. . . ." There was a distance in Holly's voice.

"When?" The bite of impatience from Rudakov.

"Next week..."

"When next week?"

"On Monday, Comrade Captain."

Rudakov looked into Holly's face, tried to read a message of defeat and was confronted only with a lackluster mask.

"Do it today."

"On Monday morning."

"You waste three more days of your life."

"On Monday morning."

There was a shrug from Rudakov. "So be it...Monday morning. Get back to your place."

Holly turned away from Rudakov, shambled away toward the wing of the front rank.

There was a flush of excitement running in Rudakov's body. His mind raced. He saw a punched tape jumping in the clamping hold of a telex machine. He saw a typed sheet being hurried from Communications along the corridors of Lubyanka. He saw the gleam of admiration playing on the face of a full colonel of state security. He saw a telegram of fulsome congratulation being drafted for transmission to Barashevo. In the bag, where all the others had failed. . . .

Rudakov turned cheerfully to Kypov.

"Commandant . . . Elena is doing Political Education on Sunday evening. She is giving a lecture, but it will be finished early. Would you care to join us afterward for dinner?"

It was the first time such an invitation had been offered.

"Your wife will hardly want to cook."

"She'll be finished quite early. She's excellent in the kitchen. She would enjoy your company, as I would." Rudakov grinned. "We'll break a bottle open. I have a little light one from Tsbilisi."

"I would enjoy that very much . . ." Kypov thought of the file that rested in the safe of his political officer. "I will look forward to the evening."

"Excellent."

Rudakov set off for his office in the administration block. Though his lips were chapped from the cold he managed to whistle. Something lively that he had picked up like a virus in Magdeburg. And he might be back there soon, in the German Democratic Republic or in Moscow, or perhaps to Prague or Warsaw, or even to Washington . . . anywhere other than the *Dubrovlag*. And when he left Barashevo he would be wearing major's pips on his epaulettes. With a jaunty step, with the tune rippling in his ears, he went to his office.

Behind him the ranks of prisoners trudged toward the gate and the transfer to the factory compound.

The perimeter path is the only place of privacy in the compound. Each night there are always a few who walk the path, sometimes in company, sometimes alone. The boot-crushed snow of the track holds no eavesdropper, the barbed wire that shields the killing zone offers no hiding place for a "stoolie."

Holly had been the first to leave the hut. There were stars for a ceiling and a misted moon. He was joined by Adimov. There was a naturalness about their meeting.

"Will you have them?"

"Cutters, food, sheets—I'll have them."

"By Sunday?"

"I'll have them. Shit, that's the easiest...."

"Give me those and I'll get you out," Holly said softly.

"Where? Where do we go out?"

There was a grating in Adimov's voice, and his glance roved up against the silhouette lines of the wire and the bare height of the wooden fence. Holly waited, ignoring the frustration of his companion. They walked on to the corner of the compound, the right-angled turn on the perimeter path. Their faces were lost in the gray shadow of the watchtower.

A slow smile from Holly. "We go out here."

Adimov darted his eyes at Holly. "Under the tower...?"

"Right."

"That's crap, that's suicide...."

"That's the safest place in the compound."

"It's right under him, under his gun."

"Under him, and out of sight of him. It's the safest place."

"I'm not having my bloody guts blown out..."

"Look at the place, look at it...." Holly had seized Adimov's sleeve, gripped him, turned his body back toward the angle and the fences and the wire. "Under the tower there is darkness. The lights are blocked by the tower and by the stilts. From the other towers they cannot look here because to do so they look into the other tower's searchlight."

"Two lots of wire, one wooden fence."

"Right."

"Shit...I'm not a coward, it's mad...."

"I said I'd get you out, Adimov."

"Under the tower, under the gun, where if we fart he'll hear us, and we cut through two wire fences and we climb a wooden fence...shit, Holly, what tells you I've the balls for it...?"

"You have a wife with cancer of the stomach, that's why you'll come with me. That's why I chose you."

As he walked away from Adimov and toward Hut 2, Holly slapped his body with his arms, trying to beat some warmth into his skin. Just once he looked back, and then not at the man that he had left but at the small, shadowed space beneath the watchtower. Above the shadowed space was a watchtower and a guard and a machine gun. A machine gun, and the targets would be at point-blank range. Nowhere else, Holly, nowhere else. He slammed the door of the hut behind him and felt the heat waft across him, and there was a shudder in his breath. Ignoring the questioning glance of Feldstein, he climbed onto his mattress and turned to the wall.

Long after the lights had been switched off, and the warmth of the stove had waned, the hut was a chilled and dark place. The old ones said that it was always coldest in Mordovia when the winter was close to running its course. A hundred men lay on their mattresses in Hut 2, and those that were lucky had found sleep, and all were wrapped tight in their blankets and had discarded only their boots for the night hours.

Anatoly Feldstein had not found sleep.

It was the hunger that made it hardest to drift into the dream world that was an escape. The hunger caught at his stomach. The hunger had stripped the flesh from his bones and those bones made him believe that he lay on a bed of stones rather than a mattress of waste straw. The bones gouged into his body, pressed on his organs and nerves. And when he was exhausted, the bitterness welled in him, and sleep was even harder to achieve.

Above him Adimov was asleep. Regular, grunted waves of breathing. He'd be counting, his mind playing at a cash register...who owed him money, who owed him tobacco, who owed him food.... The criminals could always sleep....

That was the cruelty of the *Dubrovlag*, to leave a man such as himself in the company of these animals. Pigheaded, imbecile criminals who were the fodder on which the camps fed. They could have moved Feldstein, could have sent him to Perm where they had gathered the dissidents. Not that the regime at Perm would be different to Barashevo...same stinking food, same stinking huts, same stinking regime...but he would have been with friends. The people at Perm were all together. Chained in a common purpose, weren't they? Camp 35 and Camp 36 and Camp 37 were the homes of the people that Feldstein yearned to be with, the camps of Perm where the Article 72 men rotted their lives away. Article 72—especially dangerous crimes against the State—was the net that pulled in the hard bedrock of the dissidents, that consigned them to Perm that lay 400 kilometers to the east of the *Dubrovlag*. Almost an insult, for a dissident not to be imprisoned at Perm. They were the élite, and Anatoly Feldstein was committed to a camp of criminals.

He thought of the men in the hut. Adimov was a thug, Poshekhonov was a fraud, Chernayev was a thief, Byrkin was a fool, Mamarev was an informer. Those were Anatoly Feldstein's companions. That was the knife-edge of real cruelty.

And there was Michael Holly.

Holly should have been the friend of Feldstein.

Holly should have been different to the herd. Holly who tossed on the bed close to him and sometimes cursed in the tantalizing unknown of a foreign language. Holly should have been the colleague of a political activist. Holly knew the meaning of freedom, had grown to manhood in its company.

Yet Holly barely acknowledged the existence of Anatoly Feldstein—Feldstein the dissident, the Prisoner of Conscience, the victim of the abuse of Human Rights.

Could Holly ever know what it took in courage to be an opponent of the Union of Soviet Socialist Republics? Could he know what it meant to breed the fear that this day or this month the lift would come? The lift and then the interrogation, the interrogation and then the imprisonment?

Could Holly know what it meant to fight from within? There were few enough allies. Forget the students at the university and the trainees at the laboratory. Don't look for a pillar from your mother and father and grandmother, from your brothers and sisters.

Holly should have known, Holly had lived in liberty.

Feldstein rolled on his mattress, listened to the night sounds of the hut. He heard the scrape of the springs of Holly's bed.

"Holly . . . you are awake?" A whisper, a pleading for contact.

"I'm awake."

"Sometimes we are too tired to sleep."

"You can't sleep if somebody talks to you."

A hesitation. "I'm sorry, Holly . . ."

"I didn't mean that, Feldstein . . . I take it back."

"When you came here, to Russia, when you did whatever you had to, did you think it might end in a place such as this?"

"No."

There was a rough laugh from Holly.

"Did you know of such places as this?"

"Vaguely . . . I didn't have the names and the map references."

"The people of Britain, they don't know about such places as Barashevo?"

"There are a few who tell them, not many who listen."

"If you had known this place waited for you, would you have done what you did?"

"I don't know . . . Christ, Feldstein, it's halfway through the night . . ."

"You have to know that answer."

"I have to sleep . . . I don't know."

"All of us knew, everyone in my group. Can you understand that? We knew what faced us, we knew of this camp and a hundred other camps. We knew when we started. . . ."

"Some day they'll strike you a medal."

"Why will you not talk of this, Holly?"

"Because I want to sleep . . . damn you, Feldstein, because talk doesn't help. Talk wins nothing."

"Only through talking can we win. Only that way do we succeed."

"What has your talking won you? . . . Sakharov is exiled, Scharansky and Orlov in camps, Bukovsky and Kuznetsov booted out. Bloody marvelous talkers all of them. Talked their bloody heads off, and won them nothing."

"There is no other possibility, Holly."

"Then you are doomed. For fifteen years you've been pushing round paper, collecting fifty people to stand in Pushkin Square, burying the White House in cables. You've filled the camps again, Feldstein, and nobody cares. A million people go to work each morning in London and they're thinking of the bird next to them, whether they can afford a music center, how much it's going to cost to get to Spain in the summer. They couldn't give a damn about you . . . nor about me, nor about anyone else who's plastered in flea-bites and sores and working his ass off in Mordovia."

"We knew when we started on our journey that it would bring us here."

"What do you want of me, Feldstein?"

"We chose the weapon against them that hurts them most,

we took the weapon of legality. We demanded the rights that
are owed to us through the Constitution."

"Feldstein . . . Christ, I admire you. I admire all your colleagues. You are all bloody marvelous. What I am saying . . . Christ, I'm tired . . . I'm saying you're not winning
anything. When they put you in here and they throw the bloody
key away, then you're beaten. Nobody listens to the shout of
Anatoly Feldstein. You can lift the bloody roof, and nobody
hears you. That's not winning. . . ."

"When we have a hunger strike . . ."

"Then they save on the food. They don't give a shit."

"What is your way, Michael Holly?"

"I don't know." A quaver of evasion.

"You have a different way to our way." The glint of sarcasm.

"I don't know . . . but if you fight to win, then you use the
weapons that bring victory. . . ."

"And nonviolence is not such a weapon?"

"Go to sleep, Anatoly."

"Why do you run from every question?"

"Because answering questions helps not at all. Go to sleep."

"And Zatikyan and Stepanyan and Bagdasaryan, the Ar-
menians who were shot for the Moscow bomb that killed seven
persons in the Metro—were they using the right weapon? You
have to answer that question, you have to. . . ."

Quiet fell between the bunk frames.

For a long time Feldstein waited, and he was rewarded only
with the sounds of Michael Holly's breathing. Hopelessness
consumed him. Holly preferred the company of Adimov who
was a killer, Feldstein had seen them together on the perimeter
path. There was cruelty all round him, but that was the cruelest.

Another evening, another fall of darkness, another hushing of
the life of ZhKh 385/3/I.

Elena Rudakov walked beside her husband across the compound.

She took the center of the path and her leather boots were
unsure on the diamond ice and she hugged her husband's arm
and muffled herself in the warmth of her fox fur. She was a
creature of duty. She had chosen for her text the munificence
of the aid supplied by her government to the Third World. She

had written out her speech in full. Better that she should bury her head in her script. If she looked up into the faces of her audience, she would see the animal lust of the pigs. . . . There was a meat stew in the oven of the bungalow gently simmering, potato and carrot in the saucepans waiting for the gas to be lit when she returned. For the life of her she could not comprehend why Yuri had asked Kypov to come to dinner.

In a watchtower a young guard swore at the wind that pierced the open window at the front of his platform. It was in standing orders that the window must be open and the barrel of his machine gun jutting from it. The guard saw the political officer and the political officer's woman heading for the kitchen. Great fanny, the wife of the KGB captain, and three more months until his leave. The guard stood back on the platform, tried to keep himself away from the gale that sang through the window.

The kitchen was almost full.

A woman would be talking to them. She came one Sunday a month, and still seemed as preciously rare as a winter orchid. After the woman there would be a film.

A steaming warmth of breath and bodies in the hall and a chair set on the small dais, and the men at the front would see her knees and more if she shifted her legs.

Poshekhonov was at the back. He'd see her face, and think of a story told long ago of a woman who managed a handstand and leaned her buttocks against the wall. Beside Poshekhonov, Chernayev had taken his place. In Chernayev's pocket, safe and hidden, was a letter. He had not questioned Michael Holly who had given him the letter. He had accepted it, he had promised that the next evening he would personally give it to the hand of the political officer. He had shaken Holly's hand, he had known. He had looked into the face that wore a boyish grin, almost a thing of mischief, before he had gone to find a chair at the back of the kitchen hall.

Holly and Adimov stepped down from the door of Hut 2. The quiet of the compound dripped around them.

Chapter 15

The snow fell close and thick, hiding them. Sweet, perfect snow dropping in the confetti of tickertape.

To cross the compound they used the safety of the huts, hugging the long shadows. From Hut 2 they scurried to the dark pall of the bath and laundry block. A panting pause there, and ears cocked for sounds of movement and voices. Then the short sprint to the front of Hut 6, and they sheltered against the stilts of brick that supported the building while they calmed the frantic breathing. A few stumbling, running meters and they found the padlocked, recessed door of the store. That was the waiting place, that was the last place where they would stop before the charge at the fences.

They had made the sheets into crude cloaks. The fastening on each of a single safety pin left a hole for the head to dip through, and the sheets would hang down and lie secure over their backs. Like two children engaged in unimaginative fancy dress.

God, the snow helped them, the snow that cascaded from the low cloud ceiling.

God, Holly, that was luck.

Holly waited until the searchlight on the corner tower arced away along the length of the fence. The snow made its beam mottled and disturbed. He looked up at the tower, saw it as a fleeting image, checked like a chessboard, dark shape on white snow. He saw the barely distinct outline of the torso of the guard. Far back, the bastard, where he could warm himself. The guard would have to move forward on his platform each time that he varied the aim of his searchlight, but he'd do that rarely enough. He'd move the beam when he had to, when it was necessary, he'd not be hanging through the window.

He grinned, something mad in his eyes.

"Ready, Adimov . . . ?"

"'Course I'm ready." A snarl from Adimov.

"Stay close to me."

"Right up your ass."

Holly reached out in the blackness, found Adimov's hand, felt through the wool of their gloves the trembling of the fingers. He squeezed Adimov's hand, squeezed it tight, dropped it.

"We shouldn't hang about. . . ."

Holly turned again toward the angle of the compound. He looked up again at the watchtower. He waited, and Adimov's body was pressed against him as if to propel him forward. Holly waited, and was rewarded. The shadow of the guard came to the window, and the searchlight rotated across the huts and the inner compound, swung in a great sweep before coming to rest on the opposite fence.

Holly was gone. The very speed of his movement seemed to catch Adimov unprepared. Adimov chased after the billowing white back. Snow in their faces, in their eyes, melting in their mouths, settling on their capes. Hard to keep the eyes open when they were running, when they were bent, when the iced snow landed on them. Holly stopped, he crouched, Adimov crashed against him. A second of awkwardness, balance failing, but the discipline held. No words, and the white sheets blanketed their bodies and they froze to a statue stillness. They were at the angle of the perimeter path, on the ice of the trampled walkway where the snow now painted over the boot marks. Holly had been here many times. Now the new route, now the magic road. God, he was tired. Shouldn't have been tired. Not at the start. He felt the lights all around him, the lights that stood back from the far fence, suspended from poles. And this was the most naked place, the most dangerous. This was where the guardtowers had been sited to provide maximum vision. The low wooden fence was beside him, peeping over the snow that had been taken from the perimeter path. The low wooden fence that acted as a marker for the killing zone. Have to get past the fence, have to get into the wire. When is the best time? No time is best, every time is awful . . . Shift yourself, Holly, shift yourself, or turn round and head back for that stinking bloody hut.

He looked up once, directly up toward the tower. He saw the falling snowflakes lively in the beam of the searchlight. He saw no movement. For a moment he wondered about the visibility of the guard on the next corner's watchtower. Dead, weren't they, if that guard looked, if that guard was not huddled too at the back of his platform. He saw the barrel of the machine gun, depressed so that the snowflakes could not penetrate its muzzle: the black eye of the barrel with a crest of snow lying on its foresight, the eye that laughed at him. Shift yourself.

He rose halfway to his full height. He stepped over the low wooden fence.

Into the killing zone.

His feet plunged down into the virgin snow, where no boots had trod that winter. Gentle, giving snow. He lurched three, four, five steps toward the first wire fence. There was a howl from the wind. God, bless you for the wind.

He felt Adimov's hand clasping at his sheet and the tail of his tunic. He had told the bugger to stay close, close he was, close as a bloody ball and chain. He was beside a post from which the wire was stretched. Old, rusty wire with ocher sharp barbs. He turned toward Adimov, and the man had remembered. Adimov had released his hold on Holly's back and now leaned away from him and crudely swept with his gloves the snow back over the chasms that their boots had left. God bless the snow, let it fall in the gouged holes and smooth away the sharp lines of recent movement. Holly fumbled in his pocket for the wire-cutters. Not much more than heavy pliers, the best that could be provided, and they were Adimov's ticket. . . . Adimov alone could have provided him with the cutters. . . . Everyone tries to go out in the short nights of summer. Only a fool, only Michael Holly, would try to go out in deep winter. That's your bed, Holly, lie on the bastard. He sank to his knees, grasped the cutters in both fists, cursed the impediment of the gloves. Adimov rearranged the sheet across Holly's back. Holly shivered. No time is best . . . every time is awful.

Close to them, close enough for them to feel the jarring impact, were the sounds of stamping feet on the boards above. The bastard who was in the watchtower, belting his feet on the platform, trying to cudgel some warmth into his toes. Come down here, bastard, come and feel the cold when the snow is wet through your trousers. The guard coughed, hoarse and raking, then a choking sound. God, and the bastard's crying, crying up there because it's cold, because the wind is hooked to his body. Crying for his home, crying for his mother. Keep warm, bastard, keep warm against the back of the platform.

Holly clamped the cutters on the first strand of wire. Stretched, taut wire that had been applied in patterns of six-inch squares. No wire to spare for coils. That would have finished them, if the wire had been coiled. Cut low, cut close to the snow line. Holly froze. The wire snapped. The first strand was broken. He felt the slackness, behind him was the hiss of Adimov's breathing. Holly's hand groped for the next strand. He would cut out a box, a square box that had the width of a man's shoulders. There would be a tumbler alarm wire above the line where he cut, set to explode a siren if a man bucked the fence and climbed. He was below it, he was safe from it. About the only bloody thing he was safe from.

Holly made the hole. As he crawled through, Adimov's hands protected the material of the sheet from the wire's barbs.

Holly first, Adimov following. They had crossed the killing zone, they had broken through the first wire fence. Remember what Mikk Laas had said . . . they're thorough, these pigs, good and thorough. In front of them was the high wire fence, and then the high wooden fence. Above them was the watchtower where a young guard trembled with cold, where a machine gun rested on its mounting. He closed his eyes, tried to flourish some deep strength from far inside himself.

He reached forward to feel the first strand that he would cut of the high wire fence.

A deadly, lifeless audience.

A humorless, witless speech.

She spoke against a wall of noise offered by scraping feet, moving chairs, hacking coughs. Yuri Rudakov did not always attend his wife's monthly political lecture, sometimes said to himself that it was good for her to shoulder a burden alone. She had privileges enough, it did her no damage to stand on her own feet. He was with her tonight because she had bitched so loud in the privacy of her own kitchen about the dinner invitation to Commandant Kypov. If she had spoken well, that would have given him pleasure, but she had hidden her pretty face behind her spectacles, buried herself in her script and read with a droning monotony.

". . . For many of the countries of the emerging Third World, the Soviet Union is the only friend to whom they can turn for genuine help and guidance. From the West all they will find is the desire to reimpose the chains of servility that were the way of life under the old imperialistic rule. The countries of the west have never accepted the de-slavement of the peoples whom they regard as inferior and of value only if they can be exploited. But the Soviet Union offers true friendship. I would like to tell you of some of the agricultural development programs that have been originated in Ethiopia, just one country that has rejected and expelled the yoke of American cold war politics . . ."

Rudakov winced, wondered from where she had rifled the text. Pravda? Izvestia? And the eyes of the pigs were on her. Almost dribbling, those that sat at the front. Not watching her face, not listening to her words. Staring at her knees and the skirt was too short. Prying open her thighs, they'd be, the filth and the scum that sat in front of her. Elena should not have worn that skirt, not in the kitchen hall. Then he thought of the orderly who would bring Michael Holly. They would start early, straight after roll call. He'd have the coffee again. . . . That made him smile. . . . He would speak to Elena about her skirt. Not tonight, not so that he provoked a row with the Commandant coming to dinner, not with the precious excitement of the morning beckoning. But he would find a time to speak to her about the length of skirt she wore in front of the scum.

Holly had taken between his fingers the last strand of wire that he must cut to fashion the hole in the high wire fence.

Behind him Adimov sighed in impatience. What did the bugger expect. He wasn't snipping bloody roses. Bloody life and death wasn't it? And each time that the cutters bit down on the wire and separated it, then there had been the crack of the parting and they had lain still for a moment, covering their breath, not able to believe that the sounds would not be heard. They were almost underneath the watchtower now. The bastard would have to forsake his shelter, he'd have to lean through the open window to see them, he'd have to peer down at the base of the wood stilts if he were to notice the twin crouched figures. For Christ's sake, Holly . . . there's a path across the killing zone, smoothed a bit, cosmeticized by Adimov's efforts and by the steady falling snow, but for all that a path. There's a hole in the inner wire fence. If the bastard goes to the window, if he looks out in front of him . . . if he sees nothing then he's blind.

The strands were loose, the square of wire could be bent back to make space for them.

The high wooden wall was in front.

Yes, Mikk Laas, yes, they're thorough. A killing zone, two wire fences, a high wooden fence, and the prisoners that the barricades have been built to hold are half-starved, half-dead from tiredness. Yes, they're thorough, old Mikk Laas from Estonia. You never forget Mikk Laas, the encyclopedia that made it possible, you always remember him. But if you remember Mikk Laas then you remember a partisan, and a partisan means reprisal, and reprisal is a road to a *zek* in the Central Investigation Prison at Yavas. That man will die, Michael Holly. And if you remember him then you remember also a letter in the pocket of Chernayev . . . God, God . . . and all the memories lead to a hole cut with heavy pliers in the high wire fence.

His legs were wet, his trousers sodden. Water slopped in his boots.

Dreaming, Holly, and dreaming is death. Adimov was pushing him. Adimov who was the fellow traveler was heaving, shoving, persuading Holly into the hole. Holly snapped the images from his mind. His elbows edged forward, he dragged himself through the gap. He heard the gasp of relief from Adimov.

He was through.

He rested for a moment against the thick beam support of the watchtower. Only the high wooden fence, only that barrier left. What did they say? That the little camp was only a microcosm of the big camp, and the big camp stretched forever, the big camp compound was a thousand miles across, wasn't that what they said? Wrap it. . . . He took Adimov's hand, pulled him a few inches, released a wire barb from Adimov's sheet.

Adimov joined him, slumped on top of him. They tried together to catch their breath, to subdue the pounding. They lay together in the snow under the high wooden fence. Holly could no longer feel his toes and his fingers were brilliant with pain.

It was Adimov who heard the ice slither of the skis.

First the skis, then the patter of the dog's feet and the panting of his breath. It was Adimov who reacted, pressing Holly face-down into the snow. Skis and a dog approaching on the far side of the high wooden fence. A scuffling of paws on the far side of the high wooden fence. Was this where it finished, gin-trapped between an attack dog and a belt-fed machine gun?

"All quiet?"

"Yes, sergeant, all quiet. . . ." A chilled, unhappy voice from above.

"Fucking awful night."

"Yes, sergeant."

"All right for you in your shelter."

"Yes, sergeant."

"Fucking awful night to be out . . . and the dog, silly bitch, doesn't notice it. Have you been throwing food down?"

"Perhaps, perhaps a bit of sandwich, sergeant."

"You eat your food in the barracks, you don't take bloody sandwiches on duty. Right?"

"Right, sergeant. I'm sorry, sergeant."

"Don't let me catch you again . . . come on, you stupid bitch, you're fed enough without having to dig the snow for a crust. . . ."

The dog growled, a soft rumble in her throat.

"I'm sorry, sergeant."

Then the hiss of the skis and the oath for the dog to follow, and the stamp of the feet above them. Holly and Adimov held each other for comfort. Holly grinned, Adimov bit his lip to suffocate a laugh of relief.

The high wooden fence was dark with creosote. The top was two feet above Holly's head when he stood. He reached up with his hands, felt the rough-cut wood through his gloves. It was the last mountain to be climbed. He stood a long time, waiting for the strength to return.

The words had passed him by. Chernayev cared nothing for the lecture of Elena Rudakov. He had sat for near to an hour rigid in his seat. He had listened only for the hammer of gunfire, the agony scream of the perimeter siren. The letter burned in his pocket, the letter he had been charged by Michael Holly to hand to Captain Yuri Rudakov on the following afternoon. And Holly was running... Holly who had no words for the thief once he had returned to the hut from the SHIzo block. Happy enough to talk with Chernayev before he went to the SHIzo, glad enough then to hint of revolution. But the SHIzo had changed him.... How many times had Chernayev tried to talk with him since he had come back? Half-a-dozen times, a dozen times? And nothing given in return, nothing until the last. When the letter had been passed, that had been the Holly he knew. The man who was going to the wire, the man who could crack a grin, the man who was going to run and who asked a friend to give a letter to the captain of KGB. Shit, that was style. Chernayev had been seventeen years in the *Dubrovlag* and had never known of a man succeed in running loose from the camps.

There was no applause when she finished her speech.

The senior man from Internal Order shouted for them to come to their feet and they stood in silence and watched the departure of the political officer and his woman. He was smart in his uniform greatcoat, she was velvet in the warmth of her fur. And she wore her scent, the bitch, because her scent would save her nose from the smell of the men that gaped at her. Chernayev flopped again to his chair and waited for a film to be shown—and for the gunfire, and for the sirens.

Run with the wind, Holly. They'll hunt you as they would a rat in a chicken coop. And in winter.... Run hard. An old thief was allowed to cry. There was no shame in crying for a young man who ran at the wire.

"What's the film called?" Chernayev asked.

"The title is irrelevant. The important thing is that it lasts two hours," replied Poshekhonov comfortably.

He had needed Adimov to push him up. Without Adimov he could not have found the muscle necessary to scale the high wooden fence. When Holly jumped, Adimov grasped his shins and forced them up so Holly could swing his leg and straddle the summit of the fence. For a moment Holly was silhouetted

on the top of the fence, and he ducked his body down and tried
to lie along its length. He pulled at Adimov's wrist. Adimov
was strong. The man who was at the front of the food line in
the kitchen, who had not spent fifteen days in the SHIzo block
on half-rations. He could climb for himself. They were together
on the fence. A deafening noise they seemed to have made.
Holly saw the ski tracks and the footprints of the dog. He held
the top of the fence in a steel grip of his hurt fingers, he swung
the other leg, he hung from his fingers.

He fell and his body crumpled on the snow and the blood
flushed to his head and his ears screamed with the noise of his
landing. He thought of a guard who stood a few feet above
him, he thought of a balaclava and a forage cap with ear
muffs . . . Adimov fell beside him.

They crouched low. Each for the other they spread out the
sheet tangle to cover their backs. The camouflage of the white
winter fox.

The guard shifted on his platform, his feet beat on the
planked flooring. Over the fence and the high wire and the low
wire came the drift of voices, the spill from the kitchen, those
who were leaving before the start of the film. Incredible, to
hear those voices from beyond the fences.

It was as though Holly had performed his task. Adimov's
fist rested on Holly's elbow, ready to propel him toward the
darkness of the tree line. Holly had said he would take Adimov
out, Holly had been good to his word. Like a team that could
work in tandem, the leadership was exchanged without question. Adimov pointed to the snow surface, made a smoothing
motion with his hand.

Forty meters to the tree line.

Adimov went first, awkward, charging.

Holly watched him go. His legs shook. He lost Adimov in
the haze of trees.

Holly's turn. But he must go backward, his back to the
trees. He must be bent so that he could push the snow again
into the holes that their feet had left. Forty yards to cover while
his glance wavered between the snow pits and the back of the
guard in the watchtower. Don't turn, you bastard, don't turn.
He remembered Feldstein's question: "If you had known that
this place waited for you would you have done what you
did?" . . . and a miserable answer he had given. Of course he

hadn't known of ZhKh 385/3/I, of course he hadn't known of two wire fences and a high wooden fence and a guard above him with a machine gun and clear fire field....

Did Alan Millet know? Holly wanted to shout the question, found it rising in him. Did the man who gave him sandwiches and beer in a pub near the Thames and a package to take to Moscow, did he know? When he was out... when... he'd find Alan Millet.

Adimov clutched him, twisted him toward the abyss of the woods. No gun had been cocked. No siren button had been depressed.

At first they went in caution, doubled beneath the lower branches of the firs and larches and wild birch. Sometimes where the trees were set thickest there was little snow, but when they came to places of more open planting they would fall up to their waists into drifts. They blundered in the blackness with an arm raised to protect their faces from the whiplash of loose young branches. When the lights over the perimeter of the camp could no longer be seen, they went faster. They cared less for noise now. The pace increasing, the exhaustion surging. And through all the hours of darkness they must never stop, never break the rhythm of distancing themselves from the fences.

"We're going north?"

"As I said we would, Holly."

"How far, like this?"

"Till we reach the railway that runs north from Barashevo."

"We will go along the line?"

"The line is safer than the roads."

"I thought... I thought there would be a greater excitement...."

Adimov leading, not looking back, the snow falling from the branches that he disturbed onto Holly's face and body.

"Excitement at what?"

"At getting out. Stupid, I thought I'd be singing."

"Stupid, Holly... it's not a bloody Pioneer ramble.... You want to know what chance you have of getting out, right out, over the frontier? None. You've done all this just to be brought back, and when you're back it will be worse... And for me, what is there?"

"There is your wife, Adimov...."

"My wife who is dying. To see her, should that make me excited?"

In morose silence they trudged on through the woods. There were tears in the sheets where they had caught against branches. Neither man was willing to stop to remove the drapes, and they would need them when they came to the railway line.

No excitement, Holly. Only the pain, only the waiting for the siren to reach out for them.

He missed little. He noticed everything that broke the pattern of the hut.

Mamarev had strolled with an inoffensive innocence the length of the aisle between the bunks.

As he had gone by the bunks he was watched but not spoken to. They all knew which was the "stoolie" among them. And they tolerated him because his person was sacrosanct. He was protected by the death penalty, he was kept safe by the threat of the SHIzo block. A nine-year stretch—a stretch for taking a girl into a truck park. Loud and clear she'd said "yes," till her fucking pants were at her ankles. A nine-year stretch and they'd said they'd halve his time. He had been a clerk, he had worked in the offices of the administration of transport in Novosibirsk. He was not a part of this place, he owed nothing to these creatures in the bunk beds of Hut 2, he owed it only to himself to get clear of this stinking cesspit camp.

Two bunks were empty when the ceiling lights were switched off. Adimov and Holly. He had seen them together earlier at the perimeter path, and now their bunks were empty.

The Englishman was nothing, he had no fear of the Englishman, but Adimov was different . . . Adimov carried a knife.

The trusty from Internal Order slept at the far end of the hut to the bunks of Adimov and Holly, a double bunk-frame to himself, and a curtain to shield him from the common *zeks*. Mamarev had allowed an hour to pass from the dousing of the lights before he slid from his bed and went on his toes toward the drawn curtain. A wraith moving along the rough-floored aisle of the hut. Let the bastard trusty inform on the bastard "baron." He drew the curtain aside, he insinuated himself behind it. He shook the shoulder of the sleeping man until he woke. He whispered into the ear of the trusty.

"There are two beds that are empty. Adimov's and Holly's. . . ."

"You little shit. . . ."

With the "baron's" help the trusty could run an easy hut. Not that they could be friends, of course, but they need not cross each other. A "baron" was a bad enemy, even for a trusty.

"Two beds are empty. I've told you . . . what are you going to do?"

"Fucking strangle you, that's what I could do about it."

"And lose your precious curtain, and good conduct, and your red stripe, and your fucking life."

"Get back to your bunk. . . ." the trusty spat the words in a rare savagery.

The trusty heard the fall of the curtain, the drift of a light footfall. He had no choice. He pulled on his boots. He slipped into his jacket with the bright red band on the upper right arm. He switched on his flashlight and walked the length of the hut. He saw the two folded blankets. He cursed quietly, sadly. When he came back between the bunk ends his flashlight showed him Mamarev sitting upright on his mattress, smiling. No choice. The trusty opened the door of Hut 2, bent his head and began to walk to the guardhouse.

They had reached the railway line. Behind them were the blurred lights of Barashevo railway station. In front the twin rails stood out in the half-gloom between the black cloud and the whiteness covering the sleepers and chip stones.

Holly put his hand on Adimov's shoulder. "Well done . . . well done."

Adimov did not reply.

The wind was at their backs. The sheets were pressed against their bodies. Two ghosts going north from the village along the railway track. Outside the confines of the camp Holly felt the terrible nakedness of the fugitive. And the little camp was exchanged for the big camp. It was a thousand miles to the perimeter path of the big camp. Into the night, into the driving snow, into the short horizon of the narrowing railway lines.

The sergeant was sprawled in a chair in front of the stove of the guardhouse. His dog lay beside his feet close to the opened

doors where the flames curled from the heaped coke. The
sergeant was near to sleep, the dog snored. On a better night
he would have gone out again, toured the fence a second time
as midnight approached. Buggered if he would on such a night.
Get himself soaked and half-frozen, and he could lose a good
dog in a snow blizzard, get her cold again when she'd not dried
out her fur, that was the way to kill a good dog. The radio
played quietly on the table beside him. He had his tobacco.
He had mugs of tea brought by one of the kids each time he
shouted for it. Buggered if he'd go out again. His skis stood
against the outside wall of the guardhouse and they'd stay there.

"Sergeant, the Internal Order prisoner from Hut 2 wishes
to speak with you. . . ."

The sergeant straightened, swung in his chair to face the
duty orderly. His fingers flicked nervously at the buttons of
his tunic. The dog stirred. When the sergeant saw the snow-
covered, muffled shape of the trusty framed by the doorway
he felt the premonition of crisis.

"I am sorry to disturb you, sergeant. I thought you should
know. Two men are missing from Hut 2."

"So tomorrow you have the Englishman?"

"Tomorrow I have him."

"You've played it strangely, I'll say that, Rudakov, bloody
strangely . . . and now you are to be rewarded for your eccentricity."

"For each fish there is a different bait."

"And when you've milked him, will he be on his way?"

"He thinks so, that's what he believes."

The Commandant laughed. Major Vasily Kypov shook in
merriment and his shoulders heaved and his jaw wobbled, and
the burst of his amusement splayed out over the small front
garden of Yuri Rudakov's bungalow. Rudakov laughed with
him, and the cigars glowed from the porch. On the road beyond
the white-painted palisade the Commandant's driver started the
engine of the jeep.

"That's what he believes. . . . That's very good . . . very funny.
Bloody spy. An excellent evening, Rudakov. I'm more than
grateful to your wife. Fine meal, and damn good hospitality
afterward. . . . Won't be forgotten, not by me. Shit, we dented
those bottles."

Kypov swayed against Rudakov. The political officer wondered how the Commandant would negotiate the snowbound path to the gate.

"It's been my pleasure and my privilege to entertain you, Major."

"Vasily, please. . . . Again my best wishes and my thanks to your wife."

He made it to the jeep, not easily, but he arrived. The lights sparked, the engine roared.

Rudakov smiled, sweetly, privately, went back into the bungalow and locked the front door. He was hurrying now. Through the living room and the kitchen to turn off the lights, to make up the fire for the night, to peel off his tunic and kick off his shoes. The bedroom was in darkness. He could hear Elena's breathing, erratic and excited. More of the scent that he had bought for her, that she knew he liked her to wear. Shaking out of his trousers, wriggling from his shirt, discarding his socks. Elena would have sensed his mood, known the anticipation that gripped him while the banalaties were traded with a boring fool on the front porch. Her arms greeted him, slender and naked. Naked as her breast and her stomach and her thighs. He swam beneath the comforter, he slid over the sheets warmed by her body. Beautiful, wonderful, dry, clean skin resting, rolling against his. Her hands finding the sinew in the small of his back, his fingers scouring for her nipples. Her hands diving over the flatness of his belly, his fingers plunging for the richness of heat and moisture and opened legs. Her hands holding and squeezing, his fingers prying and searching. And he had sat with the file open, with the typed words battering his mind, when this was waiting for him. Idiot, Yuri . . . her mouth was over his, her tongue forced his back. There was a whisper in her ear, an entreaty. He began to climb onto her, to submerge her beneath him.

He heard the siren.

Turn the bastard thing off . . . kill it. But the siren at Camp 3 can never be switched off. It must scream its course. The softness had fled Elena. He felt her rigid against him. A new sound with the siren call, sharper and more urgent. He might have sobbed, and Elena pulled the bed clothes around her as he reached for the telephone.

"Rudakov. . . ."

He listened.

The hand that had gloried in the skin of Elena was now white and clenched on the telephone. Abruptly he replaced it, then sagged back onto the bed. Though the room was dark his hands covered his face. For a full minute he lay quite still on the bed, not caring to cover his nakedness, then he dragged himself from the coverlet and started a haphazard search across the floor for the items of his uniform. He let himself into the living room where he would dress. Because Elena Rudakov's head was deep beneath her pillow he did not hear her weeping.

He had lost a jewel, a jewel that would have adorned his crown.

On the railway line, beyond the reach of the village lights, two men heard the far cry of pursuit, the siren's howl, and tried to run faster.

Chapter 16

There had been a long night of confusion in the hut.

The *zeks* lay on their beds as they had been ordered and were drowned by the blazing ceiling lights. None were to leave their beds. The counting had been long ago; now they lay submissive on their mattresses, witnesses to the anger of the high and mighty of the camp who came to inspect the insult of two empty bunks and two folded blankets. The *zeks* were forbidden to talk, but they watched each move of the investigators. Ever since the siren had awakened them the *zeks* had been alert to the drama of the night. The Commandant had come, glowered at the unused mattresses, stalked the length of the hut, departed, and had returned. The political officer had been three times to Hut 2, as if some factor in the outrage of escape had first eluded him, and there was fury on his face for every time that he stamped the boards of the hut to the far wall where guards and warders stood, useless as statues.

Each man in the hut read the message. Escape was the great weapon. Escape was a cudgel that whipped across the shoulders of the men of authority. The anger of Vasily Kypov, the fury of Yuri Rudakov, were twin witnesses of the wound that had been done to them. He would have been a brave man who sniggered in their hearing, an idiot man who smirked in their sight. The *zeks* were silent, the *zeks* averted their eyes from the faces of the men in authority.

All the men in the hut would reckon that they knew Adimov. Only a few could claim to be familiar with the Englishman.

Chernayev from his bunk watched the two camp officers who would coordinate the hunting down of Holly and Adimov, and against his vest was the letter that he had been charged to hand to Rudakov when the late afternoon came. Byrkin who in his time had been a petty officer and so was familiar with command and instruction saw the pacing frustration of the Commandant. Poshekhonov turned to his pillow and pretended to sleep so that he might better hear the whispered conversations of Kypov and Rudakov when they came close to the mother heat of the stove.

"Right under the corner tower they went out." A snapped accusation from Rudakov.

"Under a tower? And the tower was manned?"

"Of course it was manned. . . ."

"You have a trail?"

"Something that is nothing. We have a trail that is under twenty centimeters of snow. Two sets of wire cut, and then a trail to the woods on the north side. . . . If we have the dogs out blundering in the trees in darkness we screw all the scent that's left. If we leave it till first light we have another twenty centimeters sitting on the scent. . . . It's a bloody shambles."

"How could that happen?"

Vasily Kypov spoke almost to himself, as if the question bemused him.

He won no charity from Rudakov.

"They had wire-cutters. They went out underneath a tower. I'm not responsible for fence security. . . ."

"Holly was yours. You were responsible for him. Full enough last night with your boasts of success." Kypov flared in retaliation, and the memory of hospitality received a few hours earlier fled.

"If he had not been able to walk out of your camp—to walk through two wire fences and over a wooden fence—then he would have been mine."

"You should have observed your man better."

"You should have secured your perimeter. Isn't that what they teach the serving officer?" Rudakov sneered.

"They'll singe us for this."

"They'll have our asses."

Kypov cocked his head, peered out through the window into the stinging snowfall.

"Where can they go?"

"How can they go anywhere? They can only run, freeze, starve."

"There will have to be an inquiry."

"When a prisoner escapes there is always an inquiry. They will say that escape is not possible from an efficiently run camp."

"The search parties will start at dawn."

Kypov bit at his lip, tucked his chin to his chest, and stamped out of the hut into the last moments of the night. Trailing behind him were his adjutant and a radio operator whose set crackled static across the compound.

Rudakov stood by himself close to the stove. He felt the frail, local warmth.

They were all watching him, but if he raised his eyes all would turn away. He was hated here. Scum, weren't they? They could be beaten till they fell, they could be starved till they tumbled, but to the moment of death they would hate, loathe him. He understood the source of that strength. Holly and Adimov had given it to them. An escape through two wire fences, and over a high wooden fence, and under a watchtower. He felt a private wound. He had offered freedom to Michael Holly and had been given an obscenity for a reply. Rudakov threaded between the guards and the warders to the far end, to the empty bunks. He crouched beside Feldstein's.

"Did you know, Feldstein?"

"Know what, Captain?"

"Don't piss with me, did you know?"

"Would I tell you, Captain, if I had?"

"Do you want to go to the SHIzo block?"

"I . . . I did not."

"Why did they go?"

"You want to know?" A grimness in Feldstein's voice.

"I want to know."

"They had the courage to say that what happens in a concentration camp is not inevitable, is not irreversible. Every man in this hut shouts in his heart for their success."

Rudakov whispered beside the ear of Feldstein. "If they are not shot . . . if they are returned here then what has been the value of their courage?"

Feldstein laughed without mirth. "They have damaged the institution of the camp, they have kicked the authority of the comrade Commandant, they have battered the dignity of the comrade political officer. I have to tell you that?"

"If for this escape there is collective punishment against all the men in the camp, what then is the value of their courage?"

"We have nothing. If you have nothing what then can be taken from you . . . ?"

At first light a convoy of trucks and jeeps arrived at Camp 3. A hundred cold, cursing men who had been pulled early from their barracks' beds at Yavas. They brought with them their trained tracker dogs and their skis and their rifles. The troops stayed under the tarpaulin covers of their vehicles, the officers gathered in Vasily Kypov's office.

There was a large-scale map unfolded on the Commandant's table. One centimeter to five hundred meters. A full colonel had come from Yavas and there was the hint that the general himself might follow. Kypov, bruised with embarrassment, prodded his finger at the map and at the camp diagram that he had drawn himself. He explained the detail of the escape. When he had finished he was eased without apology by the colonel from the central point in front of the map.

"Visibility is no more than a hundred meters, perhaps not even that."

Kypov asked with caution. "You have road blocks out?"

"I have road blocks, I have the stations watched. I have men who could be better employed waiting in reserve. I have a bloody army ready."

"In this weather surely they cannot go far?"

"More luck to you if they don't. . . . I have a helicopter if the bastard thing can fly."

The colonel strode out into the snow, shouting his first orders. The men fell from the tailboards of their trucks and the dogs plunged in the drifts. He spoke to Kypov's adjutant who scurried into the compound to return with two folded blankets. The column skirted the perimeter of the camp and came to the northwest corner watchtower. The troops stood back, the blankets were thrown onto the snow for the dogs to sniff at. There were faint indentations in the snow surface, something of the start of a trail that headed across the open ground toward the trees. The dogs buried their nostrils in the blankets and patterned the snow with their footprints before they were satisfied.

They moved into the trees. Four dogs pulling their handlers after them and a hundred men fanned out in line behind. As they entered the tree line there was the rippling clatter of weapons being armed.

Chernayev and Poshekhonov on the perimeter path, walking before the breakfast bell.

"Did you see him, the bastard Kypov? Did you see his face? Like the world had fallen on him. . . ." Poshekhonov was animated, bubbling. "Best thing I've seen in five bastard years. Your friend did that for us, Chernayev. I could kiss him, if I ever see him again."

"Perhaps you will see Holly again, perhaps not," Chernayev said softly.

The trusty from Internal Order took a place at the end of a rank of five. A long snake column heading through the gates of the compound for the factory. Byrkin was at the trusty's shoulder.

"They've no chance, have they?"

"Quiet, look to the front."

Byrkin ignored the instruction. He would not have done that before, a small courage flushed to his cheeks. "The alarm went too early. They had to have all of the night . . ."

"You want the SHIzo for fifteen days?"

"Why did the alarm go?"

"I've warned you."

"How did the alarm go?"

The trusty hesitated, seemed to look only at his boots in the snow, seemed to take a decision of loyalty, to span a crevasse. "There was an informer . . ."

"You . . . ?"

"Mamarev. . . ."

Byrkin smacked the fist of his hand against his thigh.

"Thank you. . . ."

"I have told you nothing."

They made wooden dolls in the factory wing of the women's zone. Chubby dolls with wide smiles and hollow so that a smaller replica could fit inside the two halves.

This week Irina Morozova painted the faces. Twin pink

blobs on the cheeks, coy black eyelashes, a petite ruby mouth.
Down the line another woman would paint the yellow of the
headscarf, another the red and blue and gold of the traditional
peasant dress. The tourists beavering for presents in the hotel
stores in Moscow or Leningrad would never know that a doll
so full of life came from the work bench of a young girl with
a pale face and hollowed eyes. Irina Morozova's fingers were
quick. She was a pianist, though she had not seen a piano for
twenty-seven months. She was of minor concert standard and
had not known an audience's applause since her arrest. She
could meet the daily norm. She could satisfy her supervisor.

The thunder of the rotor blades distracted her. A huge beast
with black and dun-colored camouflage stripes on its hull hovered beside the window of the factory above the perimeter
fence. The roof staggered under the force of the downblast.
She saw the crew man at the opened door, the microphone at
his mouth as he talked the pilot to the ground.

She had heard the siren in the night, but she had not spoken
of it to any of the other women in their small dormitory hut.
She was the "intellectual," and that was a dreaded label in a
criminal compound. The prostitutes and thieves of the dormitory were vicious toward any that claimed a superiority over
them. She might have won a protector, but she had kicked her
boot at the cow's finger grope and earned herself three nights
in the SHIzo. And she had no friends because the bitches were
fast to sneer at an Article 58 "intellectual."

"Why is the helicopter here?"

There were times when she could not help herself, when
she could not survive the isolation wall around her.

"The Commandant didn't tell me." The woman who painted
the headscarves cackled in laughter.

"I heard the siren, there were trucks arriving early this morning, now a helicopter. . . ."

"Go and ask the Commandant, darling, she'll tell you, a
clever bitch like you."

Article 58—a typed letter to the United Nations Commission of Human Rights in Switzerland. She had been an idiot
to have believed that the letter would ever reach its destination.
A complaint on the persecution of the Tartar minority, and she
not even a Tartar. A four-year sentence—an exemplary penalty

the judge had described it. The dissemination of anti-Soviet propaganda, the spreading of lies about her country. Her letter had traveled no further than Lubyanka.

"Has there been an escape?"

"Well, it's not Brezhnev come to kiss us goodnight. . . . 'Course there's been a fucking escape. Out of Zone I. One of the "barons" and an Englishman as well. Wish the bastards had managed it in here. . . . Not that you'd be interested, would you, darling?"

"An Englishman . . . ?"

"Some bastard spy . . . good looking stud. We'd have hidden him well enough." She laughed again and her breath whistled in the gap where two upper teeth were missing.

Morozova's fingers trembled on the narrow stem of the brush. The helicopter's engine was a diminishing whine, slipping below the fence. She dipped her brush in the paint pot. She took again in her hand the wooden shell of the doll. She remembered a man who had stood tall among those around him while the women waited for the column to pass between the factory and Zone I. She had seen a name that was strange in its lettering. The man had stared at her. Of all the women it was she at whom he had stared.

There was another memory, a memory of a shout through the wall of a SHIzo cell. A different accent, an accent that was as strange as the lettering of a name.

"Don't please them with your tears," the man had shouted through the bricks of the cell wall. She had not cried since.

The Englishman was running, the man who had called to her through the cell wall, the man who had picked her from a crowd as she had watched the *zeks* go by.

God, keep you safe.

God. Something from her childhood that the elementary school and the Pioneer Corps and the Academy of Music had never painted over. A shadow that stayed with her.

She could not recall the letters on his tunic. She did not know his name. She only knew that a helicopter had come to join the men who hunted for him.

The senior official of the Ministry of the Interior picked at his nose as he waited in the anteroom outside the office of the procurator. He wondered how long he must wait before he was permitted to enter the sanctum and display the latest of the telex messages to have come from Saransk concerning events at ZhKh 385/3/I.

He was adept at his work, this senior official. When he had been ushered into the procurator's presence and sat humbly on the edge of his chair, he was ready with his denunciation.

"You will remember, Procurator, that this is not the first incident involving Camp 3 at Barashevo this year. Within the last month we have had the fire, as yet unexplained, that burned down the Commandant's office. We have had the dysentery epidemic that claimed the life of a guard and hospitalized seventeen others. Now we have an escape. I should draw your attention, Procurator, to the identity of one of those who is missing. Michael Holly, an Englishman serving a fifteen-year sentence for espionage against the State. He was a Red Stripe prisoner and yet he was able to acquire wire-cutters and cut through two wire fences, and scale a wall, right underneath a watchtower. Already I have had Lubyanka on the telephone, they describe this man as a prisoner of maximum importance. I think you will agree, Procurator, that the matter is a disgrace...."

"Who is the Commandant at Camp 3?"

"Major Vasily Kypov, formerly paratroop."

"How is my diary next week?"

"You are in Moscow—routine."

"Make the travel arrangements."

The train had spurred them on, driven them forward with fresh hope.

When they had heard its approach, slow in the dawn light, they had been staggering along the path of chipstones and snow-covered sleepers. They had plunged together into the snow at the side of the line and tried to arrange their sheets across their backs. It was an old steam engine, pulling a crocodile line of freight cars and belching black smoke, forcing the snow from the line with an angled fender. The train lumbered past them, scattering soot over their bodies. Holly had seen the value of the train. He had seen the way it had scoured the track of surplus snow, tossed it on one side, and spilled down a debris of coke and dirt. The dogs would have a hard time of it, a hard time following the scent now that the train had passed. Desperately tired, he had dragged Adimov up from the snow, on down the track. It was a chance that must be taken. Adimov had cursed him, and Holly's grip on his tunic had tightened. They had gone on together, two gray shadows on the embankment of the track.

They had walked another hour after dawn and then they had seen the farm hut a few yards from the line.

While Adimov wrenched at the door, Holly smoothed their snowprints flat.

A windowless hut, with a floor covering of wet hay. A palace to two fugitives.

They sank to the rough floor.

They eyed each other.

One thing to be friends when the momentum of escape drove them forward. Another matter when they were alone, isolated inside four tin walls. Almost a shyness between them. Holly knew why. Adimov had the food and Adimov had never shared his food with any *zek* in the camp.

"We have to eat, Adimov," Holly said.

The bastard wants me sleeping, Holly thought. On my back and cold and out, and then he'll stuff the bloody food down his throat.

"We're going to share the food, Adimov. Crumb for crumb we're going to share it."

"I don't need you . . . not now."

"Get the food out."

Both men on their knees now and the brightness of anger in their faces. Bitter, locked eyes.

"I gave you the cutters, you took me through the wire— that's where it ended."

"It ends when I say. Get the food and share it."

On their knees because they had walked all night and neither had the sinew to stand. Ready to fight over half a loaf of hard black bread, and a cube of cheese, and a pinched paper filled with sugar.

Adimov reached between the buttons of his tunic.

"You want the food, you get the food . . ."

Holly remembered the blade, steel sharp against the blanket

of a bunk in Hut 2. He lurched forward, swung his weight against Adimov. Had to go fast. Find the wrist, hold it. One blow, one harsh stroke. The glaze was in Adimov's eyes. Beaten, destroyed by one punch. Holly reached inside Adimov's tunic, took the handle of the knife and the plastic bag of food. He crawled to the door, pushed it a few inches open and threw the knife as far as his strength allowed. The snow still fell, the hiding place would be covered, lost until the spring thaw.

The cheese could wait, and the sugar too. They would be needed on the second day and the third. He would break into the bread alone. He tore off a quarter of half a loaf and then divided that quarter. He crawled across the floor of the hut toward Adimov and the man shrank away from him until he was against the wall and could go no further. Holly put an arm around Adimov's shoulder.

"Together we have a chance, alone we are beaten. Eat, Adimov."

When the old *zek* had closed the door Yuri Rudakov tore open the gummed-down envelope. He read the words, written in a strong decisive hand, with a growing astonishment.

> Captain Rudakov,
> You have a man accused of the poisoning of the barracks water supply. He is not guilty of that offense. I alone was responsible. On the question of my escape I want you to know that Adimov was not the instigator of the attempt. Again I take full responsibility. With this knowledge I hope you will take the appropriate actions.
> Sincerely,
> Michael Holly

Chapter 17

They lay together, two gray bundles of quilted rags, and the cold burrowed against their bones.

Holly remembered when he had taken Adimov for that first time to the perimeter path and talked of escape. To get through the wire had then been the summit of their aspirations. Bloody daft, bloody idiot thought. . . . To get through the wire was nothing. To get away and clear, that was everything. And they lay on the floor of a farmer's hut a few short kilometers from the camp, soaked and frozen, they were starved close to exhaustion. What had he been thinking of when he had taken Adimov to the perimeter path? There had been no plan. Only the blazing anxiety to get clear of the camp because he had consigned a man to the condemned cells of Yavas and, if Michael Holly could break out, and leave a pathetic note for Rudakov to read, then he could in some way scrub his conscience clean. Escape was an absolution, a few fleeting hours of the hair shirt and the whip. Holly had thought that escape would purge him of the responsibility for the man who would be shot at Yavas. Bloody naïve. Escape should have been a symphony of electric excitement, it should have been a dream of fresh flowers and springtime. Escape was a body draped in wet clothes, without heat, without food, without hope. . . .

Without hope, Holly?

Lying on the floor of the hut he believed that he knew why men bent the knee and turned the cheek in the camp.

They had managed nothing, nothing that was worthwhile. They had exchanged one prison for another. He almost yearned for the bunk in Hut 2, he almost wished to hear the dragging of the main gate shut behind him. God, Holly, bloody beaten, and not out of the bloody place eighteen hours. Is that all you're worth? Eighteen bloody hours. . . . And this was only the be-

ginning, only the first short footstep. Barely out of sight of the
camp, barely beyond the range of the lights set above the high
wooden fence, a thousand miles to travel.

"We have to have a fire, Holly. . . ."

A fire meant smoke, and smoke meant a trail, and a trail
meant capture.

"No."

"We have to warm ourselves. We have to dry our clothes."

"If you want a fire then you walk back along the track to
Barashevo. All the way to Barashevo and the fire in Hut 2.
That's where the bloody fire is."

Holly listened to his own words, heard their spite. He was
not willing to mitigate it.

"Why did you come out?"

They would have to walk through the night. They must be
alert for the blocks and cordons. Out beyond the short snow
horizon an army would be mobilized. They had to sleep through
the day's hours, they had to rest. God, he wished that he had
come alone. Adimov had said that they no longer needed each
other. But they were bound together, bound by a chain of
dependence.

"Because to stay there is to be defeated. To accept their
rule is to be beaten."

"That's shit."

"No one has shown you another color, Adimov, you only
know the color of the *Dubrovlag*. If you stay there you make
it easy for them."

There was a laugh from Adimov that veered to hysteria.

"The camps are a part of us, a part of Russia. Can we beat
that? Adimov and Holly can run away from Camp 3, and that
helps to beat the camps. That's shit, Holly."

"We have to do it for ourselves. . . ."

He remembered the hut of the Commandant that had burned.
He remembered the reinforcement platoon that had come to
replace the guards taken to the hospital beds. He remembered
the wail of the siren at his back. We have to do it for ourselves.
And each hour of the day, each day of the year a million men
rotted in the camps, and a million men had not found the way
to win . . . Christ, what an arrogance, Holly. What a conceit.
A million men do not fight, and yet to Holly the answer of
combat is crystal clear.

"If they take you back ... ?"

"It will still have been worth it."

"We split at Gorki. I go to Moscow."

"When we get to Gorki I decide where I go."

"We have to have a fire."

"No."

Adimov sighed, slumped back again to the floor. "You'll kill us without a fire."

"No."

For a long time Yuri Rudakov had sat in his office pondering the letter. The single sheet of paper was locked away now, secure in the inner drawer of his safe. He had shouted at his orderly that he wanted to be left alone.

The dilemma tore at the peace of his mind.

Outside his window was the howl of a helicopter landing. Impossible to think with the battering noise of the engine piercing the window of his room. He must go home, back to Elena. His head shook slowly, imperceptibly.

Was the innocence of a *zek* a question that should absorb him? Had innocence ever played a part in determining punishment?

He was in a pit, a dark and stinking hole. His hands could not reach the rim of the sides. If the letter were suppressed a man who was innocent would die. If he admitted to the letter then the bright career of Captain Yuri Rudakov was a mess of broken china on the floor. This was how Holly had repaid him. The bastard should have been grateful. Bastard, Holly....

He walked out of the office and to his jeep. They were loading a searchlight through the open doorway of the helicopter. They would fly through the night. There would be no refuge from the dogs and searchers and helicopters. They would have him back. And when he was returned, with his wrists manacled, then the letter written by Michael Holly would be snug in the safe. He surged away in his jeep and drove recklessly over the ice-covered road to his bungalow.

Inside the living room of his home he opened his soul to Elena. Never before had he felt such desperation and uncertainty. He stood with his back to the log fire, and she sat pretty and blonde and clean in her chair. He talked of the letter and of a man in the condemned cell at Yavas. He talked of the prize that had been so nearly gained should Michael Holly have broken in interrogation. He talk:d of the disgrace of failure that would shower on him.

"You must not interfere with the man at Yavas," Elena said quietly, and her cheeks were smooth and rosy from the fire's heat.

"Then an innocent man dies."

She laughed shrilly. "And he would be the first?"

Rudakov knelt beside her chair, and his arms were around her neck, and his head was hard against her breast, and through the thin wool of her jersey she felt the panting of his breathing. Neither looked up, nor broke away from each other, as the helicopter shuddered away over the roof of their bungalow to resume its search.

There were nail holes in the tin walls of the hut, and through them Adimov could see that the light outside was failing. Holly was in deep sleep, his mouth at peace and his forehead unlined. He lay on his side and his body was curled tight, knees against his chest. Adimov stayed very still for a full minute watching the pull and give of Holly's breathing. When he was satisfied he crawled across the floor of the hut to the doorway and eased his shoulder against it to open it a few centimeters.

The snow had stopped. There was a misted haze over the smoothed white ground. Away to his left were the dim outlines of the telegraph poles beside the railway.

Even from the cab of a train a driver would only have a scant impression of the smoke, it would merge in the coming darkness. Better if there had been a hole in the roof through which the smoke could escape because then he could have prepared his fire inside the hut. No hole, and therefore he must make his fire in the doorway. He worked in a scrabbling haste. He pushed what dry hay he could find into a small central heap, and his groping hands found lengths of old planking. He took his matches from his pocket and silently praised himself for having remembered to wrap them in plastic. Five matches only. He lit the first, nestled it against the hay, watched it spark, felt the heave of the wind, watched it splutter, watched it die. Adimov swore. He lit the second and it was a poor match which flamed for a moment and then was gone before he had hidden it in the hay. The third match was alive now and Adimov gazed at the brightness of its flame and tucked it into the hole he had fashioned, and slid strands of hay across it, and cupped his hands to protect the flicker of light from the wind, and blew softly with his mouth.

He built his fire, and when it had caught he stood up and, above the short flames, he held his sheet high so that the smoke bounced against it and was directed through the doorway. He felt the heat against his legs and when the first of the wood embers were alight he nudged his boot against the fire and pushed the center of the burning further into the doorway, and added more wood. Only a portion of the smoke now peeled back into the hut. Adimov dropped again to the ground and dragged at his boots that were wet solid and difficult to bend from his feet, and he stripped off his socks, and placed the boots close to the fire and his socks over them.

The smoke climbed, the flames tickled, the heat breathed over him. Behind Adimov Holly slept on.

Adimov lay on the ground and the warmth of the small flames was like a narcotic. If his boots were dried then, perhaps, he could manage to walk again through the night. He leaned forward to take his feet in his hands and rubbed them and chafed the white skin. The smoke from the wood played at his nostrils, the odor was sapping and softening. There were many thoughts in Adimov's mind . . . of a wife bedded down with cancer . . . of a woman outside a bank and crossing a road . . . of a tobacco store abandoned in a prison hut . . . of punishment cells and loss of privilege . . . of the smile that would break on the pained cheeks of a woman in sickness. He would walk through the night for that smile. And across the hut, Holly's regular breathing comforted Adimov. His hand settled on another plank, dusty and dry in its rottenness, and he twisted to drop it into the heart of the fire, and his head sagged to the crook of his arm.

Holly already sleeping, and Adimov now asleep, and the fire bright and the smoke crawling toward the clouds from the doorway of a farm hut.

Like a hawk that alternately hovers and then surges forward at speed, the helicopter ranged over the map coordinates that had been issued to its crew. The side doors behind the fliers had been removed and on each flank of the helicopter sat a machine gunner with a mounted armament, protected from the cold by electrically heated flying suits. They flew low, the altitude needle bouncing on either side of the 200-meter marker on the dial, and the cloud was a ceiling just above them that the pilot avoided. It was hard for them to see any great distance ahead or sideways because the further they looked then the more obscure was the graying mist of evening and darkness. The men in the helicopter placed little trust in the searchlight with which they were now equipped. Any search for fugitives was enough of a needle in a haystack operation, but to rely on a narrow cone of light when daylight vision had failed was to hope for the miraculous.

Beneath them was the snow carpet, a vanishing expanse which played tricks on the eyes. The railway line was their marker guide, and they had used its dark river slash as a reference to be married to the map that was folded under a plastic cover on the thigh of the second pilot.

The pilot of the helicopter was not required to make his own decisions on areas of search. The earphones in his flying cap carried the instructions that he must follow. He was aware of a growing frustration in the staccato commands that he was given by the signals officer who controlled him from Barashevo.

He was very young, the pilot, fifty days past his twenty-second birthday. He had been born six years after the death of Joseph Stalin but he knew little of the camps that were Stalin's legacy, except that it was necessary to find a suitable place for the minority scum who were parasites on the State. He barely thought of the two men hiding somewhere beneath him. He sought only to find them, before darkness negated his efforts.

The helicopter hovered. The second pilot pointed to the map with a fur-gloved finger, indicated their position. The pilot acknowledged, switched the button for his mouth transmitter.

"Area C . . . east of the track. Nothing. Over. . . ."

There was the stamp of static in his earphones, then the distortion of a mechanical voice.

"Hold your position for further instructions. . . ."

The helicopter yawed, the wind tossed through the thunder of the rotor blades. There were occasional snow flurries across the perspex, and the wipers smeared the pilots' vision ahead. The second pilot did not speak because he knew that the young man beside him was waiting, concentrating, for the new instructions. But he tugged at his arm, and when he had achieved attention he pointed ahead to the blurred horizon where mist and snow were mingled. Something there. Something trickling upward from the vague outline that might be a snow-sheltered hut.

The pilot nodded.

"Command . . . I have smoke, approximately two kilometers, ahead. I think there is a hut there. . . ."

"Give your position." A keener note to the voice in his ears.

"Over the railway track, eight kilometers north from Barashevo."

"Wait."

Didn't the buggers know the light was half gone?

"For your information, we have no record of an occupied dwelling close to the line and approximately ten kilometers north from Barashevo. Investigate."

The engine roared forward, a great camouflaged bird of prey racing from the darkness of the cloud ceiling.

He was dreaming.

The same repetitious dream that led to the same tunnel, the same crevice. Always the setting was the ground floor flat, her clothes on the bedroom floor, her sink in the kitchen filled with unwashed saucepans, her wanting to take in a film when he had arranged to go to Hampton Wick. Piffling excuses for a row. And when he tidied her clothes, and washed her saucepans, and canceled his arrangements, then she would scream at him. His only weapon against her scream was morose quiet, and that was the catalyst that raised her voice. The dream always ended with her in full cry.

The scream had become a thunder. As if when she screamed the very ceiling fell on her. A crashing, heaving fall about her as she screamed.

Holly woke.

As he opened his eyes, the scream was cut. Not the thunder.

Thunder filled the hut, and smoke too, and there was a spread of light across the doorway of the hut. Short stabs of light.

Bastard helicopter.

Between Holly and the fire, Adimov sat confused.

"You lit a fire, you lit a bloody fire."

"I was cold. . . ." The defense of a trapped child.

"You've brought the helicopter."

The flames were fanned by the down blast, singed his face as he charged the doorway with Adimov following. Through the barrier of flame, through a hiss of fire. He felt the down draft of the rotors and his forage cap was torn from his head and billowed away in cartwheels toward the hiding place of the knife.

The helicopter coming down, seeking to squash him as a toad would a spider.

"My boots . . . my socks . . . they're in the hut. . . ." Adimov was holding back, trying to wrench himself clear of Holly's hold. Knowing the futility of what he did, Holly bent his back and worked Adimov's arms around his neck. With his own hands he pulled up Adimov around his hips. Holly giving Adimov a piggyback ride, as if they were part of a children's carnival. He looked up at the blackness of the helicopter's belly, just once he looked up. He reached the railway track, and where the snow was thinly spread he was able to muster the imitation of a run. A slow trot.

God, he was making good sport for them. A man running with his fellow on his back, and in pursuit was a helicopter with a ground-speed capability of 175 kph. Will they shoot? No warning if they fire. Don't look up, Holly . . . get it over, you bastards. He thought of Angela, crying in the flat. He thought of Millet, laughing as he went from his seat to go back to the bar. He thought of two old people in a terraced house at Hampton Wick, who would draw their curtains and put a kettle on the stove and weep only when they were ready to give each other strength. . . .

Get it over, you bastards. . . .

Above the thunder came the shrill crack of the gunfire.

Holly saw the pattern line of impact in front of him, he heard the singing ricochets from the chipstones. No man can run into gunfire . . . there was a man who ran at the wire . . . God, he wanted to live, and his legs refused him.

He stood still on the track and released his grip, and Adimov slid to the snow beside him. The helicopter settled gingerly down avoiding the telephone wires. A searchlight played in their faces.

"I understand about the fire, friend." Holly spoke from the side of his mouth. "Thank you for what you have done. . . ."

Adimov reached up and took Holly's hand, as if by that action he gave himself protection. Holly looked steadily into the searchlight beam. If he cowered then they might shoot. He wanted to live. To live was to be in Hut 2, to be alive was to exist behind the wire of Camp 3. He thought of Rudakov, he thought of a letter that he had written, he thought of a man in a cell at Yavas.

He pulled Adimov to his feet.

Holly put his hands on his head. He walked upright, surely, toward the helicopter.

The *zeks* were straddled in the no-man's-land between the factory and the living zone when the helicopter landed in the vehicle park. Burdened by the presence of the MVD colonel in his corridors and office, Kypov had thrown himself with his old energy into the detail of the running of the camp. If prisoners were on the move then he would be there to watch. It was his skin that would be peeled if there was future slackness. Let the men watch, Kypov had determined, let them see the degradation of the returned fugitives.

The intention was based on good sense. It went unfulfilled.

The rotor blades died, circled slowly, came to rest. The parking area was lit by headlights. Uniformed men, some straining behind taut dog leashes, ran forward.

Kypov saw Holly jump down from the helicopter.

All the *zeks* saw him.

All the guards saw him.

He jumped easily, landed as if on the balls of his feet. The helicopter crew had not come prepared from Saransk, they had carried no handcuffs, and Holly's wrists were free. Holly turned back to the helicopter doorway and he reached out with his arms and steadied and then caught Adimov who was propelled out by a boot. All the *zeks* saw the whiteness of Adimov's feet. The guards closed round Holly. Like a bobbing twig on a fast stream his head alone was visible among them, held high.

Kypov elbowed his way past the *zeks* and the guards. A swagger-stick was in his hand. He split open the cordon round Holly, and the swagger-stick was raised high in the air and whipped down on Holly's face. The swagger-stick rose and fell, and Adimov screamed from the blows that found his shoulder. All the *zeks* saw the adjutant pull Kypov away with the hesitant force that a subordinate will exercise on his superior. Holly still carried Adimov on his back and there was blood on his cheek, and there were some at the front of the ranks of *zeks* who were to swear that they saw him smile, that they saw his hand lifted in a wave of salute.

Like a tidal flow the anger moaned in the lines of prisoners, splashed and beat across the guards who gave more rein to their dogs and backed away and lifted their rifles to the aim. But the prisoners did not cower before the guns and the dancing dogs.

Poshekhonov said, "He showed no fear. He gave them nothing."

Chernayev said, "The camp has been a new place since he came. He should have been on his knees, and the bugger waved. . . ."

Byrkin said, "He is a leader, born to lead. In battle he would be forward of the frontline troops."

Feldstein said, "He could take men to hell, and he would not care if they did not return."

There was a strange music in Kypov's ears. He heard the catcalls, the jeers, the NCOs' shouts for silence that went unobeyed.

Irina Morozova climbed down from her bunk. She slept on an upper bed, and it was beside the window, so she had a vantage-point from which she could see over the high wooden fence ringing the women's zone. Her movements were deliberate, as if she had been struck a blow, as if she must be careful not to lose her footing. The noise of the helicopter descent had drawn her to the window. She had seen him jump down from the helicopter's door. She had not seen him again. There had only been the flash of his face as he had jumped. She felt a great wound, the misery that comes with the ending of hope.

Chapter 18

Security's surveillance operation had been in place a full week before word of it seeped across central London to the desk belonging to Alan Millet in the East European section at Century.

A chauffeur of the Soviet Trade Delegation, working out of their Highgate office, was the target of attention.

Late on a Monday afternoon, the memorandum requesting basic help reached Alan Millet.

A guarded little memorandum, giving little, telling less.

It was by chance that the contact had been made with the chauffeur. Routine. A leading aircraftman from the Royal Air Force base on the island of Anglesey had actually been idiot enough to write a letter to the Trade Delegation offering information for cash. And what sort of information could an LAC offer from miserable old Anglesey? An RAF station for the Hawk trainer, where once in a blue moon a squadron of Phantoms called in for low-level flying over the Irish Sea. Who would want information about such a stereotyped aircraft? There could hardly be anything in the Hawk's makeup that the Soviets didn't already know. And a fool of an LAC had dipped his nib and written off. The Soviets had sent one of the Delegation chauffeurs on a cheap day excursion from Euston to Holyhead. That was three days after the LAC's letter had been steamed open in the basement room of the post office sorting building at Mount Pleasant. Special Branch had been asked to pull a man off the ferry watch to Ireland to provide the muscle up at the far end of the line. An SB sergeant had phoned in his report while the chauffeur was slogging back to London via Chester, Crew, Stafford and Rugby. The LAC and the chauffeur had met for half an hour and no papers had been exchanged. The LAC's bank manager yielded up reluctantly the details of an overdraft of £672.89, an RAF Special Investigation Branch officer reported that the LAC had recently been on an insubordination charge, and that his wife was pregnant yet again. A boring little creep . . . and SB would probably have been left to handle it in their own sweet way if the LAC hadn't gone sick two days later and made a trip to London and been identified by the watchers at Euston, picked up by the Soviets, taken to lunch in a Wimpy bar and gone for a walk in Regent's Park with the friendly chauffeur. The LAC traveled home to his red bank balance and his bulging wife and his engine maintenance. The chauffeur returned to work and the residential compound in north London. SB in Wales could look after the LAC, security struggled with their manpower problems to maintain a 24-hour surveillance on the chauffeur. Nine men working three eight-hour shifts. Gave the buggers something to do, Millet thought, and about all they were fit for.

They might have elaborated on the memorandum, they might have flashed more images onto the single page of typescript than had been intended by its authors.

Security wanted to know if the chauffeur figured on Century's computer. Was the rank of chauffeur a cover? No major of KGB covert intelligence seemed to give a shit what his title was abroad.

Millet had taken the lift down to the library. A bit archaic, calling it the library. Precious few books there. The central floor area was set with visual display units. He had typed out the chauffeur's name, but got back damn all in return. Nothing on the chauffeur in Century's machines.

There was a silly small smile on Millet's face when he went back to the lift late that Monday afternoon. The button he pressed took the lift past the floor where East European was housed, to the office of the deputy undersecretary.

He stood in front of Maude Frobisher's desk, a suspicious and unhappy owl behind her hornrims.

"I have to see him, Miss Frobisher."

"He's clearing his desk because he has an early engagement this evening."

"I have to see him."

"If you listened to me, Mr. Millet, I said he was clearing his desk."

"I'll go in."

Millet strode past her desk, was confronted by the closed door, hesitated, then knocked. A respectful little tap. Miss Frobisher's displeasure pierced his back. He heard the muffled call. He couldn't help himself, he fingered his tie straight. But it was a bloody good idea.

Nothing wrong with this idea at all.

"I'm at an FCO dinner tonight. Our Lord and Master will be there. I could raise the matter quietly, Millet."

"It's because we've nothing in the bank to pay for Holly at the moment, sir, but we could have. We could get this wretched little driver. Nine times out of ten their operatives have diplomatic immunity, and all we can do is shove them back onto an Aeroflot. But the chauffeur doesn't have diplomatic immunity. We can hold him, we can charge and imprison him. Then we'll have currency to pay for Holly."

"It's not the most imaginative of concepts, going back twice to pee against the same tree trunk. Shouldn't we learn a new trick?"

"I couldn't think of another trick, sir." Millet gazed unhappily across the deputy undersecretary's desk. "I just thought that this way offered us the chance of a positive reaction to Michael Holly's situation."

"Another swap...." The deputy undersecretary tapped his pen cap on the desk top. "It's a plausible program."

"You told me I should not forget him."

"Indeed, I told you that. In fact, I said more than that. I said I'd break your neck if you ever forgot him."

"We're not forgetting him, if we pull the chauffeur in."

"I'm at the FCO tonight for dinner with the Secretary of State, then I'm away for a fortnight. I've an hour and a half before I leave here, so come and see me before I go. Meanwhile, talk to Security. I have to know their attitude before I'll take it any further."

"Is that quite necessary?"

"I've said what I'll do, and I've said what I want from you. I'll be waiting to hear from you, Mr. Millet."

"Does it have your support, sir?"

"You're wasting the limited time that is available to you, Mr. Millet."

* * *

They shook hands. It was nearly dark and the paths in St. James's gleamed from the yellow sodium lights and the slow drizzle of rain. Security had requested that Millet should meet the man in the park.

"Doubtfire's the name."

"I'm Millet. We've met somewhere."

"I'm stuck in a bloody office all day; that's why I suggested we meet here. Nothing spooky, just that I get almost no opportunity of fresh air. I hope you don't mind . . . I gave you a lift back from Hammersmith a few weeks ago, after the Soviet snuffed."

"I remember."

"I bought a couple of buns on the way over, for the ducks. They don't get much to eat in this weather. If you don't mind, we'll walk beside the lake."

"I don't mind where we walk."

At the lakeside among the ducks Doubtfire tore chunks from the buns, kneaded them into crumbs and flung these into the air above the rampage of birds.

They started to walk, and Doubtfire crumpled his bag into a ball and dropped it carefully into a wire rubbish bin.

"What can I do for you, Mr. Millet?"

"You sent in today a request for a search on a Highgate chauffeur. We're quite interested. What I mean is that we're quite interested in any Soviet who's misbehaving at the moment and who is not covered by immunity."

"Why?"

"We think we could benefit from the situation."

"And what the hell does that mean?"

"That if a Soviet without diplomatic immunity were to receive an Official Secrets Act conviction we would benefit from it."

"And you're asking me . . ."

"To pick him up, bring him in."

"It was a request for information, Mr. Millet, not a bloody invitation for your lot to horn in."

"There's no need to be offensive, Mr. Doubtfire."

"It's interference."

"It's a request for a spy to be charged and convicted on the evidence you already hold."

"I'll give you some facts, Mr. Millet, some facts of life.

There's no way this man will be picked up at the present time. From what we've seen of him he's a runaround, he's a nothing, too bloody small. We'll recommend no arrests until our Anglesey boy is a great deal higher up the ladder than a chauffeur contact. If we can nail someone at the top of the pecking order, then there'll be arrests. . . ."

"But anyone high will have immunity. That's the way they work."

"I'll give you another fact, Mr. Millet. Our concern is to prevent Soviet intelligence gathering in the United Kingdom, simple enough brief. We don't give a hoot whether their operatives are in jail here, or bound for home on an Aeroflot. Why do you want a man in jail?"

"We'd like to be in the barter game." Misery in Millet's admission.

"Who's so precious?"

"One of ours."

"So we blow what might be interesting, what might be trivial, to bail you out?"

"That's the request, that you give us a body."

"Is your man important?"

"We want him home. He shouldn't be there."

"Then he shouldn't have been sent."

"That's history. And you playing a pompous shit doesn't rewrite it."

Millet caught at Doubtfire's arm. The path around them was empty. The traffic murmured down the Mall behind the sentry line of trees.

"And he's your field man, Mr. Millet?"

"Christ, and you're fast at seeing the light . . . I'm sorry. He's my field man, and he shouldn't be there, and we want him home, and I have to report to the deputy undersecretary in twenty-five minutes, and my field man has in front of him fourteen years of Strict Regime in a Correctional Labor Colony. That's why I want a chauffeur without immunity charged and convicted."

Doubtfire watched the water rippling around two fighting drakes. He took a handkerchief from his pocket and slowly, loudly, blew his nose, then folded it again and returned it to his trousers. The rainwater ran down his nose.

"Very eloquent, Mr. Millet . . . I'll give you some more of

the facts of life. Such a thing would be above deputy under-secretary and director general level. That's a ministerial matter. If you want to involve the clowns, that's your affair. Foreign Secretary will have to talk to Home Secretary. That's how it will have to be."

"We're supposed to be on the same side and fighting the same enemy, Mr. Doubtfire."

"An interesting concept—we'll just have to see if Home Office and Foreign Office agree."

"Thanks for nothing."

"Not fair, Mr. Millet. For someone who's cocked something rotten, I think we're being rather kind to you. I hope we can reach an agreement through the clowns. I'd hate to think of a man stuck in those camps for fourteen years with nothing to think about but the incompetence of the chappie who sent him."

"You're a right bugger."

"And that's better than being a failure, Mr. Millet."

They parted on the lakeside path, Millet striding fast back toward Century, Doubtfire ambling slowly in the direction of Charing Cross underground station.

Rocking with the motion of a puppet manipulated by uneven lengths of twine, the senior official of the procurator general trailed his damaged foot along the corridor toward his superior's office. The procurator general always worked late into the evening, and his senior official stayed close to the seat of power until the departure of the black limousine from the Ministry's courtyard. The senior official fed from the procurator general's table, and he was not one to leave before every useful crumb had been gobbled.

He was only just in time.

"Yes?"

"I thought you would like to know, Comrade Procurator, that the men who escaped last night from ZhKh 385/3/I have been recaptured . . ."

"That couldn't wait till the morning?"

"It was right that you should know the details at the earliest possible moment, since the escape involves State Security."

"How is State Security involved in that crap pile?"

"One of the prisoners to break out was an Englishman, but of Soviet parentage, and serving fourteen years for espionage."

"A fucking spy was allowed to break out?"

"You will remember I have drawn attention to Major Vasily Kypov's command twice in the past few weeks. Events in that camp have shown a disturbing laxity. I have to report a certain criticism from State Security that a prisoner of such sensitivity should have been able to cut his way out of the camp."

The procurator general's gaze sharpened. "In the face of this criticism, what is the wish of the State Security in relation to the spy?"

"He will be moved."

"Soon?"

"Within a few days, when arrangements have been made."

"And the criticism . . . ?"

"It was sharp."

"The prisoner will be in the punishment cells until he is moved?"

"Of course."

"Thank you."

"Good night, Comrade Procurator, I wish you a safe journey home."

"I'm bored to tears with Intelligence. Do you understand me?"

The Foreign Secretary poked a bony index finger into the shirt front of the deputy undersecretary. They stood beside a curtained window away from the table where a dozen guests sat among brandy glasses and cigar smoke.

"Nevertheless I wanted to bring the matter to your attention before my departure for Washington."

"You've let yourself down, man, you know that. Something pressing, you said, and I've a damned table full of people to look after. You reckon this is pressing? Eh? You're obsessed with Intelligence. You forget other people are not."

The Foreign Secretary looked with longing over the shoulder of the deputy undersecretary toward his guests, the decanter, their conversation.

"So what do you want from me?"

"Only some sort of commitment."

"Commitment to what?"

"To argue our corner with Security."

"And supposing what you call 'our corner' diverges from policy, the policy of Her Majesty's Government."

"I don't understand you, sir."

"Straightforward, I would have thought . . . Intelligence is covert warfare. I am responsible for gathering Intelligence, I am also responsible for diplomacy. Diplomacy is not a battle-ground, it is an exercise in building bridges of trust."

"I don't understand you, sir."

"Policy accepted by Cabinet is currently directed toward a renewal of détente between our side and the Soviets, in words of one syllable. If I support the dredging into custody of a nondescript Trade Delegation chauffeur and his subsequent conviction in a blare of publicity, then I can hardly be accused of pursuing a policy of détente with enthusiasm. Charge this driver and I'll lose the Parliamentary delegation to Moscow next week. Stands to reason that they have to retaliate. . . . What's the name of this fellow you want back? Remind me."

"Michael Holly. He's there because of our mistake, Foreign Secretary."

"Because of your department's mistake, I should ride across HMG policy?"

"We would greatly appreciate it if you would argue our corner with Security."

"You're not prepared to forget about this young man, this Michael Holly?"

"I said to the desk officer who dispatched him that if he ever forgot about Michael Holly I'd break his neck."

With an involuntary and sharp little movement, the Foreign Secretary stepped back as if suddenly intimidated. He gazed into the face of the deputy undersecretary but met only the clear hazel eyes, unblinking and without emotion. A slow smile spread across the Foreign Secretary's mouth.

"I believe you're bullying me, Deputy Undersecretary."

"Sir?"

"I'll argue your corner."

"Thank you, sir."

"If you hadn't used that one word, I would never have agreed. Whenever the time comes I would like to meet this Holly who so stirred the conscience of the Service."

"If you're sure you wouldn't be bored, sir."

They laughed together, in quiet conspiracy. And the pointed fingers of the Foreign Secretary tapped on the deputy undersecretary's shoulder in happy rhythm at the secrecy of their joke.

Millet was a lonely passenger off the last train.

It was more than an hour since the deputy undersecretary had telephoned through to the East European desk where Millet had waited throughout the evening in the company of the night staff. Alan Millet was to prepare a paper that would go to Foreign and Commonwealth. And the conclusion was better than DUS had thought possible. Not all victory, of course; a bit of give and take. Security would be offered complete freedom to decide when any pickup might be effected.

And, of course, they might not bite. Taking everything for granted, Millet reckoned. There was nothing to say the Soviets wanted a creepy chauffeur back so badly that they would be prepared to wipe out Alan Millet's failure. But it was a beginning, it was a journey started.

Late at night, past midnight, and Alan Millet was heading for the one person that he must tell of his efforts for Michael Holly's release.

He paused in front of the door. What the hell was he doing there? Smearing his failure around the southwest London suburbs. Out of his mind he must have been, to believe that he could spread that failure and then drape over it a boast of his success. Loud, lively music cascaded over him, dancing music. Perhaps his nerve would not hold against the barrage of noise—shouting, singing, movement and happiness. Perhaps he would walk away, find a telephone booth and ring for a minicab home. The door mocked him. He was cold, he was wet, he was part of a faraway camp. That camp had no place in the life blood of a party. The door shut out the camp. His fingers found the bell button and pressed.

A young man opened the door, glass in hand. A young man who was a little drunk and trying to relate to an intruder in a wet raincoat standing in the doorway.

"Yes?"

"I've come to see Angela."

His eyebrows flickered upward, surprised. He giggled. "She's a bit busy . . ."

Millet pushed his way past the young man. He stepped over the legs of a couple twined on the floor in the corridor. He came to the entrance of the living room, stared into the hushed light, winced at the noise, searched for the face of the woman he must speak with.

"Did you bring a bottle, squire . . . ?" The young man shouted behind him.

He might have been black, he might have had the plague. The dancers watched him, the couples on the floor watched him, those on the sofa watched him. The music boomed at his ears. He felt the dampness in his shoes, he felt the wetness of his trouser legs. The heat and the smoke were suffocating.

He couldn't see her. Among all the faces grinning at him as if he was a zoo freak, he could not find her.

He turned back to the young man who had opened the door to him. "I have to speak to Angela."

Again the giggle. "I said she was busy."

"Get her," Alan Millet said. He'd pissed about long enough with these idiots.

"Who the bloody hell do you think you are, bloody secret police . . . ?"

"Get her."

Millet's voice slashed the shriek of the young man's laughter.

"Please yourself, squire."

The young man went to the bedroom door, closed. He knocked lightly and when it opened an inch he whispered into the crack. Millet couldn't hear what he said against the force of the record player. The dancers now swirled around him, ignoring him. He was isolated from these people, cocooned from them, kept apart by the wire of a camp across a continent, like a membrane. What did these shits know of a man in a strict regime Correctional Labor Colony. What did any man know? What did Alan Millet know?

The door opened. She came out, her face expectant and puzzled and her fingers fiddling with the blouse buttons. Millet was sweating in the damp closeness of his raincoat. He thought he might be sick. An unstubbed cigarette burned smoke into his nose. She hadn't tucked her blouse into her jeans. She was barefoot. Her hair fell half across her face.

She saw Millet. She blinked at him, confused.

"What are you doing here?"

"I had to see you."

"What about?"

The dancers veered between them. A man with a loose beard stood behind her in the doorway, trying to play protector, his hand resting confidently on her shoulder. He looked annoyed.

"About Michael Holly."

"You bloody promised . . . you promised you'd never come again . . . it's my birthday, you know that . . . you're barging in on my birthday. . . ."

"I have to talk to you about Holly."

The young man behind Millet said, "You're out of turn, squire."

No dancing now. The living room and the corridor to the bedroom door were a cockpit. Conflict, anger, rising across the space between Millet and Angela.

"Quit while you're in one piece," the man behind her said.

She brushed away the hand on her shoulder, shrugged helplessly and pushed back her hair. She came to Millet and took his hand and led him through an aisle of hostility into the kitchen. She jerked with her thumb toward the door for those in there to leave. She kicked the door shut behind the last of them.

"You'd better take your coat off. Will you drink something?"

"I won't, thank you."

She pulled out a kitchen chair, slid it toward Millet, and perched herself on a stool.

"What must you talk to me about?"

Better if he had never come. Better if he had turned away at the door. Better if he had not seen the small reddened swell at her neck.

"I came to talk about Holly."

"I'm not involved with Michael Holly."

"I came to tell you what was happening about Holly, what we hope will happen."

"It's not my business what happens to Michael Holly."

"I came to say that we hope we can free him, not immediately, not tomorrow . . . but we hope it will be soon."

"You haven't been listening, Mr. Millet. We were divorced. Our lives have separated."

The tiredness billowed through Millet. He started to unbutton his raincoat.

"I just thought you'd want to know."

"You came here just to tell me that?"

"For Christ's sake. . . ." Millet's hand hit the table. The food bowls jarred, a glass wobbled above a narrow stem. "I thought it might mean something. I thought . . . I'm sorry."

He stood up and started for the door.

She waved him back to the chair. The tears were bright on her cheeks.

"You couldn't understand, Mr. Millet."

"I thought you'd want to know."

"I shall never see Holly again. I didn't want that. Holly said it. Holly said I would never see him again. Listen to me, Mr. Millet. Don't interrupt. . . ."

Her head was in her hands and she spoke through the fingers that spread across her face.

"I won't interrupt."

"I went to the divorce hearing. I don't know why I went. I suppose a woman has a tidy mind and wants to see something through, see it settled and final. I was to have gone with a friend, but she cried off in the morning, rang me just before I was due to leave the apartment. I went on my own. I'd never thought he'd be there, and if I'd considered for a moment that he would be there, then I'd never have gone myself. If you didn't realize, Mr. Millet, it's a pretty stark occasion. The court was just about empty, and there were only the two of us in the public pit. Two of us, and we sat at opposite ends of a great long bench, and there was a mile of cold polished wood between us. It doesn't last long, it's an express job—that way it's cheap—and we never looked at each other all the time that the bloody lawyers droned away. I didn't take in a word that was said. It was so stupid; I was at my own divorce hearing and all I wanted to do was to run the length of that bench and hold onto him, hold him and say that it was ridiculous, that it wasn't happening to us, and that we should go home. We never looked at each other, not once. I didn't look at him, I just loved him. I loved him, Mr. Millet, loved him with a mile of polished bloody wood between us. At the end, he stood up and I stood up, and he went out fast and I went slowly. I walked out of the Court, and I was a free woman and I was blubbering like a baby. I don't know why, I don't usually do it, I went across the Strand and into the first pub I saw, and I went up

to the bar and ordered a double something, and I found a seat
and sat down. I sat down next to Holly. Shit . . . can you see
that, Mr. Millet? I sat down next to him. He was crying. I
suppose that's why there was a seat beside him in the pub, I
mean, nobody wants to sit next to a grown man who is crying.
And we couldn't help each other. We just sat there, and sipped
our drinks, and bloody cried. And it was too late . . . too late
for both of us. He went and bought me a pork pie, a horrible
thing, all fatty, and he said that he had never cried in his life
before, at least not since he was a small child. He held my
hand and he told me that nobody would ever see him cry again.
He said that if he ever saw me again, I would make him cry.
All the time that he spoke he held my hand, he squeezed it so
that it hurt first and then was white and numbed. Something
in him died that day, Mr. Millet. It wasn't all my fault, you
know. He killed it himself, but something died. Perhaps it was
the will to love that died. Perhaps it was the dependence on
another living and breathing soul that died. If he comes home
or if he stays in the place where he is now, still that death will
be final. I could never meet him again, I could never bear to
see him cry again. It's taken me three years to try to lose the
memory of Holly weeping. I'll never lose it, Mr. Millet. Holly
will never cry again, he'll never love again. . . . Suddenly he
stood up, and his beer wasn't finished and his pie wasn't eaten
and he wiped his sleeve across his face as if nobody was looking
and half the pub was, and he waved to me as if we'd only
known each other for half an hour and he walked out through
the door. So you see, Mr. Millet, Holly is none of my business.
The man that I knew is dead, dead in his tears."

Millet stood up.

"I hope I haven't spoiled your party."

Chapter 19

"What was it worth?" Mikk Laas asked.

"It was worth nothing," Holly said.

"Does freedom have a rare taste?"

"For me it had nothing."

"To have gone through the wire you must have believed in that freedom?"

"And not found it."

"On the outside, you saw people?"

"Not until the helicopter came."

"You saw the face of no man who was free?"

"The first face I saw was that of the helicopter marksman."

"Was it luck that beat you?"

"It was inevitable."

"The escape was wasted?"

"It was lunatic, we were exhausted, we were hungry, we had nowhere to go," Holly said bitterly. "I hadn't thought it out. I hadn't reckoned on the tiredness. I told Adimov that I had thought I would find an excitement when we were clear of the wire, a great breath of fresh excitement, and I felt nothing. Once you hear the siren there is no freedom. Out of the little camp and into the big camp, that's what they say, isn't it? Near my country is Ireland, they have a sport there that they call 'coursing.' They release a hare and the fastest dogs they have chase it. For the hare there is a moment of something like freedom because it can run. But the dogs are faster. The hare has only a moment of freedom, and its freedom is spent with the blood spurting in its heart. That's not freedom, Mikk Laas."

"Others before you have tried, others after you will try."

"Then they're better men."

"And now you will bend to them?"

"They drag it out of you, don't they? They drag the guts and bowels out of you. You start by trying to fight. You run against a wall, you beat your head against their bricks. You kick, you punch the wall, but you cannot hurt the bricks. I've tried...."

"How have you tried?"

Michael Holly looked across the narrow width of the SHIzo cell toward the old Estonian. They had not talked the previous evening, but morning now, the morning after recapture, and he could talk. But he felt an impatience at the veteran's bleak questions. He felt the requirement of justification.

"I burned down the Commandant's hut."

"You did that?" Mikk Laas nodded, an academic's approval.

"I did that. I poisoned the garrison water supply."

"That too?"

"I escaped, I cut through their bloody wire."

"And now you will bend to them?"

"I... I don't know...."

"Have you achieved anything by the burning, the poisoning, the escape? Anything of value?"

"You tell me."

"Time alone will tell you. Perhaps you have lit some fire in the camp."

"Did I have the right to do those things, Mikk Laas?" He thought of a man taken to Yavas to face capital trial, a man whom he had never seen.

"When we were last together you spoke of reprisal, I remember. If at the end, Michael Holly, you have won a victory then you were justified. If now you bend the knee to them, then you have no right to do those things."

"Thank you, Mikk Laas."

An incredible old man. In the camps from before the time Holly was born. An old fighter, an old idiot, who did not know when to bend to them. Not a spare pinch of flesh on his body, and he had strength to give away. He had never met a man like Mikk Laas before. He had to travel a thousand miles inside the frontiers of the big camp to find him. Holly squeezed the frail fingers in affection.

A warder unbolted the door of the cell and dumped inside

a bucket and a broom of bound twigs. They should slop out
and clean the cell, and after that Mikk Laas would go to the
workshop and Michael Holly would be taken to the office of
the political officer. The door slammed shut.

Holly was on his knees picking up the dirt between his
forefinger and thumb.

"There is a man at Yavas who will die because I poisoned
the water."

"Only a victory can balance that man's life."

An old voice, a voice that shuffled between the close walls
of the cell.

It is not easy to administer with success the daily life of an
organism as complex as a prison camp.

The traditional way, the way of the Commandants of the
Dubrovlag, is the iron-gloved routine. In theory the weight of
repression and penalty is sufficient to make the inmates accept
their demilife behind the fences. For a thousand days, or ten
thousand days, the tough way will insure a pliability from the
zeks. Short of food, short of rest, short of dignity, the prisoners
will seek the one course that will permit their survival. They
will strive above all to live. But one day, they refuse to lie
down before the steamroller wheel of camp routine. From the
offices of senior officials of the Ministry of Interior in far away
and comfortable Moscow right down to the stink of the living
huts in the camps, there is no known science to explain those
few and long separated moments when the prisoners' tolerance
of their condition is overwhelmed.

At the camp with the designated title of ZhKh 385/3/I that
one day—the day that follows a thousand, the day that follows
ten thousand—was a Tuesday in the last week of February.

A report now rests in the basement filing library of the
Ministry of the Interior, compiled from laborious interviews
with Vasily Kypov, Yuri Rudakov, an assortment of officers
and NCOs under their command, trusties from Internal Order,
and senior warders. The report seeks to explain the events that
were linked, in Zone I of Camp 3, on a Tuesday in the last
week of the month of February, with the name of Michael
Holly.

Michael Holly, however, cannot be directly related to the

initial action on that Tuesday morning—that point was to be most precisely made by the Ministry's senior official who was to be the final author and arbiter of the report. Michael Holly was isolated in the SHIzo punishment block with only a senile Estonian for company. But his name was spoken often on that Tuesday morning. Men conjured with that name, took it as a faith's cross, whispered it as a healing herb. Around the camp was a low wooden fence, and then a killing zone, and then two fences of barbed wire, and then a high wooden fence. Around the camp were watchtowers, guards, guns, dogs. Around the camp was an impasse of snow emptiness. Behind those barriers, in spite of those barriers, a defiance was born. On that Tuesday morning an anger fluttered, a spirit tickled and, in ways that could sometimes be touched and that were at other moments intangible, the name of Michael Holly grasped at the consciousness of the prisoners. There are many errors in the report of the Ministry of the Interior, but when the heavy typewritten sheets point to the central position of Michael Holly they do not lie.

On that Tuesday morning from his bunk in Hut 2, Anatoly Feldstein declared that he had begun a hunger strike.

When the body is semi-starved, when the diet provides sufficient calories and protein only to keep the prisoner as a working creature, then a hunger strike is no easy weapon for a man to take with his fist.

Feldstein lay on his mattress and the hut around him was quiet. All the *zeks* had gone for exercise and breakfast, and then for roll call before the march to the factory zone. The trusty was the last who had spoken to him, sworn at him, cursed him.

Not an easy weapon to hold, the self-denial of food. But he had seen a man jump down from the cabin of a helicopter on the previous evening, a man who had crawled in the snow to slice through the strands of wire that bound them all to the compound, a man who had run before the hunting troops with the scream of the siren betraying his action, a man who had carried his friend, a man who had managed to wave to the *zeks* who watched his homecoming.

He had seen a man who had fought back.

Bukovsky, Orlov, Scharansky, Kuznetsov—they were in the folklore of the dissident fighters. Bukovsky had led the hunger strike at Perm 35. Orlov, who was in Perm 37 and shadowed even in the camp by two KGB officers, alternated between hunger strike and the SHIzo punishment cell. Scharansky, while in the hard Christopol jail, had organized a ten-day strike in solidarity with "the Peoples struggling against Russian-Soviet Imperialism and Colonialism." Kuznetsov had not compromised even under the sentence of death. They were the cream, they were the leaders who were known beyond the borders of their country. Anatoly Feldstein was a minnow in their company.

He had been serving out his time, whiling away the months of his captivity. He had been in the SHIzo just once, for failing to remove his cap in the presence of an officer. He had dreamed of an exile in the west. The Englishman had nudged his guilt. Where before he had seen no value in confrontation, he now saw its worth. When he had passed the *samizdat* writings in Moscow he had known of the penalties, he had told Michael Holly that he knew of them. Now, as he lay on his mattress, he thought of the further penalties that he would face.

Let the bastards come. When you have nothing, what then can be taken from you? This was his gesture. . . .

Four men around the bunk. Two warders with truncheons drawn, the trusty who had brought them, Captain Yuri Rudakov because Feldstein was political.

"Get up, you little Jew shit," from the first warder.

"Off your ass before we kick you off," from the second warder.

"Why are you not at roll call, Feldstein?" A coldness from Rudakov.

Words hammering around Feldstein's ears, and he felt small and vulnerable and beneath the swing of their fists and truncheons he waited for the blows.

"I declare a hunger strike in protest against the violation of my constitutional rights. . . ."

"It's not like you to be stupid, Feldstein. . . ."

The boy saw the beginning of puzzlement on Rudakov's forehead, as if the political officer were weighted by another preoccupation.

"In addition to a hunger strike I declare a work strike in

protest against the labor conditions of the camp, which are illegal under Soviet law because they contravene Soviet safety standards."

"In five minutes you'll be off that bed and on roll call and that's generous. If you want to diet, that's your business. You can diet to death for all I bloody care."

"I declare a hunger strike, I declare a work strike."

He saw the political officer step back. Rudakov's fingers snapped in annoyance.

"I'm going back to my office. In five minutes Feldstein will be in the compound."

Above him he saw white hands that stroked the length of their truncheons.

The officers did not notice a change of mood among the *zeks* lined in front of them to hear the names called. They were familiar only with docility. If the *zeks* stood straighter in their lines, if their eyes gazed more questioningly around them, if they had shed a little of their apathy, it was lost on the men in uniform.

On that Tuesday morning the *zeks* missed nothing.

They saw the captain of KGB stamp out from Hut 2, the annoyance large on his face. From line to line the whisper spread that Feldstein, who was a political, had declared a hunger strike. The story of this small act of rebellion slipped from tongue to ear in a quiet murmur. Rebellion frightened some, excited others, but no man could be indifferent to it. A political on hunger strike, and two days before that a pair of men had cut their way out through the wire, and two weeks before that the guards' barracks had been struck by dysentery, and a week before that the office of the Commandant had been razed to the ground. A pulse ran along the lines.

A name called and a name answered. A tedious rhythm of shout and countershout.

Mamarev sensed the difference. He, and all the pervert prisoners who lived in the split world between captor and captive, could sense the small current of aggression that flowed steadily, imperceptibly, through the ranks of the prisoners. He felt a fear in his own body, he felt the pull of anticipation around him.

Every man in the compound heard Feldstein's shout.

In front of the parade, from the doorway of Hut 2, Anatoly Feldstein was pitched out into the snow.

A boot swung, a truncheon lashed.

"I declare a hunger strike, I protest against the violation of my constitutional rights. . . ."

A boot thudded his voice to a whimper, a truncheon smacked him flat to the ground.

"I declare a work strike against illegal safety standards. . . ."

His head was deep in snow, his hands protected his genitals. He screamed the high-flung shriek of pain. As if a color sergeant had howled a command at a squad of conscripts, so the *zeks* reacted, stiffened, stood erect.

Of course, they had seen pain before. Each man of eight hundred had known for himself what it was to be hit. On a thousand days, on ten thousand days, they would have turned the cheek, dropped the eye.

Not on this Tuesday morning.

A growl ran through the lines, something heavy with menace.

The two warders picked Feldstein up under his arms and dragged him across the snow so that his hanging legs made a tramline track between the imprint of their own boots. The growl had turned to a whistle. The whistle of the supporters who watch the home team defeated in the Lenin stadium. A whistle of derision. The warders took Feldstein to the edge of the rear rank, dropped him, scuttled back. Feldstein was not wearing his boots, his socks were black with the wet from the snow. He was bent double, the whistling sang in his ears. He wore no gloves, and blue tinged the fingers that were still tight around his groin.

"Call the names." The adjutant shouted to his sergeant, and there was the smear of nervousness in his eyes.

"Chernayev. . . ."

The shout soared over the spilling noise of the whistle.

Afterward he could not say why he took the action that he did. He had been seventeen years in the camps, seventeen years of preventive detention from the only trade that he knew, the work of thieving. He had been a model prisoner through the years of his second term. He had offended nobody. A docile and anonymous creature who had merged into the life of the camp. He heard his name called, listened as if he were a stranger to the shout. No answer slipped his tongue. His mind was far distanced. He thought of the perimeter path, he thought of evening when the *zeks* had gathered in their huts, he thought of walking with Michael Holly beside the killing zone. "If everybody says that they cannot be beaten then that will be true." Those were Holly's words, and now Feldstein had joined him hand in hand. Timid Feldstein who hid behind what he believed to be his intellectual superiority. Feldstein who had never known a knife fight. Feldstein who buried himself in books to escape the surroundings of Hut 2. "If everybody says that they cannot be beaten then that will be true."

"Chernayev. . . ."

The repetition of the shout. Between the shoulders of the *zeks* in front he saw the reddening face of the sergeant. It was a caricature of pomposity. He found its fury amusing.

Chernayev sat down.

He sat down in the snow. He felt the wetness seep through the seat of his trousers, tickle against his skin. He was smiling as if a light-headed calm had captured him. It had been so easy, easier than he could ever have believed. He did not think of the truncheons and boots that had struck Feldstein. He thought of nothing but the contentment of sitting in the snow, and the ruddy anger of the sergeant's face. He reached up with his hand and tugged at Byrkin's tunic then pointed to the squeezed mess of slush beside Byrkin's boots. Byrkin responded, Byrkin settled beside him. Chernayev saw Byrkin's chin jut out, take on the gaunt point of a rock's edge.

The whistling had stopped. There was a great quiet clouding the compound. The guards cradled their rifles and looked to their sergeant. The sergeant studied his board with the lists of names, then turned to the adjutant for guidance. The adjutant clasped and unclasped his fingers behind his back and stared at the window of the Commandant's office in administration as if from the steamed panes of glass might come salvation.

The gate of the compound opened. Just a few feet, sufficient to allow the passage of a prisoner who wore manacles on his wrists, and two warders who gripped his arms. The prisoner was being taken from the SHIzo punishment block to the administration building.

Chernayev saw Michael Holly and his escort, Byrkin too. They watched him as he walked, eyes straight ahead, before he was lost to their view behind the mass of legs.

Poshekhonov saw Michael Holly. Poshekhonov who was the survivor, who had slept in a death cell, who now had the bunk beside the stove in Hut 2. He had never joined the company of the whiners and dissenters. Lucky to be alive, wasn't he? He had faced the executioner's bullet, and any life was better than a dawn death in a prison yard. He intended to walk out through those prison gates one day and collect the suit he had been wearing at the time of his arrest—it wouldn't fit him well, it would be a give away at every station between Barashevo and the Black Sea—and take his railway warrant and go home to dream of a bank account in Zürich gathering interest and dust. He'd find a way to get there. Bloody well swim the Black Sea if he had to. Poshekhonov was a survivor. That's what he had told Holly, told him that his weapon was the humor that won him small victories. And Holly had dismissed him. "Little victories win nothing. . . ." Extraordinary, that Chernayev had sat down. Sensible old goat, he'd always reckoned Chernayev. Byrkin, well Byrkin was different—half mad, wasn't he? Everyone knew that Byrkin was touched. And who wouldn't be if they'd been locked in a cabin below the waterline with the bombs falling. "Little victories win nothing. . . ." Feldstein on hunger strike, Chernayev sitting down, Byrkin following him, that wasn't a little victory, only an inconvenience. But if the whole of Hut 2 sat down, what then? Perhaps it would be a big victory if the whole of Hut 2 sat in the snow. He looked to the man on the right of him, who was described as a "parasite to society," and saw that his gaze was questioned. He looked to the man on the left, who was described as a "hooligan," and saw that his action was waited for. You're not mad, are you, Poshekhonov? You're not going to play crazy? If the whole of Hut 2 were to sit down. . . .

The prison diet had not entirely stripped away his fat. Poshekhonov made a faintly ridiculous sight as he rolled down onto his buttocks.

And the *zek* on his right followed him, and the *zek* on his left.

First the fraud, then the parasite, then the hooligan.

And like a line of tin soldiers who will keel over when one is pushed, the *zeks* of Hut 2 sat down.

For a moment only Mamarev was standing, and he looked hard at the adjutant and saw only indecision, then he too lowered himself to the snow.

The adjutant pursed his cold-chapped lips, wet them with his tongue. Behind five ranks of standing prisoners a whole line was sinking, dropping from his sight.

"Request Major Kypov to come here, and suggest to him that his attendance is immediate."

The adjutant rasped the instruction to an NCO, who turned and ran toward the administration building.

It was a familiar place, almost a place that was home.

As Holly was led inside Yuri Rudakov's office he felt the warmth worm beneath his clothes. He looked warily at Rudakov while the warder's keys unfastened his manacles. He saw on the political officer's face the smile of studied friendship.

"Sit down."

"Thank you."

"You have suffered no injury during your . . . your expedition?"

"There is no heating in the SHIzo, my clothes are still wet."

"Of course. Put your tunic on the radiator, your socks too."

"Thank you."

Holly laid his tunic on the hot pipes and the worn socks beside them and the heat tingled his fingers.

"Your shirt, your trousers?"

"They're all right. Thank you again."

"Coffee? Something to eat?"

"No, thank you."

Yuri Rudakov rested his elbows on the desk, balanced his chin against his hands. They could have been friends, they might have been companions. Two educated young men. Their smells divided them—Rudakov rich with the talc from his bathroom, Holly ripe with the sweat stains from his flight. Their cheeks separated them—Rudakov close shaven, Holly raw with a week's stubble.

"I would not have credited that you could have been so crass, so stupid," Rudakov said. "You believed in the possi-

bility of escape, Holly. You believed so strongly in the possibility of running clear that you even sent me a little letter.
That showed a touching faith in your ability to leave us." There
seemed a mocking serenity in Rudakov. That was his outward
armor. There were two paths he could take. There was friendship, there was the fist. His choice was based not on kindness
but on expediency. "You have confessed to murder. You make
a confession and at the same time you run away like a truant
from a teacher. Did no one ever tell you how many get clear
from the *Dubrovlag?* You know, Holly, down the road is Camp
5 where we keep the foreigners—addicts, currency offenders,
drunks, religious maniacs—never has one of them done anything as stupid as to try to break out. For a foreigner it is
impossible. . . ."

"What are you going to do?"

"Why should I do anything, Holly? It is on you that we
wait."

"No riddles, please. You don't sleep when you're running,
nor when you're on a concrete floor."

"If I do not have your statement then I do not interfere in
the case of a man held at Yavas. If I have your statement then
I take upon myself a different course of action. That is not a
riddle."

"You're a pig, Rudakov, a stinking, lousy pig."

"You don't have to be theatrical, Michael. If you did not
want to meet me you could have stayed in England. If you did
not wish to make a statement to me you could have avoided
introducing excrement in the water supply of the barracks."
There was a change now in Rudakov, a cut of hard steel. "He
was a young boy who died. He was a conscript. He served his
country, he had done no harm to you. You had no right to
murder him."

"What guarantees do you give me?"

"You cannot ask for guarantees, you are owed nothing. You
have to trust me when I say that an innocent man will not die
at Yavas because of what you have done. You have no alternative but to trust me."

Holly looked down at the floor, saw the blisters on the joints
of his toes where the skin had been rubbed away by boots that
were sufficient for the slow shuffle of the prisoner, inadequate

for the gallop of the escaper. He was no longer certain. He had boasted of his strength, and his strength was found out and false. The life and death of a man at Yavas had rotted it.

He could have cried out the name of Mikk Laas, he could have cried for an older fighter's forgiveness.

"You'd better get a sheet of paper," Holly whispered.

Vasily Kypov strode across the compound. He glowered at the front lines that stood in dumb hostile insolence. Relief at his coming lit the face of the adjutant.

He recognized the signs. Any trained and experienced officer would have recognized the signs of approaching mutiny. You catch mutiny early, he had been told that at some long ago staff officers' course, you catch it early and you belt the balls off it. He saw the widely spaced cordon of guards around the lines of prisoners, and the three small groups of warders who huddled together with only their truncheons to sustain them. Too few men, he decided.

He reached the adjutant, but did not concern himself with returning the salute.

"I want every man out of the barracks," Kypov hissed. "And I want the perimeter guard doubled."

"Most of the men who are in reserve are at visitors' reception. . . ."

"Get them here."

"Who is to supervise the visits? There is the searching of visitors. . . ."

"Fuck the visits, fuck the visitors. I want them out."

The *zeks* in the front rank had heard. The adjutant watched the bitter hardening of their faces. Visits were the cornerstone of their lives. Visits were precious.

"Is that wise, Commandant?"

"I will say what is wise."

In a camp of strict regime such as ZhKh 385/3/I, prisoners are entitled by law to two brief and one prolonged visit each year. A brief visit may last up to a maximum of four hours, a prolonged visit may be extended to three days with prisoner and relative sleeping together in small rooms set aside in a secure section of the administration block. Before and after both brief

and prolonged visits, the men and women and children who
have traveled to the camp to see their loved ones are subjected
to a vigorous and painstaking body search.

Weakened by their winter journey, depressed by the surroundings, the relatives on this Tuesday morning sat in the
wooden hut beyond the outer door of the administration building and waited to be strip-searched. The hut was full, the search
cubicles already occupied, when Kypov's order found its destination.

The daughter, aged twelve, of a fifteen-year man was in
one cubicle, her skirt up around her waist, her knickers at her
ankles, feeling the fingers of a wardress pry her open in the
hut for contraband.

A farmer from a collective outside Kazah, and past seventy
years and the father of an army deserter, was in the second
cubicle, with his trousers on the floor and his body bent forward
to expose his anus.

The mother of a thief, who had traveled eight hundred kilometers and made five connections, tipped the contents of her
plastic handbag onto the search table.

The son of an Adventist with four years to serve looked at
the crumbled wreckage of a cake first torn apart and then passed
for inspection.

These people, and those crowding the benches at the side
of the hut, were informed of the order given by the camp
Commandant. They wailed in plaintive union, and the guards
linked arms and jostled them out through the door, back into
the cold and the snow. Prisoners' scum. The women shouted
the loudest. They screamed at the smooth dark surface of the
high wooden fence, they shouted at the young men in their
high watchtowers.

Holly heard the screaming. Cocked his head for a moment,
then ignored the noise of disturbance.

"As a teenager I occasionally went with my father to meetings of the OUN—that is the Organization of Ukrainian Na-
tionalists. I don't remember that I was ever particularly interested
in what I heard there. I thought it was pretty sterile."

"You will have been on their files from that time, Michael,
the files of the Intelligence people."

"I suppose so. When I left school I went to Technical College. I was studying to be an engineer. . . ."

Yuri Rudakov was hunched over his desk, writing in a fast scrawl. It was not easy for him to mask his exhilaration. Holly was waffling, Holly was telling it his own way, in his own time. Rudakov would not interrupt, just write until his arm ached.

Kypov heard the screaming.

The *zeks* in their lines heard the screaming.

The guards who circled the prisoners heard the screaming, and they looked into the burning eyes of many hundreds of men and saw a hatred, and among the conscripts none had seen that loathing so coordinated before.

The detachment doubled into the compound.

A dozen more armed men. Kypov's army was augmented to twenty-five guards from the MVD force, fifteen warders with truncheons, four dog handlers. And he had wire fences behind him, and the watchtowers with their mounted machine guns. He would use the detachment as a wedge to break up the mass of prisoners. He would break the will of one rank, then the second, then the third.

Hut 3 formed the forward line.

"Front rank, form into fives . . . Move! Move, you bastards! . . ."

Kypov might have yelled at a mountain. The front rank stayed solid. Not even the trusties moved, not even the "stoolies." The trusties and "stoolies" had visits.

"Put a dog in, break them up."

The sergeant handler was positioned behind the lines of prisoners. He faced the sitting backs of the men of Hut 2. His dog was king, master of the pack. A black and tawny German shepherd, huge within its long and rough-haired coat, weighing 35 kilos. He slipped the leash at the collar. The dog was trained to attack the *zeks,* taught from the time it had been a puppy. The dog ran forward, low and devastating in its assault. The white teeth buried themselves into Poshekhonov's shoulder.

It was the moment that the dam burst. For two, three brief seconds, the sergeant handler saw his dog worrying at the shoulder of a small, fat prisoner who scrabbled to get clear of the animal's jaws. Then dog and prisoner were engulfed. The *zeks* from either side, the *zeks* who stood to the front, threw themselves upon his dog. Once the sergeant handler thought he heard a yelp of pain. He saw the pounding movement of the *zeks*. And as suddenly as they had moved, they parted, and as the stillness fell upon the *zeks* the sergeant handler reached for the holster flap at his waist.

His dog had a strip of padded tunic material clamped in its jaws. His dog was lying on its side, strangely twisted. His dog had been killed by the *zeks*.

Around the prisoners from the cordon of guards was the noise of bullets sliding into the breeches of rifles.

"Over their heads. . . . Fire!" Kypov shouted.

"This firm I was working for, Letterworth Engineering and Manufacturing Company had several contracts from the Soviet Union. SovImport wasn't the biggest of our clients but it was a healthy one, one that we kept sweet with. Well, it was a turbine order that we were chasing, worth two million sterling to us. We're not a big firm and that was good money. Along tripped Afghanistan, then we had the Olympic fracas. Our contract was in the pipeline but stuck there. Mark Letterworth wanted it unstuck but he wasn't the man to have the time on his hands to be sitting around Moscow. He asked me to go. Seemed obvious really. I speak the language, I'd worked on the specifications. . . ."

The sound of gunfire crashed through the room.

Instinctively Holly fell to the floor from his chair.

After the first volley another was fired, then a third.

Rudakov was on his knees clawing open the lower drawer of his desk, finding the strapping of the shoulder holster that carried the small Makharov pistol, threading it over his chest and back. He crawled across the floor to the doorway. He yelled for an orderly. He was greeted with silence, an empty corridor, deserted offices. His place was in the compound and he had no escort to take Michael Holly back to the SHIzo block. He swore, he caught at Holly's arm as the Englishman was pulling on his socks and boots and tunic. He delayed long enough for the tunic to be over Holly's shoulders, not for his boots to be tied. He propelled Holly out of the office, down the corridor, out into the compound. He gasped at the sight in front of him.

In a great flattened antheap the prisoners of Camp 3, Zone I, knelt and lay prone. In the snow beside the long boots of the guards was the twinkle of discharged cartridge cases. He barely noticed as Holly drifted from him into the fallen mess of men and was lost to his sight. He hurried to Kypov.

"They won't go to work, we've fired over their heads."

Rudakov did not hesitate, knew no caution with his advice. "Better to calm them than confront them. Withdraw the troops and the dogs—the 'stoolies' will give us the names. Once you've fired over their heads you can only fire into them, and that's a bloodbath, that's the end of us all."

"You're yellow, Rudakov, you're a bastard coward."

Rudakov yelled back, "I'm not a coward, I'm not stupid. Your way we lose, my way we win."

"It's running away."

"Call me a coward again, and I'll break you. . . ."

Rudakov, a bright young officer with a future on the KGB ladder did not know of the beating of Feldstein. Nor did he know of the sit-down in the snow, by Chernayev first and then by all the men of Hut 2. Nor did he know of the killing of the sergeant handler's dog. Rudakov's sure confidence won the day over the wavering uncertainty of his Commandant.

As they backed out through the compound's gates inside a porcupine of rifles, Rudakov said, "Within two hours we'll be back . . . when they're cold and hungry."

Chapter 20

The compound was a new place. A new place because the great gates had closed behind the withdrawal of the Commandant and the guards and the warders. Never before in any man's time in the zone had the forces of the regime scuttled to safety behind those gates.

Who now were the prisoners?

Only the guards in the watchtowers were visible to the men on the inside, and they were distant dolls high above their ladders and half-hidden by the sides of their platforms. It was unbelievable to the *zeks*, it was rich wine to these long stretch men on strict regime. It had never happened before.

How were they to respond?

As the gates slipped shut behind the retreat of Kypov and his force, the *zeks* had risen from their stomachs and their knees.

They swept the snow from their tunics and trousers and felt the excitement that comes only from unscheduled success. Kypov had fled from his own camp. So unbelievable, so extraordinary that the delight was merged with fast suspicion. From where would the hammer blow come?

Without a leader the *zeks* were pulled as if by a magnet toward the very center of the compound. They gathered between the living huts and close to the north wall of the kitchen. There seemed a certain security there, and for many the sight of the wire and the watchtowers was blocked off by the buildings.

Eight hundred men and each offering his opinion or listening to that of another, and interrupting, and shouting and whispering. But there was still the sight of the steel-clad stack of the factory chimney. Only a narrow smoke column drifted from the chimney top. No work in the factory. The civilian foreman would be beside the lathes and saws and varnish pots. One hour . . . perhaps a few hours, and then the Commandant would seek to lead them back to the factory.

Most men felt their freedom as a passing pleasure.

A shimmer of a whisper sped among the prisoners. Fingers pointed toward the northwest corner of the compound. A guard was climbing the ladder to a watchtower and he held the rungs with one hand, and in the other was the dark outline of a machine gun, and his body was wrapped in belt ammunition. They watched him climb. Then the pointing fingers changed direction as the flock of birds will turn to another course. The fingers pointed to the southwest corner watchtower, and another guard was climbing and another machine gun was carried to a vantage platform. And the fingers swung again and the direction was southeast. And swung again, and to the northeast.

It had been a tidbit of freedom. The happiness died under the barrels of the newly-placed machine guns. A man in freedom must own a certain privacy. What privacy could there be under the sights of eight machine guns? Now the prisoners watched the gates. The gates were massive and shut and held their secret. Behind the gates the force that Kypov had mustered would be collecting, absorbing its orders. The whisper had gone. Voices raised now in argument, in confusion.

Men from Hut 1 talking with men from Hut 3 and men from Hut 5. The thief with the drug addict. The speculator with the rapist. The killer with the homosexual. The first tide of fear, fear that hissed over a shingle beach.

Fear recalled the pain at Anatoly Feldstein's bruised groin, fear carried once more the dull ache to Poshekhonov's savaged shoulder, reminded Byrkin of the thunder of falling bombs above a water-line cabin. Feldstein, Poshekhonov, Byrkin, and Chernayev . . . all together, and a crush of men around them. Men pressing against them, men listening and waiting and hoping. . . .

Feldstein who had been strong on his bunk, brave in the snow when the boots and truncheons flew, now small and frightened and hurt and cold.

"What will they do?"

Poshekhonov who had sat down only after others had made the gesture and who still felt the teeth marks in his skin and the chill from the rip of his tunic.

"They'll give us one chance, then they'll fire."

Chernayev who had taken the action he would never have considered before on any day of the seventeen years that he had labored in the camps.

"They will subdue us. We'll all be for the courts at Yavas."

Byrkin who had only followed, who had never initiated.

"They have the names, they have the faces. There'll be ten years 'special' regime at best, fifteen years at Vladimir or Christopol at worst."

Feldstein said, "It wasn't supposed to be like this. Just an individual protest. . . ."

Poshekhonov said, "It's no longer one silly bastard's hunger strike. It's collective bloody mutiny. They stamp out mutiny, they make an example of it. Down the line, in the camp at Lesnoy, there was a mutiny in '77, they shot two boys for that, neither more than twenty years old."

Chernayev said, "They'll kill us, or they'll let us rot."

"We're wrecked. . . ." said Feldstein.

"We can't find an end to what was started," said Poshe-khonov.

"Holly started it, Holly is the beginning," said Chernayev.

"Holly fought them from the first bloody day he was here. We have drifted this far, if we drift further we might as well run at the wire," said Byrkin.

Each man's opinion now must count. This is not the outside world. In the small camp the minority cannot dictate to the majority. The decision must be collective.

Chernayev could see Holly. Over the close pack of heads he saw that Holly stood apart from the mass, leaning against the door frame of Hut 2. He had isolated himself from the debate, he was no part of the crowd that had come together in the heart of the compound. A calmness seemed to bandage his face. He leaned with his hands in his trouser pockets.

A group of men is a herd. It follows a leader. It gives ground to the loudest, to the most certain. Those with faint hearts stand back, though they have the opportunity to speak they will not take advantage of that opportunity. Those in the crowd who spoke with certainty were those who believed in the retaliation of Kypov that would fall on their heads, all of their heads.

"They'll butcher us when they come in. . . ."

"If we live we'll have a fifteen on top of what's there. . . ."

"If we stand together we have strength, if we're apart they'll eat us. . . ."

"They ran, the shit bastards are frightened. . . ."

Chernayev listened to the litany of confrontation. Seventeen years in the camps, more to go, and there would be another fifteen to run. Additional sentences were always consecutive, never concurrent. Why had he sat down in the snow? Abruptly Chernayev elbowed his way through the crowd that mouthed the brave words of fight and resistance. They'd learn, they'd learn what the fine words meant.

He shoved a path for himself, his eyes locked on Michael Holly.

"You were wrong with your advice. I was wrong to have accepted it."

"When you have fired over the top you have only one option left to you." For the fourth time since they had left the compound, Rudakov explained his reasoning to the Commandant. "After that you can only fire into them. Then you have a massacre. As it is, we have a problem, a small problem that will go away. They're milling about in there, all piss and wind, no leaders and no plan."

He wished he believed in his own words.

They stood together a few meters from the gate.

Vasily Kypov was restless. He stamped and pirouetted, and seemed prepared to listen only with a minimum of attention to his political officer. As if he were rousing himself before combat, Rudakov thought, and shuddered. The bloody man had no sensitivity. The sledgehammer was all he understood.

"In twenty minutes we go."

Close to the two men a small phalanx of guards waited. They wore full riot gear—helmets with plastic visors, gas canisters fastened to their webbing, infantry assault rifles alternating with long wooden sticks.

"Before we return to the compound I will address the men over the loudspeaker system."

"You can do what you like, you have nineteen minutes. Then we're going in."

*   *   *

"Go away."

"You are a part of us, Holly."

"Play your games on your own."

"It's not a game, not when Zone 1 stands together."

"I'm not a part of you."

"You're of our blood."

"I am nothing to you."

"You are everything to us, Holly."

They were beside the doorway to Hut 2. Holly on the step and Chernayev dwarfed beneath him.

"They have a dream of fighting, Holly."

"With what?" The scorn of Holly.

"Perhaps with fire, perhaps with a fouled water pipe, perhaps with wire-cutters. . . ."

"You would do better to go back and form lines, to call your own names, ask them to open the gates so that you can go to work."

"You believe that?"

"You say they have a dream of fighting, I say that is a dream of madness."

Holly saw in front of him the face of an old man. It was a puckered, weathered face, with gnarled veins bright under a white skin and sores at the mouth that were the inheritance of the camp diet.

Chernayev croaked at him, an old man near to tears. "Join us, Holly."

"You should go back to the factory. What you call a dream of fighting is pathetic, it's suicide."

"You fought, Holly, the dream was good enough for you."

"And lost, Chernayev, and lost. . . . Perhaps if you have lost it would have been better not to fight."

"That's shit."

"Tell them to go back to their ranks."

"They want a leader. Look at them." Chernayev waved his arm toward the center of the compound. All the eyes were on Holly, and on Chernayev, who played the emissary. Many hundreds of faces, faces of men that Holly had never spoken with.

Holly looked beyond the crowd, and his gaze circled as far as the twist of his neck would take him. Watchtowers, gun-barrels, wire fences, wooden fences.

"Tell them to go back to their lines, Chernayev. To go back before it is too late for them."

Chernayev clawed at Holly's sleeve. "You showed them, Holly. You were the man that roused them. Where do you think they found the courage to do what they have done this morning?"

"Silly rubbish."

"I'll tell you of the courage they found this morning. Feldstein was on a hunger strike, clever creepy little Feldstein, he declared a hunger strike and a work strike." Chernayev was shouting now, shouting and pleading. "An old man who has never kicked against them, he sat down in the snow, he refused to go to the factory."

"Who was that old man?"

"That was me."

A smile wreathed Holly's face.

"You brave sweet old bugger. You daft old bugger."

"And Poshekhonov and Byrkin, and the whole of Hut 2. Even the trusty sat down. And not one man from another hut would go to work."

"You knew what you were doing?"

"Of course we didn't know what we were bloody doing. And they put a dog on us, a sodding dog as big as a man, and we killed it."

Holly came down the step. His arm was around Chernayev's shoulder. They walked toward the waiting *zeks*. There was a faltering in Holly's stride, as if he crossed an unknown room.

"What do you want of me now?" Holly asked Chernayev.

"We want your commitment to fight."

"It cannot be the fight of one man."

"It will be the fight of us all."

The static whine of the loudspeakers burst upon them.

". . . Attention . . . Attention."

Holly recognized the voice of Yuri Rudakov. He thought of the confession that would be lying in the room of the political officer. Holly had weakened, Holly had collapsed, Holly had started to dictate a statement. And Feldstein had declared a hunger strike, and Chernayev had sat in the snow, and Poshekhonov and Byrkin with him, and a dog had been killed, and Kypov had ordered gunfire in the air, and Holly had been saved from his confession. Silently he uttered the words of his own commitment. He would never sit again in Yuri Rudakov's office. He would never place his chair again close to the warm pipes in Yuri Rudakov's office.

"...Attention...All men in the compound have precisely ten minutes to form up in their ranks preparatory to roll call and dispatch to the factory zone. If you do that immediately, there will be no reprisals taken. Failure to observe these instructions will lead to heavy penalties against all inmates of the camp. You have ten minutes...."

A hundred men were close around Holly, and behind them were another hundred, and behind them another hundred. Bleak, bowed men, with the counsel of suspicion and fear in their faces. Your army, Holly, an army of refuse and offal. Shrunken, starved bodies, hungry for leadership. Where will you lead them, Holly? Bloody fools....

He was lifted up. He swayed on the shoulders of a dozen men, his legs hanging limp against their chests. Less than ten minutes to go, and the fever of rebellion burned in them. And you started it, Holly. You started it with fire, with excrement, with wire-cutters. And how will you finish it?

Less than ten minutes until the gates of the compound were opened.

"Do you want to fight?" Holly called from his roost on the bucking shoulders.

A thunder of agreement buffeted around him. And the bright mouths of hope gleamed back at him. Bright mouths, gap teeth, pinched lips.

"Is there gas or paraffin in the compound?"

A voice shouted back, anonymous among the bee-swarm faces. "In the store at the back of the kitchen there is paraffin— a reserve if the electricity is cut."

"And there are glass bottles in the compound?"

Another voice, another hidden face. "In the shop there are bottles of lemonade."

"Who has matches?"

More voices that clamored for inclusion. "I have matches...I have a box...I have a lighter...."

"I want a dozen bottles filled with paraffin. I want a little

paraffin soaked into rags that will seal the neck of the bottles.
I want them here in three minutes." He saw men detach themselves from the main group. He saw men run when before he
had only known them slouch and stumble ". . . I want every
man on the perimeter path—'stoolies,' Internal Order, 'barons'—everyone. And I want a man on the roof of the kitchen
building, someone to wave to me when they come."

There was a wasp nest of activity around Holly. The men
who had not run to the kitchen store nor the kitchen shop nor
to their huts for the hoarded matches now sidled away toward
the edges of the compound and took a place on the stamped-
down path. God, they trusted him.

He eased himself down from the shoulders that had supported him. Chernayev smiled, Poshekhonov grinned, Byrkin
showed him the fierce anticipation of a combat-trained ser-
viceman. The bloody fools, and so bloody proud. . . .

He saw Feldstein, and there was something haunted in the
stolen glance of the young Jew.

"It's not your way, Anatoly?"

"It is not my way."

"You would lie down in front of them?"

"I would humiliate them by nonviolence."

"They'd spit on you."

"Your way they will not spit on us, they will shoot us."

"You can go out of the compound."

Feldstein looked steadily into Holly's eyes. "Don't try to
cheapen me. I said when you were brought back that you would
take men to hell and would not care if they returned. Do you
take us to hell, Holly? Do you care if we ever return?"

Holly smelt the paraffin. He turned away from Feldstein's
persistent gaze. A dozen men came to him with bottles and a
wad of rags oozed from each neck. Matches rattled in their
boxes. A thin, reed voice carried from the roof of the kitchen.

The group around Holly headed for the perimeter path.
Three bottles of paraffin would be underneath each of the corner
watchtowers.

Holly walked across the compound to join the line of gray-
uniformed men who ringed the huts and the kitchen and the
bath and the store and the parade area. He whispered something
to Byrkin, that could not be heard by Chernayev and Poshe-

khonov, and Byrkin nodded, and went on his way like a soldier.

"What are we going to do?" asked Chernayev.

"Start something they won't forget, not quickly."

"Are we going to die?" asked Poshekhonov.

"I shouldn't think so, not yet. . . ."

Holly was facing inwards toward the center of the camp. He linked arms with the *zek* on either side of him, elbow to elbow with fists clenched across the stomach. The gesture was imitated, the movement rippled. A chain of men was formed, a chain that was broken only in front of the gates into the compound.

They were not paratroops. They were a callow collection of conscripts and reserve NCOs. They were all that was available to Major Vasily Kypov. And they were nervous. He could read that, he thought that he could smell their fear. He would keep them close, a nugget group. Five ranks of five, and he would be at the front, and Rudakov would be at the rear. A magazine of live ammunition to each rifleman, and his own pistol was loaded, and Rudakov's too. He'd heard Rudakov's broadcast over the loudspeakers. Crap, he'd thought it, not hard enough, unnecessary crap.

"Rudakov, we're going." Kypov straightened himself. "Get the gates open. What are they at in there?"

Rudakov was behind the Commandant. "They are on the perimeter path."

"Any weapons?"

"Nothing that the watchtowers have reported."

"Together in formation, men, only act on my orders. Exactly on my orders."

Best foot forward, Vasily Kypov marched his men into the mouth of the camp. They were a pretty sight. They might have had a band playing because each man was in step, and as they progressed across the snow toward the center of the compound the snow flew smartly from their boots. Kypov kept his head erect, glanced to the side with the shift of his eyes. He must dominate, that was the first rule in handling a rabble. Dominate and control. When Rudakov had said they were on the perimeter path, he could not register the significance of that information. Kypov saw the significance when he was fifty meters into the camp. He was marching into a vacuum. The *zeks* were distanced from him, he could not reach out and touch them with the power of his small force. The silence and the linked arms were unnerving. He had reached the center of the camp, the very center. Between the huts, beyond the buildings, the line of *zeks* confronted him. Small blurred figures in front of him, and on either side. Blurred because of the water at his eyes, the water of frustration, of biting anger. If he marched his men to the left then he gave up all contact with the prisoners on his right. If he marched further forward then he could not dominate those behind him. If he held the center ground then he must bellow to be heard. Among the scum was a brain that had bettered his. He stamped to a halt. Where was Rudakov? Rudakov should have known. Rudakov had let him march onto shifting ground. Rudakov, at the bloody back. He turned to face his men. He saw them fidget, finger their rifles. And they had not taken the dog out, the bastard dog was still wet in the snow. Every soldier had seen the dog. Twisted neck, blue tongue, helpless teeth, bruised fur. Shit. And which way to face, when he addressed the scum? Shit. And if he made his speech, what was his message, conciliation or threat? Whose was the brain that had bettered him? Shit. Only the silence, only the linked arms of solidarity.

The training of the paratrooper won out. He took a deep sighing breath. He repeated to himself his first sentence. He was a toad puffed up to frighten the distant creatures.

"You are to form into your ranks. If my order is not obeyed the most severe penalties will be exacted on all prisoners. The troops with me are armed. If you do not move immediately I will order them to open fire at random upon you. You are completely surrounded, and there are additional machine guns sited in the towers."

He turned slowly on his heel. He looked for a movement, for the first man to break the chain and step forward. Silence beat over him, and the linked arms mocked him.

Three men stood under each of the four towers and watched Michael Holly for the signal.

He was very tense, and around him was the hiss of anticipation. Eight hundred men, and they waited for him. The hunger was forgotten, the cold was stripped away, the tiredness had gone. A racing excitement clawed him. Away behind the outlines of the low roofs of Hut 2 and Hut 3 he saw Kypov and behind him the guns, and behind them Rudakov.

"In thirty seconds I will give the order for random fire. Whoever has led you to this is a fool. You have been misled, turn your backs on this idiocy, you have less than half a minute. . . ."

He saw the rifles ease up to the shoulders, he saw the barrels waver to select a target. He heard the smatter of sound as the catches were nudged from "safety." He heard the bleat of Kypov's voice.

"You have fifteen seconds. These are automatic rifles, above you are machine guns. I am going to count the last ten seconds. I am going to start to count."

Holly swung his right arm away from the grip of the man next to him and raised it like a banner. He looked to the northeast tower and saw a sharp flash of light. He looked to the southeast tower and saw a bottle climb slowly, somersaulting, toward the open window and dark-uniformed guards.

A sheet of flame in the northwest tower. The crash of an explosion in the southwest tower. A terror scream in the northeast tower. A man beating at fire that was running across his greatcoat shoulders in the southeast tower. Black smoke spilled from the towers, and orange light sucked through the interiors.

He saw a man who was ablaze jump from the top of a watchtower ladder and dive for the salvation of the snow beneath.

He did not look behind him. Byrkin, who they said was mad, would know his job, Byrkin would be on the wire and climbing. There was the first clatter of exploding ammunition.

He hooked his right arm inside the elbow of the man next to him. He locked his hands, closed his fingers tight. The first step forward. Along the length of the line there was a shimmer of movement, a stutter. The line lurched, rolled, bent. The line straightened, the line advanced. He wondered if their nerve would hold. And why should it? If the line broke, if it broke just once, they would be massacred. God, help the line to hold. He saw Kypov, spinning like a top in a child's game. Kypov looking right, left, front, behind. He should have opened fire,

Holly thought soberly. Stupid Kypov. The line was level with the rear of Hut 2 and Hut 3. Here it could break, only here. Holly led, he was half a stride in front of the men on either side of him. Tracers streaked in brilliant lines, dividing a gray sky. Some of Kypov's detachment were on their knees as if they mistook the danger of the wild bullets. The perimeter of the line was closing in. In one place the line had not moved. The pathway to the gate was clear. The road of retreat was empty.

They came slowly now, the *zeks* with their arms linked, slowly and with purpose. They edged over the snow, and the sound of their boots was a perpetual, menacing shuffle.

Vasily Kypov could not utter the necessary command for his men to shoot. His pistol hung limp in his hand, its barrel rotating over the caps of his boots.

He heard Rudakov's voice behind him. What was Rudakov shouting? Why was Rudakov pulling at the arm of his coat?

Should it be gas, should it be rapid fire? What would rapid fire manage against this creeping ramshackle crowd? There were no weapons in their hands. They carried nothing in their hands. Rapid fire . . . too late to use gas. He had to find the words before the stinking rabble broke over him. Rapid fire . . . where was his bastard voice? Rudakov still pulling at the arm of his coat, still shouting.

"What is it?"

"Don't shoot—whatever you fucking do, don't shoot."

"Rapid fire, that's for them."

"Don't fucking shoot."

He could see their eyes, he could read the names on their tunics, he could see the cotton darning round the kneecap patches and the boots sliding toward him across the snow.

"But they're going to kill us."

"Only if you shoot. Remember the dog, Kypov, don't forget the fucking dog. . . ."

Kypov could smell them. He could not remember when last he had smelled the *zeks*. A hideous smell of waste, of dirt, of old death. They could not beat him. A rabble in a camp could not be permitted to gain victory over a major of paratroops. He knew he was raising the pistol in his hand. His arm was rising and there was the hard hold of the pistol's butt in his hand. He felt Rudakov's fist clamp on his forearm, and his arm slid back, relaxed.

"We'll be killed, Major. If one shot is fired, every last one of us...." Rudakov's voice was kindly.

He led Kypov past his troops. Out of step, out of mind, they returned to the gate. Kypov was weeping. If Rudakov had not supported him he would have fallen to the ground.

The line followed them.

The linked arms broke only when the gates had closed.

"What did you get?"

"Two of the mounted machine guns."

"Better than I'd hoped," Holly smacked Byrkin across the shoulders.

"Not better, they're all charred to hell."

The cold came fast to Holly's face. "We don't have a gun that'll fire?"

"Nothing that'll fire... I'm sorry."

Chapter 21

Holly stood near to the wire and above him was the angled, subsiding structure of the southeast watchtower. He heard the smashing of glass, the breaking of the windows of the shop and the store and the library. There was the thudding of a wooden pole used as a ram against the door of the shed behind the kitchen where the week's rations for eight hundred men were kept. The windows of the administration block that looked through barbed wire into the compound were deserted. There would be men on the roof, and the guards in the towers over-looking the hospital to the east, the factory to the north, the women's zone to the west would have a slanted and partial view into the camp.

In his mind he tried to shun responsibility for the fracturing glass, for the splintering doors. They had come to him, they had taken the step of conspiracy. But responsibility is no easy garment to cast off. Responsibility is worn tight, buttoned surely. Chernayev had told him that he, Michael Holly, had breathed the kiss of life courage into the *zeks*. He would lead them to hell, Feldstein had accused, would he care if they returned . . . ?

What is the price to be paid for pride, what is the reward of the humble?

"The price of pride is crippling. The reward of the humble is survival."

Bloody words, Michael Holly, daft words. And outside the fences they would be mustering an army, and inside the fences we're at play smashing and destroying.

He walked away from the fences and toward the kitchen. Half a dozen men were sitting on the step outside the doorway of Hut 6. They were drunk. They had broken open the store of distilled alcohol that had been the property of the hut's "baron." That was democracy, that was power to the people. The capitalist had been overthrown. They were from Georgia, dark-skinned and curly-haired, singing and belching and hiccuping.

You started it, Holly.

He walked past the back of the kitchen where the store door sagged away from its upper hinge. An old *zek* came out trying to stuff potatoes down into his trouser pockets. They were raw potatoes and he would have no way of cooking them adequately, but a man who has been starved of potato for half a decade does not have to concern himself with the niceties of cooking. He had yellow rat teeth that could handle raw potato. Another man chewed uncooked semi-frozen herrings, gulped at the gray-white meat. Another bit and worried at a length of tripe stomach-lining that would make him vomit. They would be fighting soon, those who already crowded the store and blocked its entrance, and those who shouted outside the door for access.

You started it, Holly.

He walked along the side of the kitchen and saw the broken windows. The breaking served no purpose. The snow would come in, and later the rain, the kitchen would be a worse place for the *zeks* of the future. . . . Perhaps, perhaps they do not believe in the future of the camp. Perhaps that is why they have begun to damage systematically everything that is the camp. That can be a man's freedom. A man's freedom can be to damage systematically all the apparatus of the *Dubrovlag*.

He walked to the door of the kitchen, where a knot of men with their backs to him formed an inverted triangle. They craned forward to see something at their feet. He heard the oaths and the whimper of a man who had once been privileged. Of course there would be beatings, the settling of age-old scores. Hands pulled Holly closer, he was invited to watch. He saw Mamarev on the ground. The snow was dark with mud and bright with blood. Blood dripped from the boy's mouth, from his nose. Two *zeks* kneeled above him and scrabbled with each other for the chance to strike the next blow. One of the *zeks* was Poshekhonov. Holly thought he might be sick. He reached forward and tore the two men back, and there was sudden surprise drifting to anger from Poshekhonov. Holly didn't speak. He picked Mamarev up from the ground. The sobbing gratitude of the boy shrilled in Holly's head.

You started it, Holly.

He carried Mamarev into the kitchen.

A meeting had started. Among the debris of furniture one table and two benches had been retrieved. A dozen men, perhaps fifteen, were round the table. He heard a cacophony of raised voices. Argument, dissent, discussion. Poor bastards . . . poor, stupid bastards. They had begun something incredible and they had not known what they had done. They were debating what to do next. That was a kind of freedom.

Holly let Mamarev slide down to the floor. He wondered how the men, some from each of the six huts, had been chosen. They were the doomed ones, they were the condemned men. When it was over, these names would be on Yuri Rudakov's desk. They would shoot these men in the yard of the Central Investigation Prison at Yavas. *Zeks* rule, OK . . . and for how long? For a day? For a day and a night? Chernayev and Byrkin were the representatives of Hut 2. Some of the other men he recognized, some he had never spoken with.

You started it, Holly.

He raised his hand, cut the squabble.

"It won't be a small force the next time, they'll come in strength. Now they'll be waiting for reinforcement. This time they will shoot. We have no guns. . . . When the big force arrives they will again offer us a choice, surrender or take the consequences. This is your camp, not mine, you must decide for yourselves which way you will fall."

"You led us before, Holly," Chernayev said mildly.

"When you had already made your decision. You either give in now or you finish what has begun."

The voices that Holly had hushed were raised again.

"If we give in, all of us will be shot or get fifteens . . . we'll be behind wire for the rest of our natural . . . how can we fight them when we have no guns . . . we slid into this, if we slide further we're screwed . . ."

Brave men. Men out of the gutters, men who were unable to read the page of a newspaper, men who had thieved and killed for a petty purse of rubles. Michael Holly could never walk away from them.

Holly said, "There was a riot some years ago in the *Dubrovlag*, what was the reaction of the military?"

"They brought in helicopters."

"They used the down-blast to flatten everybody."

"When everyone was on the ground, the guards and warders came in."

"They used chains on the men."

Holly asked, "What is the stomach of the camp for a fight?"

"Don't underestimate their hate."

He breathed deeply, screwed his eyes shut. There would be no going back. "Any man who wants to leave the compound should be given the chance to do so immediately. I want wire and I want rope and I want blankets. I want every man who wishes to stay inside the kitchen in fifteen minutes. There is no going back. We have to finish what has been begun. . . ."

"Where is that finish?" The *zek* from Hut 4, a big man with a bulbous mole set halfway up his nose, and mud streaks on his cheeks.

"There is the possibility, just the possibility, that the very weight of our action will frighten them. There is the possibility that they will step back, try to talk with us."

"And the probability?"

"They will hit us with everything they have."

There was silence round the table. One man slowly drummed his fingers on the wood boards, another fished in his pocket for a loose cigarette, another snorted into a rag handkerchief.

Byrkin scraped his chair, stood up. "I'll start looking for wire and the rope and blankets. I'll pass the word for the meeting."

Vasily Kypov put down the telephone.

He looked across his desk toward Yuri Rudakov, who was hunched on the edge of an easy chair.

"Yavas is sending a hundred men, a company and a colonel general. Saransk is sending four helicopters. That was staff at Yavas, a shitty lieutenant, he was almost fucking laughing at me."

The telephone rang. Kypov grimaced, reached out for it, listened intently.

Rudakov watched him for a moment, then resumed his own

brooding. The political officer was responsible for gauging the mood of the compound. It had all happened at such speed, with such fury. He was baffled. He doubted if Kypov had ever considered the prospect of mutiny. Why should he have done? Rudakov had never entertained the thought. Smart ass, wasn't he? And he'd never entertained an anxiety of mutiny.

Kypov wrapped over the telephone, guarding it from his voice. "It's bloody Moscow . . . the big bastard boss from Interior. . . ." and he was listening again and Rudakov knew the connection had been made because Kypov seemed to straighten in his chair. "Good morning, Comrade Procurator . . . yes, the situation is contained. There is no chance of a breakout. I am sorry if you disagree with my decision to withdraw . . . I was on the spot, in the compound myself . . . the reinforcement troops are expected very soon . . . no, I have not yet identified the clique of leadership . . . tomorrow, you are coming, tomorrow? I am sure that by then we will have the compound returned to normal working. . . . Goodbye, Comrade Procurator."

Rudakov scratched sharply at the back of his neck. "All we wanted."

"What troops are being sent?"

"Buggers from the far east. Regular army, none of this MVD shit."

"It's not easy to get soldiers to fire on crowds."

"They're straight off the steppes, slant eyes, they'll shoot," Kypov said, and the pencil in his hand was broken in two short halves.

They made a grim, halting procession out of the kitchen. The *zeks* whistled their going in derision, slow-clapped in contempt. Holly led them out.

They were the "stoolies," and the trusties, and the "barons." They were the outsiders who had cheated themselves of the full rigors of the camp. They were the compromisers who had sealed their deals with the regime. Each had stood in line earlier in the morning with a faint heart, because each had believed that the second stage of rebellion would be the reprisals. Until they stood in the sharp air of the compound each one had believed he might yet be the victim of a cruel trick. And now they were outside and there was no deceit.

Holly held Mamarev's arm as they started out for the gates.

"They would have killed you this morning, you know that?"

"I thought I was dead."

"When you came into the kitchen you heard what we talked of."

"A little."

"You can buy your debt from me."

"How?" Mamarev looked up at Holly, into the hard and chiseled face.

"You will say there are divisions and factions, that they are frightened of the helicopters coming, that some want to surrender but are not allowed to leave the camp."

"That is all?"

Holly stopped thirty yards short of the gates. Everything changed beyond the gate. He could hear the revving of heavy trucks and in the distance was the throb of a helicopter engine.

"Tell them what I have told you."

The blood was dry at Mamarev's mouth, dark and congealed at his nostrils. A bruise was forming on his right cheek. "It was me that reported you as missing two nights ago. I informed on you."

"On your way."

Holly turned. He started to walk back along the line of deserters. If he heard Mamarev's shout, he gave no sign.

"Do you forgive me?"

Byrkin supervised the work.

A table leg that was nearly a meter long was tied to ten meters of electrical wire stripped from the kitchen ceiling, the wire was tied to another ten meters of heavy rope taken from the building store, the rope was tied to two blankets knotted together and stripped from the bunks of the defectors. They had the material to make up nine lengths. The men that Byrkin had chosen had one thing in common. All had served their conscription duty in the army of the Soviet Union. It was the role of a petty officer to carry out orders. Holly had given him his orders. He bustled between his chosen few, checking the strength of the joins and the coiling of the heaps of wood, wire, rope and blanket. They were the best men he could have found, and much was expected of them.

He heard the faraway engine drive of the first helicopter. He looked out of the broken window at the back of the kitchen. The *zeks* were out in the compound where they had been told to wait.

He felt a sort of happiness, a happiness he had not known since the sailing of the Storozhevoy from Riga harbor.

Mikk Laas heard the helicopter coming.

He was a blind man in his cell in the SHIzo block. He heard many sounds that were new and strange, he saw nothing. The window was high above him, beyond his reach.

He had heard shooting.

He had heard the outer door of the cell block locked, and after that no movement of warders down the outer corridor.

He had heard the arrival of trucks with a different engine whine to those of the commercial vehicles that visited the camp.

He kicked the cell wall.

"Who is there?" The cry of an old man without eyes.

"Adimov. . . ."

"What is happening out there?"

"There is mutiny, I heard the warders talk. We're better here. . . ."

"Where is Holly?"

"How can I know?"

Mikk Laas crawled away across the concrete floor. He knew Holly would be in the compound. His ears told him that the trucks were bringing troops to Barashevo, that the helicopters were swarming down to Barashevo.

The colonel general sat easily on the corner of Kypov's desk. He was a youngish man, assured and certain. A good-looking man beneath his steel battle helmet. Kypov warmed to him, because this man did not sneer. The colonel general talked briefly, factually, alternating the direction of his remarks between Kypov and his political officer.

"They're big beasts, the helicopters. We'll bring them down to three, four meters and nobody will be standing under them. You get blown flat. We'll give them a minute or so, then in with the troops. We'll split them into groups of thirty, forty, then I'll have your force in . . . shouldn't be a problem."

The competence of the colonel general encouraged Yuri Rudakov.

"I'm told there are divisions within whatever leadership they have, there is a faction that believes the thing has already gone too far. They know that the helicopters will come, I think the majority of them are scared half out of their minds."

"What sort of prisoners does the camp hold?"

"Scum," said Kypov decisively.

"Criminals, pretty low intelligence," said Rudakov.

There was a knock at Kypov's door. News from the adjutant. All four helicopters had now landed in the vehicle park. The perimeter of the camp was secure. The storm-squad was in position behind the gates. Marksmen were in place on the administration block roof.

"Will you be flying yourself, Colonel General?" Kypov asked.

"Of course."

They were experienced men, the pilots of the helicopters. They accepted this mission with an amused resignation. They were accustomed to flying into actual or simulated machine gun fire. They were familiar with the evasion techniques necessary against ground-to-air missiles. Their machines carried armorplating a centimeter thick to protect the soft belly beneath their seats. Apart from his copilot each captain carried two machine gunners. And they were to be used as flyswatters. The pilots talked to each other by radio, they livened their engines, the colonel general climbed on board. The helicopters rolled, as a drunkard on ice, and lifted.

Holly stood white-lipped in the center of the compound.

Beyond the high wooden fence the bedlam of the helicopters was growing. He could see Byrkin fifty yards to his right and close to the wire. Chernayev was behind him, further than fifty yards. And there were men whose names he did not know and whose faces he might not recall, and they too were beyond reach.

He was the talisman of the compound. All the men watched him. If he broke they would all break. The *zeks* were spread out across the zone, as he had wished. Their posture was aimless. When the helicopters rose and peeped for the first time over the high wooden fence they would see only confusion. Let the bastards come. . . .

Anatoly Feldstein was beside Holly.

"If it works, your plan, will men die?"

"Not necessarily. . . ."

"And if you win this time, what of the next time?"

"I have not won this time, not yet," Holly yelled brutally.

The nose of the lead helicopter sidled above the fence, a monster that had crawled from a cave and now flexed itself.

"We're not reading your bloody *samizdat* in a Moscow flat, we're not having wet dreams over a Solzhenitsyn type-script. . . ."

Three more helicopters creeping into close formation above the first, clawing into the dull sky, climbing for altitude.

". . . We're not sending telegrams to Ronald bloody Reagan. Nobody outside this camp gives a hell for us. We're on our own, understand that."

Holly craned his head, following the gray undercarriages of the helicopters. They'd rise to a thousand feet, then drop. A controlled fall down onto the compound, down onto men who had nothing but nine coils of table leg, wire, rope, and blanket.

Feldstein held Holly's head, shouted in his ear. "Can you know what it is to read *samizdat?* It's wonderful. It is true freedom to read *samizdat.* . . ."

"Shut up and watch. Watch and I'll show you freedom. Watch the helicopters."

He pushed Feldstein away.

The sky darkened, the noise of the rotors pounded, thrashed the air. Holly saw the machine gunners, saw them grinning as they peered from their opened doors, leaning out safe on the tether of their lifelines. Let the bastards come. . . . He depended on nine men, the nerve of nine men.

The *zeks* began to run, began to form into four concentrations as Holly had dictated. Snow swept into the void, a white and blurring confetti, and he lost sight of Byrkin, and when he spun round Chernayev also was gone. God . . . the noise, the blasting sound. Holly and Feldstein were alone, and ignored by the pilots. The pilots had greater riches. Four man masses to occupy them. The snow swirls lay like a fog, low and held down by the rotor blades. The helicopters sat on the white mist, and the engines roared and screamed and howled.

"Now Byrkin . . . now Chernayev . . . now . . . now. . . ."

A stick was thrown in the air. Holly watched, cold and fascinated. A stick was caught by a rotor blade and swept from his sight, and a wire and a rope and two knotted blankets flew in pursuit of a tossed table leg. Beautiful Chernayev . . . beautiful Byrkin . . . beautiful all of you. Look at the captain, Holly. Look at his face roving over his instruments, his hands fighting the controls. Press the panic button. Why won't the bloody thing respond, Comrade Captain? . . . Holly heard the cry of a failing engine. He flung his arms round Feldstein.

"We might have won. . . ." he yelled.

The *zeks* knew, the *zeks* had heard the swing of the engine pitch from the high roar to the failing whine. Wire and rope and blankets were wrapped tight, bandaged, around the delicate free running spool between helicopter cabin and rotors. The *zeks* ran, broke and spread.

One machine bellyflopped in the compound.

The *zeks* would be at it like thieves at a Christmas party.

Another machine scraped over the administration block, and disappeared for a few short seconds before there was an explosion and the answering sweep of dark smoke.

The third machine cleared Hut 3 and took the outer telephone lines from the poles. It keeled against a watchtower, and fell beyond the high wooden fence.

Almost on the ground, the fourth helicopter seemed to give up the fight for height and settle only for distance. It careened between Hut 6 and the bathhouse, scattering its way through fences. Screaming wire, ripping wood, the howl of the engine. Holly saw it go, a great wounded bird fluttering to a defeated landfall. Byrkin was bellowing at him, hanging on his arm for attention.

"I have a colonel general . . . I have two pilots, two crew. We have two machine guns and ammunition."

Holly shook himself, tried to rid his head of the echoing noise. "Get the guns under Huts 3 and 6. Get the crew into the kitchen."

God . . . they had won! The *zeks* ran round him, dazed, overwhelmed, hysterical.

Holly went toward the administration block. So quiet without the rotors spinning above him. He walked past the huge downed beast. The *zeks* were in it, hyenas at a carcass.

He walked tall.

The marksmen would be locked on him.

Twenty meters in front of the administration block he stopped.

"Tell Major Kypov that we have a colonel general and two pilots and two crew alive and in our care. Tell him also that we have machine guns intact."

"I couldn't shoot," the marksman sobbed. "As soon as the helicopters came down they just chucked up the snow. I couldn't see anything. I couldn't give them covering fire. When the snow cleared, the first thing I saw was that they had our people. They had knives to their throats. They'd have butchered them if I'd fired."

His sergeant turned away, headed for the trapdoor, and the ladder and the corridor to the Commandant's office where the inquest would be raging.

The helicopter had speared first through the fences of Zone I, then across the roadway and into the fences and high wooden wall of Zone 4. It breached the barricades of the women's camp.

The women had been in their work area at the time of the helicopters' assault, not at their machines but crawling up for vantage points, peering through the glass of the upper windows. As the helicopter exhausted its flight they had streamed from the doorway and out into their compound ignoring the shouts of the wardresses.

It was a stampede.

In the single watchtower above the women's zone, the guard seemed not to watch them, but stared across the broken defenses into the men's camp.

One group ran toward the helicopter, and was laughing, screaming, at the dazed and disoriented crew strapped in their seats.

One group ran straight for the breach in the fences. Twenty women, perhaps thirty, sprinted and slithered over the snow and iced paths, shrieking in hysteria, and heading for the hole

without reason, and without care. Irina Morozova, not a part
of the group, was running with them. A small girl, slight even
in her quilted tunic and her knee-length black skirt. A single
guard ran along the roadway dividing the two zones holding
rifle at the hip and his finger, awkward in its glove, trying to
push forward the frozen catch from "Safety." The guard shouted
once, and the women swept toward him, ignored him, the sight
of the roadway in front of them, and beyond the guard the sight
of the men's camp. The knees of the women pumped below
their lifting skirts as they ran for the hole.

A sandcastle cannot staunch the tide. The guard was overwhelmed. He never fired, he never found the strength in his
gloved finger to release "safety." Beside Morozova, women
fell on the guard and toppled him to the snow and she heard
the howl of their fury and saw the scratching nails of their
hands. Morozova watched. The hands ripped at his greatcoat,
pulled at his tunic, thrust at the flys of his trousers. Morozova
watched. She saw the skin of his belly, she saw the white of
their hands. She heard the gabble of laughter, the scream of
the soldier's fear.

There was a long burst of machine gun fire into the snow
and the women scattered like sparrows disturbed from a bird-
table. Morozova saw two guards with machine pistols a hundred
meters away, on the road beside the corner of the men's fence.
The guard whimpered; his arms were outstretched and his genitals were exposed and bloodied. Some women turned back
toward their own compound. Two women ran away from the
guards and along the stretch of seemingly empty road, but the
watchtower machine gun found them and pitched them care-
lessly over. A few more women ran, hunched and bent, toward
the hole into the men's compound. Morozova wondered if she
were about to be sick, and she was running too, she was hunched
as well.

Where was she running to?

In front of her a woman cartwheeled and there was the flash
of flesh above her stockings and the white of her knickers.
Another shouted as if a victory had been won. Another wiped
the blood from her hands onto the dark material of her skirt
where it would be hidden.

Morozova saw the helicopter that was downed, she saw a

dog that was dead. She could no longer see the other women, engulfed now by the men who had charged to meet them.

"You should not have come. You have escaped to a worse prison."

A man gazed at her, a look of stupefaction on his round and fatted face.

"You have an Englishman in the camp," she said. "Where will I find him?"

"We have an Englishman. . . ." Poshekhonov shook his head and laughed. "We also have a helicopter because we have an Englishman."

Chapter 22

In the kitchen Feldstein waited on Michael Holly, at the fringe of the river-flow of men. He had twice pulled Holly's elbow for attention, he had twice been rebuffed.

"They will have photographers on the administration block. Every man, whether or not he is involved in positive action, must have torn off the name strip on his tunic. . . .

"I want the forage caps down over men's heads, if they have a scarf they should wear it across their mouths. . . .

"The machine guns should stay under Huts 3 and 6, but I want a diversion rush with anything that looks like a gun to under I and 4. The men with most recent military experience should be involved. . . .

"I want one man into the rafters of each hut and in the roof of the kitchen and the store and the bath. I want holes in the roofing, and runners to report troop movements. . . .

"What is it, Anatoly? No, the distribution of food is not my concern, that is for the committee to organize. . . . No, I am not putting a guard on the huts, that's the problem of the committee. If they want to wreck the huts that's their concern. . . . In a moment, Anatoly. . . . Are we winning? Go and ask Comrade Major Kypov whether he thinks he's winning. . . . Everything else must wait. . . . After the meeting, please, after the meeting of the committee. . . ."

He gestured his hands to show that enough had been said. The men around him backed away, respectful. In the corner of the kitchen near to the committee were the prisoners. They sat on the floor, with their backs resting against the wall and their hands were clasped on top of their heads. They watched for the first signs that they would be beaten, they waited for the rush of men with sticks and iron bars, they wondered whether before the night came they would be dangling from a taut rope.

"You have the prisoners. Don't play the idiot with the prisoners. With the prisoners we can show that we are not animals."

Holly was distracted, half-listening, threading his way between the upturned tables and benches.

"How can we show that?"

"Let the prisoners go, Holly. Let them go without condition. Release them while you are at the zenith of your power."

"Why?"

"It would be their way to shelter behind the backs of hostages. Only a coward covers himself with such a shield."

"What if that shield saves us from a massacre?"

Holly had reached the table, eased himself down onto the end of a bench.

Feldstein spoke with a rare passion. "You are a stranger, you know nothing of these people. You think they will allow a mutiny to continue because we hold one colonel general, one helicopter crew? They don't give a shit about a human being. Look at this camp and tell me I am wrong."

"Stay here, we'll listen to you."

Holly turned away, the hands of the committee reached out for him. A great gale of laughter blew among these men, and their hands slapped each other's backs, and the kisses smacked on their cheeks. Byrkin told how he had thrown a table leg up into the hurricane of the downblast, of the magic moment that he had seen the rope and the knotted blankets dragged away from the neat coil beside his feet. They laughed and they shouted and the noise echoed in the room.

"What will they do next?" Holly asked quietly, and the softness of his voice smashed through the bogus triumph.

"What any commander would do when he is beaten by an inferior force," Byrkin said. "He withdraws, he regroups, he waits for reinforcements, he attacks again. . . ."

"How long?"

"Before tonight, before darkness," said the man from Hut 4 with the mole on his nose.

"The reinforcements are available?"

"There are more than a hundred thousand men behind the wire of the *Dubrovlag,* from Barashevo to Pot'ma," said the hunchback from Hut 6. "There is a division of MVD along the

railway line, there is always a regiment of regular army in
reserve. They have more than a division to stamp on us."

"A division . . . and we have two machine guns. . . ."

He sat with his back to the door of the kitchen. He heard
Poshekhonov's voice shouting the length of the kitchen hall.

"The Chief has a visitor. A young lady has called to see
the Chief."

She looked the length of the wrecked kitchen, and felt like an
interloper. The men who sat on the benches began to turn, and
she saw the annoyance in their faces at the interruption of their
debate. He was the last to turn. She saw the sunken eyes of
exhaustion and the pursing of the forehead in surprise.

His face lightened. In place of strain there was the half grin
of amusement. She felt she had made an idiot of herself.

"Morozova, yes?"

"I am Morozova, Irina Morozova."

"There are more people looking for a way to leave this camp
than to join it."

"There was a hole in our fence. I came before the guards
blocked it. . . . I don't know your name."

"Michael Holly."

"I wanted to thank you for what you said to me . . . when I
was in the SHIzo block."

His eyes had narrowed. "I accept your thanks. You should
go back to your zone."

"It's wired now. If I wanted to I couldn't." She tossed her
head back, and her thick, black hair wavered over the collar
of her tunic. She jutted her chin, she rose to her toes to add
to her stature.

"The compound will be attacked this afternoon. . . ."

"I'm going to stay."

Holly shouted the length of the kitchen. "Morozova, if you
stay, if you go, I don't care. This committee is preparing to
fight an army. We have two machine guns. I haven't the time
to talk. I'd like to and I can't. Go away, go away and hide
yourself. Find me again after the attack, find me if I am here."

"This is not the man who spoke to me through the walls of
the SHIzo," she shouted back in anger.

"It is the same man. The same man but a different mo-

ment. . . ." Holly turned back to the committee. "Feldstein wants
to say something about the prisoners."

"I have two and a half hours more of light. I have the procurator
flying from Moscow tomorrow. I have a compound armed with
two machine guns and five hundred rounds minimum. I have
a colonel general as a hostage to inhibit me. What do I do,
what do we do?"

Kypov paced the short carpet of his office. With him now
were his adjutant, and the major who had come from Yavas
and who had now assumed command of the regular company.

"I'm not going in there against machine guns, not without
armor. And where do I find tanks? Where?"

The adjutant had been silent. His intervention now was
quietly spoken. "If you were thinking of tanks, how many
would you need?"

"One, but there are none in Mordovia," said the major.

The adjutant was not to be deflected. "There is one tank,
on the parade ground at Yavas."

"It's a T34—a museum piece. Has it even an engine?"

"There's an engine," Kypov said. "They rolled it out last
May Day and trundled it past the general. Bloody near choked
him with all the smoke out of its ass."

"Get it here, Major, that's my suggestion. Get it here before
dusk," said the adjutant mildly.

The major flipped the pages of his notebook for the number
of the duty officer at Yavas, then reached for Kypov's telephone, banging the receiver sharply for a line.

The bolt slid back.

"Get up, Adimov."

The very sight of the man made Rudakov feel unclean. His
dealings with the criminals were rare. This one he had not met
before.

"Yes, Comrade Captain."

Adimov watched the KGB officer with suspicion. Why should
the political officer concern himself with Adimov?

"I have a job for you."

"What job, Comrade Captain?"

"You are to broadcast to the camp, to tell them of the futility

of further resistance. Tell them that if there is immediate return
to normality only the leaders will be punished."

"Why ask me?"

"You have influence in Hut 2."

Adimov whined, "You know why I went out, Comrade
Captain?"

The cell stank. No slopping out that morning.

"Why?"

"My woman is in Moscow. She is dying of cancer. I went
out to see her."

"I am sorry, Adimov, believe me. Do this for me, Adimov,
and there will be a rail warrant and parole, that I promise. And
there will be a sentence review."

"I will do it."

Adimov and Rudakov left the SHIzo block together, a smelly
zek and a captain of KGB.

"Have there been any letters for me?"

"If there is one I'll get it for you." It would cost Rudakov
nothing, a small package of kindness.

Inside the administration block, Rudakov went first to the
post room. In the pigeon hole for "A" there was a letter addressed in a crude, inexpert hand. They went together down
the corridor where they had to edge their way past men in
combat fatigues, and at the far end of the corridor was the tube
of a 110mm mortar lying on a pile of four stretchers, and some
of the floor space was littered with a heap of gas masks. Rudakov held Adimov by the arm, Adimov held his letter tight
in his fist.

"Wait here. . . ."

Rudakov knocked and opened the door to the Commandant's
office. The officers were bent over Kypov's desk and a plan
of the camp.

"Commandant, the prisoner Adimov will broadcast to the
compound when you wish; he will urge surrender."

"There's a T34 coming up from Yavas. It'll be here by four.
If it's to have a wasted journey you'd better back your man up
for before that. They'll have a chance to respond, after that
they're blasted."

"At five minutes to four I'll put Adimov on the loudspeakers.
Will you want to address the camp yourself?"

"No."

Rudakov stepped back out of Kypov's office. Beside him in the corridor a soldier handed back a single sheet of paper to Adimov. There were five lines of writing. Adimov gazed at him impassively.

"We'll wait in my office, we'll have some coffee," Rudakov said. "You'll broadcast in thirty-five minutes."

"Is Holly involved?"

"I don't know."

Feldstein had finished, he stepped back from the table. For the first time since he had come to the camp he had spoken of his beliefs. He had preached the warfare of the turned cheek.

Now the storm burst among the men of the committee.

"The Jew had no right to speak. If he wants fucking non-violence let him go and sit in the fucking SHIzo. . . ."

"They're the only card we have. Stick them out in front, let the bastards shoot right through them. . . ."

"We can do a trade. No reprisals for the colonel general's life. . . ."

Holly slammed his fist into the table. The words, the swearing, the hate, had sapped him. Morozova was sitting at the far end of the kitchen talking with Poshekhonov. Silly old bugger, trying to pretend he was a big man down on the Black Sea when he was just a *zek* with half a regiment waiting to shoot out his guts.

His fingers tingled from the impact.

"I say they go free."

"If they'd been ordered to, they would have killed you happily," said Chernayev softly.

"You know why they have to go, Chernayev."

"What do we gain?"

Holly struggled for the words. "If we keep them and we do not use them, then there is no point in our having kept them. If we keep them and we use them, then we are the savages that they believe us to be. If they go out, then we will never be forgotten, we will be remembered as long as the camps exist."

"Is that what you want, Holly, to be remembered?"

"I want all of you to be remembered. If the colonel general

goes out then the memory of you all will be burned in their minds. If you are never forgotten, the power of the *Dubrovlag* is broken."

Chernayev, unfamiliar in anger, spat across the table. "And the boy who died from dysentery, where does he fit into the scheme of memories?"

Holly surged up from the bench seat, his fist leaped the table's width, he caught at the throat of Chernayev's tunic.

"There is a man in the condemned cell at Yavas. Don't sneer at me about memories."

Gently, Byrkin eased Holly's hand loose. "So be it, Holly, take them to the gate."

In a rush Feldstein came to Holly. His spindly arms were round Holly's shoulders. The girl came after him, but shyly and her hand rested hesitantly on his arm.

The clock on the wall, above the food hatch and below the broken frame of the photograph of the president, showed twenty minutes to four.

The tank had rattled out of the barracks at Yavas.

It slewed onto the main road north, skidded toward a parked car. It would take the driver several minutes to familiarize himself with the driving sticks that he had not handled for nine months.

The tank went to war ingloriously with a militia car in front, blue roof light rotating, to clear the traffic from its path.

Old the tank might be, but not obsolete, not for putting down an insurrection. Six shells for the main armament had been scrounged from the arsenal. A machine gun of 50mm caliber was mounted on the turret. If anything was wrong with the old monster, the driver thought, then it was the fitting of the turret hatch. The rubber sealing of the hatch had long ago rotted, it leaked and he sat in a pool of water. But it was only nine kilometers to Barashevo, and the pack snow on the road was good for the tracks.

When they passed the station at Lesozavad, a small crowd of villagers waved to the observer in the turret and cheered the tank on its way.

"You have not behaved to us as we would have expected."

The colonel general moved along a line of prisoners and

offered his hand as if he were a departing guest. Manicured fingers met those that were bone-thin and filthy with factory oil.

The gates opened, a gunbarrel peeped first, then a helmeted head. The gates were wide enough apart for a single man to squeeze through. The crew didn't wait, they were gone. The colonel general was slower, as though he sought an answer that as yet eluded him. He paused in front of Holly.

"If you ended it now, after what you have done for me, there would be leniency."

"You are not going through the gate because we hope for leniency."

"I think I knew that. I will not forget you."

"Goodbye."

The colonel general swung on his heel. The gates creaked as they were pushed shut. There was an emptiness now, a moment of confusion, and Holly shook himself, tried to shrug away the mood.

"It was the right thing. We fight them clean . . ."

The driver swore at the sluggish sticks as he brought the tank to a halt in front of the major.

The major skinned up over the track skirting and the paint-chipped armorplate of the turret. He carried the plan of the camp in his hand.

"We have a few minutes yet before you go," he called into the hatch. "I want the main armament readied, one in the breech. They'll use the machine guns against you, and you are authorized to use shellfire against them. You'll be hatchdown, but we'll be with you on the radio. I don't want any pissing about with those machine guns, if necessary ride right over them. As soon as they're out, the infantry goes in. Keep on the move inside."

"We heard they'd got a colonel general as prisoner," said the observer.

"They let him go."

Astonishment from the gunner.

"Other than the machine guns do they have any firing weapons?" the gunner.

"Two machine guns, that's their lot."

"Poor bastards. . . ." The driver spoke to himself from the bowels of the tank.

"There's a line in Hut 5," Poshekhonov said. He laughed because Holly did not understand him. "Hut 5 is a brothel now. That's the extent of our liberation, Holly. Home comforts for the storm troops. There's a line halfway down the hut. She wasn't the only one through the fence, you know, the little one who came to see you."

"What have we begun?" Holly seemed to lean against Poshekhonov's shoulder.

"You should know that, Holly. Of all of us, you should know what we have begun."

Holly's face was close to Poshekhonov's. "Promise me something, friend."

"It is not an easy time to make promises that can be honored."

"Promise me you will take care of the girl."

"When?"

"When they attack."

"Our iron man, our leader of more than seven hundred *zeks*, and he asks for the safety of a girl who need not have come?"

"Promise me."

Poshekhonov tried to laugh again, but when he looked hard into Holly's face he met only the steel gaze.

"I think you care for all of us, Holly."

"I care for all of you."

"I promise, Holly. I will care for the girl when they attack."

Holly punched Poshekhonov playfully on the arm and walked away.

Rudakov ushered Adimov out of his office.

Down the corridor the door to Kypov's room swung open. Rudakov saw the colonel general follow the Commandant into the passageway. Ten minutes before, the colonel general had been held in the camp kitchen. . . . What was happening? He forgot Adimov. He hurried down the corridor after the two men.

Kypov turned.

Rudakov looked at the colonel general in bewilderment. "How did it happen?"

"They let me out, myself and the flying crew."

"Why?"

"Their leader said that if they kept us and tried to use us as a shield they would be animals. He said animals would be forgotten. He said that if they freed us they would never be forgotten, never as long as the camps exist."

"What bloody use is it to them whether they're forgotten or not, when they're about to be mangled?"

"I don't know," said the colonel general drily. "I've never led a mutiny."

"Who is the leader?"

"They've all taken the name strips off their tunics. There is one who can be identified. Tall, darkish, speaks fluent Russian but with something of an accent."

"Michael Holly. . . ."

"Once the attack goes in, he's to be shot on sight," Kypov spoke with determination, a man who had at last retrieved his respect in the anticipation of combat.

"What did you think of this Michael Holly?" A hoarseness in Rudakov's voice.

"I thought rather well of him," the colonel general replied. There was a light smile at his face, as if he were not prepared to share his emotions with strangers. "They have a central committee, and every man on the committee wanted either to use us as sandbags or to hang us. Of course I think well of him. He is not a man to be underestimated."

"Get that scum of yours on the microphone," Kypov ordered.

Inside the guardhouse they found a chair for Adimov. He was sat down in front of a table, and Rudakov lifted down the microphone from the wall bracket. Adimov gripped the microphone with white knuckles. He looked round at the walls that were covered with lists and typed guard rosters and duty orders and photographs from the files of selected prisoners.

He felt Rudakov's faint tap on his shoulder.

"This is Adimov, from Hut 2. You will all recognize my voice. I want to tell you to surrender. You have been misled, you have been betrayed by your leaders. In a few minutes the gates of the camp will be opened, and those of my comrades who wish to leave the camp may do so, and they will not face

penalties. . . ." He had no script to read, he spoke as Rudakov
had tutored him. "I have been told by the comrade political
officer that only the leaders will be punished. This is your last
opportunity, I urge you to come through the gates. My friends,
all of our grievances will be most thoroughly investigated. Take
this chance, walk out of the compound. . . ."

Adimov looked over his shoulder at Rudakov, saw the nod
of satisfaction. His thumb slid purposefully along the stem of
the microphone as if he raised the switch from "on" to "off."

"Was that good, Captain Rudakov?"

"Excellent, Adimov."

The voice was distorted over the loudspeakers in the kitchen.

"And the tank attacks at four o'clock?"

"Not your concern."

A desperate hush in the kitchen, all eyes on the twin loudspeakers.

"And once the attack starts Holly is to be shot on sight?"

"What's it to you, Adimov?"

The words were ferried the width of the compound by the
exterior loudspeakers.

Then a distant shout, harder to hear.

"The microphone's live. . . ."

Rudakov was close to the microphone now, and screaming.
There was the sound of struggling.

"Bastard, stupid shit . . . stupid bastard, Adimov."

"I don't need your ticket, she's dead. The letter said she
was dead. She was dead before I went out. . . ."

The loudspeakers were severed. For a few seconds there
was ice-cold stillness inside the compound, then the *zeks* were
moving.

"I didn't know he had the guts," Holly said. "Can you deal
with a tank?"

"I can deal with a tank," Byrkin replied.

Chapter 23

The camp lay squat on the snow plains, an isolated place that seemed to fly the yellow pennant of contamination. Outside, soldiers in pairs and threes had used their trench spades to make small holes in which they could cower down from the wind with their rifles, their machine guns, their antitank rocket launchers. The dog-handlers were out with their animals and the skis. The major had told his boys whose homes were two and a half thousand kilometers from the *Dubrovlag* of the dangerous, seditious scum led by western provocateurs, who had risen in rebellion behind the creosote-covered fence. The troops did not doubt the word of their major. Let the fascists break out, let the traitors come through the fence.... There were no birds in the winter trees, no song to impede the crackle of instructions over the portable radio sets. The camp was doomed. The death of the camp would come before dusk, and dusk was hurrying across the flat snowscape of Mordovia, like a fog wall on a calm sea.

The marksmen watched the camp from their aerie on the roof of the administration building. There should have been despair among the *zeks*. The bastards knew that a tank was coming, they knew that an infantry force had gathered, they knew that their leader was a man marked in the gunsights for death.

A gray light was settling on the compound. Only the perimeter lights were lit. The huts were deep shadows. The kitchen was blurring, fading, from the view of the marksmen. They followed with difficulty the movements of men running between the huts, between the kitchen and the bathhouse, between the store and the library.

The tank was late coming. They would not use the search-

light that had been brought to the roof of the administration
building until the tank arrived in the compound.

The kitchen was built of brick and concrete, the most secure
construction in the camp. All who would not fight the action
were gathered there. The old, the useless, the sick. And the
women made a lonely group as if the liaisons of Hut 5 counted
now for nothing. There were no jokes in the kitchen, but a
desperate, close quiet, with each man listening for the low-
slung conversations of the committee who were grouped close
to the doorway. Holly stared out toward the black spaces sand-
wiched between the compound snow and the outline of the
huts. Waiting for Byrkin. Byrkin away on his rounds and sprinting from hut to hut, diving for the cover of the darkness underneath the stilted floors. Chernayev was with Holly, and
Feldstein. The girl was close to Holly, ignored and uncom-
plaining.

The loudspeakers barked at them from high on the walls.

". . . The gates have been opened. You must go immediately
to the gates. You have two minutes. There will be no further
opportunity to leave the compound before the intervention of
the military. . . ."

Kypov with his parade-ground shout.

". . . You have this last chance. Go immediately to the gates
with your hands on your heads. You will not be harmed. You
have two minutes."

Holly looked around him, watching for the first man to rise.
One man close to him with the cough of consumption, one
with a crutch and an amputated right leg, one with the tremble
of a disease that was incurable, one who could not see without
grotesque owl spectacles.

Who would be the first, Holly?

Why don't the buggers move? They can't fight. They're
helpless bloody food for the tank gun . . . why don't they go?
Holly thought of a second hand ticking on a watch face, jerking
through the movements of revolution. Two minutes only.

"You can go. . . . Any of you who want to go. There is no
shame in going . . ." Holly shouted.

They gazed back at him. Dumb cattle, quiet.

"Who are you to tell them that they can go?" Chernayev

hissed. "You think that you pull every string, Holly?"

Holly pitched himself forward toward the nearest part of the sitting mass. He dragged at the man with the consumptive cough, and the grip of his hands was flailed away. He pulled at the man with the amputated right leg and felt the crutch end spear into his stomach. He tugged at the man who could barely see and found only a weight that was dead to him. No man moved.

Holly caught at the tunic of the girl.

"You go, Morozova, you go."

"No." She looked up into his face, and there was a calmness and a sureness.

"Why . . . ?"

"You called through the wall of the cell, you called 'Don't please them with your tears.' To walk through the gate is to weep."

Holly shook his head. "Feldstein, you go, you are not a fighter."

"It is better to lie down in front of the tank than to walk out now."

Holly leaned against the doorway, and covered his face. No man should see him. God, how were they so brave? He had unleashed that bravery. Easy enough to burn the Commandant's hut, to poison the garrison's water, to cut through the two fences of barbed wire. Nothing when set against the courage of sitting cramped on the floor of the kitchen when safety beckoned through the opened gate. He felt the girl against him. He felt her arm slide surely round his waist.

"There has to be a time when we go through the gate."

She had a small, husky voice. "Not when they tell us, when they bribe us. In our own time we go through."

Clumsily Holly slipped his own arm around the girl. Through her tunic his fingers found the hard rib bones, played on them, climbed them. "Before you were here, before that . . . what did you do?"

"I was a pianist."

"When this camp no longer exists as a prison for a pianist, that is the time to go to the gates. When it is destroyed, when the camp is as if it had never been. When there is no place here for a pianist."

His cheek rested on the top of her cap. He heard the struggling whine of an engine, the clanking of tracks biting on ice and tarmac. The coming of the tank. The roar spread through the compound, through the kitchen, through Holly, through the girl who was against him.

Byrkin ran round the corner wall of the kitchen. Panting, pointing toward the gulf of the opened gate.

"You hear it, Holly?"

"I hear it." His arm fell from Morozova. "Are you ready for it?"

Byrkin grimaced. "As we'll ever be."

Holly turned toward the girl, searching her face for weakness. Only the sweet brown eyes, only the mouth firm in defiance. When he broke away, her hand tried to check him, for a moment, and then her grip was broken.

Together, hugging the shadow of the huts, sprinting on the open ground, Holly and Byrkin came to Hut 4. They crawled forward over the frozen mud, beneath the floorboards. Holly smelt the paraffin, saw the bottles, the strips of torn blanket, the unlit torches, the boxes of matches.

And all the time the coming thunder of the tank.

"Left side, behind the turret, right?"

"That's where it is . . . I heard it said once that when they went into Budapest they even had 'Gas' written on the screw cap."

Level with them was Hut 3, fifty yards away. If the tank came straight through the gates it would bisect the open space between the two huts.

Holly reached out and took a handful of blanket. He felt sick from the smell of paraffin.

The troops who would follow the tank into the compound were gathered in two squads on either side of the approach to the gates. A little way apart from them was Kypov. Apart because he was not in command. He might wear his helmet, he might carry a pistol in his hand, but would not feel the sweet joy of participation in the first assault. He would be used later, as an officer to administer prisoners already broken and defeated. His own men of the MVD guard were a full hundred meters further back with orders not to advance or in any way impede the attack by the regular troops. A bitter pill.

He was astonished to see the colonel general approaching him.

"You are not in command?" asked Kypov.

"My colleague can manage adequately."

"A strange decision."

"Perhaps . . . I haven't much stomach for this fight."

"None of us can choose our duty," Kypov shouted above the thunder of the tracks.

Adimov heard the muffled sounds of the tank through the reinforced wall of his SHIzo cell. He lay where they had tossed him, in a sludge of dull pain. The sergeant in the guardhouse had exacted the full toll from his ribs, his kidneys, the flesh at the fall of his stomach.

"Old man, next cell . . . I told them the tank was coming . . . I gave them warning. . . ."

A faint voice. "Perhaps it was better if they had not known."

"They have a better chance to fight it."

"The harder they fight, the harder they will be smashed."

"I tried. . . ."

"However long you are in the camps, wherever you are sent, you will be known for what you have done."

Adimov closed his eyes, and his cell was filled with the crescendo of the tank's advance.

"He's tall, dark-haired. Usually in a group of three or four. Very straight in the back, that's the give away. Once the tank's in, nail him."

The adjutant crawled away across the roof of the administration building, leaving the four marksmen to prepare for their work.

When he peered over the low parapet wall he saw the tank charging at the gates, full speed for the engine of 130 horse power.

They lay on their stomachs in the doorway of the kitchen. A daft place to be, but neither would miss the entrance of the tank into the compound.

"Are you afraid?" Morozova asked.

"Wetting my pants, darling," said Poshekhonov.

The tank loomed between the open gates. Above the engine howl they heard the noise of splintering wood as it took the right side gatepost in its rush. Poshekhonov reached for the girl, pulled her underneath his body. Shit, she felt good. Everyone who was near the doorway heard Poshekhonov's laughter, and thought a madness had taken him.

Feldstein and Chernayev crouched beside the window, peeping through cracked glass that distorted the armored hull of the T34.

Feldstein said, "I want them all killed. I'm ashamed of myself, I want every man in that tank killed."

Chernayev said, "If we beat the tank, then I don't care. If we beat the tank, then I don't care if they drop a bastard bomb on us."

A dimming gray light as the tank plunged into the compound. A gray-brown shape against the gray-white ground, and speeding toward the gray-black huts. A monster that mesmerized its watchers. Something foul from the time before history.

Holly had the blanket rags in his hand, felt the oil run slippery through his fingers. Byrkin gripped an uncapped bottle of paraffin in one hand, and in the other was an unlit torch made from a ring of cloth wrapped round a short stick. Another man held a crowbar. Another kept safe, in large work-scarred fists, a box of matches.

"Wait. . . ." whispered Byrkin.

The tank hammered toward the gap between Hut 3 and Hut 4.

"Wait. . . ."

God . . . how long? The tank blotted out the perimeter arc lights, it swerved in the snow, hunting for a target. The main armament barrel heaved and swung. He saw the thrashing motion of the tracks that he must clear when he hurled himself onto the platform. God. . . . What did you hold onto? Byrkin was coiled tight beside him.

From underneath Hut 3 came the sharp flash of a lit match. A second, a third.

From underneath Hut 3 came the first firing from the machine gun.

The whine, endless and onward, of the tracer ricocheting from armorplate.

The first bottle rose easily in its arc between the base of Hut 3 and the tank. A brilliant vapor of light caught the tank and its turret-number and its radio aerial and its gunbarrel. The second bottle and the third curved from Hut 3. The pitch of the engine sagged. The driver knew he must back away from the fire, so that his gunner could drop the main armament barrel for the close quarters contact.

He veered to the right, toward Hut 4, then to the left, aligning the gunbarrel toward the source of annoyance.

Closer to Hut 4 than to Hut 3. Blind to Hut 4, preoccupied only with Hut 3.

A match flashed beside Holly. A torch spluttered, caught, flung off a burning stench. Smoke sank in Holly's lungs.

Byrkin running. Beside him the man with the crowbar.

Holly pulled himself out from the shelter of the hut floorboards. He ran to catch them. Twenty yards to the tank. When does the bloody firing start? When do they start from the roof of the administration building? The barrel depressing, falling toward the base of Hut 3. Five feet up to the platform above the tracks, and the tank still moving and his hands scrabbling for a grip, and running beside the tank. Byrkin was on board, standing for a moment at his full height. God . . . and Byrkin held the torch, Byrkin would draw the firing like a moth at a bloody lamp. The man with the crowbar was beside Byrkin now, pushing him down into the lee of the turret. Byrkin on his knees, reaching down for Holly, dragging him upward, feet kicking past the ravaging tracks. He could hear the men shouting inside the tank, hear the stammer of their radio. A new concert of firing as the rifles on the administration block joined battle, and then the answering blast from under Hut 3, and then more distantly from under Hut 6.

The man with the crowbar smashed his weapon against the cap of the gas tank.

Holly held a pickax strapped to the turret. He found the driver's vision slit, and began to force the rags into the opening.

"Give me the fire, give me the bottle. . . ."

The bottle first. Holding the pickax with one hand, pouring the paraffin onto the rags. He dropped the bottle, reached for the fire. A new sound for the crowbar, the sound of a pierced hole in light metal. Holly took the torch, touched the rags, jumped. Byrkin jumped. The man with the crowbar jumped.

The sheet of flame soared at the front of the tank and beneath the gunbarrel. Holly stood transfixed. God . . . they were screaming. The main armament fired into the lower walls of the side of Hut 3.

Couldn't move . . . and the torch was in his hand and his body was alive with light, and inside the tank they were screaming.

Byrkin snatched the torch from Holly, cudgeled him to the ground, then looped the flame toward the spilling petrol tank.

There was the gas tank of the T34 to explode, there were five 100mm armor-piercing shells inside the hull to detonate.

Between the two of them they shoved and dragged Holly away from the bonfire of the tank. He would have stood there, rooted in fascination, if they had not taken him. A shell exploded, there was the whine of shrapnel alive in the air. When they reached the far end of Hut 4 and could shelter behind the brick stilts, then Holly could kneel and watch the devastation that was the work of Byrkin, the former petty officer.

The monster had been halted. A heart of light among a rippling mirror of melted snow. Another explosion, another shell ignited. Hut 3 was ablaze. Crawling from the fire were the men who had fired the machine gun, who had thrown the decoy bottles. And when they were moving they could not fire, and when they could not fire then the lone gun under Hut 6 could not stifle the shooting from the roof of the administration building.

An eye for an eye. The machine gun men in a searchlight beam.

A tooth for a tooth. The tracer finding them.

Death, where is thy sting? The sting is the tracer that tosses a man in the air, that hurtles another sideways, that breaks a gun into the useless metal of scrap.

"We have their tank, they have our throats," Holly said.

The flames from Hut 3 and from the T34 tank served to darken the compound beyond the orbit of the fires. The searchlight had moved on, seeking a new prey. Together Holly and Byrkin scurried across the snow to the men who had tried to carry away the machine gun. Blood on the snow. There was the bent shape, black and worthless, of the gun. One of the men lay still, the life frozen from him. Another writhed in a death dance. Another moved haphazardly in the dumb shock of a gunshot wound.

They started the long, crawling journey back toward the kitchen.

The colonel general now stood beside his major. Dark faced, harsh with anger.

"The tank...?"

"It's out."

A snapped instruction. "Mortar them."

"A particular target?"

"Random."

"And the marksmen."

"Everything."

"There may be seven hundred men in the kitchen."

"Then they'd better be on the floor."

"And the infantry?"

"I'm not losing more men."

"You'll destroy the camp."

"Before I lose one more man I will destroy the camp."

The mortar shells popped in the tube, sighed in the air, whistled as they fell, thundered on impact.

The machine guns traversed the ink-black space beneath the huts and ravaged through the windows. The tracers were one in four, red heat as they careered into bedding. The straw in the mattresses caught in the first flickers of fire.

The marksmen's bullets pecked sporadically at the windows of the kitchen.

The flames licked up from the living huts and were fanned by a light wind.

The machine gun under Hut 6 had fired occasionally since the full weight of the attack was directed on its position after the silencing of its partner. When the heat of that hut, burning too, became unendurable, the hiding place was abandoned. The gun crew tried the long, long run for the open doorway of the store shed. They were less than twenty meters from it when the searchlight found them. One man fell. Another stumbled, staggered inside the doorway. One man carried the machine gun inside the safety of the cement-block structure. Another joined him. With their fingers they tore away a metal ventilation strip, gave themselves an aiming tunnel at the main camp gates. Their brief burst of firing, ill-directed and inaccurate, was sufficient to harden the colonel general's resolve.

Systematically, steadily, the fabric of ZhKh 385/3/1 was razed to the ground by mortar shells, machine gun bullets and fire. The low cloud over the compound was burned a golden orange.

Holly had reached the kitchen.

In the murky light he could see only those *zeks* who were gathered at his end of the hall. The far end was a blackness of explosions, moaning, crying.

"We have more than twenty men hit here. We have nothing with which to treat them," said Morozova.

"They're massacring us, Holly, we've nothing to protect ourselves," said Poshekhonov.

"You are responsible for these people, Holly. They look to you. How much more will you ask of them?" said Feldstein.

"If you tell them to fight on, they will struggle with their teeth, with their fingers. You have their lives in your hands," said Chernayev.

"We have to go on, Holly. They're going to shoot us anyway. Better while we are standing, better while we are free. After the tank there is no mercy. If we surrender now, it is to die in handcuffs," said Byrkin.

"Do you trust me?"

"You have taken us this far," said Poshekhonov.

The girl was watching him. She had blood on her hands. A mortar shell burst close to the west wall of the kitchen, and glass crashed and wood shrieked. A man screamed. The bullets pattered on the brickwork. He would lead them to hell, would he care if they returned? Slowly, carefully, Holly unbuttoned his tunic. It was cold in the kitchen, bitter subzero cold. He shivered, then pulled off his shirt. He still wore the two vests that he had put on to crawl through the wire. The second vest was cleanest, whitest. He stripped off the under vest from his skin. The girl still watched him. He heard the sharp burst of firing from the store. She looked at him with compassion, with the pity of a mother. He let the vest slip to the floor, and then began to put on again his top vest, his shirt, his tunic.

"Trust me. . . ."

He stepped out of the doorway, waving his vest high above his head.

The searchlight caught him.

Far away there was a shouted order.

The snow crunched under his boots as he headed between the blazing huts and the burning tank toward the main gate.

Chapter 24

"Rudakov . . . Yuri Rudakov . . . I want to speak to Captain Rudakov."

Holly shouted into the white dazzle light of the beam soaking him from the roof of the administration building. He stood between Huts 3 and 4, and when his voice had died on the wind there were the sounds of the fire as company for him. A rafter that blazed and fell, the crackle of jumping sparks, a wall that trembled inward crazily. He felt the warmth of the fire on his body, a precious and solid heat that seemed to thaw away the chill of the kitchen. He could see no movement beyond the searchlight, he could not know that the sergeant marksman was crawling back along the flat roof to the opened trapdoor and the ladder down into the building. His arm ached as he held it high and the thin vest was wrapped by the breeze around his wrist, and tickled the skin that it found between his glove and the cuff of his tunic.

The *zeks* would fight while he was with them.

The *zeks* would die while he was with them.

There was the wreckage of the helicopter across to his right. There was the burned carcass of a tank behind him. How far would the *zeks* follow, Holly? They would follow him to hell. Would he care if they returned? God . . . there were seven hundred men and seven women in the kitchen, and the weight of their lives was across his shoulders, a hideous weight. Not surrender, no . . . he could not lead them to surrender. He waited for Rudakov to come, he stood straight and still with the vest above his head.

It had begun to snow again. Fast little flurries that soared in the beam of the searchlight and hissed in the flames. He felt it against his cheeks and nose. Seven hundred men, and some

were dead and some were wounded and some were afraid.
Seven hundred men, and they would fight with tooth and claw.
   You started it, Holly. . . .
   Rudakov was in front of him. He walked forward into the
orbit of the searchlight beam. His shadow was flung forward,
a black giant on the snow, and the cap nudged against Holly's
boots. He carried no weapon. His hands were clasped across
his stomach, resting on the webbing belt around his greatcoat.
   "You have no need of the flag, Holly. You can put down
your hands."
   "Thank you for coming."
   "Thank me for nothing."
   Rudakov came close. He showed no fear.
   "Do you like what you see, Captain Rudakov?"
   "You have expelled our Commandant from his compound.
You have brought down our helicopters. You have destroyed
our tank. Are you tired now of victories, Michael Holly? Are
you ready now for defeat?"
   "Just words, Captain Rudakov, and words are meaningless
now."
   "It was you that asked to talk."
   Holly looked into Rudakov's face, into the eyes that were
now shorn of ambition, pride.
   "The men want to fight on."
   "Then they are doomed."
   "I will not lead them to surrender."
   "Then they die."
   "There will be a massacre."
   "Not of our choice!"
   "If I were not with them . . . ?"
   "You are a part of them."
   "If I were not with them, they would come out."
   "I cannot save you, Michael Holly."
   "Have I asked to be saved?"
   "What I tried to do for you, Holly, in a civilized and humane
way, is finished. You played the idiot here, Holly. You had a
choice. You could respond to my help, you could ally yourself
with that shit in the kitchen. You made your choice. There is
a telex on my desk, Michael Holly. It talks of your transfer.
You will go to Vladimir, or perhaps to Chistopol. You will

never find another like me. You spat on me, you crapped on me. Perhaps they will shoot you now, perhaps they will lock you away forever. It is not my concern. My concern for you is over. I was reasonable with you, Michael Holly. How did you respond? You threw coffee at me. You chose the scum that are now in the kitchen. I tell you I would not have that scum clean out my lavatory. You made your choice. I have no need to stand here and listen to you."

"Captain Rudakov . . . I want the man that was sent to Yavas brought back here," Holly said.

A sad, bitter smile spread across Rudakov's face. "He is to be tried tomorrow. He will be sentenced tomorrow. In such a case the sentence of the court would be carried out within a week."

"I want him back here with us. I want him back before morning."

"You face the charge of murder of a guard. You face the charge of incitement and leadership of armed mutiny. You have the nerve to talk to me as if I were some bastard negotiator."

"Did they tell you of Kengir when they put the camp uniform on you . . . ?"

"I don't have to listen to you."

"Did they tell you of Kengir?"

"They told us of Kengir."

"Listen hard to me, Captain Rudakov. There was not one tank at Kengir, there were a dozen. The tanks came into the compound after forty days, the *zeks* had no weapons, they lay down in front of the tracks. Did they tell you that? They died rather than surrender."

"Kengir is history."

"It will be the same at Barashevo, Captain Rudakov."

Rudakov caught at Holly's arm. "You think I am in charge outside the gate. After four helicopters, after one tank, do you think the political officer is still in charge?"

"It will be a massacre, Captain Rudakov. Cruel. Horrible. Bloody. The camp of which Captain Yuri Rudakov was political officer will become a legend of death. You will be broken, Captain Rudakov, destroyed. . . ."

"That's shit. . . ." Rudakov shouted.

"That's true."

"I believe you." Rudakov's voice fell, a dropped stone. "You ask me to bring this man from Yavas back to the camp . . . what do you give me in return?"

Holly closed his eyes, squeezed them tight. The searchlight beam hammered onto his face.

"I give you the end of this."

"There will be reprisals, there will be executions, that is the way of these things."

"If you have the leader . . . ?"

"You ask me if the leader balances the scales. The camp is destroyed."

"You have the leader, you have the end to this."

"You would have faith in me, Michael?"

"As you would have faith in me, Yuri."

"There is one way only that the leader balances the scales."

"One way."

"I will bring the man from Yavas."

"When he has reached the kitchen, I will come to this place."

Rudakov's hand snaked out. He held Holly's two hands in his. "I will go to Yavas."

"Goodbye, Yuri."

"They are not worthy of you, that scum," said Rudakov quietly.

"I know who is worth friendship, I know seven hundred who are my friends. Let me know you, too, as a friend."

"I will do it myself."

"Goodbye."

Holly turned to walk back to the kitchen. Behind him, fading, was the brisk step of Rudakov across the snow. Images cascaded in his mind.

There was a couple who grew old in a small house in a narrow street in a country that could never be their own.

There was a factory in London where the workforce in their overalls would have lost the habit of wondering aloud whatever happened to the tall one who went to Moscow.

There was a pub behind the Elephant and Castle where the bar space would be cramped with men taking a beer and a sandwich before the train journey home, where two stools at a window table would be taken by an executive and his secretary, and neither would know of a promise that was given.

There was a man who worked high in Century House, with
a view of the evening river, who would have a new set of files
on his desk and a new set of clients at the end of his telephone.

There was a diplomat snug now in his Moscow flat who
would tell a prisoner to live within the system, not to kick it,
not to fight it.

There was a girl standing on a train, tired from eight hours
at a Building Society's typewriter, a lovely girl who had been
misused.

Such were the images in the mind of Michael Holly.

None of them relevant. Everything important was holed up
in the stench of death and pain in the kitchen hall. Where else
would you find such men, Holly? Where else but in the kitchen
hall of ZhKh 385/3/I. All the filth, all the trash. All the friends
of Michael Holly. They would never be forgotten.

For a moment Holly paused at the doorway of the store.
One dead, two alive. He saw the gleam of the cartridge cases
set neatly in their belt.

"You won't need the gun anymore. . . . Trust me."

The colonel general waited at the gates for Rudakov.

"They are coming out?"

"I want one hour."

"Why?"

"You can mortar the compound, you can flatten what little
is left of it, you can kill all of them. Give me an hour, please . . ."

"What did he say?"

"Colonel General, I want an hour, an hour of cease-fire.
You will see then what he said."

"I can order you to tell me."

"I ask you not to order me. I ask for an hour."

The colonel general looked down at the snow slush by his
boots. "You, too, he has trapped you, too. He is a persuasive
man. You have your hour. One hour only, then the mortars,
then I go in with the infantry."

"Thank you."

Kypov sat alone in his office with the telephone pressed hard
against his ear.

". . . I can only repeat what I have already told you, the

position has stabilized, the perimeter is secure. . . . I won't accept that. . . . I don't give a shit what it looks like from Moscow. . . . Yes, yes, I'll tell the procurator, I'll tell him just that. First thing in the morning he can hear it, that I don't give a shit what it looks like from Moscow. . . . Yes, yes, it will be finished by the time that he gets here. . . . Don't talk to me about casualties. Anytime you want me to hand over command, it's your decision. I understand your feelings. I would remind you that for two and a half years under my command the camp was a model of efficiency and discipline. It's only been in the last month. . . ."

He slammed down the telephone.

The bastard hadn't even heard him out. Just the screech of a dead line in his ear.

He looked around his new office. He would be able to pack everything that was personal to himself inside one small briefcase. The rest would belong to his successor.

"My uniform is your authorization." Rudakov beat his fist into the palm of his hand. He glared across the small room at the governor of the Central Investigation Prison. "I don't give a shit for your procedures. I've come for that prisoner, I'll take him out of here if I have to fucking manhandle him past every goon in this bastard place."

"Your language is offensive."

"Your behavior is obstructive. Your behavior will be dealt with at length in my report."

"There is no need for threats."

"Get him here. Now."

Who wanted to tangle with KGB? The governor sighed. He pushed a blank sheet of paper across the table.

"I shall require a signed statement from you, Captain Rudakov, that you have taken this man into your personal custody."

The girl sat with him. He and the girl were alone with each other on the floor, with their backs resting against the wall.

The men had shuffled away, drawn a few feet back so that Holly and Morozova had a small area to themselves. They knew. Because he is told nothing in the days and nights of his camp life, the *zek* is adept at reading scarce signs. When Holly sat with the girl, with no word of courage for them, then they knew their defeat. As a snake skin is shed, so the *zeks* let their spirit slip from their backs. A few comforted the injured at the far end of the kitchen. Mostly they squatted on the floor, waiting. Waiting was their trade. Waiting was their skill. The *zeks* waited, and they watched Holly and the girl.

His arm was around her, casually on her shoulder, laid without emotion.

"There is no other way?"

"No other way that I know."

"For these people you do it?"

"They deserve it."

"Nobody has made them such a gift before."

"They will stand on the battleground afterward, and it will be theirs."

"They have never won before."

"They deserve their victory."

"If you had known that it would end this way . . . ?"

"Feldstein asked if I would have started."

"What did you tell him?"

"I told him that I would have started."

"Afterward . . . what would you have wanted of us?"

"Only that you should be a witness. Only that you should never forget."

"Is that all you want of me, that I am here as a witness?"

"That what you have seen you will tell, that you will never forget."

"What has changed, Holly? Has any small thing changed today?"

"I don't know . . . if there has been a witness, if it is always remembered, then a small thing has changed."

"I'm cold, Holly . . . I'm frightened . . . you don't have to, Holly. . . ."

"I have to."

"Are you afraid?"

"It is their only weapon against us, that we are afraid. If we are not afraid they can never defeat us. Once we are frightened we are beaten."

"To me, Holly, to me alone, can you not show fear?"

"Not to you, not to anyone."

"Because you have no fear?"

Holly shuddered. His face was turned away from the girl. The line of his teeth was set hard in the chafed lower lip, and there was a trickle of blood.

"You have no right to ask that of me."

"Is there no other place for you, no other place than this camp?"

"When I came here I thought there was; now there is no other place."

"You have a home in England."

"I used to have a home, but my home now is the camp."

"In England there are people who love you."

"Morozova, listen to me...I have found a new home, I have found new people to love. There is something that is sweet and wonderful in this place that I have never found before. This place, these people, they are a thing of beauty to me. I glory in this place and these people."

"Are you afraid, Holly?"

"Be my witness, remember me."

Her head lay against his chest, and her hair bobbed against his chin with the motion of her crying.

The jeep skidded to a halt as Rudakov stamped on the brake pedal. It was a curious and confused creature that he had brought from Yavas, a pencil-thin man whose breath was foul. Rudakov had offered no explanation on the journey; the poor bastard was too timorous to ask for one. They had driven in silence, and at reckless speed. Rudakov reached across, screwed up his nose, and unlocked the man's handcuffs. He jumped out of the jeep, opened the man's door, and pulled him viciously down so that the man staggered on the ice.

A tall, helmeted figure waited beside the gates. The colonel general studied his watch, held it up to his face so that the thin light would fall on the dial. He nodded, he accepted.

Rudakov propelled his prisoner toward the gates. A soldier dragged them open, wide enough for one man to pass through. Rudakov pointed toward the kitchen, and pitched the man into the compound.

The gate closed.

Rudakov walked to the colonel general.

"I want a rifle."

"Was that your bargain, one for one?"

"One for them all. Holly for all of them that are in the kitchen."

"He is a brave man, your Holly."

"Just give me a rifle."

The man hesitated in the doorway. He blocked some of the light that filtered from the arc lamps and from the flames into the kitchen. He stopped as if he needed time to acclimatize himself. He had walked past a downed helicopter and a burnt-out tank, past huts that smoldered. He had come from the condemned cell. He had not understood the charge against him, now he did not understand the scene that greeted his return to the camp. He reached out with his hands in front of him like a blind man in a strange room. The *zeks* watched his return, they waited on Holly. From the floor Holly looked at the man in the doorspace. He saw the frail shoulders. He saw the hungry fleshless face. He saw the scabs at the mouth. This was the spear in his side, the nail in his hand.

Holly stood up. He turned his back on the man, he reached down and lifted the girl and for a few moments he held her warm and loving against the mud of his tunic. Once he kissed her forehead, a light and gentle kiss, and she trembled against him.

"I will be your witness, I will never forget," the girl said.

Feldstein came beside him. "They can rebuild the huts, but the camp is broken."

Chernayev was behind him. "The word will be heard in every camp."

Poshekhonov faced him. He tried to smile, wiping away the bright rivers from his face with the back of his glove. "Remember the woman who did handstands; when you are in the compound, remember her. . . ."

Holly walked out into the night. He wondered if they crowded the doorway to watch him go.

The fires were lower now, close to exhaustion.

A blackness around him.

God . . . I'm frightened.

What for, Holly? What was it for?

... I don't know....

Did you think you could beat them, Holly? Did you think you could win all on your own?

I don't know...Damn, damn, yes...I know. We won. We won against their helicopters and their tank and their wire.

Do they know that you won, Holly?

The bastards know. Certainly they know.

The searchlight beam exploded in his face. He was naked in the light. He was captured. They know that we won.

Lying on the roof of the administration block, Rudakov fired.

One shot.

The noise echoed away, withered on the wind and in the snow. He saw the first of the *zeks* step out of the doorway of the kitchen. The searchlight tilted up and away from the single prone figure, and found the spreading mass of men.

Away to his left the gates were opening, dogs were barking, there was the tramp of marching men.

Yuri Rudakov thought that he should have felt the clean draft of victory. He knew only the stale sweat-scent of despair.

Chapter 25

The first passengers off the Aeroflot dribbled through into the Zürich concourse. Alan Millet rummaged through his mind for the description that Century had given him. He looked at his watch again. He took a step nearer the glass "Arrivals" door. He was hot, yet he shivered. He felt as a mourner does who arrives too late at the wicket gate of a country churchyard and hears the singing of a distant hymn.

He had opened the file on Michael Holly. He would close that file. That he should seal it, bind it shut, had been an obsession with him since the end of February when the first outline of events in the *Dubrovlag* had reached Century House. A brief message from a man called Carpenter at Foreign and Commonwealth. "Your man's dead. They've informed the Embassy that he was shot during a camp riot. They buried him in the camp cemetery. We've tried to get a bit more, but they're not giving...." A telephone call from a girl in the Soviet section of Amnesty. Nice of her to have remembered him. "We get this material through from the camps—sometimes we take it as gospel, sometimes we're a bit cautious. The word is that an Englishman was involved in leading a riot at Barashevo, and that he was killed just before the rebellion folded. It's pretty thin, but that's all I have." A visit to a small house in Hampton Wick and a doorway conversation with an old man whose face was scarred and aged, and behind whom an invisible woman inquired in a frail quaver who the visitor was. "We know no more than you, Mr. Millet. It is your job to find out what happened to our boy. It was you that sent him."

After Carpenter's call he had swiveled round on his chair and gazed for some time out of the window over the dismal flow of the Thames. After the Amnesty message he had cleared

his desk, locked his drawer, gone home. After the visit to
Hampton Wick he had paced the streets through the squall
showers until midevening.

There was a young man next to him now, wearing jeans
and an aggressive red shirt under an open lightweight suede
jacket. A girl stood beside him, with high, wide cheekbones
and a trail of golden hair onto the shoulders of her blouse.
They too were waiting for a passenger.

She was smaller than he had expected.

She wore tight black trousers, a yellow jersey, and a blouse
that was clean and had once been white. She had large round
brown eyes. Her dark hair was cut short against her scalp. Her
face was pale. She came boldly to the sliding door, but when
it opened she hesitated, as if this were the final step to the new
world, courage had fled her. She looked for a friend.

The boy and girl who had been waiting bounced past Alan
Millet.

"Morozova. . . ."

"Irina. . . ."

"Alexei . . . 'Tasha . . . I hoped . . . I didn't know you would
be here."

"We met every flight this week."

"They told us from Moscow that it would be Zürich, they
didn't know which flight."

The boy and the girl and Irina Morozova made a bundle of
closed, desperate hugging and kissing. Alan Millet felt pow-
erless to intervene into the passion of the greeting. She was a
small town pianist, she was a small time *samizdat* courier, big
Mother Russia would not miss her. Every year they let out a
few like her, he thought, because it was good for their statistics,
it was good to throw in the faces of the visiting Congressmen.

The bundle broke open. The boy held Morozova's hand,
the girl had linked herself to Morozova's arm. As if it were
hard for her, as if the act were unfamiliar, a happy wide smile
split across Irina Morozova's face and her head was tilted first
to the right and then to the left as she nuzzled catlike, with
affection against the boy and girl.

"Miss Morozova, can I speak to you?" Alan Millet stepped
forward. His hand was outstretched. He spoke in Russian. He

felt strained, and in his mind was the face of a man sitting
opposite him on a low stool in a London pub with a glass of
beer and a sandwich for his lunch.

The boy turned, annoyed. "Are you a journalist? There will
be a press conference tomorrow. The news agencies will be
given the time and the address."

"I have to speak with you now, Miss Morozova."

She looked puzzled and the smile faded.

The girl narrowed her eyes at Alan Millet. "She's just come
off the plane. Can't you leave her alone? You can ask her
anything you want tomorrow."

"I'm not a journalist, Miss Morozova," Millet persisted.
"I'm from the British Foreign and Commonwealth Office. That's
the equivalent of the Soviet Foreign Affairs Ministry. You were
in Camp 3 at Barashevo, that's what I want to talk to you
about."

The fear came to Morozova's face. Her silence seemed to
ask if their long arm reached here, beyond the Customs and
Baggage Hall at Zürich.

"You've nothing to be frightened of, Miss Morozova, I
promise you. You were in Camp 3 at the end of February . . . ?"

"Leave her alone," the boy snapped.

"Miss Morozova, you were in Camp 3 at the time of the
riot?"

"You've no right to ask her such questions," cried the girl.

"Miss Morozova, when the riot happened there was an Englishman in the leadership. The women's zone is beside the
compound where the riot was. . . ."

"Michael Holly?" A small, nervous voice.

"Michael Holly was the Englishman's name."

"Did you know Michael Holly?"

"I was . . . I was his friend. My name is Alan Millet."

"Before he died he kissed me. Before he died I said to him
that I would be his witness, that I would never forget him.
They shot him like a dog . . ."

"We'll go and have some coffee."

Alan Millet took her arm. The boy and the girl fell back,
leaves in the wind.

He took a table far from the counter. Their elbows were on
the table, their heads were hunched close together, and the

coffee when it came grew cold, totally ignored. Irina Morozova spoke, Alan Millet listened. She talked for an hour. She talked of the office of Vasily Kypov, and the water supply of the garrison, and of the cut holes in the wire fences. She talked of the world of the *zeks* who sat down in the snow, and of helicopters screaming out of control, and of a tank ravished by the damage of an internal explosion. Around them the loud-speakers broadcast the news of arriving flights. Passengers gulped down their beers, swilled their soft drinks, ran for "Departures."

She talked of a kitchen building where the men were close packed, where some were wounded and mutilated, where the minute hand of a wall clock traveled over a final hour. She talked of a kiss, of the silence that followed his going, the crash of a single shot.

"Why?"

"The Authority had to be given a target for their vengeance after what had been done to them. He gave himself as their target. The *zeks* would have fought on for him, they would have been butchered. They loved him for the courage he had given to them."

"Did he win, is that an idiot question?"

"The camp was destroyed. That night the flames could be seen the length of the *Dubrovlag* railway. On the morning afterward the smoke could be seen by every man in every camp. I think he won. . . ."

"And his friends, what happened to them?"

"If you were his friend in London, you would not know the men who were his friends in Barashevo. Adimov who was a murderer is in Vladimir. Chernayev who was a thief is in Camp 9, Poshekhonov who was a fraud has been sent to Baku in the Azerbaijan SSR. Feldstein who was a dissident has gone to the political camps at Perm, Byrkin too has gone to Perm. That is what I have heard. None of them were executed, they all lived because one man died. The captain of KGB had given his word, and his word was honored. That they kept their word, that too was a victory of a sort."

Alan Millet held his hand softly over Irina Morozova's clenched fist.

"Your friends are waiting for you."

"Why was he there, Mr. Millet?"

"That's not the sort of thing I can discuss."

"Why?"

"I can't talk about that."

"You sent him?"

"I sent him . . . myself and others."

She snatched her hand away. "Do you know what that place is like, Mr. Millet?"

"I suppose I've a fair idea."

"And you left him there?"

"We tried. . . ."

"Tried?"

"We tried to get him out."

"And because you only tried, he died there."

"We did all we could."

"Find out what that place is like, Mr. Millet, because you should know that before you send another man to Barashevo."

"I understand your feelings, Miss Morozova." Millet sat miserably in his chair. "It's been a hideous experience."

"They loved him at Barashevo. People he had not known before, they *loved* him."

Millet shuffled, looked around him. "I think your friends want to go."

"I want to tell you one thing."

"Tell me."

"We heard the shot. We came out of the kitchen. Holly was dead, near to the tank. The soldiers were coming into the compound. The *zeks* surrounded Holly's body. They were all around him. They linked their arms. There was ring upon ring of men around him. The soldiers could not get to him. They stood, stupid bastards, around the *zeks,* around the rings. The colonel general came and then the Commandant and then the political officer, and told the *zeks* they could sleep on the floor of the factory. The *zeks* didn't move, no man moved throughout the whole night, even the wounded stayed out in the compound for the whole night. Two men died. The *zeks* stood in the cold. . . . Do you know that cold, Mr. Millet? . . . They stood in the cold for the whole night to protect the body. In the morning when the dawn came, some of the *zeks* spoke with the colonel general. They asked one favor of him, they said it

ARCHANGEL 311

was a small thing to set on the balance scales against his life. I never before heard of a colonel general who granted a favor to the *zeks*. This once, this one time alone, a favor was granted. When the day came the gates of the camp were opened and the strong men, those that had been Holly's friends, took him on their shoulders. The whole camp marched after them. They carried him to the cemetery, and all the *zeks* behind walked with their arms linked. The chain was never broken. They buried him in the cemetery, they walked back to the camp, they went into the factory. A procurator came that morning by air from Moscow and when he reached Barashevo they were all working, they were all in the factory."

"Thank you, Miss Morozova."

"He asked me to be his witness."

She was crying into a small handkerchief. Alan Millet stood up. He left the money for two coffees on the table and walked away toward the ticket counters.